TARZAN OF T

EDGAR RICE BURROUGHS was born in 1875. As a child and young man, Burroughs moved between schools regularly and, later, between jobs just as frequently. A short military career came to an end in 1897 when a medical examination revealed a heart murmur that led to his discharge. After more than a decade spent at various jobs, Burroughs decided to make a career out of his long hobby of writing. In 1911, he submitted his first story for publication, to *All-Story* magazine, where it was published as *Under the Moons of Mars*. In the following year, Burroughs published *Tarzan of the Apes* in the same magazine, and his writing career took off. Burroughs wrote twenty-six Tarzan books, with a twenty-seventh novel completed by another author after his death. In addition to the Tarzan books and numerous stand-alone works, Burroughs wrote other series: eleven novels founded on the first Mars story; the Pellucidar series about an underground civilization, in which Tarzan makes an occasional appearance; five works set on Venus; and a 'lost world' trilogy. It is Tarzan, however, that has become his legacy. Tarzan has been the subject of over fifty films, and has even left his mark on the US map: Burroughs started a ranch that grew into the town of Tarzana, California. Burroughs died at his home in California in 1950.

JASON HASLAM is an Associate Professor in the Department of English at Dalhousie University. He is the author of *Fitting Sentences: Identity in Nineteenth- and Twentieth-Century Prison Narratives*, co-editor of *Captivating Subjects: Writing Confinement, Citizenship, and Nationhood in the Nineteenth Century*, and editor of Constance Lytton's suffragette autobiography, *Prisons and Prisoners*.

OXFORD WORLD'S CLASSICS

EDGAR RICE BURROUGHS

Tarzan of the Apes

Edited with an Introduction and Notes by
JASON HASLAM

OXFORD
UNIVERSITY PRESS

OXFORD

UNIVERSITY PRESS

Great Clarendon Street, Oxford ox2 6DP

Oxford University Press is a department of the University of Oxford.
It furthers the University's objective of excellence in research, scholarship,
and education by publishing worldwide in

Oxford New York

Auckland Cape Town Dar es Salaam Hong Kong Karachi
Kuala Lumpur Madrid Melbourne Mexico City Nairobi
New Delhi Shanghai Taipei Toronto

With offices in

Argentina Austria Brazil Chile Czech Republic France Greece
Guatemala Hungary Italy Japan Poland Portugal Singapore
South Korea Switzerland Thailand Turkey Ukraine Vietnam

Oxford is a registered trade mark of Oxford University Press
in the UK and in certain other countries

TARZAN OF THE APES Copyright © 1912 EDGAR RICE BURROUGHS, INC.

Trademark TARZAN owned by EDGAR RICE BURROUGHS, INC., and Used By Permission

Cover illustration by Burne Hogarth,
Copyright © 1948 Edgar Rice Burroughs, Inc. All Rights Reserved.

Editorial material © Jason Haslam 2010

First published as an Oxford World's Classic 2010

British Library Cataloguing in Publication Data

Data available

Library of Congress Cataloging in Publication Data

Burroughs, Edgar Rice, 1875-1950.
Tarzan of the Apes / Edgar Rice Burroughs ;
edited with an introduction and notes by Jason Haslam.
p. cm.
Includes bibliographical references.
ISBN 978-0-19-954288-8 (pbk.)
ISBN 978-0-19-958703-2 (hbk.)
1. Tarzan (Fictitious character)—Fiction. 2. British—Africa—Fiction.
3. Wild men—Fiction. 4. Africa—Fiction. I. Haslam, Jason W.
(Jason William), 1971- II. Title.
PS3503.U687T3 2009 813'.52—dc22 2009026418

Typeset by Cepha Imaging Private Ltd., Bangalore, India
Printed in Great Britain
on acid-free paper by
Clays Ltd, St Ives plc

ISBN 978-0-19-954288-8 (pbk.)
ISBN 978-0-19-958703-2 (hbk.)

3

CONTENTS

ACKNOWLEDGEMENTS

I WOULD like to thank the personnel at the British Library and at the Killam Library, at Dalhousie, for their assistance. I would especially like to thank Karen Smith, Head of Special Collections at the Killam Library, for her invaluable work in obtaining a first edition of *Tarzan of the Apes*, and for allowing me easy access both to it and to the Killam's Charles O. Baldwin Burroughs Collection. Berenice Lara Laursen, my research assistant, also provided invaluable help with the preparation of the edition. Thanks are also due to the Social Science and Humanities Research Council of Canada for their continuing support. Finally, I would like to thank my partner, Julia M. Wright, for her always helpful advice.

INTRODUCTION

Readers who are unfamiliar with the plot may prefer to treat the Introduction as an Afterword.

THE turn of the twentieth century and its opening decades saw the creation of more than a few fictional characters that would become enduring cultural icons, including Arthur Conan Doyle's Sherlock Holmes (1887), Bram Stoker's Dracula (1897), and Jerry Siegel and Joe Schuster's Superman (1938). Among these figures, Edgar Rice Burroughs's Tarzan holds a special place. Tarzan is one of the most popular and pervasive characters arising out of the pulp publishing period of American literary history. Originally published in the October 1912 issue of the popular fiction magazine the *All-Story*, and as a book in 1914, *Tarzan of the Apes* introduces the character who would become the focus of twenty-five more books by Burroughs (if one does not include a novel written by another author based on Burroughs's notes),[1] and several novels by other authors (both authorized and not). The significance of the figure of Tarzan cannot be underestimated, certainly in relation to American culture, but arguably to global culture as well, given that the Tarzan novels have been reportedly translated into over fifty languages. *Tarzan of the Apes* even climbed over the Iron Curtain into the Soviet Union as early as 1922.[2] Just as importantly, Tarzan entered popular culture at a time when the centrality of print media was giving way to radio, television, and film.[3] Estimates vary, but it is safe to say that there are over fifty Tarzan movies, spanning every decade of the twentieth century since the novel's publication. Indeed, between the late 1920s and the 1960s, Tarzan was on the silver screen almost every year. Tarzan has also swung through almost all of the other branches of popular and so-called

[1] Sources vary on the number of sequels, generally depending on how two children's books—originally published separately but then combined—are counted. See the Select Bibliography, below.

[2] See Kristina Clark, *The Soviet Novel: History as Ritual* (Bloomington: Indiana Univ. Press, 2000), 104.

[3] See Walt Morton, 'Tracking the Sign of Tarzan: Trans-Media Representation of a Pop-Culture Icon', in Pat Kirkham and Janet Thumim (eds.), *You Tarzan: Masculinity, Movies and Men* (New York: St Martin's, 1993), 106–25.

'high' culture, including comics, radio, and stage—even song. It would not be an exaggeration to suggest that the history of US popular culture and the history of Tarzan are inseparable.

But the Tarzan of these forums is often as different from the hero of Burroughs's novel as Tarzan himself is different from T. S. Eliot's J. Alfred Prufrock, another notable literary creation of the period. People who are reading the novel for the first time will be surprised by the ending, which features not the grunting, half-literate (and less than half-clothed) ape-man of film, but instead focuses on Tarzan the cosmopolite, a French- and English-speaking, suit-wearing sophisticate who spends the final chapters of the novel more often in offices and drawing-rooms inhabited by the upper classes than he does in trees and forests inhabited by beasts of the jungle. In *Return of Tarzan*, the first sequel to the original novel (published in *New Story Magazine* in 1913, and as a book in 1915), Tarzan is, for a while, more the international gentleman spy than he is the feral child. Think James Bond in his tuxedo, rather than Johnny Weissmuller in his loincloth.

And yet it is the jungle Tarzan who remains etched in popular culture and in readers' imaginations, and even the sophisticated Tarzan we later see needs to return to the jungle on a regular basis. His reasons for doing so may not be that different, after all, from Prufrock's lament that his life is being 'measured out . . . with coffee spoons', or Huck Finn's philosophic approach to being 'sivilized'. All of these characters are concerned about the anaesthetizing effect of modern society on the individual, and especially the male individual. Tarzan just takes a different approach to the problem. Similarly, one cannot underestimate the role that Burroughs's character has played in contemporary conceptions of gender, race, imperialism, and national identity. Critical response bears this out well: many recent historical and critical studies of these issues use *Tarzan of the Apes* as a centrepiece for their arguments.[4] As Tarzan approaches

---

[4] See, e.g., Jeff Berglund, *Cannibal Fictions: American Explorations of Colonialism, Race, Gender, and Sexuality* (Madison: Univ. of Wisconsin Press, 2006); Eric Cheyfitz, *The Poetics of Imperialism: Translation and Colonization from* The Tempest *to* Tarzan (Philadelphia: Univ. of Pennsylvania Press, 1997); Catherine Jurca, *White Diaspora: The Suburb and the Twentieth-Century American Novel* (Princeton: Princeton Univ. Press, 2001); and Marianna Torgovnick, *Gone Primitive: Savage Intellects, Modern Lives* (Chicago: Univ. of Chicago Press, 1990).

his hundredth birthday, it is worth reconsidering the reasons for Tarzan's popularity, the character's eventual independence from his author's original creation, and his enduring cultural significance.

Burroughs of (and beyond) the Apes[5]

Edgar Rice Burroughs was born in 1875, the son of Mary Evaline and George Tyler Burroughs, a successful Chicago businessman and retired major of the Union army during the US Civil War, who had been a staunch supporter of the abolition of slavery. The youngest child, Edgar Burroughs moved between schools regularly. At 15, he was sent to a ranch run by two of his brothers in Idaho, a recently formed state that was just coming out of its frontier days. His time there was brief, however, as his father soon sent him to the Phillips Academy in Andover, Massachusetts. He left school, again, after a term. While there, however, he contributed cartoons and other drawings to the Academy's literary magazine, *The Mirror*, foreshadowing, albeit in a different medium, his later career as a popular artist.

Shortly after his brief career in Andover ended, his father sent him to the Michigan Military Academy, from which he rapidly deserted, though he eventually returned of his own accord to take his punishment and finish his education (both scholastic and military). The Commandant at Michigan, Charles King, was to have a significant effect on Burroughs. King was a veteran of the Civil War, and he had also fought in the wars against the aboriginal nations of America, particularly the Apache. He was also a writer of hundreds of stories and novels and was called 'America's Kipling', referencing the British writer from whom Burroughs himself would find inspiration for his famous ape-man.[6] Largely, it would seem, because of King's guidance, Burroughs graduated from the Military Academy in 1895, and shortly afterwards briefly held the position of instructor there.

[5] For this brief summary of Burroughs's life, as well as many of the facts concerning his creations, I am indebted to his biographers, especially Irwin Porges and John Taliaferro.

[6] See John Taliaferro, *Tarzan Forever: The Life of Edgar Rice Burroughs, Creator of Tarzan* (New York: Scribner, 1999), 33.

From Michigan, Burroughs decided to enlist in active duty, and became a private with the Seventh Cavalry stationed at Fort Grant, in the Arizona Territory. This was an area that was renowned for earlier fights against the Apache, but by the time Burroughs arrived, even occasional skirmishes were rare. Burroughs would return to this setting and its history in two later novels, *The War Chief* (1927) and *Apache Devil* (1933). His short military career came to an end in 1897 when a medical examination revealed a heart murmur that led to his discharge.

After his brief stay in Arizona, Burroughs was married to Emma Hulbert in January 1900 (they would divorce in 1934). His new position as a family man, and the new century, did not mean a new period of stability for Burroughs, however. A decade of various jobs and attempts to find a career followed, with Burroughs working for his father, buying a stationery store, working again for his brothers, becoming an alderman (for a month), working as a railway policeman, and running a stenographic department for Sears Roebuck, among other positions. By 1911, Burroughs decided to make a career out of his long hobby of writing (in addition to his cartoon work, he had written small pieces for newspapers, and creative works for his niece and nephew). He submitted his first story for publication to *All-Story* magazine, where it was serialized, starting in February 1912, as *Under the Moons of Mars*. Later that year, Burroughs published *Tarzan of the Apes* in the same forum, launching his writing career. In addition to the Tarzan books and numerous stand-alone works, Burroughs wrote other series: eleven novels founded on the first Mars story; the Pellucidar series about an underground civilization, in which Tarzan makes an occasional appearance; five works set on Venus; and a 'lost world' trilogy starting with *The Land that Time Forgot* (1918). It is Tarzan, however, that has become his legacy, even leaving his mark on the US map: Burroughs started a ranch that grew into the town of Tarzana, California. Burroughs died in 1950.

Tarzan of the Novel

The general plot of Burroughs's most famous novel is familiar to most: a boy is born in the jungle, raised by apes, eventually meets other human beings, and falls in love with a woman named Jane. The details that flesh out this skeleton, though, are more rich and multifaceted than the collective cultural memory of Tarzan may suggest. Explicitly engaging in discussions of colonialism and 'manliness', especially, but also class and what constitutes 'proper' education and learning, *Tarzan of the Apes* is a complex and contradictory product of its time.

Starting with a framing narrative in which we are told that the tale is supported by the 'dry official records of the British Colonial Office' (p. 5), the novel is explicitly situated within the history of the European colonization of Africa and the lingering effects of the transatlantic slave trade. The opening chapters focus on the English aristocrat John Clayton, and his pregnant wife, Lady Alice. Clayton, we are told, was 'appointed . . . to a new post in British West Africa', primarily to conduct 'a thorough investigation of the unfair treatment of black British subjects by the officers of a friendly European power' (p. 6). Clayton is thus associated, to a degree, with a liberal government policy that finds itself attempting to correct, rather than reproduce, the lingering effects of slavery and racism within the colonial space of Africa. Clayton and his wife are marooned by a mutiny on their transport ship, she gives birth to a son, and both adults are then killed by an 'anthropoid ape'. Their son, 'adopted' and raised by an ape-mother who recently lost her own child, comes to be called 'Tarzan' in the apes' language, meaning 'White-Skin' (p. 36).

At first, Tarzan is seen by his ape community as 'slow and backward in learning to care for' himself, since he does not learn to climb or feed himself as soon as his 'cousins' (p. 36). Yet, although he always remains small and physically weak compared to his adoptive family, 'by the time he was ten years old he was an excellent climber, and on the ground could do many wonderful things which were beyond the powers of his little brothers and sisters' (p. 37). It is Tarzan's ability to reason, the reader is told, that puts him above his peers. Rapidly discovering how to make and use tools (including a grass rope he weaves himself), Tarzan's individual growth allegorizes a general outline of human evolution, from 'anthropoid ape', to tool-user, to master of language. The ability to understand the written word is the most important of Tarzan's stages of development, and moves him, as the chapter titles tell us, into the 'Light of Knowledge', which helps him to develop 'Man's Reason'.

Significantly, this knowledge is both self-taught and an inheritance from his biological parents, and hence from Europe itself. After his parents are stranded, they build a secure cabin. This cabin becomes a space of European knowledge, where Tarzan's father reads English books and keeps a diary in French. They can thus both inhabit and keep separate from the African landscape. When Tarzan discovers this cabin, he has no memory of it or his human parents, but quickly and 'naturally' begins to teach himself to read and write from the books available. Burroughs leaves no doubt that he is using Tarzan as a figure for humanity itself: 'Tarzan of the apes, little primitive man, presented a picture filled, at once, with pathos and with promise—an allegorical figure of the primordial groping through the black night of ignorance toward the light of learning' (p. 50). Tarzan thus becomes a symbol not only for certain evolutionary principles, but also for the history of humanity, from its primordial origins, through its dark ages, to the Enlightenment. (Even the cultural practices of the apes of Tarzan's tribe are brought into this evolutionary narrative: they perform a ritual, the 'Dum-Dum', from which, the narrator tells us, 'has arisen, unquestionably, all the forms and ceremonials of modern church and state' (p. 54).) From here, Burroughs moves rapidly through Tarzan's early teens to the point when, at 17, 'he had learned to read the simple, child's primer and had fully realized the true and wonderful purpose of the little bugs', Tarzan's term for the letters of the alphabet (p. 52). After the discovery of the cabin and its contents, including, importantly, not only books but also a knife, Tarzan's mental and physical growth continues. This progress is then mirrored by a similar progress in his mastery of his surroundings. Through experimentation and repetition (the scientific method, that ultimate sign of 'man's reason'), he learns how to manipulate tools and his surroundings to such an extent that he eventually kills the alpha male of his tribe, declaring, in his own words, that he has become 'Tarzan, King of the Apes, mighty hunter, mighty fighter. In all the jungle there is none so great' (p. 94).

But Tarzan and his tribe are not alone for long. Early in the novel, a group of humans 'invade[ ] their jungle' (p. 67). And this is the point at which the novel begins its at best problematic, and at worst pathologically violent, portrayal of Tarzan's relationship with black Africans. The representation of Africans and black people in general throughout the Tarzan series was disturbing enough to lead to changes in later editions of some of the novels (in this novel, removing the suggestion that the fingerprints 'of the negro are less complex' than those of white people, for example). In *Tarzan of the Apes*, a few

African tribes are introduced, principally the tribe led by Mbonga, who are present for most of the novel. All of these characters are depicted as violent and joyous cannibals, who are nonetheless childlike, weak, and fearful of Tarzan. Tarzan also wantonly murders several Africans: the first, Kulonga, in an act of vengeance, after Kulonga kills Tarzan's ape-mother, Kala; the others, the book implies, because Tarzan 'joyed in killing', even though 'he killed with a joyous laugh upon his handsome lips [which] betokened no innate cruelty' (p. 74). Indeed, in places these problematic portrayals were expanded from the 1912 magazine publication to the 1914 book publication. For example, in the *All-Story* version Kulonga is described as a 'sleek thing of ebony', while in the book publication he becomes a 'sleek *and hideous* thing of ebony' (p. 69; emphasis added).

In the plot of the novel, Mbonga's tribe serves to teach Tarzan that there are other men like him in the world. But shortly after he becomes king of the Apes, he meets his first Europeans and Americans—mostly white—with whom he becomes more fascinated than he was with Mbonga's people, and towards whom he becomes more protective. Somewhat coincidentally, the beach on which the Claytons were stranded is the site of another marooning, of Tarzan's biological cousin, William Cecil Clayton, the new Lord Greystoke, and his party, consisting of Clayton's love interest, Jane Porter, her father, Professor Archimedes Q. Porter, his assistant, Samuel T. Philander, and Jane's servant, Esmeralda. Put ashore by a different group of mutineers and cut-throats, this group is amazed to find Tarzan's cabin, while Tarzan is equally amazed to see other white people for the first time in his life.

Here, as Tarzan is explicitly compared to his 'civilized' relatives, the novel begins to expand on earlier hints of a critique of civilization itself. The professor and his assistant are the prime models of the absent-minded academic: they not only lose their way in an attempt to walk back to civilization, but are also nearly devoured by a lion in the process, which the Professor absurdly assumes has escaped from a zoo. Clayton, meanwhile, is almost equally as helpless in the jungle, being unable to do much of anything with his hands, while Jane's servant, Esmeralda, drawn according to the grossest of 'Mammy' stereotypes out of the American South, is pictured as completely incapable. Jane, meanwhile, is captured by one of Tarzan's apes.

Against all of this incompetence, Tarzan comes to embody a rejuvenated white masculinity: intelligent and rational (like the Professor), noble and gentle (like—but better than—Clayton), but also physically powerful (like the men of Mbonga's village). Tarzan is seen as godlike not only by the black Africans, but also by the white Europeans. All of this combines to transform Tarzan into an archetype of robust masculinity. If civilization is represented as overly intellectual and emasculating, while the paired visions of Mbonga's village and the various European mutineers are seen as examples of degraded physical savagery, Tarzan manages to embody a hybrid of both. When Tarzan saves Clayton from a lion, Clayton sees him in just such a light:

The man before him was the embodiment of physical perfection and giant strength, yet it was not upon these he depended in his battle with the great cat, for, mighty as were his muscles, they were as nothing by comparison with Numa's. To his agility, to his brain and to his long keen knife he owed his supremacy. (p. 111)

Tarzan is at once identified with his physicality but not debased by it, and he is profoundly rational but not rendered incompetent by an 'ivory tower' intellectualism. Even Tarzan's physical description highlights his hybrid nature: Tarzan's 'brown skin' places him somewhere between the African and the European.

If Tarzan comes to symbolize an idealized masculinity, it is no surprise that the tension of the last portions of the novel centres on Tarzan's relationship with Jane. Much less simple than the 'Me Tarzan, You Jane' that has come to us from the films, Tarzan's courtship of Jane is both difficult and, ultimately (in the first novel, at least), frustrated. But, in keeping with his general evolutionary framework, Burroughs represents Tarzan and Jane's meeting as a rejuvenation of humanity itself, by portraying their meeting as awakening 'primeval' desires:

As the great muscles of the man's back and shoulders knotted beneath the tension of his efforts, and the huge biceps and forearm held at bay those mighty tusks, the veil of centuries of civilization and culture was swept from the blurred vision of the Baltimore girl.

When the long knife drank deep a dozen times of Terkoz' heart's blood, and the great carcass rolled lifeless upon the ground, it was a primeval woman who sprang forward with outstretched arms toward the primeval man who had fought for her and won her.

And Tarzan?

He did what no red-blooded man needs lessons in doing. He took his woman in his arms and smothered her upturned, panting lips with kisses.

For a moment Jane Porter lay there with half-closed eyes. For a moment—the first in her young life—she knew the meaning of love. (p. 154)

As he saves her from Terkoz, the ape who had captured her as his own, Tarzan briefly frees Jane from what Burroughs depicts as the stifling nature of civilization. Both then revert to what is portrayed as their 'natural', unimpeded gender roles.

After the party of Europeans is rescued, they remain none the wiser as to Tarzan's true identity, having discovered the bodies of his parents along with what appears to be a child's skeleton, but which is in reality the remains of the ape-child that is replaced by Tarzan. Left behind, though, is the French officer, D'Arnot, whom Tarzan saves from being cannibalized, and who subsequently teaches Tarzan to speak first French and then English. Both walk their way out of the jungle to reach colonial outposts in Africa, and from there make their way to Paris. By the end, Tarzan is a consummate gentleman, who, through the new technology of fingerprint identification, is proved to be the true Lord Greystoke. He journeys to America to find Jane, only to discover that she is engaged to Clayton. The novel ends with Tarzan repeating the falsehood that he is the offspring of an ape mother and an unknown father.

On its original magazine publication, the novel was received exceedingly well, as the readers' letters to *All-Story* demonstrate (selections from the letters are included in Appendix I, below). The ending, however, was greeted with less enthusiasm, and, in some cases, apparent anger: one reader simply states that the novel 'is a swell story, except the ending, which was rotten'. Calls for sequels began immediately. Burroughs had trouble placing the sequel with *All-Story*, though, and eventually sold the story to a competitor, *New Story*. Burroughs, who had achieved some minor success with *Under the Moons of Mars* in an earlier issue of *All-Story*, now found his career largely set.

Tarzan, Africa, and Race

Among the many sources and contexts for *Tarzan of the Apes*, Western narratives of African exploration stand out. While there were earlier explorations and colonial activities, notably by Portugal, the modern phase of the Western exploration and exploitation of Africa started in the seventeenth century, with the creation of the West and East India Companies by the Dutch, and their subsequent colonization of what is now South Africa. The transatlantic slave trade dominated European and American relations with Africa from the sixteenth to the nineteenth centuries, when tens of millions of Africans were taken from Africa and enslaved. The nineteenth century then saw the most significant increase in the European conquest and colonial settlement of Africa, especially in the latter half. By the closing decades of the nineteenth century, Belgium, England, France, and other European nations began a period of increased colonial activities throughout Africa, beginning what has been called the 'Scramble for Africa'. The continent was not only significant for trade and the development of settlements, but also became a pawn in various struggles between rival European powers.

Most important to readings of *Tarzan of the Apes* was the role played by King Leopold II of Belgium (1835–1909) in the Congo. Working under the auspices of a private company that was supposedly humanitarian in its goals, Leopold hired Welsh-American explorer Henry Morton Stanley (1841–1904) to lay the groundwork to develop a privately controlled state in the Congo. Stanley had already become famous as an explorer of Africa, having found David Livingstone who had been 'lost' in Africa. From Stanley's work, Leopold II was able to found the Congo Free State. His claim to the region was recognized at the Berlin West Africa conference (1884–5), which was held to settle various nations' colonial and economic claims to the Congo River Basin area. The conference also outlawed slave-trading in the region. Later, however, Leopold's control of the rubber trade, along with the abusive treatment and mass deaths of native Africans in the area, became the subject of significant political controversy. In 1903, the British House of Commons passed a motion that asked the government to consult with 'other powers' about how to 'abate the evils prevalent in that state'. By 1908, Leopold had lost his private control of the Congo Free State, which then became the Belgian Congo, a formal colony of Belgium.

This background haunts *Tarzan of the Apes* through the continued Belgian presence in the Congo, which sets the stage for Tarzan's father, Clayton, to go on the humanitarian mission against the actions of the 'friendly European power'. Burroughs's most detailed biographer, Irwin Porges, notes that Burroughs researched Africa in the Chicago Public Library, and stories of African exploration, including those by Stanley, were immensely popular. Tarzan's father has significant parallels to Stanley. Clayton's mission to protect 'black British subjects' is itself an echo of the controversies surrounding Stanley, who was involved with the anti-slavery movement but was condemned by many for his brutal attitude and actions toward native Africans, a complaint that echoes those against Leopold himself.[7] Clayton's trip, moreover, takes place in 1888, when Stanley was also in Africa, on the Congo, during his famous expedition to rescue Emin Pasha, the governor of Equatoria (then a province of Egypt); Stanley details this mission in his well-known work *In Darkest Africa* (1890). Clayton arguably also shares similarities with Livingstone and others, but the allusion to Stanley is cemented by the fact that Clayton's wife, Lady Alice, clearly takes her name from Stanley's boat, the *Lady Alice* (a ship named *Lady Alice* also appears in the second novel, *The Return of Tarzan*). While Stanley could also serve as a possible model for Tarzan himself, he is a closer match to the ape-man's biological father.

These connections underscore not only the relation between *Tarzan of the Apes* and early twentieth-century Anglo-American dealings with Africa, but also the novel's larger ties to imperial and racial politics. As the controversies around Leopold and Stanley indicate, the relations between native Africans and European colonizers were characterized by inequality and brutality, both of which were extended in the Atlantic slave trade and the enslavement of Africans and their descendants in the US and elsewhere. By the time Burroughs wrote *Tarzan of the Apes*, American slavery had been legally ended for close to fifty years, but its effects, in terms of racism, economic inequality, and other injustices faced by African Americans, were still very much part of daily life. Created at a time when the US

[7] For a discussion of the various controversies surrounding Stanley, including a reported use of slaves, which Stanley denied, see Felix Driver's 'Henry Morton Stanley and His Critics: Geography, Exploration and Empire', *Past and Present*, 133 (1991), 134–66.

was engaged in a significant cultural and social debate over the influx of recently freed, rural African Americans into the then largely white urban centres, and during a new influx of immigrants to the United States, Tarzan (the character and the book) reads also as a response to progressive, liberal race relations.[8] Tarzan's name, in the language of the 'anthropoid apes', after all, means 'white-skin'. Tying such politics to the 'effeminizing' effects of civilization, Burroughs creates a figure who allegorically traverses the different steps of a pseudo-scientific ladder of biological and social evolution: Tarzan's 'civilized' social background is stripped away, and he starts life as an ape, moves later towards a black African community, and finally enters the upper echelons of white European culture. Tarzan 'naturally' recognizes white superiority, and has few qualms about killing black people. In many ways, then, *Tarzan of the Apes* is a novel that at least tacitly, and in many places explicitly, reinforces contemporary ideas of specifically Anglo-Saxon superiority.

Tarzan's views towards native Africans vary in the series, and Burroughs did himself criticize some visions of imperial supremacy early in his career. He has been credited with writing one of many parodies of Rudyard Kipling's 'The White Man's Burden'. In this poem Kipling justifies Anglo-American imperial conquest of non-white peoples, portraying such conquest as a civilizing force. The anonymous 'Black Man's Burden' critiques such imperialism, much as in the opening pages of *Tarzan of the Apes*. But this parody, while effectively pointing out the hypocrisy of Kipling's vision of the necessity of imperialism, does not challenge the original's assumption of racial superiority. The poem foreshadows the attitudes of Burroughs's most famous novel. The ethical force of both works is directed to what Burroughs saw as the corrupting influence of 'civilization', which removes humanity from its empowering connection to nature, a connection, the poem argues, held in the twentieth century only by 'simple folk'. Later in his career, while covering a murder trial for the *Los Angeles Examiner*, he began to espouse seemingly eugenicist opinions (though not in a racial sense) with a view to 'dispens[ing] with' those he deemed 'moral imbeciles'.[9] *Tarzan of the Apes* trades in the racial attitudes and stereotypes

---

[8] See Cheyfitz, p. 4.
[9] See Taliaferro, 19, 225–31.

found in the popular African adventure tales, combining them with more than a smattering of the biological determinism that supported the eugenics movement, and thus not only reproduces the more problematic stereotypes, but also offers a redefinition of an idealized white masculinity, albeit one that of necessity shies away from 'white' civilization.

Tarzan, Nature, and Civilization

Part of this yearning for a 'primitive', uncivilized life is figured through Burroughs's depiction of the 'savage' wilderness of Africa itself. More fiction than accurate description (as evidenced by Burroughs's misplacement of tigers in Africa in the original *All-Story* version), Burroughs's Africa was influenced by popular descriptions from exploration narratives. One of the more intriguing of these is Paul Du Chaillu's *Explorations and Adventures in Equatorial Africa* (1861), which contains vivid descriptions of hunting, especially of gorillas (which were, at the time of Du Chaillu's explorations, largely mythical for the West). At times, Du Chaillu's accounts read like the most lurid of Tarzan's adventures. Du Chaillu describes his 'first gorilla':

Suddenly, as we were yet creeping along, in a silence which made a heavy breath seem loud and distinct, the woods were at once filled with the tremendous barking roar of the gorilla. Then the underbrush swayed rapidly just ahead, and presently before us stood an immense male gorilla. He had gone through the jungle on his all-fours; but when he saw our party he erected himself and looked us boldly in the face. He stood about a dozen yards from us, and was a sight I think never to forget. Nearly six feet high (he proved four inches shorter), with immense body, huge chest, and great muscular arms, with fiercely-glaring large deep gray eyes, and a hellish expression of face, which seemed to me like some nightmare vision: thus stood before us this king of the African forest.[10]

The reference to the 'king' of the jungle, the memorable roar (which Du Chaillu goes on to describe at great length as 'the most singular and awful noise heard in these African woods'), and the

[10] Paul Du Chaillu, *Explorations and Adventures in Equatorial Africa* (New York: Harper and Brothers, 1861; repr. New York: Negro Univ. Press, 1969), 98.

overall demonic description of the gorilla are close to Burroughs's own portrayal of Tarzan's ape family. Similarly, Robert Hartmann's early description of apes in general, in his *Anthropoid Apes* (1886), anticipates the way in which Burroughs describes the difference between Tarzan and his adopted family: 'A great chasm between man and anthropoids is constituted, as I believe, by the fact that the human race is capable of education, and is able to acquire the highest mental culture, while the most intelligent anthropoid can only receive a certain mechanical training.'[11] As in Burroughs's novel, 'Man's Reason' is held up as separating humanity from the natural world.

But, for Burroughs, increasing that gap too widely leads to a weakening of humanity. This fear of civilization and its degenerating effects connects *Tarzan of the Apes* to other cultural contexts, beyond Africa. *Tarzan of the Apes* fully participates in what one critic calls 'the cult of the primitive man'.[12] With the rise of the so-called 'New Woman' and the very active women's suffrage movement (Burroughs's novel was published during the height of the militant period of the suffragette movement), traditional masculinity was perceived as being under threat. The fascination with primitivism and its supposedly revivifying effects on masculinity thus arose as a partial response to the perceived decline of manhood and the nineteenth century's 'Cult of True Womanhood'.[13]

The related fixation on the wilderness and its beneficial effects on masculine identity finds its roots in the Transcendentalist thought of such figures as Ralph Waldo Emerson and Henry David Thoreau, who, like Burroughs, criticized the degrading effects on humanity of civilization, while simultaneously lauding the positive effects of a life in nature. Central figures in the American Transcendentalist school of writers, both Emerson and Thoreau, like the British Romantics before them, wrote extensively on the need to reconnect with the natural world, and on what they saw as the supremacy of

---

[11] Robert Hartmann, *Anthropoid Apes* (New York: D. Appleton and Co., 1886), 295.

[12] Roderick Nash, 'The American Cult of the Primitive', *American Quarterly*, 18/3 (1966), 517–37.

[13] See Barbara Welter, 'The Cult of True Womanhood: 1820–1860', *American Quarterly*, 18/2 (1966), 151–74.

an individualist approach to life. Emerson wrote philosophical essays on both topics, including 'Nature' (1836) and 'Self-Reliance' (1841). Taken together, these essays argue that only through an individual approach to life, uncluttered by the expectations of others and the trappings of the civilized world, can a person come to appreciate the transcendent truths of existence. Thoreau, meanwhile, tried to put these theories into practice, building a small cabin in the woods where he intended to live largely off the land; he published the account of his experience in the well-known book *Walden; or, Life in the Woods* (1854). Indeed, Tarzan, in one sense, is a literary culmination of Emerson's 'Self-Reliance', and his parents' cabin on the beach a version of Thoreau's famous shack at Walden Pond.

The idea that living in nature would revivify humanity and, especially, manhood, gained in popularity in the late nineteenth and early twentieth centuries, culminating in an oft-repeated desire to reconnect the civilized world to nature. One of the primary methods to bring about this reconnection was thought to be teaching the benefits of nature to young people, and to young boys especially. The principal organizations to put this method into practice were those associated with the Scouting movement. This movement has both North American and British origins, through Ernest Thompson Seton (1860–1946) and Robert Baden-Powell (1857–1941), respectively. Seton had started a group called the Woodcraft Indians in 1902. Structured around Seton's vision of aboriginal life in North America, the Woodcraft Indians taught young boys various outdoor skills. In 1906, Seton met Baden-Powell in England. Baden-Powell had earlier published a military text, *Aids to Scouting* (1899), but after meeting Seton, Baden-Powell published *Scouting for Boys* (1908), which became the foundation for the Boy Scouts movement. Like the writings of the earlier Romantics, these works espoused the benefits of a life connected to nature, as opposed to city life. Unlike the individualist Romanticism of Thoreau or Wordsworth, however, Scouting emphasized the ways in which an ordered life, connected to nature, could lead to a more 'proper' form of masculine citizenship for the boys in the organization. Like the young Tarzan of Burroughs's novel, the Scouts were to become physically and mentally fit through a relationship to their natural surroundings, creating what their leaders saw as a more proper, 'noble' masculinity formed through a

deep and personal connection to nature. Later, some Scouting-style
organizations based themselves explicitly on Burroughs's creation:
they were called the 'Tarzan Clans of America'.

These movements signalled a turn to a kind of revived Romanticism and emphasized a natural, physical existence that stood against
the industrialization, mechanization, and urbanization of life at the
time. This 'back to nature' movement is perhaps best exemplified
in the famous experiment undertaken by Joseph Knowles (who was
called by some the 'Maine Tarzan'). In his *Alone in the Wilderness*,
published in 1913, the year after Tarzan's appearance in *All-Story*,
Knowles describes how he lived alone in the woods with no civilized
accoutrements—including clothes, for he entered the woods naked:
'I believed there was too much artificial life at the present day in the
cities. I found myself comparing our present mode of living with
the wild rugged life of the great outdoors. Then, all of a sudden,
I wondered if the man of the present day could leave all his luxury
behind him and go back into the wilderness and live on what nature
intended him to have.'[14] At the end of the book, Knowles lauds the
Scouting movement. Knowles, like others in the various streams of
the 'back to nature' movements, thus echoes *Tarzan of the Apes*'s
statements about the threat posed to manhood by civilization
(although some accused Knowles's experiment of being almost as
much a fiction as *Tarzan of the Apes*).

Knowles's vision of leading a purely 'natural' life leads to a final
'natural' context for *Tarzan of the Apes*. Tarzan is the quintessential
fictional vision of the 'feral child', a term used to describe an
abandoned child, who is left with little or no human contact during his
or her formative years, and who is often portrayed as being raised by
animals. Burroughs stated that he was relying on that other allegory
of the origins of civilization, the story of Romulus and Remus, the
legendary founders of Rome, who were raised by wolves. Plutarch's
description of these mythological characters certainly bears a family
resemblance to Tarzan. He writes that Romulus and Remus 'were
found sucking the wolf. In their very infancy, the size and beauty of
their bodies intimated their natural superiority; and when they grew
up, they both proved brave and manly, attempting all enterprises

---

[14] Joseph Knowles, *Alone in the Wilderness* (Boston: Small, Maynard and Company,
1913), 4.

that seemed hazardous, and showing in them a courage altogether undaunted.'[15]

Other stories of so-called 'wild children' have been popular throughout the history of the West and elsewhere, and Burroughs's portrayal of Tarzan's physical and character traits echoes the more famous of these stories. Two of the more well-known feral children, Peter the Wild Boy and Victor, the Wild Boy of Aveyron, were made famous in the eighteenth and early nineteenth centuries respectively. As described in Henry Wilson's *Wonderful Characters* (1821), Peter was found in Hanover in Germany, in 1725, 'walking on his hands and feet, climbing trees like a squirrel, and feeding on grass and moss'.[16] Later taken to England, Peter became the subject of much popular interest. He was also the subject of more serious investigation. Having only a rudimentary control of language, Peter was considered by James Burnett, Lord Monboddo, as the perfect specimen for the study of the origin of language in humans. Like Burroughs's fictional feral child, Peter seemed to exemplify early theories of human development. Unlike Tarzan, though, this actual 'Wild Boy' never developed advanced social skills. According to Wilson, Monboddo nevertheless believed that Peter, like Tarzan, 'understood the language of birds and beasts, by which they express their appetites and feelings' and 'that his senses were more acute than those of the tame man'. Similarly, E. M. Itard, who studied Victor, the Wild Boy of Aveyron, writes that he recognized, in the behaviour of 'the savage', 'that primitive language of the human species, originally employed in the infancy of society'.[17] From Peter to Victor, and to many others before and after, the figure of the uncivilized child raised completely outside human contact has been used to discuss the origins of humanity and its societies. They, like Tarzan, highlight the anxieties and promises of civilization (especially through the general debate of 'nature vs. nurture'), while simultaneously helping to define characteristics of the 'uncivilized' wilderness.

---

[15] Plutarch, *Plutarch's Lives: The Translation Called Dryden's*, corrected from the Greek and revised by A. H. Cough, vol. i (Boston: Little Brown, 1895), 44.

[16] Henry Wilson, 'Peter the Wild Boy', *Wonderful Characters: Comprising Memoirs and Anecdotes of the Most Remarkable Persons of Every Age and Nation*, vol. ii (London: J. Robins and Co. Albion Press, Ivy Lane, Paternoster Row, 1821), 152–60.

[17] E. M. Itard, *An Historical Account of the Discovery and Education of a Savage Man, or of the First Developments, Physical and Moral, of the Young Savage Caught in the Woods Near Aveyron, in the Year 1798* (London: Richard Phillips, 1802), 106.

Tarzan's Literary and Cultural Relations

The issues raised by the uncivilized spectre of the feral child have
been examined by literary authors other than Burroughs, including,
of course, Rudyard Kipling. Burroughs drew on Kipling's *Jungle
Book* (1894) as an inspiration for his novel, though how deeply
Burroughs's text 'borrowed' or was 'inspired' by the earlier work
remains a contentious issue. (Kipling saw Burroughs as, at best, an
'imitator'.)[18] The hero of *The Jungle Book* is a 'wild boy', Mowgli. Like
Romulus and Remus he is raised by wolves, in India, where Kipling
himself was brought up. Both Tarzan and Mowgli are innocent of
colonial invasion (though that innocence is figured differently in both
works) but they nonetheless 'naturally' take a superior position in
their alien environments.

   There are other direct literary sources for Tarzan. Burroughs cited
English author H. Rider Haggard as a general influence.[19] Haggard's
King Solomon's Mines (1885) has many features in common with
Tarzan of the Apes. Set in Africa, it deals with both an undiscovered
civilization and a lost treasure; Burroughs includes the discovery of
a lost treasure in *Tarzan of the Apes* but in *Return of Tarzan* more
explicitly rewrites 'Solomon's Treasure Chamber' from Haggard's
novel into the piles of gold in the 'lost city' of Opar. Haggard's novels
also provide a foundation for the colonial context present in both
Tarzan of the Apes and *The Jungle Book*. They also display bluntly
racist attitudes towards the native Africans, while at times questioning
those same assumptions. For example, near the beginning of *King
Solomon's Mines*, Allan Quatermain meditates on the definition of
'gentleman':

And, besides, am I a gentleman? What is a gentleman? I don't quite
know, and yet I have had to do with niggers—no, I'll scratch that word
'niggers' out, for I don't like it. I've known natives who *are*, and so you'll
say, Harry, my boy, before you're done with this tale, and I have known
mean whites with lots of money and fresh out from home, too, who
ain't.[20]

[18] Irwin Porges, *Edgar Rice Burroughs: The Man Who Created Tarzan* (Provo, Utah:
Brigham Young Univ. Press, 1975), 132. Kipling's book also influenced Baden-Powell's
principles for Scouting.
   [19] See Porges, 130.
   [20] H. Rider Haggard, *King Solomon's Mines* (Oxford: OUP, 1989), 9.

Like Burroughs, Haggard trades in racial stereotypes, even as they are shown to be inadequate. Burroughs explicitly writes Tarzan back into this colonial setting, but also moves out from Victorian British and European colonialism to the American context, presenting a character who is at once more in control of the colonial situation than his British forebears and more isolated from what are represented as the emasculating effects of the civilized nations. While Tarzan may have British parents, he is very much an American creation.

In the American literary landscape, the adventure story became a staple of the popular fiction magazines of the early twentieth century. The pulp publishing market in which *Tarzan of the Apes* originally appeared provided the reading public with numerous 'genre' stories, from detective fiction, to romance stories, to tales of adventure, to fantasy and science fiction. These magazines gave rise to any number of popular characters who continue to be recognized today: Tarzan, of course, but also Buck Rogers, and the Shadow. These staples of the pulp market in turn drew from more literary forebears: James Fenimore Cooper's Leatherstocking adventures, and Jack London's naturalist analyses of the American individual. Cooper's historical novels, including *The Last of the Mohicans* (1826), describe early frontier life in America (both before and after the American Revolution), and like the Tarzan novels, feature adventure mixed with a return to a wilder, less civilized setting. Novels such as London's *The Call of the Wild* (1903) and *The Sea-Wolf* (1904) build on similar themes. Written at roughly the same time as Burroughs's novel, London's works share many of the same elements: the individual pitted against brutal, violent, and unforgiving circumstances, and not only surviving but thriving.

Tarzan could even be said to share kinship with Rousseau's 'natural man', whose innocence society's 'education and habits could corrupt but not entirely destroy',[21] and Nietzsche's *Übermensch* ('superman' or 'overman'), who will eventually shed the petty morality of civilized people. The danger of Tarzan's criticism of society, like that of Nietzsche, is that it plays into a vision of racial superiority that has proved as pernicious as the character is popular.

[21] Jean Jacques Rousseau, *Discourse on Inequality*, trans. Franklin Philip, ed. Patrick Coleman (Oxford: OUP, 1999), 25.

Tarzan's Afterlife

Burroughs continued writing Tarzan tales until his death, and in the following decades other writers, such as Fritz Lieber and Phillip José Farmer, who were sanctioned by Burroughs's estate, took up his story. Burroughs himself paved the way for the mass franchising of his ape-man. He formed his own publishing firm, 'Edgar Rice Burroughs, Inc.', in order to take full control of his creation, and continued to license the character for a wide variety of uses, from comic strips to toys.

Perhaps the most enduring of these non-literary Tarzans, however, was the first to appear, and one that began its own life well before ERB, Inc.: the Tarzan made famous in film. Burroughs's first foray into motion pictures was the production of a non-Tarzan story, *The Lad and the Lion*, which hit the screens in 1917. Ever the canny publicist, Burroughs arranged for the serial publication of that novel in *All-Story* to coincide, as closely as possible, with the film release. The first cinematic adaptation of *Tarzan of the Apes*—a silent film—appeared under that title in 1918. Split into three parts (dealing with the Claytons' arrival on the shores of Africa, Tarzan as a young child, and then his later adult life), the film became among the first to gross $1 million. The young Tarzan was played by Gordon Griffith, while the adult character was played by Elmo Lincoln. Lincoln reportedly killed a real lion on set, while filming the scene in which Tarzan drags the animal out of the cabin to save Jane.

From this auspicious beginning, Tarzan became a regular fixture in the cinema. Perhaps the image of Tarzan that most of us now have comes not directly from Burroughs's novel but from Johnny Weissmuller's portrayal of the ape-man. Weissmuller (1904–84), an Olympic gold medal swimmer, played Tarzan in twelve films between 1932 and 1948. The first of these, *Tarzan the Ape Man*, has led to most of the popular images of Tarzan, from his stilted English and the sound of his famous yell to his loincloth and the line 'Me Tarzan, You Jane' (though it never actually occurs in the film, this famous catchphrase is a fairly good summary of a lengthier, humorous scene in which Jane tries to introduce herself and learn Tarzan's name). That film also gave us the current pronunciation of Tarzan's name: Burroughs pronounced the name with the emphasis on the first syllable, with the second syllable rhyming with 'run' rather than with 'ran'. Burroughs, however, responded nonchalantly to the change: 'I don't give a damn what they call him . . . as long as their checks come regularly.'[22]

Beyond the author, even beyond the novel, Tarzan has become one of the most marketed icons of the twentieth century. And yet the continuing fascination of the original novel lies deeper than its iconic central character: it lies in a story that reflects many of the individual yearnings and social tensions of the last century.

[22] Taliaferro, 252.

NOTE ON THE TEXT

THE text used is the 1914 first book edition, published by McClurg, which has been checked against an early A. L. Burt reprint (*c*.1915), the first British edition published by Methuen in 1917, and an early Grosset and Dunlop edition (*c*.1928). Obvious typographical errors in the first edition that were corrected in later editions are silently corrected here, though in less obvious cases where the editions vary, the first edition has been followed. *Tarzan of the Apes* was first published in *All-Story* magazine in October 1912 (vol. 24, number 2), where it was subtitled on the cover 'A Romance of the Jungle'. The *All-Story* and first book edition are largely similar, though there are typographical differences, and Burroughs expanded the work for the McClurg publication. Along with some additions of description, these changes consist largely of making some of the language more robust, and correcting portions of the text (the most famous correction was to replace references to 'tigers', which do not live in Africa, with 'panther', 'leopard', or, most commonly, 'lioness'). The more significant differences are noted in the Explanatory Notes, especially where they change characterization or other important aspects of the work.

SELECT BIBLIOGRAPHY

Tarzan Books by Edgar Rice Burroughs

The editions listed are the first book publications.

Tarzan of the Apes (McClurg, 1914).
The Return of Tarzan (McClurg, 1915).
The Beasts of Tarzan (McClurg, 1916).
The Son of Tarzan (McClurg, 1917).
Tarzan and the Jewels of Opar (McClurg, 1918).
Jungle Tales of Tarzan (McClurg, 1919).
Tarzan the Untamed (McClurg, 1920).
Tarzan the Terrible (McClurg, 1921).
Tarzan and the Golden Lion (McClurg, 1923).
Tarzan and the Ant Men (McClurg, 1924).
The Tarzan Twins (P. F. Volland, 1927; for younger readers).
Tarzan, Lord of the Jungle (McClurg, 1928).
Tarzan and the Lost Empire (Metropolitan, 1929).
Tarzan at the Earth's Core (Metropolitan, 1930; also part of the Pellucidar series).
Tarzan the Invincible (Edgar Rice Burroughs, Inc., 1931).
Tarzan Triumphant (Edgar Rice Burroughs, Inc., 1932).
Tarzan and the City of Gold (Edgar Rice Burroughs, Inc., 1933).
Tarzan and the Lion Man (Edgar Rice Burroughs, Inc., 1934).
Tarzan and the Leopard Men (Edgar Rice Burroughs, Inc., 1935).
Tarzan Twins with Jad-bal-Ja (Whitman, 1936; for younger readers).
Tarzan's Quest (Edgar Rice Burroughs, Inc., 1936).
Tarzan and the Forbidden City (Edgar Rice Burroughs, Inc., 1938).
Tarzan the Magnificent (Edgar Rice Burroughs, Inc., 1939).
Tarzan and the Foreign Legion (Edgar Rice Burroughs, Inc., 1947).
Tarzan and the Madman (Canaveral, 1964).
Tarzan and the Castaways (Canaveral, 1967).
Tarzan— The Lost Adventure (Dark Horse, 1995; completed by Joe Lansdale, based on extensive notes by Burroughs).

Biography

Lupoff, Richard A., *Edgar Rice Burroughs: Master of Adventure* (New York: Ace, 1968).
Porges, Irwin, *Edgar Rice Burroughs: The Man Who Created Tarzan* (Provo, Utah: Brigham Young Univ. Press, 1975).

Taliaferro, John, *Tarzan Forever: The Life of Edgar Rice Burroughs, Creator of Tarzan* (New York: Scribner, 1999).

Letters

Brother Men: The Correspondence of Edgar Rice Burroughs and Herbert T. Weston, ed. and introd. Matt Cohen (Durham, NC: Duke Univ. Press, 2005).

Criticism

Berglund, Jeff, *Cannibal Fictions: American Explorations of Colonialism, Race, Gender, and Sexuality* (Madison: Univ. of Wisconsin Press, 2006).

Carey-Webb, Allen, '*Heart of Darkness*, *Tarzan*, and the "Third World": Canons and Encounters in World Literature, English 109', *College Literature*, 19-20/3–1 (1992), 121–41.

Cheyfitz, Eric, *The Poetics of Imperialism: Translation and Colonization from* The Tempest *to* Tarzan (Philadelphia: Univ. of Pennsylvania Press, 1997).

Cowart, David, 'The Tarzan Myth and Jung's Genesis of the Self', *Journal of American Culture*, 2/2 (1979), pp. 220–30.

Davison, Richard Allan, 'Edgar Rice Burroughs, Tarzan, and Hemingway', *North Dakota Quarterly*, 63/3 (1996), 34–9.

Galloway, Stan, 'The Greystoke Connection: Medievalism in Two Edgar Rice Burroughs Novels', *Studies in Medievalism*, 6 (1994), 100–8.

Gleason, William, 'Of Sequels and Sons: Tarzan and the Problem of Paternity', *Journal of American and Comparative Cultures*, 23/1 (2000), 41–51.

Hollow, John, 'Rereading *Tarzan of the Apes*; or "What Is It," Lady Alice Whispered, "A Man?"'', *Dalhousie Review*, 56 (1976), 83–92.

Holtsmark, Erling B., *Edgar Rice Burroughs* (Boston: Twayne, 1986).

—— *Tarzan and Tradition: Classical Myth in Popular Literature* (Westport, Conn.: Greenwood, 1981).

Jurca, Catherine, *White Diaspora: The Suburb and the Twentieth-Century American Novel* (Princeton: Princeton Univ. Press, 2001).

Morton, Walt, 'Tracking the Sign of Tarzan: Trans-Media Representation of a Pop-Culture Icon', in Pat Kirkham and Janet Thumim (eds.), *You Tarzan: Masculinity, Movies and Men* (New York: St. Martin's, 1993), 106–25.

Nash, Roderick, 'The American Cult of the Primitive', *American Quarterly*, 18/3 (1966), 517–37.

Nesteby, James R., 'Tarzan and the Ku Klux Klan: Anglo-Americanism in the Twenties', *Journal of English*, 6 (1979), 79–109.

Newsinger, John, 'Reader, He Rescued Her: Women in the Tarzan Stories', *Foundation: The Review of Science Fiction*, 39 (1987), 41–9.

Stecopoulos, Harry, 'The World According to Normal Bean: Edgar Rice Burroughs' Popular Culture', in Harry Stecopoulos and Michael Uebel (eds.), *Race and the Subject of Masculinities* (Durham, NC: Duke Univ. Press, 1997), 170–91.

Torgovnick, Marianna, *Gone Primitive: Savage Intellects, Modern Lives* (Chicago: Univ. of Chicago Press, 1990).

Trigilio, Tony, 'Staring Back in the Classroom: Genre, Identity, and the Power in Looking', *Modern Language Studies*, 26/4, (1996), 99–107.

African Exploration

Du Chaillu, Paul, *Explorations and Adventures in Equatorial Africa* (New York: Harper, 1861; repr. New York: Negro Univ. Press, 1969).

Kingsley, Mary H., *Travels in West Africa* (London: Macmillan, 1897).

Park, Mungo, *Travels in the Interior Districts of Africa: Performed in the Years 1795, 1796, and 1797* (London: Murray, 1816).

Stanley, Henry M., *The Congo and the Founding of Its Free State: A Story of Work and Exploration* (New York: Harper, 1885).

—— *How I Found Livingstone: Travels, Adventures and Discoveries in Central Africa: Including an Account of Four Months' Residence with Dr. Livingstone* (London: Low, 1872).

—— *In Darkest Africa, or the Quest Rescue and Retreat of Emin Governor of Equatoria* (London: Sampson, 1890).

Nature

Baden-Powell, Robert, *Scouting for Boys: The Original 1908 Edition*, ed. Elleke Boehmer (Oxford: OUP, 2004).

Emerson, Ralph Waldo, *Essays* (Boston: James Munroe, 1841).

Knowles, Joseph, *Alone in the Wilderness* (Boston: Small, Maynard and Company, 1913).

Seton, Ernest Thompson, *Woodcraft and Indian Lore: A Classic Guide from a Founding Father of the Boy Scouts of America* (New York: Skyhorse, 2007).

Thoreau, Henry David, *Walden*, ed. Stephen Fender (Oxford: OUP, 1997).

Feral Children

Itard, E. M., *An Historical Account of the Discovery and Education of a Savage Man, or of the First Developments, Physical and Moral, of the Young Savage Caught in the Woods Near Aveyron, in the Year 1798* (London: Richard Phillips, 1802).

Kipling, Rudyard, *The Jungle Books*, ed. W. W. Robson (Oxford: OUP, 2008).

Plutarch, *Plutarch's Lives: The Translation Called Dryden's*, corrected from the Greek and revised by A. H. Cough, vol. i (Boston: Little Brown, 1895).

Wilson, Henry, 'Peter the Wild Boy', *Wonderful Characters: Comprising Memoirs and Anecdotes of the Most Remarkable Persons of Every Age and Nation*, vol. ii (London: J. Robins and Co. Albion Press, 1821), 152–60.

Miscellaneous

Chomsky, Noam, *Aspects of the Theory of Syntax* (Cambridge, Mass.: MIT Press, 1969).

Dante Alighieri, *The Divine Comedy*, trans. Henry F. Cary (New York: P. F. Collier, 1909).

Franklin, Benjamin, *Autobiography and Other Writings*, ed. Ormond Seavey (Oxford: OUP, 1998).

Hartmann, Robert, *Anthropoid Apes* (New York: D. Appleton and Co., 1886).

Locke, John, *Second Treatise of Government*, ed. C. B. Macpherson (Indianapolis: Hackett Publishing, 1980).

Longfellow, Henry Wadsworth, *Poems and Other Writings*, ed. J. D. McClatchy (New York: Library of America, 2000).

Milton, John, *Paradise Lost*, ed. Stephen Orgel and Jonathan Goldberg (Oxford: OUP, 2004).

Moore, Thomas, *Epistles, Odes, and Other Poems* (London: Carpenter, 1806).

Nietzsche, Friedrich, *Thus Spoke Zarathustra*, trans. Graham Parkes (Oxford: OUP, 2005).

A CHRONOLOGY OF
EDGAR RICE BURROUGHS

Because Burroughs published close to seventy novels, and numerous other stories and miscellanea, only major works or those significant to his career are mentioned here. For a full list of the Tarzan novels, see the Select Bibliography, above.

1875   (1 Sept.) ERB born in Chicago to George Tyler and Mary Evaline (Zieger) Burroughs.

1891   Sent to work on his brother's ranch in the new state of Idaho; briefly attends Phillips Academy in Andover, Massachusetts.

1895   Graduates from Michigan Military Academy.

1896   Joins army before his twenty-first birthday, with permission of his father; serves as a Private for the Seventh US Cavalry in Fort Grant, Arizona.

1900   (30 Jan.) Marries Emma Hulbert.

1900–11 Holds a wide variety of jobs, none for very long.

1908   (12 Jan.) Daughter, Joan, born.

1909   (12 Aug.) Son, Hulbert, born.

1912   (Feb.–July.) *Under the Moon of Mars* published serially, in *All-Story Magazine*, under the pseudonym 'Norman Bean' (Burroughs had intended the name to read 'Normal Bean'); (Oct.) *Tarzan of the Apes* published in *All-Story*, under Burroughs's real name.

1913   (Jan.–May) *The Gods of Mars* published serially in *All-Story*; *All-Story* rejects the sequel to *Tarzan of the Apes*; (15 Feb.) father, George Tyler Burroughs, dies; (28 Feb.) son, John (Jack) Coleman, born; (June–Nov.) *The Return of Tarzan* is published serially by *All-Story*'s competitor, *New Story*.

1914   (Apr.) *At the Earth's Core* published in *All-Story*; (June) *Tarzan of the Apes* published as a book by McClurg.

1915   *Return of Tarzan* is published by McClurg.

1918   First film version of *Tarzan of the Apes* premieres; (Aug., Oct., Dec.) *The Land that Time Forgot* published as three stories in *Blue Book*.

1919   Moves to California and buys a ranch that he renames 'Tarzana Ranch'.

1920   (5 April) Mother, Mary Evaline Burroughs, dies.

1922   *At Earth's Core* published by McClurg.

1923   Edgar Rice Burroughs, Inc., founded.

1924   *The Land the Time Forgot* published by McClurg.

1928   Daughter, Joan, marries Jim Pierce, who played Tarzan in the final silent Tarzan film, *Tarzan and the Golden Lion* (1927).

1929   First *Tarzan of the Apes* comic strips appear in newspapers in the US and Canada.

1931   *Tarzan the Invincible* published, the first by ERB, Inc.

1932   First 'talkie' Tarzan film is released: *Tarzan the Ape-Man*, starring Johnny Weissmuller; first *Tarzan of the Apes* radio show is produced, starring daughter Joan and son-in-law Jim Pierce; *Pirates of Venus* serialized in *Argosy*.

1934   *Pirates of Venus* published by ERB, Inc.; (Dec.) divorces Emma.

1935   (Apr.) Marries actress Florence Gilbert Dearholt, after her own divorce.

1940   Moves to Hawaii.

1941   Divorces Florence; (7 Dec.) witnesses the Japanese attack on Pearl Harbor; at the request of the military, Burroughs begins writing a column, 'Laugh it Off', for local newspapers, designed to help with civilian morale.

1942   Receives credentials to be a war correspondent.

1944   (5 Nov.) Emma Hulbert Burroughs dies.

1945   (May–June) Works as a Navy correspondent aboard the *USS Cahaba*; (Oct.) returns to California, following the end of the war.

1950   (19 Mar.) Dies of a heart attack.

TARZAN OF THE APES

To
Emma Hulbert Burroughs

CONTENTS

CHAPTER I

OUT TO SEA

I HAD this story from one who had no business to tell it to me, or to any other. I may credit the seductive influence of an old vintage upon the narrator for the beginning of it, and my own skeptical incredulity during the days that followed for the balance of the strange tale.

When my convivial host discovered that he had told me so much, and that I was prone to doubtfulness, his foolish pride assumed the task the old vintage had commenced, and so he unearthed written evidence in the form of musty manuscript, and dry official records of the British Colonial Office* to support many of the salient features of his remarkable narrative.

I do not say the story is true, for I did not witness the happenings which it portrays, but the fact that in the telling of it to you I have taken fictitious names for the principal characters quite sufficiently evidences the sincerity of my own belief that it *may* be true.

The yellow, mildewed pages of the diary of a man long dead, and the records of the Colonial Office dovetail perfectly with the narrative of my convivial host, and so I give you the story as I painstakingly pieced it out from these several various agencies.

If you do not find it credible you will at least be as one with me in acknowledging that it is unique, remarkable, and interesting.

From the records of the Colonial Office and from the dead man's diary we learn that a certain young English nobleman, whom we shall call John Clayton, Lord Greystoke, was commissioned to make a peculiarly delicate investigation of conditions in a British West Coast African Colony from whose simple native inhabitants another European power was known to be recruiting soldiers for its native army, which it used solely for the forcible collection of rubber* and ivory from the savage tribes along the Congo and the Aruwimi.*

The natives of the British Colony complained that many of their young men were enticed away through the medium of fair and glowing promises, but that few if any ever returned to their families.

The Englishmen in Africa went even further; saying that these poor blacks were held in virtual slavery, since when their terms of enlistment expired their ignorance was imposed upon by their white officers, and they were told that they had yet several years to serve.

And so the Colonial Office appointed John Clayton to a new post in British West Africa, but his confidential instructions centered on a thorough investigation of the unfair treatment of black British subjects by the officers of a friendly European power. Why he was sent, is, however, of little moment to this story, for he never made an investigation, nor, in fact, did he ever reach his destination.

Clayton was the type of Englishman that one likes best to associate with the noblest monuments of historic achievement upon a thousand victorious battle fields—a strong, virile man—mentally, morally, and physically.

In stature he was above the average height; his eyes were gray, his features regular and strong; his carriage that of perfect, robust health influenced by his years of army training.

Political ambition had caused him to seek transference from the army to the Colonial Office and so we find him, still young, intrusted with a delicate and important commission in the service of the Queen.*

When he received this appointment he was both elated and appalled. The preferment seemed to him in the nature of a well merited reward for painstaking and intelligent service, and as a stepping stone to posts of greater importance and responsibility; but, on the other hand, he had been married to the Hon. Alice Rutherford for scarce a three months, and it was the thought of taking this fair young girl into the dangers and isolation of tropical Africa that dismayed and appalled him.

For her sake he would have refused the appointment; but she would not have it so. Instead she insisted that he accept, and, indeed, take her with him.

There were mothers and brothers and sisters, and aunts and cousins to express various opinions on the subject, but as to what they severally advised history is silent.

We know only that on a bright May morning in 1888,* John, Lord Greystoke, and Lady Alice* sailed from Dover on their way to Africa.

A month later they arrived at Freetown* where they chartered a small sailing vessel, the *Fuwalda*,* which was to bear them to their final destination.

And here John, Lord Greystoke, and Lady Alice, his wife, vanished from the eyes and from the knowledge of men.

Two months after they weighed anchor and cleared from the port of Freetown a half dozen British war vessels were scouring the south Atlantic for trace of them or their little vessel, and it was almost immediately that the wreckage was found upon the shores of St. Helena* which convinced the world that the *Fuwalda* had gone down with all on board, and hence the search was stopped ere it had scarce begun; though hope lingered in longing hearts for many years.

The *Fuwalda*, a barkantine of about one hundred tons, was a vessel of the type often seen in coastwise trade in the far southern Atlantic, their crews composed of the offscourings of the sea—unhanged murderers and cutthroats of every race and every nation.

The *Fuwalda* was no exception to the rule. Her officers were swarthy bullies, hating and hated by their crew. The captain, while a competent seaman, was a brute in his treatment of his men. He knew, or at least he used, but two arguments in his dealings with them—a belaying pin and a revolver—nor is it likely that the motley aggregation he signed would have understood aught else.

So it was that from the second day out from Freetown John Clayton and his young wife witnessed scenes upon the deck of the *Fuwalda* such as they had believed were never enacted outside the covers of printed stories of the sea.

It was on the morning of the second day that the first link was forged of what was destined to form a chain of circumstances ending in a life for one then unborn such as has probably never been paralleled in the history of man.

Two sailors were washing down the decks of the *Fuwalda*, the first mate was on duty, and the captain had stopped to speak with John Clayton and Lady Alice.

The men were working backwards toward the little party who were facing away from the sailors. Closer and closer they came, until one of them was directly behind the captain. In another moment he would have passed by and this strange narrative had never been recorded.

But just that instant the officer turned to leave Lord and Lady Greystoke, and, as he did so, tripped against the sailor and sprawled headlong upon the deck, overturning the water-pail so that he was drenched in its dirty contents.

For an instant the scene was ludicrous; but only for an instant. With a volley of awful oaths, his face suffused with the scarlet of mortification and rage, the captain regained his feet, and with a terrific blow felled the sailor to the deck.

The man was small and rather old, so that the brutality of the act was thus accentuated. The other seaman, however, was neither old nor small—a huge bear of a man, with fierce black mustachios, and a great bull neck set between massive shoulders.

As he saw his mate go down he crouched, and, with a low snarl, sprang upon the captain crushing him to his knees with a single mighty blow.

From scarlet the officer's face went white, for this was mutiny; and mutiny he had met and subdued before in his brutal career. Without waiting to rise he whipped a revolver from his pocket, firing point blank at the great mountain of muscle towering before him; but, quick as he was, John Clayton was almost as quick, so that the bullet which was intended for the sailor's heart lodged in the sailor's leg instead, for Lord Greystoke had struck down the captain's arm as he had seen the weapon flash in the sun.

Words passed between Clayton and the captain, the former making it plain that he was disgusted with the brutality displayed toward the crew, nor would he countenance anything further of the kind while he and Lady Greystoke remained passengers.

The captain was on the point of making an angry reply, but, thinking better of it, turned on his heel and black and scowling, strode aft.

He did not care to antagonize an English official, for the Queen's mighty arm wielded a punitive instrument which he could appreciate, and which he feared—England's far reaching navy.*

The two sailors picked themselves up, the older man assisting his wounded comrade to rise. The big fellow, who was known among his mates as Black Michael, tried his leg gingerly, and, finding that it bore his weight, turned to Clayton with a word of gruff thanks.

Though the fellow's tone was surly, his words were evidently well meant. Ere he had scarce finished his little speech he had turned and was limping off toward the forecastle with the very apparent intention of forestalling any further conversation.

They did not see him again for several days, nor did the captain vouchsafe them more than the surliest of grunts when he was forced to speak to them.

They messed in his cabin, as they had before the unfortunate occurrence; but the captain was careful to see that his duties never permitted him to eat at the same time.

The other officers were coarse, illiterate fellows, but little above the villainous crew they bullied, and were only too glad to avoid social intercourse with the polished English noble and his lady, so that the Claytons were left very much to themselves.

This in itself accorded perfectly with their desires, but it also rather isolated them from the life of the little ship so that they were unable to keep in touch with the daily happenings which were to culminate so soon in bloody tragedy.

There was in the whole atmosphere of the craft that undefinable something which presages disaster. Outwardly, to the knowledge of the Claytons, all went on as before upon the little vessel, but that there was an undertow leading them toward some unknown danger both felt, though they did not speak of it to each other.

On the second day after the wounding of Black Michael, Clayton came on deck just in time to see the limp body of one of the crew being carried below by four of his fellows while the first mate, a heavy belaying pin in his hand, stood glowering at the little party of sullen sailors.

Clayton asked no questions—he did not need to—and the following day, as the great lines of a British battle-ship grew out of the distant horizon, he half determined to demand that he and Lady Alice be put aboard her, for his fears were steadily increasing that nothing but harm could result from remaining on the lowering, sullen *Fuwalda*.

Toward noon they were within speaking distance of the British vessel, but when Clayton had about decided to ask the captain to put them aboard her, the obvious ridiculousness of such a request became suddenly apparent. What reason could he give the officer commanding her majesty's ship for desiring to go back in the direction from which he had just come!

Faith, what if he told them that two insubordinate seamen had been roughly handled by their officers. They would but laugh in their sleeves and attribute his reason for wishing to leave the ship to but one thing—cowardice.

John Clayton, Lord Greystoke, did not ask to be transferred to the British man-of-war, and late in the afternoon he saw her upper works fade below the far horizon, but not before he learned that which confirmed his greatest fears, and caused him to curse the false pride which had restrained him from seeking safety for his young wife a few short hours before, when safety was within reach—a safety which was now gone forever.

It was mid-afternoon that brought the little old sailor, who had been felled by the captain a few days before, to where Clayton and his wife stood by the ship's side watching the ever diminishing outlines of the great battle-ship. The old fellow was polishing brasses, and as he came edging along until close to Clayton he said, in an undertone:

"'Ell's to pay, sir, on this 'ere craft, an' mark my word for it, sir. 'Ell's to pay."*

"What do you mean, my good fellow?" asked Clayton.

"Wy, hasn't ye seen wats goin' on? Hasn't ye 'eard that devil's spawn of a capting an' 'is mates knockin' the bloomin' lights outen 'arf the crew?

"Two busted 'eads yeste'day, an' three today. Black Michael's as good as new agin an' 'e's not the bully to stand fer it, not 'e; an' mark my word for it, sir."

"You mean, my man, that the crew contemplates mutiny?" asked Clayton.

"Mutiny!" exclaimed the old fellow. "Mutiny! They means murder, sir, an' mark my word for it, sir."

"When?"

"Hit's comin', sir; hit's comin' but I'm not a-sayin' wen, an' I've said too damned much now, but ye was a good sort t'other day an' I thought it no more'n right to warn ye. But keep a still tongue in yer 'ead an' when ye hear shootin' git below an' stay there.

"That's all, only keep a still tongue in yer 'ead, or they'll put a pill* between yer ribs, an' mark my word for it, sir," and the old fellow went on with his polishing, which carried him away from where the Claytons were standing.

"Deuced cheerful outlook, Alice," said Clayton.

"You should warn the captain at once, John. Possibly the trouble may yet be averted," she said.

"I suppose I should, but yet from purely selfish motives I am almost prompted to 'keep a still tongue in my 'ead.' Whatever they do now they will spare us in recognition of my stand for this fellow

Black Michael, but should they find that I had betrayed them there would be no mercy shown us, Alice."

"You have but one duty, John, and that lies in the interest of vested authority. If you do not warn the captain you are as much a party to whatever follows as though you had helped to plot and carry it out with your own head and hands."

"You do not understand, dear," replied Clayton. "It is of you I am thinking—there lies my first duty. The captain has brought this condition upon himself, so why then should I risk subjecting my wife to unthinkable horrors in probably futile attempt to save him from his own brutal folly? You have no conception, dear, of what would follow were this pack of cutthroats to gain control of the *Fuwalda*."

"Duty is duty, my husband, and no amount of sophistries may change it. I would be a poor wife for an English lord were I to be responsible for his shirking a plain duty. I realize the danger which must follow, but I can face it with you—face it much more bravely than I could face the dishonor of always knowing that you might have averted a tragedy had you not neglected your duty."

"Have it as you will then, Alice," he answered, smiling. "Maybe we are borrowing trouble. While I do not like the looks of things on board this ship, they may not be so bad after all, for it is possible that the 'Ancient Mariner'* was but voicing the desires of his wicked old heart rather than speaking of real facts.

"Mutiny on the high sea may have been common a hundred years ago,* but in this good year 1888 it is the least likely of happenings.

"But there goes the captain to his cabin now. If I am going to warn him I might as well get the beastly job over for I have little stomach to talk with the brute at all."

So saying he strolled carelessly in the direction of the companionway through which the captain had passed, and a moment later was knocking at his door.

"Come in," growled the deep tones of that surly officer.

And when Clayton had entered, and closed the door behind him: "Well?"

"I have come to report the gist of a conversation I heard today, because I feel that, while there may be nothing to it, it is as well that you be forearmed. In short, the men contemplate mutiny and murder."

"It's a lie!" roared the captain. "And if you have been interfering again with the discipline of this ship, or meddling in affairs that don't concern you you can take the consequences, and be damned. I don't care whether you are an English lord or not. I'm captain of this here ship, and from now on you keep your meddling nose out of my business."

As he reached this peroration, the captain had worked himself up to such a frenzy of rage that he was fairly purple of face, and shrieked the last words at the top of his voice; emphasizing his remarks by a loud thumping of the table with one huge fist, shaking the other in Clayton's face.

Greystoke never turned a hair, but stood eying the excited man with level gaze.

"Captain Billings," he drawled finally, "if you will pardon my candor, I might remark that you are something of an ass, don't you know."

Whereupon he turned and left the cabin with the same indifferent ease that was habitual with him, and which was more surely calculated to raise the ire of a man of Billings's class than a torrent of invective.

So, whereas the captain might easily have been brought to regret his hasty speech had Clayton attempted to conciliate him, his temper was now irrevocably set in the mold in which Clayton had left it, and the last chance of their working together for their common good and preservation of life was gone.

"Well, Alice," said Clayton, as he rejoined his wife, "if I had saved my breath I should likewise have saved myself a bit of a calling. The fellow proved most ungrateful. Fairly jumped at me like a mad dog.

"He and his blasted old ship may go hang, for aught I care; and until we are safe off the thing I shall spend my energies in looking after our own welfare. And I rather fancy the first step to that end should be to go to our cabin and look over my revolvers. I am sorry now that we packed the larger guns and the ammunition with the stuff below."

They found their quarters in a bad state of disorder. Clothing from their open boxes and bags strewed the little apartment, and even their beds had been torn to pieces.

"Evidently someone was more anxious about our belongings than we," said Clayton. "By jove, I wonder what the bounder was after. Let's have a look around, Alice, and see what's missing."

A thorough search revealed the fact that nothing had been taken but Clayton's two revolvers and the small supply of ammunition he had saved out for them.

"Those are the very things I most wish they had left us," said Clayton, "and the fact that they wished for them and them alone is the most sinister circumstance of all that have transpired to endanger us since we set foot on this miserable hulk."

"What are we to do, John?" asked his wife. "I shall not urge you to go again to the captain for I cannot see you affronted further. Possibly our best chance for salvation lies in maintaining a neutral position.

"If the officers are able to prevent a mutiny, we have nothing to fear, while if the mutineers are victorious our one slim hope lies in not having attempted to thwart or antagonize them."

"Right you are, Alice. We'll keep in the middle of the road."

As they fell to in an effort to straighten up their cabin, Clayton and his wife simultaneously noticed the corner of a piece of paper protruding from beneath the door of their quarters. As Clayton stooped to reach for it he was amazed to see it move further into the room, and then he realized that it was being pushed inward by someone from without.

Quickly and silently he stepped toward the door, but, as he reached for the knob to throw it open, his wife's hand fell upon his wrist.

"No, John," she whispered. "They do not wish to be seen, and so we cannot afford to see them. Do not forget that we are keeping the middle of the road."

Clayton smiled and dropped his hand to his side. Thus they stood watching the little bit of white paper until it finally remained at rest upon the floor just inside the door.

Then Clayton stooped and picked it up. It was a bit of grimy, white paper roughly folded into a ragged square. Opening it they found a crude message printed in uncouth letters, with many evidences of an unaccustomed task.

Translated, it was a warning to the Claytons to refrain from reporting the loss of the revolvers, or from repeating what the old sailor had told them—to refrain on pain of death.

"I rather imagine we'll be good," said Clayton with a rueful smile. "About all we can do is to sit tight and wait for whatever may come."

CHAPTER II

THE SAVAGE HOME

NOR did they have long to wait, for the next morning as Clayton was emerging on deck for his accustomed walk before breakfast, a shot rang out, and then another, and another.

The sight which met his eyes confirmed his worst fears. Facing the little knot of officers was the entire motley crew of the *Fuwalda*, and at their head stood Black Michael.

At the first volley from the officers the men ran for shelter, and from points of vantage behind masts, wheel house and cabin they returned the fire of the five men who represented the hated authority of the ship.

Two of their number had gone down before the captain's revolver. They lay where they had fallen between the combatants.

Presently the first mate lunged forward upon his face, and at a cry of command from Black Michael the bloodthirsty ruffians charged the remaining four. The crew had been able to muster but six firearms, so most of them were armed with boathooks, axes, hatchets and crowbars.

The captain had emptied his revolver and was reloading as the charge was made. The second mate's gun had jammed, and so there were but two weapons opposed to the mutineers as they rapidly approached the officers, who now started to give back before the infuriated rush of their men.

Both sides were cursing and swearing in a frightful manner, which, together with the reports of the firearms and the screams and groans of the wounded, turned the deck of the *Fuwalda* to the likeness of a madhouse.

Before the officers had taken a dozen backward steps the men were upon them. An axe in the hands of a burly negro cleft the captain from forehead to chin,* and an instant later the others were down; dead or wounded from dozens of blows and bullet wounds.

Short and grisly had been the work of the mutineers of the *Fuwalda*, and through it all John Clayton had stood leaning carelessly beside the companionway puffing meditatively upon his pipe as though he had been but watching an indifferent cricket match.

As the last officer went down he bethought him that it was time that he returned to his wife lest some member of the crew find her alone below.

Though outwardly calm and indifferent, Clayton was inwardly apprehensive and wrought up, for he feared for his wife's safety at the hands of these ignorant, half-brutes into whose hands fate had so remorselessly thrown them.

As he turned to descend the ladder he was surprised to see his wife standing on the steps almost at his side.

"How long have you been here, Alice?"

"Since the beginning," she replied. "How awful, John. Oh, how awful! What can we hope for at the hands of such as those?"

"Breakfast, I hope," he answered, smiling bravely in an attempt to allay her fears.

"At least," he added, "I'm going to ask them. Come with me, Alice. We must not let them think we expect any but courteous treatment."

The men had by this time surrounded the dead and wounded officers, and without either partiality or compassion proceeded to throw both living and dead over the sides of the vessel. With equal heartlessness they disposed of their own wounded and the bodies of the three sailors to whom a merciful Providence had vouchsafed instant death before the bullets of the officers.

Presently one of the crew spied the approaching Claytons, and with a cry of: "Here's two more for the fishes," rushed toward them with uplifted axe.

But Black Michael was even quicker, so that the fellow went down with a bullet in his back before he had taken a half dozen steps.

With a loud roar, Black Michael attracted the attention of the others, and, pointing to Lord and Lady Greystoke, cried:

"These here are my friends, and they are to be left alone. D' ye understand?

"I'm captain of this ship now, an' what I says goes," he added, turning to Clayton. "Just keep to yourselves, and nobody'll harm ye," and he looked threateningly on his fellows.

The Claytons heeded Black Michael's instructions so well that they saw but little of the crew and knew nothing of the plans the men were making.

Occasionally they heard faint echoes of brawls and quarreling among the mutineers, and on two occasions the vicious bark of firearms rang out on the still air. But Black Michael was a fit leader for this heterogeneous band of cutthroats, and, withal, held them in fair subjection to his rule.

On the fifth day following the murder of the ship's officers, land was sighted by the lookout. Whether island or mainland, Black Michael did not know, but he announced to Clayton that if investigation showed that the place was habitable he and Lady Greystoke were to be put ashore with their belongings.

"You'll be all right there for a few months," he explained, "and by that time we'll have been able to make an inhabited coast somewheres and scatter a bit. Then I'll see that yer gover'ment's notified where you be an' they'll soon send a man-o'war to fetch ye off.

"You may be all right, but it would be a hard matter to land you in civilization without a lot o' questions being asked, an' none o' us here has any very convincin' answers up our sleeves."

Clayton remonstrated against the inhumanity of landing them upon an unknown shore to be left to the mercies of savage beasts, and, possibly, still more savage men.

But his words were of no avail, and only tended to anger Black Michael, so he was forced to desist and make the best he could of a bad situation.

About three o'clock in the afternoon they came about off a beautiful wooded shore opposite the mouth of what appeared to be a land-locked harbor.

Black Michael sent a small boat filled with men to sound the entrance in an effort to determine if the *Fuwalda* could be safely worked through the entrance.

In about an hour they returned and reported deep water through the passage as well as far into the little basin.

Before dark the barkantine lay peacefully at anchor upon the bosom of the still, mirror-like surface of the harbor.

The surrounding shores were beautiful with semi-tropical verdure, while in the distance the country rose from the ocean in hill and table land, almost uniformly clothed by primeval forest.

No signs of habitation were visible, but that the land might easily support human life was evidenced by the abundant bird and animal life of which the watchers on the *Fuwalda*'s deck caught occasional glimpses, as well as by the shimmer of a little river which emptied into the harbor, insuring fresh water in plentitude.

As darkness settled upon the earth, Clayton and Lady Alice still stood by the ship's rail in silent contemplation of their future abode. From the dark shadows of the mighty forest came the wild calls of savage beasts—the deep roar of the lion, and, occasionally, the shrill scream of a panther.

The woman shrank closer to the man in terror-stricken anticipation of the horrors lying in wait for them in the awful blackness of the nights to come, when they two should be alone upon that wild and lonely shore.*

Later in the evening Black Michael joined them long enough to instruct them to make their preparations for landing on the morrow. They tried to persuade him to take them to some more hospitable coast near enough to civilization so that they might hope to fall into friendly hands. But no pleas, or threats, or promises of reward could move him.

"I am the only man aboard who would not rather see you both safely dead, and, while I know that that's the sensible way to make sure of our own necks, yet Black Michael's not the man to forget a favor. You saved my life once, and in return I'm goin' to spare yours, but that's all I can do.

"The men won't stand for any more, and if we don't get you landed pretty quick they may even change their minds about giving you that much show. I'll put all your stuff ashore with you as well as cookin' utensils an' some old sails for tents, an' enough grub to last you until you can find fruit and game.

"So that with your guns for protection, you ought to be able to live here easy enough until help comes. When I get safely hid away I'll see to it that the British gover'ment learns about where you be; for the life of me I couldn't tell 'em exactly where, for I don't know myself. But they'll find you all right."

After he had left them they went silently below, each wrapped in gloomy forebodings.

Clayton did not believe that Black Michael had the slightest intention of notifying the British government of their whereabouts, nor was he any too sure but that some treachery was contemplated for the following day when they should be on shore with the sailors who would have to accompany them with their belongings.

Once out of Black Michael's sight any of the men might strike them down, and still leave Black Michael's conscience clear.

And even should they escape that fate was it not but to be faced with far graver dangers? Alone, he might hope to survive for years; for he was a strong, athletic man.

But what of Alice, and that other little life so soon to be launched amidst the hardships and grave dangers of a primeval world?

The man shuddered as he meditated upon the awful gravity, the fearful helplessness, of their situation. But it was a merciful Providence which prevented him from foreseeing the hideous reality which awaited them in the grim depths of that gloomy wood.*

Early next morning their numerous chests and boxes were hoisted on deck and lowered to waiting small boats for transportation to shore.

There was a great quantity and variety of stuff, as the Claytons had expected a possible five to eight years' residence in their new home, so that, in addition to the many necessities they had brought, were also many luxuries.

Black Michael was determined that nothing belonging to the Claytons should be left on board. Whether out of compassion for them, or in furtherance of his own self interests, it were difficult to say.

There is no question but that the presence of property of a missing British official upon a suspicious vessel would have been a difficult thing to explain in any civilized port in the world.

So zealous was he in his efforts to carry out his intentions that he insisted upon the return of Clayton's revolvers to him by the sailors in whose possession they were.

Into the small boats were also loaded salt meats and biscuit, with a small supply of potatoes and beans, matches, and cooking vessels, a chest of tools, and the old sails which Black Michael had promised them.

As though himself fearing the very thing which Clayton had suspected, Black Michael accompanied them to shore, and was the last to leave them when the small boats, having filled the ship's casks with fresh water, were pushed out toward the waiting *Fuwalda*.

As the boats moved slowly over the smooth waters of the bay, Clayton and his wife stood silently watching their departure— in the breasts of both a feeling of impending disaster and utter hopelessness.

And behind them, over the edge of a low ridge, other eyes watched—close set, wicked eyes, gleaming beneath shaggy brows.

As the *Fuwalda* passed through the narrow entrance to the harbor and out of sight behind a projecting point, Lady Alice threw her arms about Clayton's neck and burst into uncontrolled sobs.

Bravely had she faced the dangers of the mutiny; with heroic fortitude she had looked into the terrible future; but now that the horror of absolute solitude was upon them, her overwrought nerves gave way, and the reaction came.

He did not attempt to check her tears. It were better that nature have her way in relieving these long pent emotions, and it was many minutes before the girl—little more than a child she was—could again gain mastery of herself.

"Oh, John," she cried at last, "the horror of it. What are we to do? What are we to do?"

"There is but one thing to do, Alice," and he spoke as quietly as though they were sitting in their snug living room at home, "and that is work. Work must be our salvation. We must not give ourselves time to think, for in that direction lies madness.

"We must work and wait. I am sure that relief will come, and come quickly, when once it is apparent that the *Fuwalda* has been lost, even though Black Michael does not keep his word to us."

"But John, if it were only you and I," she sobbed, "we could endure it I know; but—"

"Yes, dear," he answered, gently, "I have been thinking of that, also; but we must face it, as we must face whatever comes, bravely and with the utmost confidence in our ability to cope with circumstances whatever they may be.

"Hundreds of thousands of years ago our ancestors of the dim and distant past faced the same problems which we must face, possibly in these same primeval forests. That we are here today evidences their victory.

"What they did may we not do? And even better, for are we not armed with ages of superior knowledge, and have we not the means of protection, defense, and sustenance which science has given us, but of which they were totally ignorant? What they accomplished, Alice, with instruments and weapons of stone and bone, surely that may we accomplish also."

"Ah, John, I wish that I might be a man with a man's philosophy, but I am but a woman, seeing with my heart rather than my head, and all that I can see is too horrible, too unthinkable to put into words.

"I only hope you are right, John. I will do my best to be a brave primeval woman, a fit mate for the primeval man."

Clayton's first thought was to arrange a sleeping shelter for the night; something which might serve to protect them from prowling beasts of prey.

He opened the box containing his rifles and ammunition, that they might both be armed against possible attack while at work, and then together they sought a location for their first night's sleeping place.

A hundred yards from the beach was a little level spot, fairly free of trees and here they decided eventually to build a permanent house, but, for the time being, they both thought it best to construct a little platform in the trees out of reach of the larger of the savage beasts in whose realm they were.

To this end Clayton selected four trees which formed a rectangle about eight feet square, and cutting long branches from other trees he constructed a framework around them, about ten feet from the ground, fastening the ends of the branches securely to the trees by means of rope, a quantity of which Black Michael had furnished him from the hold of the *Fuwalda*.

Across this framework Clayton placed other smaller branches quite close together. This platform he paved with the huge fronds of elephant's ear* which grew in profusion about them, and over the fronds he laid a great sail folded into several thickness.

Seven feet higher he constructed a similar, though lighter platform to serve as roof, and from the sides of this he suspended the balance of his sail cloth for walls.

When completed he had a rather snug little nest, to which he carried their blankets and some of the lighter luggage.

It was now late in the afternoon, and the balance of the daylight hours were devoted to the building of a rude ladder by means of which Lady Alice could mount to her new home.

All during the day the forest about them had been filled with excited birds of brilliant plumage, and dancing, chattering monkeys, who watched these new arrivals and their wonderful nest building operations with every mark of keenest interest and fascination.

Notwithstanding that both Clayton and his wife kept a sharp lookout they saw nothing of larger animals, though on two occasions they had seen their little simian neighbors come screaming and chattering from the nearby ridge, casting affrighted glances back over their little shoulders, and evincing as plainly as though by speech that they were fleeing some terrible thing which lay concealed there.

Just before dusk Clayton finished his ladder, and, filling a great basin with water from the nearby stream, the two mounted to the comparative safety of their aerial chamber.

As it was quite warm, Clayton had left the side curtains thrown back over the roof, and as they squatted, like Turks, upon their blankets,* Lady Alice, straining her eyes into the darkening shadows of the wood, suddenly reached out and grasped Clayton's arm.

"John," she whispered, "look! What is it, a man?"

As Clayton turned his eyes in the direction she indicated, he saw silhouetted dimly against the shadows beyond, a great figure standing upright upon the ridge.

For a moment it stood as though listening and then turned slowly, and melted into the shadows of the jungle.

"What is it, John?"

"I do not know, Alice," he answered gravely, "it is too dark to see so far, and it may have been but a shadow cast by the rising moon."

"No, John, if it was not a man it was some huge and grotesque mockery of man. Oh, I am afraid."

He gathered her in his arms, whispering words of courage and love into her ears, for the greatest pain of their misfortunes, to Clayton, was the mental anguish of his young wife. Himself brave and fearless, yet was he able to appreciate the awful suffering which fear entails— a rare gift, though but one of many which had made the young Lord Greystoke respected and loved by all who knew him.

Soon after, he lowered the curtain walls, tying them securely to the trees so that, except for a little opening toward the beach, they were entirely enclosed.

As it was now pitch dark within their tiny aerie they lay down upon their blankets to try to wrest, through sleep, a brief respite of forgetfulness.

Clayton lay facing the opening at the front, a rifle and a brace of revolvers at his hand.

Scarcely had they closed their eyes than the terrifying cry of a panther rang out from the jungle behind them. Closer and closer it came until they could hear the great beast directly beneath them. For an hour or more they heard it sniffing and clawing at the trees which supported their platform, but at last it roamed away across the beach, where Clayton could see it clearly in the brilliant moonlight—a great, handsome beast; the largest he had ever seen.

During the long hours of darkness they caught but fitful snatches of sleep, for the night noises of a great jungle teeming with myriad animal life kept their overwrought nerves on edge, so that a hundred times they were startled to wakefulness by piercing screams, or the stealthy moving of great bodies beneath them.

CHAPTER III

LIFE AND DEATH

MORNING found them but little, if at all refreshed, though it was with a feeling of intense relief that they saw the day dawn.

As soon as they had made their meager breakfast of salt pork, coffee, and biscuit, Clayton commenced work upon their house, for he realized that they could hope for no safety and no peace of mind at night until four strong walls effectually barred the jungle life from them.

The task was an arduous one and required the better part of a month, though he built but one small room. He constructed his cabin of small logs about six inches in diameter, stopping the chinks with clay which he found at the depth of a few feet beneath the surface soil.

At one end he built a fireplace of small stones from the beach. These also he set in clay and when the house had been entirely completed he applied a coating of the clay to the entire outside surface to the thickness of four inches.

In the window opening he set small branches about an inch in diameter both vertically and horizontally, and so woven that they formed a substantial grating that could withstand the strength of a powerful animal. Thus they obtained air and proper ventilation without fear of lessening the safety of their cabin.

The A-shaped roof was thatched with small branches laid close together and over these long jungle grass and palm fronds, with a final coating of clay.

The door he built of pieces of the packing-boxes which had held their belongings; nailing one piece upon another, the grain of contiguous layers running transversely, until he had a solid body some three inches thick and of such great strength that they were both moved to laughter as they gazed upon it.

Here the greatest difficulty confronted Clayton, for he had no means whereby to hang his massive door now that he had built it. After two days' work, however, he succeeded in fashioning two massive hard-wood hinges, and with these he hung the door so that it opened and closed easily.

The stuccoing and other final touches were added after they moved into the house, which they had done as soon as the roof was on, piling their boxes before the door at night and thus having a comparatively safe and comfortable habitation.

The building of a bed, chairs, table, and shelves was a relatively easy matter, so that by the end of the second month they were well settled, and, but for the constant dread of attack by wild beasts and the ever growing loneliness, they were not uncomfortable or unhappy.

At night great beasts snarled and roared about their tiny cabin, but, so accustomed may one become to oft repeated noises, that soon they paid little attention to them, sleeping soundly the whole night through.

Thrice had they caught fleeting glimpses of great manlike figures like that of the first night, but never at sufficiently close range to know positively whether the half-seen forms were those of man or brute.

The brilliant birds and the little monkeys had become accustomed to their new acquaintances, and as they had evidently never seen human beings before they presently, after their first fright had worn off, approached closer and closer, impelled by that strange curiosity which dominates the wild creatures of the forest and the jungle and the plain, so that within the first month several of the birds had gone so far as even to accept morsels of food from the friendly hands of the Claytons.

One afternoon, while Clayton was working upon an addition to their cabin, for he contemplated building several more rooms, a number of their grotesque little friends came shrieking and scolding through the trees from the direction of the ridge. Ever as they fled they cast fearful glances back of them, and finally they stopped near Clayton jabbering excitedly to him as though to warn him of approaching danger.

At last he saw it, the thing the little monkeys so feared—the man-brute of which the Claytons had caught occasional fleeting glimpses.

It was approaching through the jungle in a semi-erect position, now and then placing the backs of its closed fists upon the ground—a great anthropoid ape,* and, as it advanced, it emitted deep guttural growls and an occasional low barking sound.

Clayton was at some distance from the cabin, having come to fell a particularly perfect tree, for his building operations. Grown careless from months of continued safety, during which time they had seen no dangerous animals during the daylight hours, he had left his rifles and revolvers all within the little cabin, and now that he saw the great ape crashing through the underbrush directly toward him, and from a direction which practically cut him off from escape, he felt a vague little shiver play up and down his spine.

He knew that, armed only with an axe, his chances with this ferocious monster were small indeed—and Alice; O God, he thought, what will become of Alice?

There was yet a slight chance of reaching the cabin. He turned and ran toward it, shouting an alarm to his wife to run in and close the great door in case the ape cut off his retreat.

Lady Greystoke had been sitting a little way from the cabin, and when she heard his cry she looked up to see the ape springing with almost incredible swiftness, for so large and awkward an animal, in an effort to head off Clayton.

With a low cry she sprang toward the cabin, and, as she entered, gave a backward glance which filled her soul with terror, for the brute had intercepted her husband, who now stood at bay grasping his axe with both hands ready to swing it upon the infuriated animal when he should make his final charge.

"Close and bolt the door, Alice," cried Clayton. "I can finish this fellow with my axe."

But he knew he was facing a horrible death, and so did she.

The ape was a great bull, weighing probably three hundred pounds. His nasty, close-set eyes gleamed hatred from beneath his shaggy brows, while his great canine fangs were bared in a horrid snarl as be paused a moment before his prey.

Over the brute's shoulder Clayton could see the doorway of his cabin, not twenty paces distant, and a great wave of horror and fear swept over him as he saw his young wife emerge, armed with one of his rifles.

She had always been afraid of firearms, and would never touch them, but now she rushed toward the ape with the fearlessness of a lioness protecting its young.

"Back, Alice," shouted Clayton, "for God's sake, go back."

But she would not heed, and just then the ape charged, so that Clayton could say no more.

The man swung his axe with all his mighty strength, but the powerful brute seized it in those terrible hands, and tearing it from Clayton's grasp hurled it far to one side.

With an ugly snarl he closed upon his defenseless victim, but ere his fangs had reached the throat they thirsted for, there was a sharp report and a bullet entered the ape's back between his shoulders.

Throwing Clayton to the ground the beast turned upon his new enemy. There before him stood the terrified girl vainly trying to fire another bullet into the animal's body; but she did not understand the mechanism of the firearm, and the hammer fell futilely upon an empty cartridge.

Screaming with rage and pain, the ape flew at the delicate woman, who went down beneath him to merciful unconsciousness.

Almost simultaneously Clayton regained his feet, and without thought of the utter hopelessness of it, he rushed forward to drag the ape from his wife's prostrate form.

With little or no effort he succeeded, and the great bulk rolled inertly upon the turf before him—the ape was dead. The bullet had done its work.

A hasty examination of his wife revealed no marks upon her, and Clayton decided that the huge brute had died the instant he had sprung toward Alice.

Gently he lifted his wife's still unconscious form, and bore her to the little cabin, but it was fully two hours before she regained consciousness.

Her first words filled Clayton with vague apprehension. For some time after regaining her senses, Alice gazed wonderingly about the interior of the little cabin, and then, with a satisfied sigh, said:

"O, John, it is so good to be really home! I have had an awful dream, dear. I thought we were no longer in London, but in some horrible place where great beasts attacked us."

"There, there, Alice," he said, stroking her forehead, "try to sleep again, and do not worry your head about bad dreams."

That night a little son was born in the tiny cabin beside the primeval forest, while a leopard screamed before the door, and the deep notes of a lion's roar sounded from beyond the ridge.

Lady Greystoke never recovered from the shock of the great ape's attack, and, though she lived for a year after her baby was born, she was never again outside the cabin, nor did she ever fully realize that she was not in England.

Sometimes she would question Clayton as to the strange noises of the nights; the absence of servants and friends, and the strange rudeness of the furnishings within her room, but, though he made no effort to deceive her, never could she grasp the meaning of it all.

In other ways she was quite rational, and the joy and happiness she took in the possession of her little son and the constant attentions of her husband made that year a very happy one for her, the happiest of her young life.

That it would have been beset by worries and apprehension had she been in full command of her mental faculties Clayton well knew; so that while he suffered terribly to see her so, there were times when he was almost glad, for her sake, that she could not understand.

Long since had he given up any hope of rescue, except through accident. With unremitting zeal he had worked to beautify the interior of the cabin.

Skins of lion and panther covered the floor. Cupboards and bookcases lined the walls. Odd vases made by his own hand from the clay of the region held beautiful tropical flowers. Curtains of grass and bamboo covered the windows, and, most arduous task of all, with his meager assortment of tools he had fashioned lumber to neatly seal the walls and ceiling and lay a smooth floor within the cabin.

That he had been able to turn his hands at all to such unaccustomed labor was a source of mild wonder to him. But he loved the work because it was for her and the tiny life that had come to cheer them, though adding a hundredfold to his responsibilities and to the terribleness of their situation.

During the year that followed, Clayton was several times attacked by the great apes which now seemed to continually infest the vicinity of the cabin; but as he never again ventured outside without both rifle and revolvers he had little fear of the huge beasts.

He had strengthened the window protections and fitted a unique wooden lock to the cabin door, so that when he hunted for game and fruits, as it was constantly necessary for him to do to insure sustenance, he had no fear that any animal could break into the little home.

At first he shot much of the game from the cabin windows, but toward the end the animals learned to fear the strange lair from whence issued the terrifying thunder of his rifle.

In his leisure Clayton read, often aloud to his wife, from the store of books he had brought for their new home. Among these were many for little children—picture books, primers, readers—for they had known that their little child would be old enough for such before they might hope to return to England.

At other times Clayton wrote in his diary, which he had always been accustomed to keep in French, and in which he recorded the details of their strange life. This book he kept locked in a little metal box.

A year from the day her little son was born Lady Alice passed quietly away in the night. So peaceful was her end that it was hours before Clayton could awake to a realization that his wife was dead.

The horror of the situation came to him very slowly, and it is doubtful that he ever fully realized the enormity of his sorrow and the fearful responsibility that had devolved upon him with the care of that wee thing, his son, still a nursing babe.

The last entry in his diary was made the morning following her death, and there he recites the sad details in a matter of fact way that adds to the pathos of it; for it breathes a tired apathy born of long sorrow and hopelessness, which even this cruel blow could scarcely awake to further suffering:

My little son is crying for nourishment—O Alice, Alice, what shall I do?

And as John Clayton wrote the last words his hand was destined ever to pen, he dropped his head wearily upon his outstretched arms where they rested upon the table he had built for her who lay still and cold in the bed beside him.

For a long time no sound broke the deathlike stillness of the jungle mid-day save the piteous wailing of the tiny man-child.

CHAPTER IV

THE APES

IN THE forest of the table-land a mile back from the ocean old Kerchak the Ape was on a rampage of rage among his people.

The younger and lighter members of his tribe scampered to the higher branches of the great trees to escape his wrath; risking their lives upon branches that scarce supported their weight rather than face old Kerchak in one of his fits of uncontrolled anger.

The other males scattered in all directions, but not before the infuriated brute had felt the vertebra of one snap between his great, foaming jaws.

A luckless young female slipped from an insecure hold upon a high branch and came crashing to the ground almost at Kerchak's feet.

With a wild scream he was upon her, tearing a great piece from her side with his mighty teeth, and striking her viciously upon her head and shoulders with a broken tree limb until her skull was crushed to a jelly.

And then he spied Kala, who, returning from a search for food with her young babe, was ignorant of the state of the mighty male's temper until suddenly the shrill warnings of her fellows caused her to scamper madly for safety.

But Kerchak was close upon her, so close that he had almost grasped her ankle had she not made a furious leap far into space from one tree to another—a perilous chance which apes seldom if ever take, unless so closely pursued by danger that there is no alternative.

She made the leap successfully, but as she grasped the limb of the further tree the sudden jar loosened the hold of the tiny babe where it clung frantically to her neck, and she saw the little thing hurled, turning and twisting, to the ground thirty feet below.

With a low cry of dismay Kala rushed headlong to its side, thoughtless now of the danger from Kerchak; but when she gathered the wee, mangled form to her bosom life had left it.

With low moans, she sat cuddling the body to her; nor did Kerchak attempt to molest her. With the death of the babe his fit of demoniacal rage passed as suddenly as it had seized him.

Kerchak was a huge king ape, weighing perhaps three hundred and fifty pounds. His forehead was extremely low and receding, his eyes bloodshot, small and close set to his coarse, flat nose; his ears large and thin, but smaller than most of his kind.*

His awful temper and his mighty strength made him supreme among the little tribe into which he had been born some twenty years before.

Now that he was in his prime, there was no simian in all the mighty forest through which he roved that dared contest his right to rule, nor did the other and larger animals molest him.

Old Tantor, the elephant, alone of all the wild savage life, feared him not—and he alone did Kerchak fear. When Tantor trumpeted, the great ape scurried with his fellows high among the trees of the second terrace.

The tribe of anthropoids over which Kerchak ruled with an iron hand and bared fangs, numbered some six or eight families, each family consisting of an adult male with his wives and their young, numbering in all some sixty or seventy apes.

Kala was the youngest wife of a male called Tublat, meaning broken nose, and the child she had seen dashed to death was her first; for she was but nine or ten years old.

Notwithstanding her youth, she was large and powerful—a splendid, clean-limbed animal, with a round, high forehead, which denoted more intelligence than most of her kind possessed. So, also, she had a greater capacity for mother love and mother sorrow.

But she was still an ape, a huge, fierce, terrible beast of a species closely allied to the gorilla, yet more intelligent; which, with the strength of their cousin, made her kind the most fearsome of those awe-inspiring progenitors of man.

When the tribe saw that Kerchak's rage had ceased they came slowly down from their arboreal retreats and pursued again the various occupations which he had interrupted.

The young played and frolicked about among the trees and bushes. Some of the adults lay prone upon the soft mat of dead and decaying vegetation which covered the ground, while others turned over pieces of fallen branches and clods of earth in search of the small bugs and reptiles which formed a part of their food.

Others, again, searched the surrounding trees for fruit, nuts, small birds, and eggs.

They had passed an hour or so thus when Kerchak called them together, and, with a word of command to them to follow him, set off toward the sea.

They traveled for the most part upon the ground, where it was open, following the path of the great elephants whose comings and goings break the only roads through those tangled mazes of bush, vine, creeper, and tree. When they walked it was with a rolling, awkward motion, placing the knuckles of their closed hands upon the ground and swinging their ungainly bodies forward.

But when the way was through the lower trees they moved more swiftly, swinging from branch to branch with the agility of their smaller cousins, the monkeys. And all the way Kala carried her little dead baby hugged closely to her breast.

It was shortly after noon when they reached a ridge overlooking the beach where below them lay the tiny cottage which was Kerchak's goal.

He had seen many of his kind go to their deaths before the loud noise made by the little black stick in the hands of the strange white ape who lived in that wonderful lair, and Kerchak had made up his brute mind to own that death-dealing contrivance, and to explore the interior of the mysterious den.

He wanted, very, very much, to feel his teeth sink into the neck of the queer animal that he had learned to hate and fear, and because of this, he came often with his tribe to reconnoiter, waiting for a time when the white ape should be off his guard.

Of late they had quit attacking, or even showing themselves; for every time they had done so in the past the little stick had roared out its terrible message of death to some member of the tribe.

Today there was no sign of the man about, and from where they watched they could see that the cabin door was open. Slowly, cautiously, and noiselessly they crept through the jungle toward the little cabin.

There were no growls, no fierce screams of rage—the little black stick had taught them to come quietly lest they awaken it.

On, on they came until Kerchak himself slunk stealthily to the very door and peered within. Behind him were two males, and then Kala, closely straining the little dead form to her breast.

Inside the den they saw the strange white ape lying half across a table, his head buried in his arms; and on the bed lay a figure covered by a sail cloth, while from a tiny rustic cradle came the plaintive wailing of a babe.

Noiselessly Kerchak entered, crouching for the charge; and then John Clayton rose with a sudden start and faced them.

The sight that met his eyes must have frozen him with horror, for there, within the door, stood three great bull apes, while behind them crowded many more; how many he never knew, for his revolvers were hanging on the far wall beside his rifle, and Kerchak was charging.

When the king ape released the limp form which had been John Clayton, Lord Greystoke, he turned his attention toward the little cradle; but Kala was there before him, and when he would have grasped the child she snatched it herself, and before he could intercept her she had bolted through the door and taken refuge in a high tree.

As she took up the little live baby of Alice Clayton she dropped the dead body of her own into the empty cradle; for the wail of the living had answered the call of universal motherhood within her wild breast which the dead could not still.

High up among the branches of a mighty tree she hugged the shrieking infant to her bosom, and soon the instinct that was as dominant in this fierce female as it had been in the breast of his tender and beautiful mother—the instinct of mother love—reached out to the tiny man-child's half-formed understanding, and he became quiet.

Then hunger closed the gap between them, and the son of an English lord and an English lady nursed at the breast of Kala, the great ape.*

In the meantime the beasts within the cabin were warily examining the contents of this strange lair.

Once satisfied that Clayton was dead, Kerchak turned his attention to the thing which lay upon the bed, covered by a piece of sailcloth.

Gingerly he lifted one corner of the shroud, but when he saw the body of the woman beneath he tore the cloth roughly from her form and seized the still, white throat in his huge, hairy hands.

A moment he let his fingers sink deep into the cold flesh, and then, realizing that she was already dead, he turned from her, to examine the contents of the room; nor did he again molest the body of either Lady Alice or Sir John.

The rifle hanging upon the wall caught his first attention; it was for this strange, death-dealing thunder-stick that he had yearned for months; but now that it was within his grasp he scarcely had the temerity to seize it.

Cautiously he approached the thing, ready to flee precipitately should it speak in its deep roaring tones, as he had heard it speak before, the last words to those of his kind who, through ignorance or rashness, had attacked the wonderful white ape that had borne it.

Deep in the beast's intelligence was something which assured him that the thunder-stick was only dangerous when in the hands of one who could manipulate it, but yet it was several minutes ere he could bring himself to touch it.

Instead, he walked back and forth along the floor before it, turning his head so that never once did his eyes leave the object of his desire.

Using his long arms as a man uses crutches, and rolling his huge carcass from side to side with each stride, the great king ape paced to and fro, uttering deep growls, occasionally punctuated with that ear-piercing scream, than which there is no more terrifying noise in all the jungle.

Presently he halted before the rifle. Slowly he raised a huge hand until it almost touched the shining barrel, only to withdraw it once more and continue his hurried pacing.

It was as though the great brute by this show of fearlessness, and through the medium of his wild voice, were endeavoring to bolster up his courage to the point which would permit him to take the rifle in his hand.

Again he stopped, and this time succeeded in forcing his reluctant hand to the cold steel, only to snatch it away almost immediately and resume his restless beat.

Time after time this strange ceremony was repeated, but on each occasion with increased confidence, until, finally, the rifle was torn from its hook and lay in the grasp of the great brute.

Finding that it harmed him not, Kerchak began to examine it closely. He felt of it from end to end, peered down the black depths of the muzzle, fingered the sights, the breech, the stock, and finally the trigger.

During all these operations the apes who had entered sat huddled near the door watching their chief, while those outside strained and crowded to catch a glimpse of what transpired within.

Suddenly Kerchak's finger closed upon the trigger. There was a deafening roar in the little room and the apes at and beyond the door fell over one another in their wild anxiety to escape.

Kerchak was equally frightened; so frightened, in fact, that he quite forgot to throw aside the author of that fearful noise, but bolted for the door with it tightly clutched in one hand.

As he passed through the opening, the front sight of the rifle caught upon the edge of the inswung door with sufficient force to close it tightly after the fleeing ape.

When Kerchak came to a halt a short distance from the cabin and discovered that he still held the rifle, he dropped it as he might have dropped a red hot iron, nor did he again essay to recover it—the noise was too much for his brute nerves; but he was now quite convinced that the terrible stick was quite harmless by itself if left alone.

It was an hour before the apes could again bring themselves to approach the cabin to continue their investigations, and when they finally did so, they found to their chagrin that the door was closed and so securely fastened that they could not force it.

The cleverly constructed latch which Clayton had made for the door had sprung as Kerchak passed out; nor could the apes find means of ingress through the heavily barred windows.

After roaming about the vicinity for a short time, they started back for the deeper forests and the higher land from whence they had come.

Kala had not once come to earth with her little adopted babe, but now Kerchak called to her to descend with the rest, and as there was no note of anger in his voice she dropped lightly from branch to branch and joined the others on their homeward march.

Those of the apes who attempted to examine Kala's strange baby were repulsed with bared fangs and low menacing growls, accompanied by words of warning from Kala.

When they assured her that they meant the child no harm she permitted them to come close, but would not allow them to touch her charge.

It was as though she knew that her baby was frail and delicate and feared lest the rough hands of her fellows might injure the little thing.

Another thing she did, and which made traveling an onerous trial for her. Remembering the death of her own little one, she clung desperately to the new babe, with one hand, whenever they were upon the march.

The other young rode upon their mothers' backs; their little arms tightly clasping the hairy necks before them, while their legs were locked beneath their mothers' arm pits.

Not so with Kala; she held the small form of the little Lord Greystoke tightly to her breast, where the dainty hands clutched the long black hair which covered that portion of her body. She had seen one child fall from her back to a terrible death, and she would take no further chances with this.

CHAPTER V

THE WHITE APE

TENDERLY Kala nursed her little waif, wondering silently why it did not gain strength and agility as did the little apes of other mothers. It was nearly a year from the time the little fellow came into her possession before he would walk alone, and as for climbing—my, but how stupid he was!

Kala sometimes talked with the older females about her young hopeful, but none of them could understand how a child could be so slow and backward in learning to care for itself. Why, it could not even find food alone, and more than twelve moons had passed since Kala had come upon it.

Had they known that the child had seen thirteen moons before it had come into Kala's possession they would have considered its case as absolutely hopeless, for the little apes of their own tribe were as far advanced in two or three moons as was this little stranger after twenty-five.

Tublat, Kala's husband, was sorely vexed, and but for the female's careful watching would have put the child out of the way.

"He will never be a great ape," he argued. "Always will you have to carry him and protect him. What good will he be to the tribe? None; only a burden.

"Let us leave him quietly sleeping among the tall grasses, that you may bear other and stronger apes to guard us in our old age."

"Never, Broken Nose," replied Kala. "If I must carry him forever, so be it."

And then Tublat went to Kerchak to urge him to use his authority with Kala, and force her to give up little Tarzan, which was the name they had given to the tiny Lord Greystoke, and which meant "White-Skin."

But when Kerchak spoke to her about it Kala threatened to run away from the tribe if they did not leave her in peace with the child; and as this is one of the inalienable rights* of the jungle folk, if they be dissatisfied among their own people, they bothered her no more, for Kala was a fine clean-limbed young female, and they did not wish to lose her.

As Tarzan grew he made more rapid strides, so that by the time he was ten years old he was an excellent climber, and on the ground could do many wonderful things which were beyond the powers of his little brothers and sisters.

In many ways did he differ from them, and they often marveled at his superior cunning, but in strength and size he was deficient; for at ten the great anthropoids were fully grown, some of them towering over six feet in height, while little Tarzan was still but a half-grown boy.

Yet such a boy!

From early infancy he had used his hands to swing from branch to branch after the manner of his giant mother, and as he grew older he spent hour upon hour daily speeding through the tree tops with his brothers and sisters.

He could spring twenty feet across space at the dizzy heights of the forest top, and grasp with unerring precision, and without apparent jar, a limb waving wildly in the path of an approaching tornado.

He could drop twenty feet at a stretch from limb to limb in rapid descent to the ground, or he could gain the utmost pinnacle of the loftiest tropical giant with the ease and swiftness of a squirrel.

Though but ten years old he was fully as strong as the average man of thirty, and far more agile than the most practiced athlete ever becomes. And day by day his strength was increasing.

His life among these fierce apes had been happy; for his recollection held no other life, nor did he know that there existed within the universe aught else than his little forest and the wild jungle animals with which he was familiar.

He was nearly ten before he commenced to realize that a great difference existed between himself and his fellows. His little body, burned brown by exposure, suddenly caused him feelings of intense shame, for he realized that it was entirely hairless, like some low snake, or other reptile.

He attempted to obviate this by plastering himself from head to foot with mud, but this dried and fell off. Beside it felt so uncomfortable that he quickly decided that he preferred the shame to the discomfort.

In the higher land which his tribe frequented was a little lake, and it was here that Tarzan first saw his face in the clear, still waters of its bosom.

It was on a sultry day of the dry season that he and one of his cousins had gone down to the bank to drink. As they leaned over, both little faces were mirrored on the placid pool; the fierce and terrible features of the ape beside those of the aristocratic scion of an old English house.

Tarzan was appalled. It had been bad enough to be hairless, but to own such a countenance! He wondered that the other apes could look at him at all.

That tiny slit of a mouth and those puny white teeth! How they looked beside the mighty lips and powerful fangs of his more fortunate brothers!

And the little pinched nose of him; so thin was it that it looked half starved. He turned red as he compared it with the beautiful broad nostrils of his companion. Such a generous nose! Why it spread half across his face! It certainly must be fine to be so handsome, thought poor little Tarzan.

But when he saw his own eyes; ah, that was the final blow—a brown spot, a gray circle and then blank whiteness! Frightful! not even the snakes had such hideous eyes as he.

So intent was he upon this personal appraisement of his features that he did not hear the parting of the tall grass behind him as a great body pushed itself stealthily through the jungle; nor did his companion, the ape, hear either, for he was drinking and the noise of his sucking lips and gurgles of satisfaction drowned the quiet approach of the intruder.

Not thirty paces behind the two she crouched—Sabor, the huge lioness*—lashing her tail. Cautiously she moved a great padded paw forward, noiselessly placing it before she lifted the next. Thus she advanced; her belly low, almost touching the surface of the ground—a great cat preparing to spring upon its prey.

Now she was within ten feet of the two unsuspecting little playfellows—carefully she drew her hind feet well up beneath her body, the great muscles rolling under the beautiful skin.

So low she was crouching now that she seemed flattened to the earth except for the upward bend of the glossy back as it gathered for the spring.

No longer the tail lashed—quiet and straight behind her it lay.

An instant she paused thus as though turned to stone, and then, with an awful scream, she sprang.

Sabor, the lioness, was a wise hunter. To one less wise the wild alarm of her fierce cry as she sprang would have seemed a foolish thing, for could she not more surely have fallen upon her victims had she but quietly leaped without that loud shriek?

But Sabor knew well the wondrous quickness of the jungle folk and their almost unbelievable powers of hearing. To them the sudden scraping of one blade of grass across another was as effectual a warning as her loudest cry, and Sabor knew that she could not make that mighty leap without a little noise.

Her wild scream was not a warning. It was voiced to freeze her poor victims in a paralysis of terror for the tiny fraction of an instant which would suffice for her mighty claws to sink into their soft flesh and hold them beyond peradventure of escape.

In so far as the ape was concerned, Sabor reasoned correctly. The little fellow crouched trembling just an instant, but that instant was quite long enough to prove his undoing.

Not so, however, with Tarzan, the man-child. His life amidst the dangers of the jungle had taught him to meet emergencies with self-confidence, and his higher intelligence resulted in a quickness of mental action far beyond the powers of the apes.

So the scream of Sabor, the lioness, galvanized the brain and muscles of little Tarzan into instant action.

Before him lay the deep waters of the little lake, behind him certain death; a cruel death beneath tearing claws and rending fangs.

Tarzan had always hated water except as a medium for quenching his thirst. He hated it because he connected it with the chill and discomfort of the torrential rains, and he feared it for the thunder and lightning and wind which accompanied them.

The deep waters of the lake he had been taught by his wild mother to avoid, and further, had he not seen little Neeta sink beneath its quiet surface only a few short weeks before never to return to the tribe?

But of the two evils his quick mind chose the lesser ere the first note of Sabor's scream had scarce broken the quiet of the jungle, and before the great beast had covered half her leap Tarzan felt the chill waters close above his head.

He could not swim, and the water was very deep; but still he lost no particle of that self-confidence and resourcefulness which were the badges of his superior being.

Rapidly he moved his hands and feet in an attempt to scramble upward, and, possibly more by chance than design, he fell into the stroke that a dog uses when swimming, so that within a few seconds his nose was above water and he found that he could keep it there by continuing his strokes, and also make progress through the water.

He was much surprised and pleased with this new acquirement which had been so suddenly thrust upon him, but he had no time for thinking much upon it.

He was now swimming parallel to the bank and there he saw the cruel beast that would have seized him crouching upon the still form of his little playmate.

The lioness was intently watching Tarzan, evidently expecting him to return to shore, but this the boy had no intention of doing.

Instead he raised his voice in the call of distress common to his tribe, adding to it the warning which would prevent would-be rescuers from running into the clutches of Sabor.

Almost immediately there came an answer from the distance, and presently forty or fifty great apes swung rapidly and majestically through the trees toward the scene of tragedy.

In the van* was Kala, for she had recognized the tones of her best beloved, and with her was the mother of the little ape who lay dead beneath cruel Sabor.

Though more powerful and better equipped for fighting than the apes, the lioness had no desire to meet these enraged adults, and with a snarl of hatred she sprang quickly into the brush and disappeared.

Tarzan now swam to shore and clambered quickly upon dry land. The feeling of freshness and exhilaration which the cool waters had imparted to him, filled his little being with grateful surprise, and ever after he lost no opportunity to take a daily plunge in lake or stream or ocean when it was possible to do so.

For a long time Kala could not accustom herself to the sight; for though her people could swim when forced to it, they did not like to enter water, and never did so voluntarily.

The adventure with the lioness gave Tarzan food for pleasurable memories, for it was such affairs which broke the monotony of his daily life—otherwise but a dull round of searching for food, eating, and sleeping.

The tribe to which he belonged roamed a tract extending, roughly, twenty-five miles along the sea coast and some fifty miles inland.

This they traversed almost continually, occasionally remaining for months in one locality; but as they moved through the trees with great speed they often covered the territory in a very few days.

Much depended upon food supply, climatic conditions, and the prevalence of animals of the more dangerous species; though Kerchak often led them on long marches for no other reason than that he had tired of remaining in the same place.

At night they slept where darkness overtook them, lying upon the ground, and sometimes covering their heads, and more seldom their bodies, with the great leaves of the elephant's ear. Two or three might lie cuddled in each other's arms for additional warmth if the night were chill, and thus Tarzan had slept in Kala's arms nightly for all these years.

That the huge, fierce brute loved this child of another race* is beyond question, and he, too, gave to the great, hairy beast all the affection that would have belonged to his fair young mother had she lived.

When he was disobedient she cuffed him, it is true, but she was never cruel to him, and was more often caressing than chastising him.

Tublat, her husband, always hated Tarzan, and on several occasions had come near ending his youthful career.

Tarzan on his part never lost an opportunity to show that he fully reciprocated his foster father's sentiments, and whenever he could safely annoy him or make faces at him or hurl insults upon him from the safety of his mother's arms, or the slender branches of the higher trees, he did so.

His superior intelligence and cunning permitted him to invent a thousand diabolical tricks to add to the burdens of Tublat's life.

Early in his boyhood he had learned to form ropes by twisting and tying long grasses together, and with these he was forever tripping Tublat or attempting to hang him from some overhanging branch.

By constant playing and experimenting with these he learned to tie rude knots, and make sliding nooses; and with these he and the younger apes amused themselves. What Tarzan did they tried to do also, but he alone originated and became proficient.

One day while playing thus Tarzan had thrown his rope at one of his fleeing companions, retaining the other end in his grasp. By accident the noose fell squarely about the running ape's neck, bringing him to a sudden and surprising halt.

Ah, here was a new game, a fine game, thought Tarzan, and immediately he attempted to repeat the trick. And thus, by painstaking and continued practice, he learned the art of roping.

Now, indeed, was the life of Tublat a living nightmare. In sleep, upon the march, night or day, he never knew when that quiet noose would slip about his neck and nearly choke the life out of him.

Kala punished, Tublat swore dire vengeance, and old Kerchak took notice and warned and threatened; but all to no avail.

Tarzan defied them all, and the thin, strong noose continued to settle about Tublat's neck whenever he least expected it.

The other apes derived unlimited amusement from Tublat's discomfiture, for Broken Nose was a disagreeable old fellow, whom no one liked, anyway.

In Tarzan's clever little mind many thoughts revolved, and back of these was his divine power of reason.

If he could catch his fellow apes with his long arm of many grasses, why not Sabor, the lioness?

It was the germ of a thought, which, however, was destined to mull around in his conscious and subconscious mind until it resulted in magnificent achievement.

But that came in later years.

CHAPTER VI

JUNGLE BATTLES

THE wanderings of the tribe brought them often near the closed and silent cabin by the little land-locked harbor. To Tarzan this was always a source of never-ending mystery and pleasure.

He would peek into the curtained windows, or, climbing upon the roof, peer down the black depths of the chimney in vain endeavor to solve the unknown wonders that lay within those strong walls.

His little childish imagination pictured wonderful creatures within, and the very impossibility of forcing entrance added a thousandfold to his desire to do so.

He would clamber about the roof and windows for hours attempting to discover means of ingress, but to the door he paid little attention, for this was apparently as solid as the walls.

It was in the next visit to the vicinity, following the adventure with old Sabor, that, as he approached the cabin, Tarzan noticed that from a distance the door appeared as though an independent part of the wall in which it was set, and for the first time it occurred to him that this might prove the means of entrance which had so long eluded him.

He was alone, as was often the case when he visited the cabin, for the apes had no love for it; the story of the thunder-stick having lost nothing in the telling during these ten years had quite surrounded the white man's deserted abode with an atmosphere of weirdness and terror for the simians.

The story of his own connection with the cabin had never been told him. The language of the apes has so few words that they could talk but little of what they had seen in the cabin, having no words to accurately describe either the strange people or their belongings, and so, long before Tarzan was old enough to understand, the subject had been forgotten by the tribe.

Only in a dim, vague way had Kala explained to him that his father had been a strange white ape, but he did not know that Kala was not his own mother.

On this day, then, he went directly to the door and spent hours examining it and fussing with the hinges, the knob and the latch.

Finally he stumbled upon the right combination, and the door swung creakingly open before his astonished eyes.

For some minutes he did not dare venture within, but finally, as his eyes became accustomed to the dim light of the interior he slowly and cautiously entered.

In the middle of the floor lay a skeleton, every vestige of flesh gone from the bones to which still clung the mildewed and mouldered remnants of what had once been clothing. Upon the bed lay a similar grewsome thing, but smaller, while in a tiny cradle nearby was a third, a wee mite of a skeleton.

To none of these evidences of a fearful tragedy of a long dead day did little Tarzan give but passing heed. His wild jungle life had inured him to the sight of dead and dying animals, and had he known that he was looking upon the remains of his own father and mother he would have been no more greatly moved.

The furnishings and other contents of the room it was which riveted his attention. He examined many things minutely—strange tools and weapons, books, papers, clothing—what little had withstood the ravages of time in the humid atmosphere of the jungle coast.

He opened chests and cupboards, such as did not baffle his small experience, and in these he found the contents much better preserved.

Among other things he found a sharp hunting knife, on the keen blade of which he immediately proceeded to cut his finger. Nothing daunted he continued his experiments, finding that he could hack and hew splinters of wood from the table and chairs with this new toy.

For a long time this amused him, but finally tiring he continued his explorations. In a cupboard filled with books he came across one with brightly colored pictures—it was a child's illustrated alphabet—

> A is for Archer
> Who shoots with a bow.
> B is for Boy,
> His first name is Joe.

The pictures interested him greatly.

There were many apes with faces similar to his own, and further over in the book he found, under "M," some little monkeys such as he saw daily flitting through the trees of his primeval forest. But nowhere was pictured any of his own people; in all the book was none that resembled Kerchak, or Tublat, or Kala.

At first he tried to pick the little figures from the leaves, but he soon saw that they were not real, though he knew not what they might be, nor had he any words to describe them.

The boats, and trains, and cows and horses were quite meaningless to him, but not quite so baffling as the odd little figures which appeared beneath and between the colored pictures—some strange kind of bug he thought they might be, for many of them had legs though nowhere could he find one with eyes and a mouth. It was his first introduction to the letters of the alphabet, and he was over ten years old.

Of course he had never before seen print, or never had spoken with any living thing which had the remotest idea that such a thing as a written language existed, nor ever had he seen anyone reading.

So what wonder that the little boy was quite at a loss to guess the meaning of these strange figures.

Near the middle of the book he found his old enemy, Sabor, the lioness, and, further on, coiled Histah, the snake.

Oh, it was most engrossing! Never before in all his ten years had he enjoyed anything so much. So absorbed was he that he did not note the approaching dusk, until it was quite upon him and the figures were blurred.

He put the book back in the cupboard and closed the door, for he did not wish anyone else to find and destroy his treasure, and as he went out into the gathering darkness he closed the great door of the cabin behind him as it had been before he discovered the secret of its lock, but before he left he had noticed the hunting knife lying where he had thrown it upon the floor, and this he picked up and took with him to show to his fellows.

He had taken scarce a dozen steps toward the jungle when a great form rose up before him from the shadows of a low bush. At first he thought it was one of his own people but in another instant he realized that it was Bolgani, the huge gorilla.

So close was he that there was no chance for flight and little Tarzan knew that he must stand and fight for his life; for these great beasts were the deadly enemies of his tribe, and neither one or the other ever asked or gave quarter.

Had Tarzan been a full grown bull ape of the species of his tribe he had been more than a match for the gorilla, but being only a little English boy, though enormously muscular for such, he stood no show against his cruel antagonist. In his veins, though, flowed the blood of the best of a race of mighty fighters, and back of this was the training of his short lifetime among the fierce brutes of the jungle.

He knew no fear, as we know it; his little heart beat the faster but from the excitement and exhilaration of adventure. Had the opportunity presented itself he would have escaped, but solely because his judgment told him he was no match for the great thing which confronted him. And since reason showed him that successful flight was impossible he met the gorilla squarely and bravely without a tremor of a single muscle, or any sign of panic.

In fact he met the brute midway in its charge, striking its huge body with his closed fists and as futilely as he had been a fly attacking an elephant. But in one hand he still clutched the knife he had found in the cabin of his father, and as the brute, striking and biting, closed upon him the boy accidentally turned the point toward the hairy breast. As it sank deep into the body of him the gorilla shrieked in pain and rage.

But the boy had learned in that brief second a use for his sharp and shining toy, so that, as the tearing, striking beast dragged him to earth he plunged the blade repeatedly and to the hilt into its breast.

The gorilla, fighting after the manner of its kind, struck terrific blows with its open hand, and tore the flesh at the boy's throat and chest with its mighty tusks.

For a moment they rolled upon the ground in the fierce frenzy of combat. More and more weakly the torn and bleeding arm struck home with the long sharp blade, then the little figure stiffened with a spasmodic jerk, and Tarzan, the young Lord Greystoke, rolled lifeless upon the dead and decaying vegetation which carpeted his jungle home.

A mile back in the forest the tribe had heard the fierce challenge of the gorilla, and, as was his custom when any danger threatened, Kerchak called his people together, partly for mutual protection against a common enemy, since this gorilla might be but one of a party of several, and also to see that all members of the tribe were accounted for.

It was soon discovered that Tarzan was missing, and Tublat was strongly opposed to sending assistance. Kerchak himself had no liking for the strange little waif, so he listened to Tublat, and, finally, with a shrug of his shoulders, turned back to the pile of leaves on which he had made his bed.

But Kala was of a different mind; in fact, she had not waited but to learn that Tarzan was absent ere she was fairly flying through the matted branches toward the point from which the cries of the gorilla were still plainly audible.

Darkness had now fallen, and an early moon was sending its faint light to cast strange, grotesque shadows among the dense foliage of the forest.

Here and there the brilliant rays penetrated to earth, but for the most part they only served to accentuate the Stygian blackness* of the jungle's depths.

Like some huge phantom, Kala swung noiselessly from tree to tree; now running nimbly along a great branch, now swinging through space at the end of another, only to grasp that of a further tree in her rapid progress toward the scene of the tragedy her knowledge of jungle life told her was being enacted a short distance before her.

The cries of the gorilla proclaimed that it was in mortal combat with some other denizen of the fierce wood. Suddenly these cries ceased, and the silence of death reigned throughout the jungle.

Kala could not understand, for the voice of Bolgani had at the last been raised in the agony of suffering and death, but no sound had come to her by which she possibly could determine the nature of his antagonist.

That her little Tarzan could destroy a great bull gorilla she knew to be improbable, and so, as she neared the spot from which the sounds of the struggle had come, she moved more warily and at last slowly and with extreme caution she traversed the lowest branches, peering eagerly into the moon-splashed blackness for a sign of the combatants.

Presently she came upon them, lying in a little open space full under the brilliant light of the moon—little Tarzan's torn and bloody form, and beside it a great bull gorilla, stone dead.

With a low cry Kala rushed to Tarzan's side, and gathering the poor, blood-covered body to her breast, listened for a sign of life. Faintly she heard it—the weak beating of the little heart.

Tenderly she bore him back through the inky jungle to where the tribe lay, and for many days and nights she sat guard beside him, bringing him food and water, and brushing the flies and other insects from his cruel wounds.

Of medicine or surgery the poor thing knew nothing. She could but lick the wounds, and thus she kept them cleansed, that healing nature might the more quickly do her work.

At first Tarzan would eat nothing, but rolled and tossed in a wild delirium of fever. All he craved was water, and this she brought him in the only way she could, bearing it in her own mouth.

No human mother could have shown more unselfish and sacrificing devotion than did this poor, wild brute for the little orphaned waif whom fate had thrown into her keeping.

At last the fever abated and the boy commenced to mend. No word of complaint passed his tight set lips, though the pain of his wounds was excruciating.

A portion of his chest was laid bare to the ribs, three of which had been broken by the mighty blows of the gorilla. One arm was nearly severed by the giant fangs, and a great piece had been torn from his neck, exposing his jugular vein, which the cruel jaws had missed but by a miracle.

With the stoicism of the brutes who had raised him he endured his suffering quietly, preferring to crawl away from the others and lie huddled in some clump of tall grasses rather than to show his misery before their eyes.

Kala, alone, he was glad to have with him, but now that he was better she was gone longer at a time, in search of food; for the devoted animal had scarcely eaten enough to support her own life while Tarzan had been so low, and was in consequence, reduced to a mere shadow of her former self.*

CHAPTER VII

THE LIGHT OF KNOWLEDGE

AFTER what seemed an eternity to the little sufferer he was able to walk once more, and from then on his recovery was rapid, so that in another month he was as strong and active as ever.

During his convalescence he had gone over in his mind many times the battle with the gorilla, and his first thought was to recover the wonderful little weapon which had transformed him from a hopelessly outclassed weakling to the superior of the mighty terror of the jungle.

Also, he was anxious to return to the cabin and continue his investigations of its wondrous contents.

So, early one morning, he set forth alone upon his quest. After a little search he located the clean-picked bones of his late adversary, and close by, partly buried beneath the fallen leaves, he found the knife, now red with rust from its exposure to the dampness of the ground and from the dried blood of the gorilla.

He did not like the change in its former bright and gleaming surface; but it was still a formidable weapon, and one which he meant to use to advantage whenever the opportunity presented itself. He had in mind that no more would he run from the wanton attacks of old Tublat.

In another moment he was at the cabin, and after a short time had again thrown the latch and entered. His first concern was to learn the mechanism of the lock, and this he did by examining it closely while the door was open, so that he could learn precisely what caused it to hold the door, and by what means it released at his touch.

He found that he could close and lock the door from within, and this he did so that there would be no chance of his being molested while at his investigations.

He commenced a systematic search of the cabin; but his attention was soon riveted by the books which seemed to exert a strange and powerful influence over him, so that he could scarce attend to aught else for the lure of the wondrous puzzle which their purpose presented to him.

Among the other books were a primer, some child's readers, numerous picture books, and a great dictionary. All of these he examined, but the pictures caught his fancy most, though the strange little bugs which covered the pages where there were no pictures excited his wonder and deepest thought.

Squatting upon his haunches on the table top in the cabin his father had built—his smooth, brown, naked little body bent over the book which rested in his strong slender hands, and his great shock of long, black hair falling about his well shaped head and bright, intelligent eyes—Tarzan of the apes, little primitive man, presented a picture filled, at once, with pathos and with promise—an allegorical figure of the primordial groping through the black night of ignorance toward the light of learning.*

His little face was tense in study, for he had partially grasped, in a hazy, nebulous way, the rudiments of a thought which was destined to prove the key and the solution to the puzzling problem of the strange little bugs.

In his hands was a primer opened at a picture of a little ape similar to himself, but covered, except for hands and face, with strange, colored fur, for such he thought the jacket and trousers to be. Beneath the picture were three little bugs—

BOY

And now he had discovered in the text upon the page that these three were repeated many times in the same sequence.

Another fact he learned—that there were comparatively few individual bugs; but these were repeated many times, occasionally alone, but more often in company with others.

Slowly he turned the pages, scanning the pictures and the text for a repetition of the combination *b-o-y*. Presently he found it beneath a picture of another little ape and a strange animal which went upon four legs like the jackal and resembled him not a little. Beneath this picture the bugs appeared as:

A BOY AND A DOG

There they were, the three little bugs which always accompanied the little ape.

And so he progressed very, very slowly, for it was a hard and laborious task which he had set himself without knowing it—a task which might seem to you or me impossible—learning to read without having the slightest knowledge of letters or written language, or the faintest idea that such things existed.

He did not accomplish it in a day, or in a week, or in a month, or in a year; but slowly, very slowly, he learned after he had grasped the possibilities which lay in those little bugs, so that by the time he was fifteen he knew the various combinations of letters which stood for every pictured figure in the little primer and in one or two of the picture books.

Of the meaning and use of the articles and conjunctions, verbs and adverbs and pronouns he had but the faintest and haziest conception.

One day when he was about twelve he found a number of lead pencils in a hitherto undiscovered drawer beneath the table, and in scratching upon the table top with one of them he was delighted to discover the black line it left behind it.

He worked so assiduously with this new toy that the table top was soon a mass of scrawly loops and irregular lines and his pencil-point worn down to the wood. Then he took another pencil, but this time he had a definite object in view.

He would attempt to reproduce some of the little bugs that scrambled over the pages of his books.

It was a difficult task, for he held the pencil as one would grasp the hilt of a dagger, which does not add greatly to ease in writing nor to the legibility of the results.

But he persevered for months, at such times as he was able to come to the cabin, until at last by repeated experimenting he found a position in which to hold the pencil that best permitted him to guide and control it, so that at last he could roughly reproduce any of the little bugs.

Thus he made a beginning at writing.

Copying the bugs taught him another thing, their number; and though he could not count as we understand it yet he had an idea of quantity, the base of his calculations being the number of fingers upon one of his hands.

His search through the various books convinced him that he had discovered all the different kinds of bugs most often repeated in combination, and these he arranged in proper order with great ease because of the frequency with which he had perused the fascinating alphabet picture book.

His education progressed; but his greatest finds were in the inexhaustible storehouse of the huge illustrated dictionary, for he learned more through the medium of pictures than text, even after he had grasped the significance of the bugs.

When he discovered the arrangement of words in alphabetical order he delighted in searching for and finding the combinations with which he was familiar, and the words which followed them, their definitions, led him still further into the mazes of erudition.

By the time he was seventeen he had learned to read the simple, child's primer and had fully realized the true and wonderful purpose of the little bugs.

No longer did he feel shame for his hairless body or his human features, for now his reason told him that he was of a different race from his wild and hairy companions. He was a M-A-N, they were A-P-E-S, and the little apes which scurried through the forest top were M-O-N-K-E-Y-S. He knew, too, that old Sabor was a L-I-O-N-E-S-S, and Histah a S-N-A-K-E, and Tantor an E-L-E-P-H-A-N-T. And so he learned to read.*

From then on his progress was rapid. With the help of the great dictionary and the active intelligence of a healthy mind endowed by inheritance with more than ordinary reasoning powers he shrewdly guessed at much which he could not really understand, and more often than not his guesses were close to the mark of truth.

There were many breaks in his education, caused by the migratory habits of his tribe, but even when removed from recourse to his books his active brain continued to search out the mysteries of his fascinating avocation.

Pieces of bark and flat leaves and even smooth stretches of bare earth provided him with copy books whereon to scratch with the point of his hunting knife the lessons he was learning.

Nor did he neglect the sterner duties of life while following the bent of his inclination toward the solving of the mystery of his library.

He practiced with his rope and played with his sharp knife, which he had learned to keep keen by whetting upon flat stones.

The tribe had grown larger since Tarzan had come among them, for under the leadership of Kerchak they had been able to frighten the other tribes from their part of the jungle so that they had plenty to eat and little or no loss from predatory incursions of neighbors.

Hence the younger males as they became adult found it more comfortable to take wives from their own tribe, or if they captured one of another tribe to bring her back to Kerchak's band and live in amity with him rather than attempt to set up a new establishment of their own, or fight with the redoubtable Kerchak for supremacy at home.

Occasionally one more ferocious than his fellows would attempt this latter alternative, but none had come yet who could wrest the palm of victory* from the fierce and brutal ape.

Tarzan held a peculiar position in the tribe. They seemed to consider him one of them and yet in some way different. The older males either ignored him entirely or else hated him so vindictively that but for his wondrous agility and speed and the fierce protection of the huge Kala he would have been dispatched at an early age.

Tublat was his most consistent enemy, but it was through Tublat that, when he was about thirteen, the persecution of his enemies suddenly ceased and he was left severely alone, except on the occasions when one of them ran amuck in the throes of one of those strange, wild fits of insane rage which attacks the males of many of the fiercer animals of the jungle. Then none was safe.

On the day that Tarzan established his right to respect, the tribe was gathered about a small natural amphitheater which the jungle had left free from its entangling vines and creepers in a hollow amongst some low hills.*

The open space was almost circular in shape. Upon every hand rose the mighty giants of the untouched forest, with the matted undergrowth banked so closely between the huge trunks that the only opening into the little, level arena was through the upper branches of the trees.

Here, safe from interruption, the tribe often gathered. In the center of the amphitheater was one of those strange earthen drums which the anthropoids build for the queer rites the sounds of which men have heard in the fastnesses of the jungle, but which none has ever witnessed.

Many travelers have seen the drums of the great apes, and some have heard the sounds* of their beating and the noise of the wild,

weird revelry of these first lords of the jungle, but Tarzan, Lord
Greystoke, is, doubtless, the only human being who ever joined in
the fierce, mad, intoxicating revel of the Dum-Dum.

From this primitive function has arisen, unquestionably, all the
forms and ceremonials of modern church and state, for through all
the countless ages, back beyond the last, uttermost ramparts of a
dawning humanity our fierce, hairy forebears danced out the rites
of the Dum-Dum to the sound of their earthen drums, beneath the
bright light of a tropical moon in the depth of a mighty jungle which
stands unchanged today as it stood on that long forgotten night in the
dim, unthinkable vistas of the long dead past when our first shaggy
ancestor swung from a swaying bough and dropped lightly upon the
soft turf of the first meeting place.*

On the day that Tarzan won his emancipation from the persecution
that had followed him remorselessly for twelve of his thirteen years
of life, the tribe, now a full hundred strong, trooped silently through
the lower terrace of the jungle trees and dropped noiselessly upon the
floor of the amphitheater.

The rites of the Dum-Dum marked important events in the life
of the tribe—a victory, the capture of a prisoner, the killing of some
large fierce denizen of the jungle, the death or accession of a king, and
were conducted with set ceremonialism.

Today it was the killing of a giant ape, a member of another tribe,
and as the people of Kerchak entered the arena two mighty bulls
might have been seen bearing the body of the vanquished between
them.

They laid their burden before the earthen drum and then squatted
there beside it as guards, while the other members of the community
curled themselves in grassy nooks to sleep until the rising moon
should give the signal for the commencement of their savage orgy.

For hours absolute quiet reigned in the little clearing, except as it
was broken by the discordant notes of brilliantly feathered parrots,
or the screeching and twittering of the thousand jungle birds flitting
ceaselessly amongst the vivid orchids and flamboyant blossoms which
festooned the myriad, moss covered branches of the forest kings.

At length as darkness settled upon the jungle the apes commenced
to bestir themselves, and soon they formed a great circle about the
earthen drum. The females and young squatted in a thin line at the

outer periphery of the circle, while just in front of them ranged the adult males. Before the drum sat three old females, each armed with a knotted branch fifteen or eighteen inches in length.

Slowly and softly they began tapping upon the resounding surface of the drum as the first faint rays of the ascending moon silvered the encircling tree-tops.

As the light in the amphitheater increased the females augmented the frequency and force of their blows until presently a wild, rhythmic din pervaded the great jungle for miles in every direction. Huge, fierce brutes stopped in their hunting, with up-pricked ears and raised heads, to listen to the dull booming that betokened the Dum-Dum of the apes.

Occasionally one would raise his shrill scream or thunderous roar in answering challenge to the savage din of the anthropoids, but none came near to investigate or attack, for the great apes, assembled in all the power of their numbers, filled the breasts of their jungle neighbors with deep respect.

As the din of the drum rose to almost deafening volume Kerchak sprang into the open space between the squatting males and the drummers.

Standing erect he threw his head far back and looking full into the eye of the rising moon he beat upon his breast with his great hairy paws and emitted his fearful roaring shriek.

Once—twice—thrice that terrifying cry rang out across the teaming solitude of that unspeakably quick, yet unthinkably dead, world.

Then, crouching, Kerchak slunk noiselessly around the open circle, veering far away from the dead body lying before the altar-drum, but, as he passed, keeping his little, fierce, wicked, red eyes upon the corpse.

Another male then sprang into the arena, and, repeating the horrid cries of his king, followed stealthily in his wake. Another and another followed in quick succession until the jungle reverberated with the now almost ceaseless notes of their bloodthirsty screams.

It was the challenge and the hunt.

When all the adult males had joined in the thin line of circling dancers the attack commenced.

Kerchak, seizing a huge club from the pile which lay at hand for the purpose, rushed furiously upon the dead ape, dealing the corpse a terrific blow, at the same time emitting the growls and snarls of combat. The din of the drum was now increased, as well as the frequency of the blows, and the warriors, as each approached the victim of the hunt and delivered his bludgeon blow, joined in the mad whirl of the Death Dance.

Tarzan was one of the wild, leaping horde. His brown, sweat-streaked, muscular body, glistening in the moonlight, shone supple and graceful among the uncouth, awkward, hairy brutes about him.

None more craftily stealthy in the mimic hunt, none more ferocious than he in the wild ferocity of the attack, nor none who leaped so high into the air in the Dance of Death.

As the noise and rapidity of the drum beats increased the dancers apparently became intoxicated with the wild rhythm and the savage yells. Their leaps and bounds increased, their bared fangs dripped saliva, and their lips and breasts were flecked with foam.

For half an hour the weird dance went on, until, at a sign from Kerchak, the noise of the drums ceased, the female drummers scampering hurriedly through the line of dancers toward the outer rim of squatting spectators. Then, as one man, the males rushed headlong upon the thing which their terrific blows had reduced to a mass of hairy pulp.

Flesh seldom came to their jaws in satisfying quantities, so a fit finale to their wild revel was a taste of fresh killed meat, and it was to the purpose of devouring their late enemy that they now turned their attention.

Great fangs sunk into the carcass tearing away huge hunks, the mightiest of the apes obtaining the choicest morsels, while the weaker circled the outer edge of the fighting, snarling pack awaiting their chance to dodge in and snatch a dropped tit-bit or filch a remaining bone before all was gone.

Tarzan, more than the apes, craved and needed flesh. Descended from a race of meat eaters, never in his life, he thought, had he once satisfied his appetite for animal food, and so now his agile little body wormed its way far into the mass of struggling, rending apes in an endeavor to obtain a share which his strength would have been unequal to the task of winning for him.

At his side hung the hunting knife of his unknown father in a sheath self-fashioned in copy of one he had seen among the pictures of his treasure-books.

At last he reached the fast disappearing feast and with his sharp knife slashed off a more generous portion than he had hoped for, an entire hairy forearm, where it protruded from beneath the feet of the mighty Kerchak, who was so busily engaged in perpetuating the royal prerogative of hogging that he failed to note the act of *lese-majesté*.*

So little Tarzan wriggled out from beneath the struggling mass, clutching his grisly prize close to his breast.

Among those circling futilely the outskirts of the banqueters was old Tublat. He had been among the first at the feast, but had retreated with a goodly share to eat in quiet, and was now forcing his way back for more.

So it was that he spied Tarzan as the boy emerged from the clawing, pushing throng with that hairy forearm hugged firmly to his body.

Tublat's little, close-set, blood-shot, pig eyes shot wicked gleams of hate as they fell upon the object of his loathing. In them, too, was greed for the toothsome dainty the boy carried.

But Tarzan saw his arch enemy as quickly, and divining what the great beast would do he leaped nimbly away toward the women and children, hoping to hide himself among them. Tublat, however, was close upon his heels, so that he had no opportunity to seek a place of concealment, but saw that he would be put to it to escape at all.

Swiftly he sped toward the surrounding trees and with an agile bound gained a lower limb with one hand, and then, transferring his burden to his teeth, he climbed rapidly upward, closely followed by Tublat.

Up, up he went to the waving pinnacle of a lofty monarch of the forest where his heavy pursuer dared not follow him. There he perched, hurling taunts and insults at the raging, foaming beast fifty feet below him.

And then Tublat went mad.

With horrifying screams and roars he rushed to the ground, among the females and young, sinking his great fangs into a dozen tiny necks and tearing great pieces from the backs and breasts of the females who fell into his clutches.

In the brilliant moonlight Tarzan witnessed the whole mad carnival of rage. He saw the females and the young scamper to the safety of the trees. Then the great bulls in the center of the arena felt the mighty fangs of their demented fellow, and with one accord they melted into the black shadows of the over-hanging forest.

There was but one in the amphitheater beside Tublat, a belated female running swiftly toward the tree where Tarzan perched, and close behind her came the awful Tublat.

It was Kala, and as quickly as Tarzan saw that Tublat was gaining on her he dropped with the rapidity of a falling stone, from branch to branch, toward his foster mother.

Now she was beneath the overhanging limbs and close above her crouched Tarzan, waiting the outcome of the race.

She leaped into the air grasping a low hanging branch, but almost over the head of Tublat, so nearly had he distanced her. She should have been safe now but there was a rending, tearing sound, the branch broke and precipitated her full upon the head of Tublat, knocking him to the ground.

Both were up in an instant, but as quick as they had been Tarzan had been quicker, so that the infuriated bull found himself facing the man-child who stood between him and Kala.

Nothing could have suited the fierce beast better, and with a roar of triumph he leaped upon the little Lord Greystoke. But his fangs never closed in that nut brown flesh.

A muscular hand shot out and grasped the hairy throat, and another plunged a keen hunting knife a dozen times into the broad breast. Like lightning the blows fell, and only ceased when Tarzan felt the limp form crumple beneath him.

As the body rolled to the ground Tarzan of the Apes* placed his foot upon the neck of his lifelong enemy and raising his eyes to the full moon threw back his fierce young head and voiced the wild and terrible cry of his people.

One by one the tribe swung down from their arboreal retreats and formed a circle about Tarzan and his vanquished foe. When they had all come Tarzan turned toward them.

"I am Tarzan," he cried. "I am a great killer. Let all respect Tarzan of the Apes and Kala, his mother. There be none among you as mighty as Tarzan. Let his enemies beware."

Looking full into the wicked, red eyes of Kerchak, the young Lord Greystoke beat upon his mighty breast and screamed out once more his shrill cry of defiance.

CHAPTER VIII

THE TREE-TOP HUNTER

THE morning after the Dum-Dum the tribe started slowly back through the forest toward the coast.

The body of Tublat lay where it had fallen, for the people of Kerchak do not eat their own dead.

The march was but a leisurely search for food. Cabbage-palm and gray plum, pisang and scitamine* they found in abundance, with wild pineapple, and occasionally small mammals, birds, eggs, reptiles, and insects. The nuts they cracked between their powerful jaws, or, if too hard, broke by pounding between stones.

Once old Sabor, crossing their path, sent them scurrying to the safety of the higher branches, for if she respected their number and their sharp fangs, they on their part held her cruel and mighty ferocity in equal esteem.

Upon a low hanging branch sat Tarzan directly above the majestic, supple body as it forged silently through the thick jungle. He hurled a pineapple at the ancient enemy of his people. The great beast stopped and, turning, eyed the taunting figure above her.

With an angry lash of her tail she bared her yellow fangs, curling her great lips in a hideous snarl that wrinkled her bristling snout in serried ridges and closed her wicked eyes to two narrow slits of rage and hatred.

With back-laid ears she looked straight into the eyes of Tarzan of the Apes and sounded her fierce, shrill challenge.

And from the safety of his overhanging limb the ape-child sent back the fearsome answer of his kind.

For a moment the two eyed each other in silence, and then the great cat turned into the jungle, which swallowed her as the ocean engulfs a tossed pebble.

But into the mind of Tarzan a great plan sprang. He had killed the fierce Tublat, so was he not therefore a mighty fighter? Now would he track down the crafty Sabor and slay her likewise. He would be a mighty hunter, also.

At the bottom of his little English heart beat the great desire to cover his nakedness with *clothes* for he had learned from his picture books that all *men* were so covered, while *monkeys* and *apes* and every other living thing went naked.

Clothes therefore, must be truly a badge of greatness; the insignia of the superiority of *man* over all other animals, for surely there could be no other reason for wearing the hideous things.

Many moons ago, when he had been much smaller, he had desired the skin of Sabor, the lioness, or Numa,* the lion, or Sheeta, the leopard to cover his hairless body that he might no longer resemble hideous Histah, the snake; but now he was proud of his sleek skin for it betokened his descent from a mighty race, and the conflicting desires to go naked in prideful proof of his ancestry, or to conform to the customs of his own kind and wear hideous and uncomfortable apparel found first one and then the other in the ascendency.

As the tribe continued their slow way through the forest after the passing of Sabor, Tarzan's head was filled with his great scheme for slaying his enemy, and for many days thereafter he thought of little else.

On this day, however, he presently had other and more immediate interests to attract his attention.

Of a sudden it became as midnight; the noises of the jungle ceased; the trees stood motionless as though in paralyzed expectancy of some great and imminent disaster. All nature waited—but not for long.

Faintly, from a distance, came a low, sad moaning. Nearer and nearer it approached, mounting louder and louder in volume.

The great trees bent in unison as though pressed earthward by a mighty hand. Further and further toward the ground they inclined, and still there was no sound save the deep and awesome moaning of the wind.

Then, suddenly, the jungle giants whipped back, lashing their mighty tops in angry and deafening protest. A vivid and blinding light flashed from the whirling, inky clouds above. The deep cannonade of roaring thunder belched forth its fearsome challenge. The deluge came—all hell broke loose upon the jungle.

The tribe huddled, shivering from the cold rain, at the bases of great trees. The lightning darting and flashing through the blackness, showed wildly waving branches, whipping streamers and bending trunks.

Now and again some ancient patriarch of the woods, rent by a flashing bolt, would crash in a thousand pieces among the surrounding trees, carrying down numberless branches and many smaller neighbors to add to the tangled confusion of the tropical jungle.

Branches, great and small, torn away by the ferocity of the tornado, hurtled through the wildly waving verdure, carrying death and destruction to countless unhappy denizens of the thickly peopled world below.

For hours the fury of the storm continued without surcease, and still the tribe huddled close in shivering fear. In constant danger from falling trunks and branches and paralyzed by the vivid flashing of lightning and the bellowing of thunder they crouched in pitiful misery until the storm passed.

The end was as sudden as the beginning. The wind ceased, the sun shone forth—nature smiled once more.

The dripping leaves and branches, and the moist petals of gorgeous flowers glistened in the splendor of the returning day. And, so—as Nature forgot, her children forgot also. Busy life went on as it had been before the darkness and the fright.

But to Tarzan a dawning light had come to explain the mystery of *clothes*. How snug he would have been beneath the heavy coat of Sabor! And so was added a further incentive to the adventure.

For several months the tribe hovered near the beach where stood Tarzan's cabin, and his studies took up the greater portion of his time, but always when journeying through the forest he kept his rope in readiness, and many were the smaller animals that fell into the snare of the quick thrown noose.

Once it fell about the short neck of Horta, the boar, and his mad lunge for freedom toppled Tarzan from the overhanging limb where he had lain in wait and from whence he had launched his sinuous coil.

The mighty tusker turned at the sound of his falling body, and, seeing only the easy prey of a young ape, he lowered his head and charged madly at the surprised youth.

Tarzan, happily, was uninjured by the fall, alighting catlike upon all fours far outspread to take up the shock. He was on his feet in an instant and, leaping with the agility of the monkey he was, he gained the safety of a low limb as Horta, the boar, rushed futilely beneath.

Thus it was that Tarzan learned by experience the limitations as well as the possibilities of his strange weapon.

He lost a long rope on this occasion, but he knew that had it been Sabor, who had thus dragged him from his perch the outcome might have been very different, for he would have lost his life, doubtless, into the bargain.

It took him many days to braid a new rope, but when, finally, it was done he went forth purposely to hunt, and lie in wait among the dense foliage of a great branch right above a well-beaten trail that led to water.

Several small animals passed unharmed beneath him. He did not want such insignificant game. It would take a strong animal to test the efficacy of his new scheme.

At last came she whom Tarzan sought, with lithe sinews rolling beneath shimmering hide; fat and glossy came Sabor, the lioness.

Her great padded feet fell soft and noiseless on the narrow trail. Her head was high in ever alert attention; her long tail moved slowly in sinuous and graceful undulations.

Nearer and nearer she came to where Tarzan of the Apes crouched upon his limb, the coils of his long rope poised ready in his hand.

Like a thing of bronze, motionless as death, sat Tarzan. Sabor passed beneath. One stride beyond she took—a second, a third, and then the silent coil shot out above her.

For an instant the spreading noose hung above her head like a great snake, and then, as she looked upward to detect the origin of the swishing sound of the rope, it settled about her neck. With a quick jerk Tarzan snapped the noose tight about the glossy throat, and then he dropped the rope and clung to his support with both hands.

Sabor was trapped.

With a bound the startled beast turned into the jungle, but Tarzan was not to lose another rope through the same cause as the first. He had learned from experience. The lioness had taken but half her second bound when she felt the rope tighten about her neck; her body turned completely over in the air and she fell with a heavy crash upon her back. Tarzan had fastened the end of the rope securely to the trunk of the great tree on which he sat.

Thus far his plan had worked to perfection, but when he grasped the rope, bracing himself behind a crotch of two mighty branches, he found that dragging the mighty, struggling, clawing, biting, screaming mass of iron-muscled fury up to the tree and hanging her was a very different proposition.

The weight of old Sabor was immense, and when she braced her huge paws nothing less than Tantor, the elephant, himself, could have budged her.

The lioness was now back in the path where she could see the author of the indignity which had been placed upon her. Screaming with rage she suddenly charged, leaping high into the air toward Tarzan, but when her huge body struck the limb on which Tarzan had been, Tarzan was no longer there.

Instead he perched lightly upon a smaller branch twenty feet above the raging captive. For a moment Sabor hung half across the branch, while Tarzan mocked, and hurled twigs and branches at her unprotected face.

Presently the beast dropped to the earth again and Tarzan came quickly to seize the rope, but Sabor, had now found that it was only a slender cord that held her, and grasping it in her huge jaws severed it before Tarzan could tighten the strangling noose a second time.

Tarzan was much hurt. His well laid plan had come to naught, so he sat there screaming at the roaring creature beneath him and making mocking grimaces at it.

Sabor paced back and forth beneath the tree for hours; four times she crouched and sprang at the dancing sprite above her, but as well have clutched at the illusive wind that murmured through the tree tops.

At last Tarzan tired of the sport, and with a parting roar of challenge and a well-aimed ripe fruit that spread soft and sticky over the snarling face of his enemy, he swung rapidly through the trees, a hundred feet above the ground, and in a short time was among the members of his tribe.

Here he recounted the details of his adventure, with swelling chest and so considerable swagger that he quite impressed even his bitterest enemies, while Kala fairly danced for joy and pride.

CHAPTER IX

MAN AND MAN

Tᴀʀᴢᴀɴ of the Apes lived on in his wild, jungle existence with little change for several years, only that he grew stronger and wiser, and learned from his books more and more of the strange words which lay somewhere outside his primeval forest.

To him life was never monotonous or stale. There was always Pisah the fish, to be caught in the many streams and the little lakes, and Sabor, with her ferocious cousins to keep one ever on the alert and give zest to every instant that one spent upon the ground.

Often they hunted him, and more often he hunted them, but though they never quite reached him with those cruel, sharp claws of theirs, yet there were times when one could scarce have passed a thick leaf between their talons and his smooth hide.

Quick was Sabor, the lioness, and quick were Numa and Sheeta, but Tarzan of the Apes was lightning.

With Tantor, the elephant, he made friends. How? Ask me not. But this is known to the denizens of the jungle, that on many moonlit nights Tarzan of the Apes and Tantor, the elephant, walked together, and where the way was clear Tarzan rode, perched high upon Tantor's mighty back.

All else of the jungle were his enemies, except his own tribe, among whom he now had many friends.

Many days during these years he spent in the cabin of his father, where still lay, untouched, the bones of his parents and the little skeleton of Kala's baby. At eighteen he read fluently and understood nearly all he read in the many and varied volumes on the shelves.

Also could he write, with printed letters, rapidly and plainly, but script he had not mastered, for though there were several copy books among his treasure, there was so little written English in the cabin that he saw no use for bothering with this other form of writing, though he could read it, laboriously.

Thus, at eighteen, we find him, an English lordling, who could speak no English, and yet who could read and write his native language. Never had he seen a human being other than himself, for the little area traversed by his tribe was watered by no great river to bring down the savage natives of the interior.*

High hills shut it off on three sides, the ocean on the fourth. It was alive with lions and leopards and poisonous snakes. Its untouched mazes of matted jungle had as yet invited no hardy pioneer from the human beasts beyond its frontier.

But as Tarzan of the Apes sat one day in the cabin of his father delving into the mysteries of a new book, the ancient security of his jungle was broken forever.

At the far eastern confine a strange cavalcade strung, in single file, over the brow of a low hill.

In advance were fifty black warriors armed with slender wooden spears with ends hard baked over slow fires, and long bows and poisoned arrows. On their backs were oval shields, in their noses huge rings, while from the kinky wool of their heads protruded tufts of gay feathers.

Across their foreheads were tattooed three parallel lines of color, and on each breast three concentric circles. Their yellow teeth were filed to sharp points, and their great protruding lips added still further to the low and bestial brutishness of their appearance.

Following them were several hundred women and children, the former bearing upon their heads great burdens of cooking pots, household utensils and ivory. In the rear were a hundred warriors, similar in all respects to the advance guard.

That they more greatly feared an attack from the rear than whatever unknown enemies lurked in their advance was evidenced by the formation of the column; and such was the fact, for they were fleeing from the white man's soldiers who had so harassed them for rubber and ivory that they had turned upon their conquerors one day and massacred a white officer and a small detachment of his black troops.

For many days they had gorged themselves on meat, but eventually a stronger body of troops had come and fallen upon their village by night to revenge the death of their comrades.

That night the black soldiers of the white man had had meat a-plenty,* and this little remnant of a once powerful tribe had slunk off into the gloomy jungle toward the unknown, and freedom.

But what meant freedom and the pursuit of happiness* to these savage blacks meant consternation and death to many of the wild denizens of their new home.

For three days the little cavalcade marched slowly through the heart of this unknown and untracked forest, until finally, early in the fourth day, they came upon a little spot, near the banks of a small river, which seemed less thickly overgrown than any ground they had yet encountered.

Here they set to work to build a new village, and in a month a great clearing had been made, huts and palisades erected, plantains, yams and maize planted, and they had taken up their old life in their new home. Here there were no white men, no soldiers; nor any rubber or ivory to be gathered for cruel and thankless taskmasters.

Several moons passed by ere the blacks ventured far into the territory surrounding their new village. Several had already fallen prey to old Sabor, and because the jungle was so infested with these fierce and blood thirsty cats, and with lions and leopards, the ebony warriors hesitated to trust themselves far from the safety of their palisades.

But one day, Kulonga, a son of the old king, Mbonga,* wandered far into the dense mazes to the west. Warily he stepped, his slender lance ever ready, his long oval shield firm grasped in his left hand close to his sleek ebony body.

At his back his bow, and in the quiver upon his shield many slim, straight arrows, well smeared with the thick, dark, tarry substance that rendered deadly their tiniest needle prick.*

Night found Kulonga far from the palisades of his father's village, but still headed westward, and climbing into the fork of a great tree he fashioned a rude platform and curled himself for sleep.

Three miles to the west of him slept the tribe of Kerchak.

Early the next morning the apes were astir, moving through the jungle in search of food. Tarzan, as was his custom, prosecuted his search in the direction of the cabin so that by leisurely hunting on the way his stomach was filled by the time he reached the beach.

The apes scattered by ones, and twos, and threes in all directions, but ever within sound of a signal of alarm.

Kala had moved slowly along an elephant track toward the east, and was busily engaged in turning over rotted limbs and logs in search of esculent bugs and fungi, when the faintest shadow of a strange noise brought her to startled attention.

For fifty yards before her the trail was straight, and down this leafy tunnel she saw the stealthily advancing figure of a strange and fearful creature.

It was Kulonga.

Kala did not wait to see more, but, turning, moved rapidly back along the trail. She did not run; but, after the manner of her kind when not aroused, sought rather to avoid than to escape.

Close after her came Kulonga. Here was meat. He could make a killing and feast well this day. On he hurried, his spear poised for the throw.

At a turning of the trail he came in sight of her again upon another straight stretch. His spear-hand went far back, the muscles rolled, lightning-like, beneath the sleek hide. Out shot the arm, and the spear sped toward Kala.

A poor cast. It but grazed her side.

With a cry of rage and pain the she-ape turned upon her tormentor. In an instant the trees were crashing beneath the weight of her hurrying fellows, swinging rapidly toward the scene of trouble in answer to Kala's scream.

As she charged, Kulonga unslung his bow and fitted an arrow with almost unthinkable quickness. Drawing the shaft far back he drove the poisoned missile straight into the heart of the great anthropoid.

With a horrid scream Kala plunged forward upon her face before the astonished members of her tribe.

Roaring and shrieking the apes dashed toward Kulonga, but that wary savage was fleeing down the trail like a frightened antelope.

He knew something of the ferocity of these wild, hairy men, and his one desire was to put as many miles between himself and them as he possibly could.

They followed him, racing through the trees, for a long distance, but finally one by one they abandoned the chase and returned to the scene of the tragedy.

None of them had ever seen a man before, other than Tarzan, and so they wondered vaguely what strange manner of creature it might be that had invaded their jungle.

On the far beach, by the little cabin Tarzan heard the faint echoes of the conflict and knowing that something was seriously amiss among the tribe he hastened rapidly toward the direction of the sound.

When he arrived he found the entire tribe gathered jabbering about the dead body of his slain mother.

Tarzan's grief and anger were unbounded. He roared out his hideous challenge time and again. He beat upon his great chest with his clenched fists, and then he fell upon the body of Kala and sobbed out the pitiful sorrowing of his lonely heart.

To lose the only creature in all one's world who ever had manifested love and affection for one, is a great bereavement indeed.

What though Kala was a fierce and hideous ape! To Tarzan she had been kind, she had been beautiful.

Upon her he had lavished, unknown to himself, all the reverence and respect and love that a normal English boy feels for his own mother. He had never known another, and so to Kala was given, though mutely, all that would have belonged to the fair and lovely Lady Alice had she lived.

After the first outburst of grief Tarzan controlled himself, and questioning the members of the tribe who had witnessed the killing of Kala he learned all that their meagre vocabulary could vouchsafe him.

It was enough, however, for his needs. It told him of a strange, hairless, black ape with feathers growing upon its head, who launched death from a slender branch, and then ran, with the fleetness of Bara, the deer, toward the rising sun.

Tarzan waited no longer, but leaping into the branches of the trees sped rapidly through the forest. He knew the windings of the elephant trail along which Kala's murderer had flown, and so he cut straight through the jungle to intercept the black warrior who was evidently following the tortuous detours of the trail.

At his side was the hunting knife of his unknown sire, and across his shoulders the coils of his own long rope. In an hour he struck the trail again, and coming to earth examined the soil minutely.

In the soft mud on the bank of a tiny rivulet he found footprints such as he alone in all the jungle had ever made, but much larger than his. His heart beat fast. Could it be that he was trailing a MAN—one of his own race?

There were two sets of imprints pointing in opposite directions. So his quarry had already passed on his return along the trail. As he examined the newer spoor a tiny particle of earth toppled from the outer edge of one of the footprints to the bottom of its shallow depression—ah, the trail was very fresh, his prey must have but scarcely passed.

Tarzan swung himself to the trees once more, and with swift noiselessness sped along high above the trail.

He had covered barely a mile when he came upon the black warrior standing in a little open space. In his hand was his slender bow to which he had fitted one of his death dealing arrows.

Opposite him across the little clearing stood Horta, the boar, with lowered head and foam flecked tusks, ready to charge.

Tarzan looked with wonder upon the strange creature beneath him—so like him in form and yet so different in face and color. His books had portrayed the *negro*, but how different had been the dull, dead print to this sleek and hideous thing of ebony, pulsing with life.

As the man stood there with taught drawn bow Tarzan recognized in him not so much the *negro* as the *Archer* of his picture book—

A stands for Archer

How wonderful! Tarzan almost betrayed his presence in the deep excitement of his discovery.

But things were commencing to happen below him. The sinewy black arm had drawn the shaft far back; Horta, the boar, was charging, and then the black released the little poisoned arrow, and Tarzan saw it fly with the quickness of thought and lodge in the bristling neck of the boar.

Scarcely had the shaft left his bow ere Kulonga had fitted another to it, but Horta, the boar, was upon him so quickly that he had no time to discharge it. With a bound the black leaped entirely over the rushing beast and turning with incredible swiftness planted a second arrow in Horta's back.

Then Kulonga sprang into a nearby tree.

Horta wheeled to charge his enemy once more, a dozen steps he took, then he staggered and fell upon his side. For a moment his muscles stiffened and relaxed convulsively, then he lay still.

Kulonga came down from his tree.

With the knife that hung at his side he cut several large pieces from the boar's body, and in the center of the trail he built a fire, cooking and eating as much as he wanted. The rest he left where it had fallen.

Tarzan was an interested spectator. His desire to kill burned fiercely in his wild breast, but his desire to learn was even greater. He would follow this savage creature for a while and know from whence he came. He could kill him at his leisure later, when the bow and deadly arrows were laid aside.

When Kulonga had finished his repast and disappeared beyond a near turning of the path, Tarzan dropped quietly to the ground. With his knife he severed many strips of meat from Horta's carcass, but he did not cook them.

He had seen fire, but only when Ara, the lightning, had destroyed some great tree. That any creature of the jungle could produce the red-and-yellow fangs which devoured wood and left nothing but fine dust surprised Tarzan greatly, and why the black warrior had ruined his delicious repast by plunging it into the blighting heat was quite beyond him. Possibly Ara was a friend with whom the Archer was sharing his food.

But, be that as it may, Tarzan would not ruin good meat in any such foolish manner, so he gobbled down a great quantity of the raw flesh, burying the balance of the carcass beside the trail where he could find it upon his return.

And then Lord Greystoke wiped his greasy fingers upon his naked thighs and took up the trail of Kulonga, the son of Mbonga, the king; while in far-off London another Lord Greystoke, the younger brother of the real Lord Greystoke's father, sent back his chops to the club's *chef* because they were underdone, and when he had finished his repast he dipped his finger-ends into a silver bowl of scented water and dried them upon a piece of snowy damask.

All day Tarzan followed Kulonga, hovering above him in the trees like some malign spirit. Twice more he saw him hurl his arrows of destruction—once at Dango, the hyena, and again at Manu, the monkey. In each instance the animal died almost instantly, for Kulonga's poison was very fresh and very deadly.

Tarzan thought much on this wondrous method of slaying as he swung slowly along at a safe distance behind his quarry. He knew that alone the tiny prick of the arrow could not so quickly dispatch these wild things of the jungle, who were often torn and scratched and gored in a frightful manner as they fought with their jungle neighbors, yet as often recovered as not.

No, there was something mysterious connected with these tiny slivers of wood which could bring death by a mere scratch. He must look into the matter.

That night Kulonga slept in the crotch of a mighty tree and far above him crouched Tarzan of the Apes.

When Kulonga awoke he found that his bow and arrows had disappeared. The black warrior was furious and frightened, but more frightened than furious. He searched the ground below the tree, and he searched the tree above the ground; but there was no sign of either bow or arrows or of the nocturnal marauder.

Kulonga was panic-stricken. His spear he had hurled at Kala and had not recovered; and, now that his bow and arrows were gone, he was defenseless except for a single knife. His only hope lay in reaching the village of Mbonga as quickly as his legs would carry him.

That he was not far from home he was certain, so he took to the trail at a rapid trot.

From a great mass of impenetrable foliage a few yards away emerged Tarzan of the Apes to swing quietly in his wake.

Kulonga's bow and arrows were securely tied high in the top of a giant tree from which a patch of bark had been removed by a sharp knife near to the ground, and a branch half cut through and left hanging about fifty feet higher up. Thus Tarzan blazed the forest trails and marked his caches.

As Kulonga continued his journey Tarzan closed up on him until he traveled almost over the black's head. His rope he now held coiled in his right hand; he was almost ready for the kill.

The moment was delayed only because Tarzan was anxious to ascertain the black warrior's destination, and presently he was rewarded, for they came suddenly in view of a great clearing, at one end of which lay many strange lairs.

Tarzan was directly over Kulonga, as he made the discovery. The forest ended abruptly and beyond lay two hundred yards of planted fields between the jungle and the village.

Tarzan must act quickly or his prey would be gone; but Tarzan's life training left so little space between decision and action when an emergency confronted him that there was not even room for the shadow of a thought between.

So it was that as Kulonga emerged from the shadow of the jungle a slender coil of rope sped sinuously above him from the lowest branch of a mighty tree directly upon the edge of the fields of Mbonga, and ere the king's son had taken a half dozen steps into the clearing a quick noose tightened about his neck.

So quickly did Tarzan of the Apes drag back his prey that Kulonga's cry of alarm was throttled in his windpipe. Hand over hand Tarzan drew the struggling black until he had him hanging by his neck in midair; then Tarzan climbed to a larger branch drawing the still threshing victim well up into the sheltering verdure of the tree.*

Here he fastened the rope securely to a stout branch, and then, descending, plunged his hunting knife into Kulonga's heart. Kala was avenged.

Tarzan examined the black minutely, never had he seen any other human being. The knife with its sheath and belt caught his eye; he appropriated them. A copper anklet also took his fancy, and this he transferred to his own leg.

He examined and admired the tattooing on the forehead and breast. He marveled at the sharp filed teeth. He investigated and appropriated the feathered head-dress, and then he prepared to get down to business, for Tarzan of the Apes was hungry, and here was meat; meat of the kill, which jungle ethics permitted him to eat.

How may we judge him, by what standards, this ape-man with the heart and head and body of an English gentleman, and the training of a wild beast?

Tublat, whom he had hated and who had hated him, he had killed in fair fight, and yet never had the thought of eating Tublat's flesh entered his head. It would have been as revolting to him as is cannibalism to us.

But who was Kulonga that he might not be eaten as fairly as Horta, the boar, or Bara, the deer? Was he not simply another of the countless wild things of the jungle who preyed upon one another to satisfy the cravings of hunger?

Of a sudden, a strange doubt stayed his hand. Had not his books taught him that he was a man? And was not The Archer a man, also?

Did men eat men? Alas, he did not know. Why, then, this hesitancy! Once more he essayed the effort, but of a sudden a qualm of nausea overwhelmed him. He did not understand.

All he knew was that he could not eat the flesh of this black man, and thus hereditary instinct, ages old, usurped the functions of his untaught mind and saved him from transgressing a world-wide law of whose very existence he was ignorant.

Quickly he lowered Kulonga's body to the ground, removed the noose, and took to the trees again.

CHAPTER X

THE FEAR-PHANTOM

FROM a lofty perch Tarzan viewed the village of thatched huts across the intervening plantation.

He saw that at one point the forest touched the village, and to this spot he made his way, lured by a fever of curiosity to behold animals of his own kind, and to learn more of their ways and view the strange lairs in which they lived.

His savage life among the fierce wild brutes of the jungle left no opening for any thought that these could be aught else than enemies. Similarity of form led him into no erroneous conception of the welcome that would be accorded him should he be discovered by these, the first of his own kind he had ever seen.

Tarzan of the Apes was no sentimentalist. He knew nothing of the brotherhood of man. All things outside his own tribe were his deadly enemies, with the few exceptions of which Tantor, the elephant, was a marked example.

And he realized all this without malice or hatred. To kill was the law of the wild world he knew. Few were his primitive pleasures, but the greatest of these was to hunt and kill, and so he accorded to others the right to cherish the same desires as he, even though he himself might be the object of their hunt.

His strange life had left him neither morose nor bloodthirsty. That he joyed in killing, and that he killed with a joyous laugh upon his handsome lips betokened no innate cruelty. He killed for food most often, but, being a man, he sometimes killed for pleasure, a thing which no other animal does; for it has remained for man alone among all creatures to kill senselessly and wantonly for the mere pleasure of inflicting suffering and death.

And when he killed for revenge, or in self-defense, he did that also without hysteria, but it was a very businesslike proceeding which admitted of no levity.

So it was that now, as he cautiously approached the village of Mbonga, he was quite prepared either to kill or be killed should he be discovered. He proceeded with unwonted stealth, for Kulonga had taught him great respect for the little sharp splinters of wood which dealt death so swiftly and unerringly.

At length he came to a great tree, heavy laden with thick foliage and loaded with pendant loops of giant creepers. From this almost impenetrable bower above the village he crouched, looking down upon the scene below him, wondering over every feature of this new, strange life.

There were naked children running and playing in the village street. There were women grinding dried plantain in crude stone mortars, while others were fashioning cakes from the powdered flour. Out in the fields he could see still other women hoeing, weeding, or gathering.

All wore strange protruding girdles of dried grass about their hips and many were loaded with brass and copper anklets, armlets and bracelets. Around many a dusky neck hung curiously coiled strands of wire, while several were further ornamented by huge nose-rings.

Tarzan of the Apes looked with growing wonder at these strange creatures. Dozing in the shade he saw several men, while at the extreme outskirts of the clearing he occasionally caught glimpses of armed warriors apparently guarding the village against surprise from an attacking enemy.

He noticed that the women alone worked. Nowhere was there evidence of a man tilling the fields or performing any of the homely duties of the village.

Finally his eyes rested upon a woman directly beneath him.

Before her was a small cauldron standing over a low fire and in it bubbled a thick, reddish, tarry mass. On one side of her lay a quantity of wooden arrows the points of which she dipped into the seething substance, then laying them upon a narrow rack of boughs which stood upon her other side.

Tarzan of the Apes was fascinated. Here was the secret of the terrible destructiveness of The Archer's tiny missiles. He noted the extreme care which the woman took that none of the matter should touch her hands, and once when a particle spattered upon one of her fingers he saw her plunge the member into a vessel of water and quickly rub the tiny stain away with a handful of leaves.

Tarzan of the Apes knew nothing of poison, but his shrewd reasoning told him that it was this deadly stuff that killed, and not the little arrow, which was merely the messenger that carried it into the body of its victim.

How he should like to have more of those little death dealing slivers. If the woman would only leave her work for an instant he could drop down, gather up a handful, and be back in the tree again before she drew three breaths.

As he was trying to think out some plan to distract her attention he heard a wild cry from across the clearing. He looked and saw a black warrior standing beneath the very tree in which he had killed the murderer of Kala an hour before.

The fellow was shouting and waving his spear above his head. Now and again he would point to something on the ground before him.

The village was in an uproar instantly. Armed men rushed from the interior of many a hut and raced madly across the clearing toward the excited sentry. After them trooped the old men, and the women and children until, in a moment, the village was deserted.

Tarzan of the Apes knew that they had found the body of his victim, but that interested him far less than the fact that no one remained in the village to prevent his taking a supply of the arrows which lay below him.

Quickly and noiselessly he dropped to the ground beside the cauldron of poison. For a moment he stood motionless, his quick, bright eyes scanning the interior of the palisade.

No one was in sight. His eyes rested upon the open doorway of a nearby hut. He would take a look within, thought Tarzan, and so, cautiously, he approached the low thatched building.

For a moment he stood without, listening intently. There was no sound, and he glided into the semi-darkness of the interior.

Weapons hung against the walls—long spears, strangely shaped knives, a couple of narrow shields. In the center of the room was a cooking pot, and at the far end a litter of dry grasses covered by woven mats which evidently served the owners as beds and bedding. Several human skulls* lay upon the floor.

Tarzan of the Apes felt of each article, hefted the spears, smelled of them, for he "saw" largely through his sensitive and highly trained nostrils. He determined to own one of these long, pointed sticks, but he could not take one on this trip because of the arrows he meant to carry.

One by one, as he took each article from the walls, he placed them in a pile in the center of the room, and on top of all he placed the cooking pot, inverted, and on top of this he laid one of the grinning skulls, upon which he fastened the head-dress of the dead Kulonga.

Then he stood back and surveyed his work, and grinned. Tarzan of the Apes was a joker.

But now he heard, without, the sounds of many voices, and long mournful howls, and mighty wailing. He was startled. Had he remained too long? Quickly he reached the doorway and peered down the village street toward the village gate.

The natives were not yet in sight, though he could plainly hear them approaching across the plantation. They must be very near.

Like a flash he sprang across the opening to the pile of arrows. Gathering up all he could carry under one arm, he overturned the seething cauldron with a kick, and disappeared into the foliage above just as the first of the returning natives entered the gate at the far end of the village street. Then he turned to watch the proceeding below, poised like some wild bird ready to take swift wing at the first sign of danger.

The natives filed up the street, four of them bearing the dead body of Kulonga. Behind trailed the women, uttering strange cries and weird lamentation. On they came to the portals of Kulonga's hut, the very one in which Tarzan had wrought his depredations.

Scarcely had half a dozen entered the building ere they came rushing out in wild, jabbering confusion. The others hastened to gather about. There was much excited gesticulating, pointing, and chattering; then several of the warriors approached and peered within.

Finally an old fellow with many ornaments of metal about his arms and legs, and a necklace of dried human hands depending upon his chest, entered the hut.

It was Mbonga, the king, father of Kulonga.

For a few moments all were silent. Then Mbonga emerged, a look of mingled wrath and superstitious fear writ upon his hideous countenance. He spoke a few words to the assembled warriors, and in an instant the men were flying through the little village searching minutely every hut and corner within the palisade.

Scarcely had the search commenced than the overturned cauldron was discovered, and with it the theft of the poisoned arrows. Nothing more they found, and it was a thoroughly awed and frightened group of savages which huddled around their king a few moments later.

Mbonga could explain nothing of the strange events that had taken place. The finding of the still warm body of Kulonga—on the very verge of their fields and within easy earshot of the village—knifed and stripped at the door of his father's home, was in itself sufficiently mysterious, but these last awesome discoveries within the village, within the dead Kulonga's own hut, filled their hearts with dismay, and conjured in their poor brains only the most frightful of superstitious explanations.

They stood in little groups, talking in low tones, and ever casting affrighted glances behind them from their great rolling eyes.

Tarzan of the Apes watched them for a while from his lofty perch in the great tree. There was much in their demeanor which he could not understand, for of superstition he was ignorant, and of fear of any kind he had but a vague conception.

The sun was high in the heavens. Tarzan had not broken fast this day, and it was many miles to where lay the toothsome remains of Horta the boar.

So he turned his back upon the village of Mbonga and melted away into the leafy fastness of the forest.

CHAPTER XI

"KING OF THE APES"

IT WAS not yet dark when he reached the tribe, though he stopped to exhume and devour the remains of the wild boar he had cached the preceding day, and again to take Kulonga's bow and arrows from the tree top in which he had hidden them.

It was a well-laden Tarzan who dropped from the branches into the midst of the tribe of Kerchak.

With swelling chest he narrated the glories of his adventure and exhibited the spoils of conquest.

Kerchak grunted and turned away, for he was jealous of this strange member of his band. In his little evil brain he sought for some excuse to wreak his hatred upon Tarzan.

The next day Tarzan was practicing with his bow and arrows at the first gleam of dawn. At first he lost nearly every bolt he shot, but finally he learned to guide the little shafts with fair accuracy, and ere a month had passed he was no mean shot; but his proficiency had cost him nearly his entire supply of arrows.

The tribe continued to find the hunting good in the vicinity of the beach, and so Tarzan of the Apes varied his archery practice with further investigation of his father's choice though little store of books.

It was during this period that the young English lord found hidden in the back of one of the cupboards in the cabin a small metal box. The key was in the lock, and a few moments investigation and experimentation were rewarded with the successful opening of the receptacle.

In it he found a faded photograph of a smooth faced young man, a golden locket studded with diamonds, linked to a small gold chain, a few letters and a small book.

Tarzan examined these all minutely.

The photograph he liked most of all, for the eyes were smiling, and the face was open and frank. It was his father.

The locket, too, took his fancy, and he placed the chain about his neck in imitation of the ornamentation he had seen to be so common among the black men he had visited. The brilliant stones gleamed strangely against his smooth, brown hide.

The letters he could scarcely decipher for he had learned little or nothing of script, so he put them back in the box with the photograph and turned his attention to the book.

This was almost entirely filled with fine script, but while the little bugs were all familiar to him, their arrangement and the combinations in which they occurred were strange, and entirely incomprehensible.

Tarzan had long since learned the use of the dictionary, but much to his sorrow and perplexity it proved of no avail to him in this emergency. Not a word of all that was writ in the book could he find, and so he put it back in the metal box, but with a determination to work out the mysteries of it later on.

Poor little ape-man! Had he but known it that tiny, baffling mystery held between its seal covers the key to his origin; the answer to the strange riddle of his strange life.

It was the diary of John Clayton, Lord Greystoke—kept in French, as had always been his custom.

Tarzan replaced the box in the cupboard, but always thereafter he carried the features of the strong, smiling face of his father in his heart, and in his head a fixed determination to solve the mystery of the strange words in the little black book.

At present he had more important business in hand, for his supply of arrows was exhausted, and he must needs journey to the black men's village and renew it.

Early the following morning he set out, and, traveling rapidly, he came before midday to the clearing. Once more he took up his position in the great tree, and, as before, he saw the women in the fields and the village street, and the cauldron of bubbling poison directly beneath him.

For hours he lay awaiting his opportunity to drop down unseen and gather up the arrows for which he had come; but nothing now occurred to call the villagers away from their homes. The day wore on, and still Tarzan of the Apes crouched above the unsuspecting woman at the cauldron.

Presently the workers in the fields returned. The hunting warriors emerged from the forest, and when all were within the palisade the gates were closed and barred.

Many cooking pots were now in evidence about the village. Before each hut a woman presided over a boiling stew, while little cakes of plantain, and cassava puddings were to be seen on every hand.

Suddenly there came a hail from the edge of the clearing.

Tarzan looked.

It was a party of belated hunters returning from the north, and among them they half led, half carried a struggling animal.

As they approached the village the gates were thrown open to admit them, and then, as the people saw the victim of the chase, a savage cry rose to the heavens, for the quarry was a man.

As he was dragged, still resisting, into the village street, the women and children set upon him with sticks and stones, and Tarzan of the Apes, young and savage beast of the jungle, wondered at the cruel brutality of his own kind.

Sheeta, the leopard,* alone of all the jungle folk, tortured his prey. The ethics of all the others meted a quick and merciful death to their victims.

Tarzan had learned from his books but scattered fragments of the ways of human beings.

When he had followed Kulonga through the forest he had expected to come to a city of strange houses on wheels, puffing clouds of black smoke from a huge tree stuck in the roof of one of them—or to a sea covered with mighty floating buildings which he had learned were called, variously, ships and boats and steamers and craft.

He had been sorely disappointed with the poor little village of the blacks, hidden away in his own jungle, and with not a single house as large as his own cabin upon the distant beach.

He saw that these people were more wicked than his own apes, and as savage and cruel as Sabor, herself. Tarzan began to hold his own kind in but low esteem.

Now they had tied their poor victim to a great post near the center of the village, directly before Mbonga's hut, and here they formed a dancing, yelling circle of warriors about him, alive with flashing knives and menacing spears.

In a larger circle squatted the women, yelling and beating upon drums. It reminded Tarzan of the Dum-Dum, and so he knew what to expect. He wondered if they would spring upon their meat while it was still alive. The Apes did not do such things as that.

The circle of warriors about the cringing captive drew closer and closer to their prey as they danced in wild and savage abandon to the maddening music of the drums. Presently a spear reached out and pricked the victim. It was the signal for fifty others.

Eyes, ears, arms and legs were pierced; every inch of the poor writhing body that did not cover a vital organ became the target of the cruel lancers.

The women and children shrieked their delight. The warriors licked their hideous lips in anticipation of the feast to come, and vied with one another in the savagery and loathsomeness of the cruel indignities with which they tortured the still conscious prisoner.

Then it was that Tarzan of the Apes saw his chance. All eyes were fixed upon the thrilling spectacle at the stake. The light of day had given place to the darkness of a moonless night, and only the fires in the immediate vicinity of the orgy had been kept alight to cast a restless glow upon the restless scene.

Gently the lithe boy dropped to the soft earth at the end of the village street. Quickly he gathered up the arrows—all of them this time, for he had brought a number of long fibers to bind them into a bundle.

Without haste he wrapped them securely, and then, ere he turned to leave, the devil of capriciousness entered his heart. He looked about for some hint of a wild prank to play upon these strange, grotesque creatures that they might be again aware of his presence among them.

Dropping his bundle of arrows at the foot of the tree, Tarzan crept among the shadows at the side of the street until he came to the same hut he had entered on the occasion of his first visit.

Inside all was darkness, but his groping hands soon found the object for which he sought, and without further delay he turned again toward the door.

He had taken but a step, however, ere his quick ear caught the sound of approaching footsteps immediately without. In another instant the figure of a woman darkened the entrance of the hut.

Tarzan drew back silently to the far wall, and his hand sought the long, keen hunting knife of his father. The woman came quickly to the center of the hut. There she paused for an instant feeling about with her hands for the thing she sought. Evidently it was not in its accustomed place, for she explored ever nearer and nearer the wall where Tarzan stood.

So close was she now that the ape-man felt the animal warmth of her naked body. Up went the hunting knife, and then the woman turned to one side and soon a guttural "ah" proclaimed that her search had at last been successful.

Immediately she turned and left the hut, and as she passed through the doorway Tarzan saw that she carried a cooking pot in her hand.

He followed closely after her, and as he reconnoitered from the shadows of the doorway he saw that all the women of the village were hastening to and from the various huts with pots and kettles. These they were filling with water and placing over a number of fires near the stake where the dying victim now hung, an inert and bloody mass of suffering.

Choosing a moment when none seemed near, Tarzan hastened to his bundle of arrows beneath the great tree at the end of the village street. As on the former occasion he overthrew the cauldron before leaping, sinuous and catlike, into the lower branches of the forest giant.

Silently he climbed to a great height until he found a point where he could look through a leafy opening upon the scene beneath him.

The women were now preparing the prisoner for their cooking pots, while the men stood about resting after the fatigue of their mad revel. Comparative quiet reigned in the village.

Tarzan raised aloft the thing he had pilfered from the hut, and, with aim made true by years of fruit and cocoanut throwing, launched it toward the group of savages.

Squarely among them it fell, striking one of the warriors full upon the head and felling him to the ground. Then it rolled among the women and stopped beside the half butchered thing they were preparing to feast upon.

All gazed in consternation at it for an instant, and then, with one accord, broke and ran for their huts.

It was a grinning human skull which looked up at them from the ground. The dropping of the thing out of the open sky was a miracle well aimed to work upon their superstitious fears.

Thus Tarzan of the Apes left them filled with terror at this new manifestation of the presence of some unseen and unearthly evil power which lurked in the forest about their village.

Later, when they discovered the overturned cauldron, and that once more their arrows had been pilfered, it commenced to dawn upon them that they had offended some great god who ruled this part of the jungle by placing their village there without propitiating him. From then on an offering of food was daily placed below the great tree from whence the arrows had disappeared, in an effort to conciliate the mighty one.

But the seed of fear was deep sown, and had he but known it, Tarzan of the Apes had laid the foundation for much future misery for himself and his tribe.

That night he slept in the forest not far from the village, and early the next morning set out slowly on his homeward march, hunting as he traveled. Only a few berries and an occasional grub worm rewarded his search, and he was half famished when, looking up from a log he had been rooting beneath, he saw Sabor, the lioness, standing in the center of the trail not twenty paces from him.

The great yellow eyes were fixed upon him with a wicked and baleful gleam, and the red tongue licked the longing lips as Sabor crouched, worming her stealthy way with belly flattened against the earth.

Tarzan did not attempt to escape. He welcomed the opportunity for which, in fact, he had been searching for days past, not now armed only with a rope of grass.

Quickly he unslung his bow and fitted a well daubed arrow, and as Sabor sprang, the tiny missile leaped to meet her in mid air. At the same instant Tarzan of the Apes jumped to one side, and as the great cat struck the ground beyond him another death-tipped arrow sunk deep into Sabor's loin.

With a mighty roar the beast turned and charged once more, only to be met with a third arrow full in one eye; but this time she was too close upon the ape-man for the latter to sidestep the on-rushing body.

Tarzan of the Apes went down beneath the great body of his enemy, but with gleaming knife drawn and striking home. For a moment they lay there, and then Tarzan realized that the inert mass lying upon him was beyond power ever again to injure man or ape.

With difficulty he wriggled from beneath the great weight, and as he stood erect and gazed down upon the trophy of his skill, a mighty wave of exultation swept over him.

With swelling breast, he placed a foot upon the body of his powerful enemy, and throwing back his fine young head, roared out the awful challenge of the victorious bull ape.

The forest echoed to the savage and triumphant pæan. Birds fell still, and the larger animals and beasts of prey slunk stealthily away, for few there were of all the jungle who sought for trouble with the great anthropoids.

And in London another Lord Greystoke was speaking to *his* kind in the House of Lords, but none trembled at the sound of his soft voice.

Sabor proved unsavory eating even to Tarzan of the Apes, but hunger served as a most efficacious disguise to toughness and rank taste, and ere long, with well filled stomach, the ape-man was ready to sleep again. First, however, he must remove the hide, for it was as much for this as for any other purpose that he had desired to encompass the destruction of Sabor.

Deftly he removed the great pelt, for he had practiced often on smaller animals. When the task was finished he carried his trophy to the fork of a high tree, and there, curling himself securely in a crotch, he fell into deep and dreamless slumber.

What with loss of sleep, arduous exercise, and a full belly, Tarzan of the Apes slept the sun around, awakening about noon of the following day. He straightway repaired to the carcass of Sabor, but was angered to find the bones picked clean by other hungry denizens of the jungle.

Half an hour's leisurely progress through the forest brought to sight a young deer, and before ever the little creature knew that an enemy was near a tiny arrow had lodged in its neck.

So quickly the virus worked that at the end of a dozen leaps the deer plunged headlong into the undergrowth, dead. Again did Tarzan feast well, but this time he did not sleep.

Instead, he hastened on toward the point where he had left the tribe, and when he had found them proudly exhibited the skin of Sabor, the lioness.

"Look!" he cried, "Apes of Kerchak. See what Tarzan, the mighty killer, has done. Who else among you has ever killed one of Numa's people? Tarzan is mightiest amongst you for Tarzan is no ape. Tarzan is—" But here he stopped, for in the language of the anthropoids there was no word for man, and Tarzan could only write the word in English; he could not pronounce it.

The tribe had gathered about to look upon the proof of his wondrous prowess, and to listen to his words.

Only Kerchak hung back, nursing his hatred and his rage.

Suddenly something snapped in the wicked little brain of the anthropoid. With a frightful roar the great beast sprang among the assemblage.

Biting, and striking with his huge hands, he killed and maimed a dozen ere the balance could escape to the upper terraces of the forest.

Frothing and shrieking in the insanity of his fury, Kerchak looked about for the object of his greatest hatred, and there, upon a nearby limb, he saw him sitting.

"Come down, Tarzan, great killer," cried Kerchak. "Come down and feel the fangs of a greater! Do mighty fighters fly to the trees at the first approach of danger?" And then Kerchak emitted the volleying challenge of his kind.

Quietly Tarzan dropped to the ground. Breathlessly the tribe watched from their lofty perches as Kerchak, still roaring, charged the relatively puny figure.

Nearly seven feet stood Kerchak on his short legs. His enormous shoulders were bunched and rounded with huge muscles. The back of his short neck was as a single lump of iron sinew which bulged beyond the base of his skull, so that his head seemed like a small ball protruding from a huge mountain of flesh.

His back-drawn, snarling lips exposed his great fighting fangs, and his little, wicked, bloodshot eyes gleamed in horrid reflection of his madness.

Awaiting him stood Tarzan, himself a mighty muscled animal, but his six feet of height and his great rolling sinews seemed pitifully inadequate to the ordeal which awaited them.

His bow and arrows lay some distance away where he had dropped them while showing Sabor's hide to his fellow apes, so that he confronted Kerchak now with only his hunting knife and his superior intellect to offset the ferocious strength of his enemy.

As his antagonist came roaring toward him, Lord Greystoke tore his long knife from its sheath, and with an answering challenge as horrid and blood-curdling as that of the beast he faced, rushed swiftly to meet the attack. He was too shrewd to allow those long hairy arms to encircle him, and just as their bodies were about to crash together, Tarzan of the Apes grasped one of the huge wrists of his assailant, and, springing lightly to one side, drove his knife to the hilt into Kerchak's body, below the heart.

Before he could wrench the blade free again, the bull's quick lunge to seize him in those awful arms had torn the weapon from Tarzan's grasp.

Kerchak aimed a terrific blow at the ape-man's head with the flat of his hand, a blow which, had it landed, might easily have crushed in the side of Tarzan's skull.

The man was too quick, and, ducking beneath it, himself delivered a mighty one, with clenched fist, in the pit of Kerchak's stomach.

The ape was staggered, and what with the mortal wound in his side had almost collapsed, when, with one mighty effort he rallied for an instant—just long enough to enable him to wrest his arm free from Tarzan's grasp and close in a terrific clinch with his wiry opponent.

Straining the ape-man close to him, his great jaws sought Tarzan's throat, but the young lord's sinewy fingers were at Kerchak's own before the cruel fangs could close on the sleek brown skin.

Thus they struggled, the one to crush out his opponent's life with those awful teeth, the other to close forever the windpipe beneath his strong grasp, the while he held the snarling mouth from him.

The greater strength of the ape was slowly prevailing, and the teeth of the straining beast were scarce an inch from Tarzan's throat when, with a shuddering tremor, the great body stiffened for an instant and then sank limply to the ground.

Kerchak was dead.

Withdrawing the knife that had so often rendered him master of far mightier muscles than his own, Tarzan of the Apes placed his foot upon the neck of his vanquished enemy, and once again, loud through the forest rang the fierce, wild cry of the conqueror.

And thus came the young Lord Greystoke into the kingship of the Apes.

CHAPTER XII

MAN'S REASON

THERE was one of the tribe of Tarzan who questioned his authority, and that was Terkoz, the son of Tublat, but he so feared the keen knife and the deadly arrows of his new lord that he confined the manifestation of his objections to petty disobediences and irritating mannerisms; Tarzan knew, however, that he but waited his opportunity to wrest the kingship from him by some sudden stroke of treachery, and so he was ever on his guard against surprise.

For months the life of the little band went on much as it had before, except that Tarzan's greater intelligence and his ability as a hunter were the means of providing for them more bountifully than ever before. Most of them, therefore, were more than content with the change in rulers.

Tarzan led them by night to the fields of the black men, and there, warned by their chief's superior wisdom, they ate only what they required, nor ever did they destroy what they could not eat, as is the way of Manu, the monkey, and of most apes.

So, while the blacks were wroth at the continued pilfering of their fields, they were not discouraged in their efforts to cultivate the land, as would have been the case had Tarzan permitted his people to lay waste the plantation wantonly.

During this period Tarzan paid many nocturnal visits to the village, where he often renewed his supply of arrows. He soon noticed the food always standing at the foot of the tree which was his avenue into the palisade, and after a little, he commenced to eat whatever the blacks put there.

When the awe-struck savages saw that the food disappeared over night they were filled with consternation and awe, for it was one thing to put food out to propitiate a god or a devil, but quite another thing to have the spirit really come into the village and eat it. Such a thing was unheard of, and it filled their superstitious minds with all manner of vague fears.

Nor was this all. The periodic disappearance of their arrows, and the strange pranks perpetrated by unseen hands, had wrought them to such a state that life had become a veritable burden in their new home, and now it was that Mbonga and his head men began to talk of abandoning the village and seeking a site further on in the jungle.

Presently the black warriors began to strike further and further south into the heart of the forest when they went to hunt, looking for a site for a new village.

More often was the tribe of Tarzan disturbed by these wandering huntsmen. Now was the quiet, fierce solitude of the primeval forest broken by new, strange cries. No longer was there safety for bird or beast. Man had come.

Other animals passed up and down the jungle by day and by night—fierce, cruel beasts—but their weaker neighbors only fled from their immediate vicinity to return again when the danger was past.

With man it is different. When he comes many of the larger animals instinctively leave the district entirely, seldom if ever to return; and thus it has always been with the great anthropoids. They flee man as man flees a pestilence.

For a short time the tribe of Tarzan lingered in the vicinity of the beach because their new chief hated the thought of leaving the treasured contents of the little cabin forever. But when one day a member of the tribe discovered the blacks in great numbers on the banks of a little stream that had been their watering place for generations, and in the act of clearing a space in the jungle and erecting many huts, the apes would remain no longer, and so Tarzan led them inland for many marches to a spot as yet undefiled by the foot of a human being.

Once every moon Tarzan would go swinging rapidly back through the swaying branches to have a day with his books, and to replenish his supply of arrows. This latter task was becoming more and more difficult, for the blacks had taken to hiding their supply away at night in granaries and living huts.

This necessitated watching by day on Tarzan's part to discover where the arrows were being concealed.

Twice had he entered huts at night while the inmates lay sleeping upon their mats, and stolen the arrows from the very sides of the warriors. But this method he realized to be too fraught with danger, and so he commenced picking up solitary hunters with his long, deadly noose, stripping them of weapons and ornaments and dropping their bodies from a high tree into the village street during the still watches of the night.

These various escapades again so terrorized the blacks that, had it not been for the monthly respite between Tarzan's visits, in which they had opportunity to renew hope that each fresh incursion would prove the last, they soon would have abandoned their new village.

The blacks had not as yet come upon Tarzan's cabin on the distant beach, but the ape-man lived in constant dread that, while he was away with the tribe, they would discover and despoil his treasure. So it came that he spent more and more time in the vicinity of his father's last home, and less and less with the tribe. Presently the members of his little community began to suffer on account of his neglect, for disputes and quarrels constantly arose which only the king might settle peaceably.

At last some of the older apes spoke to Tarzan on the subject, and for a month thereafter he remained constantly with the tribe.

The duties of kingship among the anthropoids are not many or arduous.

In the afternoon comes Thaka, possibly, to complain that old Mungo* has stolen his new wife. Then must Tarzan summon all before him, and if he finds that the wife prefers her new lord he commands that matters remain as they are, or possibly that Mungo give Thaka one of his daughters in exchange.

Whatever his decision, the apes accept it as final, and return to their occupations satisfied.

Then comes Tana, shrieking and holding tight her side from which blood is streaming. Gunto, her husband, has cruelly bitten her! And Gunto, summoned, says that Tana is lazy and will not bring him nuts and beetles, or scratch his back for him.

So Tarzan scolds them both and threatens Gunto with a taste of the death-bearing slivers if he abuses Tana further, and Tana, for her part, is compelled to promise better attention to her wifely duties.

And so it goes, little family differences for the most part, which, if left unsettled would result finally in greater factional strife, and the eventual dismemberment of the tribe.

But Tarzan tired of it as he found that kingship meant the curtailment of his liberty. He longed for the little cabin and the sun-kissed sea—for the cool interior of the well built house, and for the never-ending wonders of the many books.

As he had grown older, he found that he had grown away from his people. Their interests and his were far removed. They had not kept pace with him, nor could they understand aught of the many strange and wonderful dreams that passed through the active brain of their human king. So limited was their vocabulary that Tarzan could not even talk with them of the many new truths, and the great fields of thought that his reading had opened up before his longing eyes, or make known ambitions which stirred his soul.

Among the tribe he no longer had friends and cronies as of old. A little child may find companionship in many strange and simple creatures, but to a grown man there must be some semblance of equality in intellect as the basis for agreeable consociation.

Had Kala lived, Tarzan would have sacrificed all else to remain near her, but now that she was dead, and the playful friends of his childhood grown into fierce and surly brutes he felt that he much preferred the peace and solitude of his cabin to the irksome duties of leadership amongst a horde of wild beasts.

The hatred and jealousy of Terkoz, son of Tublat, did much to counteract the effect of Tarzan's desire to renounce his kingship among the apes, for, stubborn young Englishman that he was, he could not bring himself to retreat in the face of so malignant an enemy.

That Terkoz would be chosen leader in his stead he knew full well, for time and again the ferocious brute had established his claim to physical supremacy over the few bull apes who had dared resent his savage bullying.

Tarzan would have liked to subdue the ugly beast without recourse to knife or arrows. So much had his great strength and agility increased in the period following his maturity that he had come to believe that he might master the redoubtable Terkoz in a hand to hand fight were it not for the terrible advantage the anthropoid's huge fighting fangs gave him over the poorly armed Tarzan.

The entire matter was taken out of Tarzan's hands one day by force of circumstances, and his future left open to him, so that he might go or stay without any stain upon his savage escutcheon.

It happened thus:

The tribe was feeding quietly, spread over a considerable area, when a great screaming arose some distance east of where Tarzan lay upon his belly beside a limpid brook, attempting to catch an elusive fish in his quick, brown hands.

With one accord the tribe swung rapidly toward the frightened cries, and there found Terkoz holding an old female by the hair and beating her unmercifully with his great hands.

As Tarzan approached he raised his hand aloft for Terkoz to desist, for the female was not his, but belonged to a poor old ape whose fighting days were long over, and who, therefore, could not protect his family.

Terkoz knew that it was against the laws of his kind to strike the woman of another, but being a bully, he had taken advantage of the weakness of the female's husband to chastise her because she had refused to give up to him a tender young rodent she had captured.

When Terkoz saw Tarzan approaching without his arrows, he continued to be-labor the poor woman in a studied effort to affront his hated chieftain.

Tarzan did not repeat his warning signal, but instead rushed bodily upon the waiting Terkoz.

Never had the ape-man fought so terrible a battle since that long-gone day when, Bolgani, the great king gorilla had so horribly manhandled him ere the new-found knife had, by accident, pricked the savage heart.

Tarzan's knife on the present occasion but barely offset the gleaming fangs of Terkoz, and what little advantage the ape had over the man in brute strength was almost balanced by the latter's wonderful quickness and agility.

In the sum total of their points, however, the anthropoid had a shade the better of the battle, and had there been no other personal attribute to influence the final outcome, Tarzan of the Apes, the young Lord Greystoke, had died as he had lived—an unknown savage beast in equatorial Africa.

But there was that which had raised him far above his fellows of the jungle—that little spark which spells the whole vast difference between man and brute—Reason. This it was which saved him from death beneath the iron muscles and tearing fangs of Terkoz.

Scarcely had they fought a dozen seconds ere they were rolling upon the ground, striking, tearing and rending—two great savage beasts battling to the death.

Terkoz had a dozen knife wounds on head and breast, and Tarzan was torn and bleeding—his scalp in one place half torn from his head so that a great piece hung down over one eye, obstructing his vision.

But so far the young Englishman had been able to keep those horrible fangs from his jugular and now, as they fought less fiercely for a moment, to regain their breath, Tarzan formed a cunning plan. He would work his way to the other's back and, clinging there with tooth and nail, drive his knife home until Terkoz was no more.

The maneuver was accomplished more easily than he had hoped, for the stupid beast, not knowing what Tarzan was attempting, made no particular effort to prevent the accomplishment of the design.

But when, finally, he realized that his antagonist was fastened to him where his teeth and fists alike were useless against him, Terkoz hurled himself about upon the ground so violently that Tarzan could but cling desperately to the leaping, turning, twisting body, and ere he had struck a blow the knife was hurled from his hand by a heavy impact against the earth, and Tarzan found himself defenseless.

During the rollings and squirmings of the next few minutes, Tarzan's hold was loosened a dozen times until finally an accidental circumstance of those swift and ever-changing evolutions gave him a new hold with his right hand, which he soon realized was absolutely unassailable.

His arm was passed beneath Terkoz' arm from behind and his hand and forearm encircled the back of Terkoz' neck. It was the half-Nelson of modern wrestling which the untaught ape-man had stumbled upon, but divine reason showed him in an instant the value of the thing he had discovered. It was the difference to him between life and death.

And so he struggled to encompass a similar hold with the left hand, and in a few moments Terkoz' bull neck was creaking beneath a full-Nelson.

There was no more lunging about now. The two lay perfectly still upon the ground, Tarzan upon Terkoz' back. Slowly the bullet head of the ape was being forced lower and lower upon his chest.

Tarzan knew what the result would be. In an instant the neck would break. Then there came to Terkoz' rescue the same thing that had put him in these sore straits—a man's reasoning power.

"If I kill him," thought Tarzan, "what advantage will it be to me? Will it not but rob the tribe of a great fighter? And if Terkoz be dead, he will know nothing of my supremacy, while alive he will ever be an example to the other apes."

"*Ka-goda?*" hissed Tarzan in Terkoz' ear, which, in ape tongue, means, freely translated: "Do you surrender?"

For a moment there was no reply, and Tarzan added a few more ounces of pressure, which elicited a horrified shriek of pain from the great beast.

"*Ka-goda?*" repeated Tarzan.

"*Ka-goda!*" cried Terkoz.

"Listen," said Tarzan, easing up a trifle, but not releasing his hold. "I am Tarzan, King of the Apes, mighty hunter, mighty fighter. In all the jungle there is none so great.

"You have said: '*Ka-goda*' to me. All the tribe have heard. Quarrel no more with your king or your people, for next time I shall kill you. Do you understand?"

"*Huh,*" assented Terkoz.

"And you are satisfied?"

"*Huh,*" said the ape.

Tarzan let him up, and in a few minutes all were back at their vocations, as though naught had occurred to mar the tranquility of their primeval forest haunts.

But deep in the minds of the apes was rooted the conviction that Tarzan was a mighty fighter and a strange creature. Strange because he had had it in his power to kill his enemy, but had allowed him to live—unharmed.

That afternoon as the tribe came together, as was their wont before darkness settled on the jungle, Tarzan, his wounds washed in the limpid waters of the stream, called the old males about him.

"You have seen again today that Tarzan of the Apes is the greatest among you," he said.

"*Huh,*" they replied with one voice, "Tarzan is great."

"Tarzan," he continued, "is not an ape. He is not like his people. His ways are not their ways, and so Tarzan is going back to the lair of his own kind by the waters of the great lake which has no further shore. You must choose another to rule you, for Tarzan will not return."

And thus young Lord Greystoke took the first step toward the goal which he had set—the finding of other white men like himself.

CHAPTER XIII

HIS OWN KIND

THE following morning, Tarzan, lame and sore from the wounds of his battle with Terkoz, set out toward the west and the sea coast.

He traveled very slowly, sleeping in the jungle at night, and reaching his cabin late the following morning.

For several days he moved about but little, only enough to gather what fruit and nuts he required to satisfy the demands of hunger.

In ten days he was quite sound again, except for a terrible, half-healed scar, which, starting above his left eye ran across the top of his head, ending at the right ear. It was the mark left by Terkoz when he had torn the scalp away.

During his convalescence Tarzan tried to fashion a mantle from the skin of Sabor, which had lain all this time in the cabin. But he found the hide had dried as stiff as a board, and as he knew naught of tanning, he was forced to abandon his cherished plan.

Then he determined to filch what few garments he could from one of the black men of Mbonga's village, for Tarzan of the Apes had decided to mark his evolution from the lower orders in every possible manner, and nothing seemed to him a more distinguishing badge of manhood than ornaments and clothing.

To this end, therefore, he collected the various arm and leg ornaments he had taken from the black warriors who had succumbed to his swift and silent noose, and donned them all after the way he had seen them worn.

About his neck hung the golden chain from which depended the diamond encrusted locket of his mother, the Lady Alice. At his back was a quiver of arrows slung from a leathern shoulder belt, another piece of loot from some vanquished black.

About his waist was a belt of tiny strips of rawhide fashioned by himself as a support for the home-made scabbard in which hung his father's hunting knife. The long bow which had been Kulonga's hung over his left shoulder.

The young Lord Greystoke was indeed a strange and warlike figure, his mass of black hair falling to his shoulders behind and cut with his hunting knife to a rude bang upon his forehead, that it might not fall before his eyes.

His straight and perfect figure, muscled as the best of the ancient Roman gladiators must have been muscled, and yet with the soft and sinuous curves of a Greek god, told at a glance the wondrous combination of enormous strength with suppleness and speed.

A personification, was Tarzan of the Apes, of the primitive man, the hunter, the warrior.

With the noble poise of his handsome head upon those broad shoulders, and the fire of life and intelligence in those fine, clear eyes, he might readily have typified some demi-god of a wild and warlike bygone people of his ancient forest.

But of these things Tarzan did not think. He was worried because he had no clothing to indicate to all the jungle folks that he was a man and not an ape, and grave doubt often entered his mind as to whether he might not yet become an ape.

Was not hair commencing to grow upon his face? All the apes had hair upon theirs, but the black men were entirely hairless, with very few exceptions.

True, he had seen pictures in his books of men with great masses of hair upon lip and cheek and chin, but, nevertheless, Tarzan was afraid. Almost daily he whetted his keen knife and scraped and whittled at his young beard to eradicate this degrading emblem of apehood.

And so he learned to shave—rudely and painfully, it is true—but, nevertheless, effectively.

When he felt quite strong again, after his bloody battle with Terkoz, Tarzan set off one morning towards Mbonga's village. He was moving carelessly along a winding jungle trail, instead of making his progress through the trees, when suddenly he came face to face with a black warrior.

The look of surprise on the savage face was almost comical, and before Tarzan could unsling his bow the fellow had turned and fled down the path crying out in alarm as though to others before him.

Tarzan took to the trees in pursuit, and in a few moments came in view of the men desperately striving to escape.*

There were three of them, and they were racing madly in single file through the dense undergrowth.

Tarzan easily distanced them, nor did they see his silent passage above their heads, nor note the crouching figure squatted upon a low branch ahead of them beneath which the trail led them.

Tarzan let the first two pass beneath him, but as the third came swiftly on, the quiet noose dropped about the black throat. A quick jerk drew it taut.

There was an agonized scream from the victim, and his fellows turned to see his struggling body rise as by magic slowly into the dense foliage of the trees above.

With affrighted shrieks they wheeled once more and plunged on in their efforts to escape.

Tarzan dispatched his prisoner quickly and silently; removed the weapons and ornaments, and—oh, the greatest joy of all—a handsome doeskin breechcloth, which he quickly transferred to his own person.

Now indeed was he dressed as a man should be. None there was who could now doubt his high origin. How he should liked to have returned to the tribe to parade before their envious gaze this wondrous finery.

Taking the body across his shoulder, he moved more slowly through the trees toward the little palisaded village, for he again needed arrows.

As he approached quite close to the enclosure he saw an excited group surrounding the two fugitives, who, trembling with fright and exhaustion, were scarce able to recount the uncanny details of their adventure.

Mirando, they said, who had been ahead of them a short distance, had suddenly come screaming toward them, crying that a terrible white and naked warrior was pursuing him. The three of them had hurried toward the village as rapidly as their legs would carry them.

Again Mirando's shrill cry of mortal terror had caused them to look back, and there they had seen the most horrible sight—their companion's body flying upwards into the trees, his arms and legs beating the air and his tongue protruding from his open mouth. No other sound did he utter nor was there any creature in sight about him.

The villagers were worked up into a state of fear bordering on panic, but wise old Mbonga affected to feel considerable skepticism regarding the tale, and attributed the whole fabrication to their fright in the face of some real danger.

"You tell us this great story," he said, "because you do not dare to speak the truth. You do not dare admit that when the lion sprang upon Mirando you ran away and left him. You are cowards."

Scarcely had Mbonga ceased speaking when a great crashing of branches in the trees above them caused the blacks to look up in renewed terror. The sight that met their eyes made even wise old Mbonga shudder, for there, turning and twisting in the air, came the dead body of Mirando, to sprawl with a sickening reverberation upon the ground at their feet.

With one accord the blacks took to their heels; nor did they stop until the last of them was lost in the dense shadows of the surrounding jungle.

Again Tarzan came down into the village and renewed his supply of arrows, and ate of the offering of food which the blacks had made to appease his wrath.

Before he left he carried the body of Mirando to the gate of the village, and propped it up against the palisade in such a way that the dead face seemed to be peering around the edge of the gate-post down the path which led to the jungle.

Then Tarzan returned, hunting, always hunting, to the cabin by the beach.

It took a dozen attempts on the part of the thoroughly frightened blacks to re-enter their village, past the horrible, grinning face of their dead fellow, and when they found the food and arrows gone they knew, what they had only too well feared, that Mirando had seen the evil spirit of the jungle.

That now seemed to them the logical explanation. Only those who saw this terrible god of the jungle died; for was it not true that none left alive in the village had ever seen him? Therefore, those who had died at his hands must have seen him and paid the penalty with their lives.

As long as they supplied him with arrows and food he would not harm them unless they looked upon him, so it was ordered by Mbonga that in addition to the food offering there should also be laid out an offering of arrows for this Munango-Keewati, and this was done from then on.

If you ever chance to pass that far off African village you will still see before a tiny thatched hut, built just without the village, a little iron pot in which is a quantity of food, and beside it a quiver of well-daubed arrows.

When Tarzan came in sight of the beach where stood his cabin, a strange and unusual spectacle met his vision.

On the placid waters of the land-locked harbor floated a great ship, and on the beach a small boat was drawn up.

But, most wonderful of all, a number of white men like himself were moving about between the beach and his cabin.

Tarzan saw that in many ways they were like the men of his picture books. He crept closer through the trees until he was quite close above them.

There were ten men. Swarthy, sun-tanned, villainous looking fellows. Now they had congregated by the boat and were talking in loud, angry tones, with much gesticulating and shaking of fists.

Presently one of them, a little, mean-faced, black-bearded fellow with a countenance which reminded Tarzan of Pamba, the rat, laid his hand upon the shoulder of a giant who stood next him, and with whom all the others had been arguing and quarreling.

The little man pointed inland, so that the giant was forced to turn away from the others to look in the direction indicated. As he turned, the little, mean-faced man drew a revolver from his belt and shot the giant in the back.

The big fellow threw his hands above his head, his knees bent beneath him, and without a sound he tumbled forward upon the beach, dead.

The report of the weapon, the first that Tarzan had ever heard, filled him with wonderment, but even this unaccustomed sound could not startle his healthy nerves into even a semblance of panic.

The conduct of the white strangers it was that caused him the greatest perturbation. He puckered his brows into a frown of deep thought. It was well, thought he, that he had not given way to his first impulse to rush forward and greet these white men as brothers.

They were evidently no different from the black men—no more civilized than the apes—no less cruel than Sabor.

For a moment the others stood looking at the little, mean-faced man and the giant lying dead upon the beach.

Then one of them laughed and slapped the little man upon the back. There was much more talk and gesticulating, but less quarreling.

Presently they launched the boat and all jumped into it and rowed away toward the great ship, where Tarzan could see other figures moving about upon the deck.

When they had clambered aboard, Tarzan dropped to earth behind a great tree and crept to his cabin, keeping it always between himself and the ship.

Slipping in at the door he found that everything had been ransacked. His books and pencils strewed the floor. His weapons and shields and other little store of treasures were littered about.

As he saw what had been done a great wave of anger surged through him, and the new made scar upon his forehead stood suddenly out, a bar of inflamed crimson against his tawny hide.

Quickly he ran to the cupboard and searched in the far recess of the lower shelf. Ah! He breathed a sigh of relief as he drew out the little tin box, and, opening it, found his greatest treasures undisturbed.

The photograph of the smiling, strong-faced young man, and the little black puzzle book were safe.

What was that?

His quick ear had caught a faint but unfamiliar sound.

Running to the window Tarzan looked toward the harbor, and there he saw that a boat was being lowered from the great ship beside the one already in the water. Soon he saw many people clambering over the sides of the larger vessel and dropping into the boats. They were coming back in full force.

For a moment longer Tarzan watched while a number of boxes and bundles were lowered into the waiting boats, then, as they shoved off from the ship's side, the ape-man snatched up a piece of paper, and with a pencil printed on it for a few moments until it bore several lines of strong, well-made, almost letter-perfect characters.

This notice he stuck upon the door with a small sharp splinter of wood. Then gathering up his precious tin box, his arrows, and as many bows and spears as he could carry, he hastened through the door and disappeared into the forest.

When the two boats were beached upon the silvery sand it was a strange assortment of humanity that clambered ashore.

Some twenty souls in all there were, if the fifteen rough and villainous appearing seamen could have been said to possess that immortal spark, since they were, forsooth, a most filthy and bloodthirsty looking aggregation.

The others of the party were of different stamp.

One was an elderly man, with white hair and large rimmed spectacles. His slightly stooped shoulders were draped in an ill-fitting, though immaculate, frock-coat; a shiny silk hat added to the incongruity of his garb in an African jungle.

The second member of the party to land was a tall young man in white ducks,* while directly behind came another elderly man with a very high forehead and a fussy, excitable manner.

After these came a huge negress clothed like Solomon as to colors.* Her great eyes rolling in evident terror first toward the jungle and then toward the cursing band of sailors who were removing the bales and boxes from the boats.

The last member of the party to disembark was a girl of about nineteen, and it was the young man who stood at the boat's bow to lift her high and dry upon land. She gave him a brave and pretty smile of thanks, but no words passed between them.

In silence the party advanced toward the cabin. It was evident that whatever their intentions, all had been decided upon before they left the ship; and so they came to the door, the sailors carrying the boxes and bales, followed by the five who were of so different a class. The men put down their burdens, and then one caught sight of the notice which Tarzan had posted.

"Ho, mates!" he cried. "What's here? This sign was not posted an hour ago or I'll eat the cook."

The others gathered about, craning their necks over the shoulders of those before them, but as few of them could read at all, and then only after the most laborious fashion, one finally turned to the little old man of the top hat and frock-coat.

"Hi, perfesser," he called, "step for'rd and read the bloomin' notis."

Thus addressed, the old man came slowly to where the sailors stood, followed by the other members of his party. Adjusting his spectacles he looked for a moment at the placard and then, turning away, strolled off muttering to himself: "Most remarkable—most remarkable!"

"Hi, old fossil," cried the man who had first called on him for assistance, "did je think we wanted of you to read the bloomin' notis to yourself? Come back here and read it out loud, you old barnacle."

The old man stopped and, turning back, said: "Oh, yes, my dear sir, a thousand pardons. It was quite thoughtless of me, yes—very thoughtless. Most remarkable—most remarkable!"

Again he faced the notice and read it through, and doubtless would have turned off again to ruminate upon it had not the sailor grasped him roughly by the collar and howled into his ear.

"Read it out loud, you blithering, old idiot."

"Ah, yes indeed, yes indeed," replied the professor softly, and adjusting his spectacles once more he read aloud:

> THIS IS THE HOUSE OF
> TARZAN,* THE KILLER OF
> BEASTS AND MANY BLACK
> MEN. DO NOT HARM THE
> THINGS WHICH ARE TAR-
> ZAN'S. TARZAN WATCHES.
> TARZAN OF THE APES.

"Who the devil is Tarzan?" cried the sailor who had before spoken.

"He evidently speaks English," said the young man.

"But what does 'Tarzan of the Apes' mean?" cried the girl.

"I do not know, Miss Porter," replied the young man, "unless we have discovered a runaway simian from the London Zoo who has brought back a European education to his jungle home. What do you make of it, Professor Porter?" he added, turning to the old man.

Professor Archimedes Q. Porter* adjusted his spectacles.

"Ah, yes, indeed; yes indeed—most remarkable, most remarkable!" said the professor; "but I can add nothing further to what I have already remarked in elucidation of this truly momentous occurrence," and the professor turned slowly in the direction of the jungle.

"But, papa," cried the girl, "you haven't said anything about it yet."

"Tut—tut, child; tut—tut," responded Professor Porter, in a kindly and indulgent tone, "do not trouble your pretty head with such weighty, and abstruse problems," and again he wandered slowly off in still another direction, his eyes bent upon the ground at his feet, his hands clasped behind him beneath the flowing tails of his coat.

"I reckon the daffy old bounder don't know no more'n we do about it," growled the rat-faced sailor.

"Keep a civil tongue in your head," cried the young man, his face paling in anger, at the insulting tone of the sailor. "You've murdered our officers, and robbed us. We are absolutely in your power, but you'll treat Professor Porter and Miss Porter with respect or I'll break that vile neck of yours with my bare hands—guns or no guns," and the young fellow stepped so close to the rat-faced sailor that the latter, though he bore two revolvers and a villainous looking knife in his belt, slunk back abashed.

"You damned coward," cried the young man. "You'd never dare shoot a man until his back was turned. You don't dare shoot me even then," and he deliberately turned his back full upon the sailor and walked nonchalantly away as if to put him to the test.

The sailor's hand crept slyly to the butt of one of his revolvers; his wicked eyes glared vengefully at the retreating form of the young Englishman. The gaze of his fellows was upon him, but still he hesitated. At heart he was even a greater coward than Mr. William Cecil Clayton had imagined.

What he would have done will never be known, for there was another factor abroad which none of the party had yet guessed would enter so largely into the problems of their life on this inhospitable African shore.

Two keen eyes had watched every move of the party from the foliage of a nearby tree. Tarzan had seen the surprise caused by his notice, and while he could understand nothing of the spoken language of these strange people their gestures and facial expressions told him much.

The act of the little rat-faced sailor in killing one of his comrades had aroused a strong dislike in Tarzan, and now that he saw him quarreling with the fine-looking young man his animosity was still further stirred.

Tarzan had never seen the effects of a firearm before, though his books had taught him something of them, but when he saw the rat-faced one fingering the butt of his revolver he thought of the scene he had witnessed so short a time before, and naturally expected to see the young man murdered as had been the huge sailor earlier in the day.

So Tarzan fitted a poisoned arrow to his bow and drew a bead upon the rat-faced sailor, but the foliage was so thick that he soon saw the arrow would be deflected by the leaves or some small branch, and instead he launched a heavy spear from his lofty perch.

Clayton had taken but a dozen steps. The rat-faced sailor had half drawn his revolver; the other sailors stood watching the scene intently.

Professor Porter had already disappeared into the jungle, whither he was being followed by the fussy Samuel T. Philander,* his secretary and assistant.

Esmeralda, the negress, was busy sorting her mistress' baggage from the pile of bales and boxes beside the cabin, and Miss Porter had turned away to follow Clayton, when something caused her to turn again toward the sailor.

And then three things happened almost simultaneously—the sailor jerked out his weapon and leveled it at Clayton's back, Miss Porter screamed a warning, and a long, metal-shod spear shot like a bolt from above and passed entirely through the right shoulder of the rat-faced man.

The revolver exploded harmlessly in the air, and the seaman crumpled up with a scream of pain and terror.

Clayton turned and rushed back toward the scene. The sailors stood in a frightened group, with drawn weapons, peering into the jungle. The wounded man writhed and shrieked upon the ground.

Clayton, unseen by any, picked up the fallen revolver and slipped it inside his shirt, then he joined the sailors in gazing, mystified, into the jungle.

"Who could it have been?" whispered Jane Porter, and the young man turned to see her standing, wide-eyed and wondering, close beside him.

"I dare say Tarzan of the Apes is watching us all right," he answered, in a dubious tone. "I wonder, now, who that spear was intended for. If for Snipes, then our ape friend is a friend indeed.

"By Jove, where are your father and Mr. Philander? There's some one or something in that jungle, and it's armed, whatever it is. Ho! Professor! Mr. Philander!" young Clayton shouted. There was no response.

"What's to be done, Miss Porter?" continued the young man, his face clouded by a frown of worry and indecision.*

"I can't leave you here alone with these cutthroats, and you certainly can't venture into the jungle with me; yet some one must go in search of your father. He is more than apt to wandering off aimlessly, regardless of danger or direction, and Mr. Philander is only a trifle less impractical than he. You will pardon my bluntness, but our lives are all in jeopardy here, and when we get your father back something must be done to impress upon him the dangers to which he exposes you as well as himself by his absent-mindedness."

"I quite agree with you," replied the girl, "and I am not offended at all. Dear old papa would sacrifice his life for me without an instant's hesitation, provided one could keep his mind on so frivolous a matter for an entire instant. There is only one way to keep him in safety, and that is to chain him to a tree. The poor dear is *so* impractical."

"I have it!" suddenly exclaimed Clayton. "You can use a revolver, can't you?"

"Yes. Why?"

"I have one. With it you and Esmeralda will be comparatively safe in this cabin while I am searching for your father and Mr. Philander. Come, call the woman and I will hurry on. They can't have gone far."

Jane Porter did as he suggested and when he saw the door close safely behind them Clayton turned toward the jungle.

Some of the sailors were drawing the spear from their wounded comrade and, as Clayton approached, he asked if he could borrow a revolver from one of them while he searched the jungle for the professor.

The rat-faced one, finding he was not dead, had regained his composure, and with a volley of oaths directed at Clayton refused in the name of his fellows to allow the young man any firearms.

This man, Snipes, had assumed the role of chief since he had killed their former leader, and so little time had elapsed that none of his companions had as yet questioned his authority.

Clayton's only response was a shrug of the shoulders, but as he left them he picked up the spear which had transfixed Snipes, and thus primitively armed, the son of the then Lord Greystoke strode into the dense jungle.

Every few moments he called aloud the names of the wanderers. The watchers in the cabin by the beach heard the sound of his voice growing ever fainter and fainter, until at last it was swallowed up by the myriad noises of the primeval wood.

When Professor Archimedes Q. Porter and his assistant, Samuel T. Philander, after much insistence on the part of the latter, had finally turned their steps toward camp, they were as completely lost in the wild and tangled labyrinth of the matted jungle as two human beings well could be, though they did not know it.

It was by the merest caprice of fortune that they headed toward the west coast of Africa, instead of toward Zanzibar on the opposite side of the dark continent.*

When in a short time they reached the beach, only to find no camp in sight, Philander was positive that they were north of their proper destination, while, as a matter of fact they were about two hundred yards south of it.

It never occurred to either of these impractical theorists to call aloud on the chance of attracting their friends' attention. Instead, with all the assurance that deductive reasoning from a wrong premise induces in one, Mr. Samuel T. Philander grasped Professor Archimedes Q. Porter firmly by the arm and hurried the weakly protesting old gentleman off in the direction of Cape Town,* fifteen hundred miles to the south.

When Jane Porter and Esmeralda found themselves safely behind the cabin door the negress's first thought was to barricade the portal from the inside. With this idea in mind she turned to search for some means of putting it into execution; but her first view of the interior of the cabin brought a shriek of terror to her lips, and like a frightened child the huge black ran to bury her face on her mistress' shoulder.

Jane Porter, turning at the cry, saw the cause of it lying prone upon the floor before them—the whitened skeleton of a man. A further glance revealed a second skeleton upon the bed.

"What horrible place are we in?" murmured the awestruck girl. But there was no panic in her fright.

At last, disengaging herself from the frantic clutch of the still shrieking Esmeralda, Jane Porter crossed the room to look into the little cradle, knowing what she should see there before ever the tiny skeleton disclosed itself in all its pitiful and pathetic frailty.

What an awful tragedy these poor mute bones proclaimed! The girl shuddered at thought of the eventualities which might lie before herself and her friends in this ill-fated cabin; the haunt of mysterious, perhaps hostile, beings.

Quickly, with an impatient stamp of her little foot, she endeavored to shake off the gloomy forebodings, and turning to Esmeralda bade her cease her wailing.

"Stop, Esmeralda; stop it this minute!" she cried. "You are only making it worse. Why, I never saw such a big baby."

She ended lamely, a little quiver in her own voice as she thought of the three men, upon whom she depended for protection, wandering in the depth of that awful forest.

Soon the girl found that the door was equipped with a heavy wooden bar upon the inside, and after several efforts the combined strength of the two enabled them to slip it into place, the first time in twenty years.

Then they sat down upon a bench with their arms about one another, and waited.

CHAPTER XIV

AT THE MERCY OF THE JUNGLE

AFTER Clayton had plunged into the jungle, the sailors—mutineers of the *Arrow*—fell into a discussion of their next step; but on one point all were agreed—that they should hasten to put off to the anchored *Arrow*, where they could at least be safe from the spears of their unseen foe. And so, while Jane Porter and Esmeralda were barricading themselves within the cabin, the cowardly crew of cutthroats were pulling rapidly for their ship in the two boats that had brought them ashore.

So much had Tarzan seen that day that his head was in a whirl of wonder. But the most wonderful sight of all, to him, was the face of the beautiful white girl.

Here at last was one of his own kind; of that he was positive. And the young man and the two old men; they, too, were much as he had pictured his own people to be.

But doubtless they were as ferocious and cruel as other men he had seen. The fact that they alone of all the party were unarmed might account for the fact that they had killed no one. They might be very different if provided with weapons.

Tarzan had seen the young man pick up the fallen revolver of the wounded Snipes and hide it away in his breast; and he had also seen him slip it cautiously to the girl as she entered the cabin door.

He did not understand anything of the motives behind all that he had seen; but, somehow, intuitively he liked the young man and the two old men, and for the girl he had a strange longing which he scarcely understood. As for the big black woman, she was evidently connected in some way to the girl, and so he liked her, also.

For the sailors, and especially Snipes, he had developed a great hatred. He knew by their threatening gestures and by the expressions upon their evil faces that they were enemies of the others of the party, and so he decided to watch them closely.

Tarzan wondered why the men had gone into the jungle, nor did it ever occur to him that one could become lost in that maze of undergrowth which to him was as simple as is the main street of your own home town to you.

When he saw the sailors row away toward the ship, and knew that the girl and her companion were safe in his cabin, Tarzan decided to follow the young man into the jungle and learn what his errand might be. He swung off rapidly in the direction taken by Clayton, and in a short time heard faintly in the distance the now only occasional calls of the Englishman to his friends.

Presently Tarzan came up with the white man, who, almost fagged, was leaning against a tree wiping the perspiration from his forehead. The ape-man, hiding safe behind a screen of foliage, sat watching this new specimen of his own race intently.

At intervals Clayton called aloud and finally it came to Tarzan that he was searching for the old man.

Tarzan was on the point of going off to look for them himself, when he caught the yellow glint of a sleek hide moving cautiously through the jungle toward Clayton.

It was Sheeta, the leopard. Now, Tarzan heard the soft bending of grasses and wondered why the young white man was not warned. Could it be he had failed to note the loud warning? Never before had Tarzan known Sheeta to be so clumsy.

No, the white man did not hear. Sheeta was crouching for the spring, and then, shrill and horrible, there rose upon the stillness of the jungle the awful cry of the challenging ape, and Sheeta turned, crashing into the underbrush.

Clayton came to his feet with a start. His blood ran cold. Never in all his life had so fearful a sound smote upon his ears. He was no coward; but if ever man felt the icy fingers of fear upon his heart, William Cecil Clayton, eldest son of Lord Greystoke of England, did that day in the fastness of the African jungle.

The noise of some great body crashing through the underbrush so close beside him, and the sound of that blood-curdling shriek from above, tested Clayton's courage to the limit; but he could not know that it was to that very voice he owed his life, nor that the creature who hurled it forth was his own cousin—the real Lord Greystoke.

The afternoon was drawing to a close, and Clayton, disheartened and discouraged, was in a terrible quandary as to the proper course to pursue; whether to keep on in search of Professor Porter, at the almost certain risk of his own death in the jungle by night, or to return to the cabin where he might at least serve to protect Jane Porter from the perils which confronted her on all sides.

He disliked to return to camp without her father; still more, he shrank from the thought of leaving her alone and unprotected in the hands of the mutineers of the *Arrow*, or to the hundred unknown dangers of the jungle.

Possibly, too, he thought, ere this the professor and Philander had returned to camp. Yes, that was more than likely. At least he would return and see, before he continued what bade fare to be a most fruitless quest. And so he started, stumbling back through the thick and matted underbrush in the direction that he thought the cabin lay.

To Tarzan's surprise the young man was heading further into the jungle in the general direction of Mbonga's village, and the shrewd young ape-man was convinced that he was lost.

To Tarzan this was scarcely comprehensible; but his judgment told him that no man would venture toward the village of the cruel blacks armed only with a spear which, from the awkward way in which he carried it, was evidently an unaccustomed weapon to this white man. Nor was he following the trail of the old men. That, they had crossed and left long since, though it had been fresh and plain before Tarzan's eyes.

Tarzan was perplexed. The fierce jungle would make easy prey of this unprotected stranger in a very short time if he were not guided quickly to the beach.

Yes, there was Numa, the lion, even now, stalking the white man a dozen paces to the right.

Clayton heard the great body paralleling his course, and now there rose upon the evening air the beast's thunderous roar. The man stopped with upraised spear and faced the brush from which issued the awful sound. The shadows were deepening, darkness was settling in.

God! To die here alone, beneath the fangs of wild beasts; to be torn and rended; to feel the hot breath of the brute on his face as the great paw crushed down upon his breast!

For a moment all was still. Clayton stood rigid, with raised spear. Presently a faint rustling of the bush apprised him of the stealthy creeping of the thing behind. It was gathering for the spring. At last he saw it, not twenty feet away—the long, lithe, muscular body and tawny head of a huge black-maned lion.

The beast was upon its belly, moving forward very slowly. As its eyes met Clayton's it stopped, and deliberately, cautiously gathered its hind quarters beneath it.

In agony the man watched; fearful to launch his spear; powerless to fly.

He heard a noise in the tree above him. Some new danger, he thought, but he dared not take his eyes from the yellow green orbs before him. There was a sharp twang as of a broken banjo-string, and at the same instant an arrow appeared in the yellow hide of the crouching lion.

With a roar of pain and anger the beast sprang; but, somehow, Clayton stumbled to one side, and as he turned again to face the infuriated king of beasts, he was appalled at the sight which confronted him. Almost simultaneously with the lion's turning to renew the attack a naked giant dropped from the tree above squarely on the brute's back.

With lightning speed an arm that was banded layers of iron muscle encircled the huge neck, and the great beast was raised from behind, roaring and pawing the air—raised as easily as Clayton would have lifted a pet dog.

The scene he witnessed there in the twilight depths of the African jungle was burned forever into the Englishman's brain.

The man before him was the embodiment of physical perfection and giant strength, yet it was not upon these he depended in his battle with the great cat, for, mighty as were his muscles, they were as nothing by comparison with Numa's. To his agility, to his brain and to his long keen knife he owed his supremacy.

His right arm encircled the lion's neck, while the left hand plunged the knife time and again into the unprotected side behind the left shoulder. The infuriated beast, pulled up and backwards until he stood upon his hind legs, struggled impotently in this unnatural position.

Had the battle been of a few seconds' longer duration the outcome might have been different, but it was all accomplished so quickly that the lion had scarce time to recover from the confusion of its surprise ere it sank lifeless to the ground.

Then the strange figure which had vanquished it stood erect upon the carcass, and throwing back the wild and handsome head, gave out the fearsome cry which a few moments earlier had so startled Clayton.

Before him he saw the figure of a young man, naked except for a loin cloth and a few barbaric ornaments about arms and legs; on the breast a priceless diamond locket gleaming against a smooth brown skin.

The hunting-knife had been returned to its homely sheath, and the man was gathering up his bow and quiver from where he had tossed them, when he leaped to attack the lion.

Clayton spoke to the stranger in English, thanking him for his brave rescue and complimenting him on the wondrous strength and dexterity he had displayed, but the only answer was a steady stare and a faint shrug of the mighty shoulders, which might betoken either disparagement of the service rendered, or ignorance of Clayton's language.

When the bow and quiver had been slung to his back the wild man, for such Clayton now thought him, once more drew his knife and deftly carved a dozen large strips of meat from the lion's carcass. Then, squatting upon his haunches, he proceeded to eat, first motioning Clayton to join him.

The strong white teeth sank into the raw and dripping flesh in apparent relish of the meal, but Clayton could not bring himself to share the uncooked meat with his strange host; instead he watched him, and presently there dawned upon him the conviction that this was Tarzan of the Apes, whose notice he had seen posted upon the cabin door that morning.

If so, he must speak English.

Again Clayton essayed speech with the ape-man; but the replies, now vocal, were in a strange tongue, which resembled the chattering of monkeys mingled with the growling of some wild beast.

No, this could not be Tarzan of the Apes, for it was very evident that he was an utter stranger to English.

When Tarzan had completed his repast he rose and, pointing in a very different direction from that which Clayton had been pursuing, started off through the jungle toward the point he had indicated.

Clayton, bewildered and confused, hesitated to follow him, for he thought he was but being led more deeply into the mazes of the forest; but the ape-man, seeing him disinclined to follow, returned, and, grasping him by the coat, dragged him along until he was convinced that Clayton understood what was required of him. Then he left him to follow voluntarily.

The Englishman, finally concluding that he was a prisoner, saw no alternative open but to accompany his captor, and thus they traveled slowly through the jungle while the sable mantle of the impenetrable forest night fell about them, and the stealthy footfalls of padded paws mingled with the breaking of twigs and the wild calls of the savage life that Clayton felt closing in upon him.

Suddenly Clayton heard the faint report of a firearm—a single shot, and then silence.

In the cabin by the beach two thoroughly terrified women clung to each other as they crouched upon the low bench in the gathering darkness.

The negress sobbed hysterically, bemoaning the evil day that had witnessed her departure from her dear Maryland, while the white girl, dry eyed and outwardly calm, was torn by inward fears and forebodings. She feared not more for herself than for the three men whom she knew to be wandering in the abysmal depths of the savage jungle, from which she now heard issuing the almost incessant shrieks and roars, barkings and growlings of its terrifying and fearsome denizens as they sought their prey.

And now there came the sound of a heavy body brushing against the side of the cabin. She could hear the great padded paws upon the ground without. Then, for an instant, all was silence; even the bedlam of the forest died to a faint murmur; then she distinctly heard the beast without sniffing at the door, not two feet from where she crouched. Instinctively the girl shuddered, and shrank closer to the black woman.

"Hush!" she whispered. "Hush, Esmeralda," for the woman's sobs and groans seemed to have attracted the thing that stalked there just beyond the thin wall.

A gentle scratching sound was heard on the door. The brute tried to force an entrance; but presently this ceased, and again she heard the great pads creeping stealthily around the cabin. Again they stopped—beneath the window on which the terrified eyes of the girl now glued themselves.

"God!" she murmured, for now, silhouetted against the moonlit sky beyond, she saw framed in the tiny square of the latticed window the head of a huge lioness. The gleaming eyes were fixed upon her in intent ferocity.

"Look, Esmeralda!" she whispered. "For God's sake, what shall we do? Look! Quick! The window!"

Esmeralda, cowering still closer to her mistress, took one affrighted glance toward the little square of moonlight, just as the lioness emitted a low, savage snarl.

The sight that met the poor black's eyes was too much for the already overstrung nerves.

"Oh, Gaberelle!"* she shrieked, and slid to the floor an inert and senseless mass.

For what seemed an eternity the great brute stood with its fore paws upon the sill, glaring into the little room. Presently it tried the strength of the lattice with its great talons.

The girl had almost ceased to breathe, when, to her relief, the head disappeared and she heard the brute's footsteps leaving the window. But now they came to the door again, and once more the scratching commenced; this time with increasing force until the great beast was tearing at the massive panels in a perfect frenzy of eagerness to seize its defenseless victims.

Could Jane Porter have known the immense strength of that door, builded* piece by piece, she would have felt less fear of the lioness reaching her by this avenue.

Little did John Clayton imagine when he fashioned that crude but mighty portal that one day, twenty years later, it would shield a fair American girl, then unborn, from the teeth and talons of a man-eater.

For fully twenty minutes the brute alternately sniffed and tore at the door, occasionally giving voice to a wild, savage cry of baffled rage. At length, however, she gave up the attempt, and Jane Porter heard her returning toward the window, beneath which she paused for an instant, and then launched her great weight against the time-worn lattice.

The girl heard the wooden rods groan beneath the impact; but they held, and the huge body dropped back to the ground below.

Again and again the lioness repeated these tactics, until finally the horrified prisoner within saw a portion of the lattice give way, and in an instant one great paw and the head of the animal were thrust within the room.

Slowly the powerful neck and shoulders spread the bars apart, and the lithe body protruded further and further into the room.

As in a trance, the girl rose, her hand upon her breast, wide eyes staring horror-stricken into the snarling face of the beast scarce ten feet from her. At her feet lay the prostrate form of the negress. If she could but arouse her, their combined efforts might possibly avail to beat back the fierce and blood-thirsty intruder.

Jane Porter stooped to grasp the black woman by the shoulder. Roughly she shook her.

"Esmeralda! Esmeralda!" she cried. "Help me, or we are lost."

Esmeralda slowly opened her eyes. The first object they encountered was the dripping fangs of the hungry lioness.

With a horrified scream the poor woman rose to her hands and knees, and in this position scurried across the room, shrieking: "O Gaberelle! O Gaberelle!" at the top of her lungs.

Esmeralda weighed some two hundred and eighty pounds, which enhanced nothing the gazelle-like grace of her carriage when walking erect, and her extreme haste, added to her extreme corpulency, produced a most amazing result when Esmeralda elected to travel on all fours.

For a moment the lioness remained quiet with intense gaze directed upon the flitting Esmeralda, whose goal appeared to be the cupboard, into which she attempted to propel her huge bulk; but, as the shelves were but nine or ten inches apart, she only succeeded in getting her head in, whereupon, with a final screech, which paled the jungle noises into insignificance, she fainted once again.

With the subsidence of Esmeralda the lioness renewed her efforts to wriggle her huge bulk through the weakening lattice.

The girl, standing pale and rigid against the further wall, sought with ever-increasing terror for some loop-hole of escape. Suddenly her hand, tight-pressed against her bosom, felt the hard outline of the revolver that Clayton had left with her earlier in the day.

Quickly she snatched it from its hiding-place, and, leveling it full at the lioness's face, pulled the trigger.

There was a flash of flame, the roar of the discharge, and an answering roar of pain and anger from the beast.

Jane Porter saw the great form disappear from the window, and then she, too, fainted, the revolver falling at her side.

But Sabor was not killed. The bullet had but inflicted a painful wound in one of the great shoulders. It was the surprise at the blinding flash and the deafening roar that had caused her hasty, though but temporary, retreat.

In another instant she was back at the lattice, and with renewed fury was clawing at the aperture, but with lessened effect, since the wounded member was almost useless.

She saw her prey—the two women—lying senseless upon the floor; there was no longer any resistance to be overcome. Her meat lay before her, and Sabor had only to worm her way through the lattice to claim it.

Slowly she forced her great bulk, inch by inch, through the opening. Now her head was through, now one great forearm and shoulder.

Carefully she drew up the wounded member to insinuate it gently beyond the tight pressing bars.

A moment more and both shoulders through, the long, sinuous body and the narrow hips would glide quickly after.

It was on this sight that Jane Porter again opened her eyes.

CHAPTER XV

THE FOREST GOD

WHEN Clayton heard the report of the firearm he fell into an agony of fear and apprehension. He knew that one of the sailors might be the author of it; but the fact that he had left the revolver with Jane Porter, together with the overwrought condition of his nerves, made him morbidly positive that she was threatened with some great danger; perhaps even now attempting to defend herself against some savage man or beast.

What were the thoughts of his strange captor or guide Clayton could only vaguely conjecture; but that he had heard the shot, and was in some manner affected by it was quite evident, for he quickened his pace so appreciably that Clayton, stumbling blindly in his wake, was down a dozen times in as many minutes in a vain effort to keep pace with him, and soon was left hopelessly behind.

Fearing that he would again be irretrievably lost, he called aloud to the wild man ahead of him, and in a moment had the satisfaction of seeing him drop lightly to his side from the branches above.

For a moment Tarzan looked at the young man closely, as though undecided as to just what was best to do; then, stooping down before Clayton, he motioned him to grasp him about the neck, and, with the white man upon his back, Tarzan took to the trees.

The next few minutes were such as the young Englishman never forgot. High into bending and swaying branches he was borne with what seemed to him incredible swiftness, while Tarzan chafed at the slowness of his progress.

From one lofty branch the agile creature swung with Clayton through a dizzy arc to a neighboring tree; then for a hundred yards maybe the sure feet threaded a maze of interwoven limbs, balancing like a tightrope walker high above the black depths of verdure beneath.

From the first sensation of chilling fear Clayton passed to one of keen admiration and envy of those giant muscles and that wondrous instinct or knowledge which guided this forest god through the inky blackness of the night as easily and safely as Clayton could have strolled a London street at high noon.

Occasionally they would enter a spot where the foliage above was less dense, and the bright rays of the moon lit up before Clayton's wondering eyes the strange path they were traversing.

At such times the man fairly caught his breath at sight of the horrid depths below them, for Tarzan took the easiest way, which often led over a hundred feet above the earth.

And yet with all his seeming speed, Tarzan was in reality feeling his way with comparative slowness, searching constantly for limbs of adequate strength for the maintenance of this double weight.

Presently they came to the clearing before the beach. Tarzan's quick ears had heard the strange sounds of Sabor's efforts to force her way through the lattice, and it seemed to Clayton that they dropped a straight hundred feet to earth, so quickly did Tarzan descend. Yet when they struck the ground it was with scarce a jar; and as Clayton released his hold on the ape-man he saw him dart like a squirrel for the opposite side of the cabin.

The Englishman sprang quickly after him just in time to see the hind quarters of some huge animal about to disappear through the window of the cabin.

As Jane Porter opened her eyes to a realization of the again imminent peril which threatened her, her brave young heart gave up at last its final vestige of hope, and she turned to grope for the fallen weapon that she might mete to herself a merciful death ere the cruel fangs tore into her fair flesh.

The lioness was almost through the opening before Jane found the weapon, and she raised it quickly to her temple to shut out forever the hideous jaws gaping for their prey.

An instant she hesitated, to breathe a short and silent prayer to her Maker, and as she did so her eyes fell upon her poor Esmeralda lying inert, but alive, beside the cupboard.

How could she leave the poor, faithful thing to those merciless, yellow fangs? No, she must use one cartridge on the senseless woman ere she turned the cold muzzle toward herself again.

How she shrank from the ordeal! But it had been cruelty a thousand times less justifiable to have left the loving black woman who had reared her from infancy with all a mother's care and solicitude, to regain consciousness beneath the rending claws of the great cat.

Quickly Jane Porter sprang to her feet and ran to the side of the black. She pressed the muzzle of the revolver tight against that devoted heart, closed her eyes, and—

Sabor emitted a frightful shriek.

The girl, startled, pulled the trigger and turned to face the beast, and with the same movement raised the weapon against her own temple.

She did not fire a second time,* for to her surprise she saw the huge animal being slowly drawn back through the window, and in the moonlight beyond she saw the heads and shoulders of two men.

As Clayton rounded the corner of the cabin to behold the animal disappearing within, it was also to see the ape-man seize the long tail in both hands, and, bracing himself with his feet against the side of the cabin, throw all his mighty strength into the effort to draw the beast out of the interior.

Clayton was quick to lend a hand, but the ape-man jabbered to him in a commanding and peremptory tone something which Clayton knew to be orders, though he could not understand them.

At last, under their combined efforts, the great body commenced to appear farther and farther without the window, and then there came to Clayton's mind a dawning conception of the rash bravery of his companion's act.

For a naked man to drag a shrieking, clawing man-eater forth from a window by the tail to save a strange white girl, was indeed the last word in heroism.

In so far as Clayton was concerned it was a very different matter, since the girl was not only of his own kind and race, but was the one woman in all the world whom he loved.

Though he knew that the lioness would make short work of both of them, he pulled with a will to keep it from Jane Porter. And then he recalled the battle between this man and the great, black-maned lion which he had witnessed a short time before, and he commenced to feel more assurance.

Tarzan was still issuing orders which Clayton could not understand.

He was trying to tell the stupid white man to plunge his poisoned arrows into Sabor's back and sides, and to reach the savage heart with the long, thin hunting knife that hung at Tarzan's hip; but the man would not understand, and Tarzan did not dare release his hold to do the things himself, for he knew that the puny white man never could hold mighty Sabor alone, for an instant.

Slowly the lioness was emerging from the window. At last her shoulders were out.

And then Clayton saw a thing done which not even the eternal heavens had ever seen before. Tarzan, racking his brains for some means to cope single-handed with the infuriated beast, had suddenly recalled his battle with Terkoz; and as the great shoulders came clear of the window, so that the lioness hung upon the sill only by her forepaws, Tarzan suddenly released his hold upon the brute.

With the quickness of a striking rattler he launched himself full upon Sabor's back, his strong young arms seeking and gaining a full-Nelson upon the beast, as he had learned it that other day during his bloody, wrestling victory over Terkoz.

With a shriek the lioness turned completely over upon her back, falling full upon her enemy; but the black-haired giant only closed tighter his hold.

Pawing and tearing at earth and air, Sabor rolled and threw herself this way and that in an effort to dislodge this strange antagonist; but ever tighter and tighter drew the iron bands that were forcing her head lower and lower upon her tawny breast.

Higher crept the steel forearms of the ape-man about the back of Sabor's neck. Weaker and weaker became the lioness's efforts.

At last Clayton saw the immense muscles of Tarzan's shoulders and biceps leap into corded knots beneath the silver moonlight. There was a long sustained and supreme effort on the ape-man's part—and the vertebræ of Sabor's neck parted with a sharp snap.

In an instant Tarzan was upon his feet, and for the second time that day Clayton heard the bull ape's savage roar of victory. Then he heard Jane Porter's agonized cry:

"Cecil—Mr. Clayton! Oh, what is it? What is it?"

Running quickly to the cabin door, Clayton called out that all was right, and bade her open. As quickly as she could she raised the great bar and fairly dragged Clayton within.

"What was that awful noise?" she whispered, shrinking close to him.

"It was the cry of the kill from the throat of the man who has just saved your life, Miss Porter. Wait, I will fetch him that you may thank him."

The frightened girl would not be left alone, so she accompanied Clayton to the side of the cabin where lay the dead body of the lioness.

Tarzan of the Apes was gone.

Clayton called several times, but there was no reply, and so the two returned to the greater safety of the interior.

"What a frightful sound!" cried Jane Porter, "I shudder at the mere thought of it. Do not tell me that human throat voiced that hideous and fearsome shriek."

"But it did, Miss Porter," replied Clayton; "or at least if not a human throat that of a forest god."

And then he told her of his experiences with this strange creature—of how twice the wild man had saved his life—of the wondrous strength, and agility, and bravery—of the brown skin and the handsome face.

"I cannot make it out at all," he concluded. "At first I thought he might be Tarzan of the Apes; but he neither speaks nor understands English, so that theory is untenable."

"Well, whatever he may be," cried the girl, "we owe him our lives, and may God bless him and keep him in safety in his wild and savage jungle!"

"Amen," said Clayton, fervently.

"Fo' de good Lawd's sake, ain' Ah daid?"

The two turned to see Esmeralda sitting upright upon the floor, her great eyes rolling from side to side as though she could not believe their testimony as to her whereabouts.

The lioness's shriek, as Jane Porter had been about to put a bullet into poor Esmeralda, had saved the black's life, for the little start the girl gave had turned the muzzle of the revolver to one side, and the bullet had passed harmlessly into the floor.

And now, for Jane Porter, the reaction came, and she threw herself upon the bench, screaming with hysterical laughter.

CHAPTER XVI

"MOST REMARKABLE"

SEVERAL miles south of the cabin, upon a strip of sandy beach, stood two old men, arguing.

Before them stretched the broad Atlantic; at their backs the Dark Continent; close around them loomed the impenetrable blackness of the jungle.

Savage beasts roared and growled; noises, hideous and weird, assailed their ears. They had wandered for miles in search of their camp; but always in the wrong direction. They were as hopelessly lost as though they suddenly had been transported to another world.

At such a time indeed must every fiber of their combined intellects have been concentrated upon the vital question of the minute—the life-and-death question to them of retracing their steps to camp.

Samuel T. Philander was speaking.

"But, my dear professor," he was saying, "I still maintain that but for the victories of Ferdinand and Isabella over the fifteenth-century Moors in Spain* the world would be today a thousand years in advance of where we now find ourselves.

"The Moors were essentially a tolerant, broad-minded, liberal race of agriculturists, artisans and merchants—the very type of people that has made possible such civilization as we find today in America and Europe—while the Spaniards—"

"Tut, tut, dear Mr. Philander," interrupted Professor Porter; "their religion positively precluded the possibilities you suggest, Moslemism* was, is, and always will be, a blight on that scientific progress which has marked—"

"Bless me! Professor," interjected Mr. Philander, who had turned his gaze toward the jungle, "there seems to be someone approaching."

Professor Archimedes Q. Porter turned in the direction indicated by the nearsighted Mr. Philander.

"Tut, tut, Mr. Philander," he chided. "How often must I urge you to seek that absolute concentration of your mental faculties which alone may permit you to bring to bear the highest powers of intellectuality upon the momentous problems which naturally fall to the lot of great minds? And now I find you guilty of a most flagrant breach of courtesy in interrupting my learned discourse to call attention to a mere quadruped of the genus *Felis*.* As I was saying, Mr.—"

"Heavens, Professor, a lion?" cried Mr. Philander, straining his weak eyes toward the dim figure outlined against the dark tropical underbrush.

"Yes, yes, Mr. Philander, if you insist upon employing slang in your discourse, a 'lion.' But as I was saying—"

"Bless me, Professor," again interrupted Mr. Philander; "permit me to suggest that doubtless the Moors who were conquered in the fifteenth century will continue in that most regrettable condition for the time being at least, even though we postpone discussion of that world calamity until we may attain the enchanting view of yon *Felis carnivora** which distance proverbially is credited with lending."

In the meantime the lion had approached with quiet dignity to within ten paces of the two men, where he stood curiously watching them.

The moonlight flooded the beach, and the strange group stood out in bold relief against the yellow sand.

"Most reprehensible, most reprehensible," exclaimed Professor Porter, with a faint trace of irritation in his voice.

"Never, Mr. Philander, never before in my life have I known one of these animals to be permitted to roam at large from its cage. I shall most certainly report this outrageous breach of ethics to the directors of the adjacent zoological garden."

"Quite right, Professor," agreed Mr. Philander, "and the sooner it is done the better. Let us start now."

Seizing the professor by the arm, Mr. Philander set off in the direction that would put the greatest distance between themselves and the lion.

They had proceeded but a short distance when a backward glance revealed to the horrified gaze of Mr. Philander that the lion was following them. He tightened his grip upon the protesting professor and increased his speed.

"As I was saying, Mr. Philander," repeated Professor Porter.

Mr. Philander took another hasty glance rearward. The lion also had quickened his gait, and was doggedly maintaining an unvarying distance behind them.

"He is following us!" gasped Mr. Philander, breaking into a run.

"Tut, tut, Mr. Philander," remonstrated the professor, "this unseemly haste is most unbecoming men of letters.

"What will our friends think of us, who may chance to be upon the street and witness our frivolous antics? Pray let us proceed with more decorum."

Mr. Philander stole another observation astern.

Horrors! The lion was bounding along in easy leaps scarce five paces behind.

Mr. Philander dropped the professor's arm, and broke into a mad orgy of speed that would have done credit to any varsity track team.

"As I was saying, Mr. Philander—" screamed Professor Porter, as, metaphorically speaking, he himself "threw her into high." He, too, had caught a fleeting backward glimpse of cruel yellow eyes and half open mouth within startling proximity of his person.

With streaming coat-tails and shiny silk hat Professor Archimedes Q. Porter fled through the moonlight close upon the heels of Mr. Samuel T. Philander.

Before them a point of the jungle ran out toward a narrow promontory, and it was for the haven of the trees he saw there that Mr. Samuel T. Philander directed his prodigious leaps and bounds; while from the shadows of this same spot peered two keen eyes in interested appreciation of the race.

It was Tarzan of the Apes who watched, with face a-grin, this odd game of follow-the-leader.

He knew the two men were safe enough from attack in so far as the lion was concerned. The very fact that Numa had foregone such easy prey at all convinced the wise forest craft of Tarzan that Numa's belly already was full.

The lion might stalk them until hungry again; but the chances were that if not angered he would soon tire of the sport, and slink away to his jungle lair.

Really, the one great danger was that one of the men might stumble and fall, and then the yellow devil would be upon him in a moment and the joy of the kill would be too great a temptation to withstand.

So Tarzan swung quickly to a lower limb in line with the approaching fugitives; and as Mr. Samuel T. Philander came panting and blowing beneath him, already too spent to struggle up to the safety of the limb, Tarzan reached down and, grasping him by the collar of his coat, yanked him to the limb by his side.

Another moment brought the professor within the sphere of the friendly grip, and he, too, was drawn upward to safety just as the baffled Numa, with a roar, leaped to recover his vanishing quarry.

For a moment the two men clung panting to the great branch, while Tarzan squatted with his back to the stem of the tree, watching them with mingled curiosity and amusement.

It was the professor who first broke the silence.

"I am deeply pained, Mr. Philander, that you should have evinced such a paucity of manly courage in the presence of one of the lower orders, and by your crass timidity have caused me to exert myself to such an unaccustomed degree in order that I might resume my discourse.

"As I was saying, Mr. Philander, when you interrupted me, the Moors—"

"Professor Archimedes Q. Porter," broke in Mr. Philander, in icy tones, "the time has arrived when patience becomes a crime and mayhem appears garbed in the mantle of virtue. You have accused me of cowardice. You have insinuated that you ran only to overtake me, not to escape the clutches of the lion.

"Have a care, Professor Archimedes Q. Porter! I am a desperate man. Goaded by long-suffering patience the worm will turn."

"Tut, tut, Mr. Philander, tut, tut!" cautioned Professor Porter; "you forget yourself."

"I forget nothing as yet, Professor Archimedes Q. Porter; but, believe me, sir, I am tottering on the verge of forgetfulness as to your exalted position in the world of science, and your gray hairs."

The professor sat in silence for a few minutes, and the darkness hid the grim smile that wreathed his wrinkled countenance. Presently he spoke.

"Look here, Skinny Philander," he said, in belligerent tones, "if you are lookin' for a scrap, peel off your coat and come on down on the ground, and I'll punch your head just as I did sixty years ago in the alley back of Porky Evans' barn."

"Ark!" gasped the astonished Mr. Philander. "Lordy, how good that sounds! When you're human, Ark, I love you; but somehow it seems as though you had forgotten how to be human for the last twenty years."

The professor reached out a thin, trembling old hand through the darkness until it found his old friend's shoulder.

"Forgive me, Skinny," he said, softly. "It hasn't been quite twenty years, and God alone knows how hard I have tried to be 'human' for Jane's sake, and yours, too, since He took my other Jane away."

Another old hand stole up from Mr. Philander's side to clasp the one that lay upon his shoulder, and no other message could better have translated the one heart to the other.

They did not speak for some minutes. The lion below them paced nervously back and forth. The third figure in the tree was hidden by the dense shadows near the stem. He, too, was silent—motionless as a graven image.*

"You certainly pulled me up into this tree just in time," said the professor at last. "I want to thank you. You saved my life."

"But I didn't pull you up here, Professor," said Mr. Philander. "Bless me! The excitement of the moment quite caused me to forget that I myself was drawn up here by some outside agency—there must be someone or something in this tree with us."

"Eh?" ejaculated Professor Porter. "Are you quite positive, Mr. Philander?"

"Most positive, Professor," replied Mr. Philander, "and," he added, "I think we should thank the party. He may be sitting right next to you now, Professor."

"Eh? What's that? Tut, tut, Mr. Philander, tut, tut!" said Professor Porter, edging cautiously nearer to Mr. Philander.

Just then it occurred to Tarzan of the Apes that Numa had loitered beneath the tree for a sufficient length of time, so he raised his young head toward the heavens, and there rang out upon the terrified ears of the two old men the awful warning challenge of the anthropoid.

The two friends, huddled trembling in their precarious position on the limb, saw the great lion halt in his restless pacing as the blood-curdling cry smote his ears, and then slink quickly into the jungle, to be instantly lost to view.

"Even the lion trembles in fear," whispered Mr. Philander.

"Most remarkable, most remarkable," murmured Professor Porter, clutching frantically at Mr. Philander to regain the balance which the sudden fright had so perilously endangered. Unfortunately for them both, Mr. Philander's center of equilibrium was at that very moment hanging upon the ragged edge of nothing, so that it needed but the gentle impetus supplied by the additional weight of Professor Porter's body to topple the devoted secretary from the limb.

For a moment they swayed uncertainly, and then, with mingled and most unscholarly shrieks, they pitched headlong from the tree, locked in frenzied embrace.

It was quite some moments ere either moved, for both were positive that any such attempt would reveal so many breaks and fractures as to make further progress impossible.

At length Professor Porter essayed an attempt to move one leg. To his surprise, it responded to his will as in days gone by. He now drew up its mate and stretched it forth again.

"Most remarkable, most remarkable," he murmured.

"Thank God, Professor," whispered Mr. Philander, fervently, "you are not dead, then?"

"Tut, tut, Mr. Philander, tut, tut," cautioned Professor Porter, "I do not know with accuracy as yet."

With infinite solicitude Professor Porter wiggled his right arm—joy! It was intact. Breathlessly he waved his left arm above his prostrate body—it waved!

"Most remarkable, most remarkable," he said.

"To whom are you signaling, Professor?" asked Mr. Philander, in an excited tone.

Professor Porter deigned to make no response to this puerile inquiry. Instead he raised his head gently from the ground, nodding it back and forth a half-dozen times.

"Most remarkable," he breathed. "It remains intact."

Mr. Philander had not moved from where he had fallen; he had not dared the attempt. How indeed could one move when one's arms and legs and back were broken?

One eye was buried in the soft loam; the other, rolling sidewise, was fixed in awe upon the strange gyrations of Professor Porter.

"How sad!" exclaimed Mr. Philander, half aloud. "Concussion of the brain, superinducing total mental aberration. How very sad indeed! and for one still so young!"

Professor Porter rolled over upon his stomach; gingerly he bowed his back until he resembled a huge tom cat in proximity to a yelping dog. Then he sat up and felt of various portions of his anatomy.

"They are all here," he ejaculated. "Most remarkable!"

Whereupon he arose, and, bending a scathing glance upon the still prostrate form of Mr. Samuel T. Philander, he said:

"Tut, tut, Mr. Philander; this is no time to indulge in slothful ease. We must be up and doing."*

Mr. Philander lifted his other eye out of the mud, and gazed in speechless rage at Professor Porter. Then he attempted to rise; nor could there have been any more surprised than he when his efforts were immediately crowned with marked success.

He was still bursting with rage, however, at the cruel injustice of Professor Porter's insinuation, and was on the point of rendering a tart rejoinder when his eyes fell upon a strange figure standing a few paces away, scrutinizing them intently.

Professor Porter had recovered his shiny silk hat, which he had brushed carefully upon the sleeve of his coat and replaced upon his head. When he saw Mr. Philander pointing to something behind him he turned to behold a giant, naked but for a loin cloth and a few metal ornaments, standing motionless before him.

"Good evening, sir!" said the professor, lifting his hat.

For reply the giant motioned them to follow him, and set off up the beach in the direction from which they had recently come.

"I think it the part of discretion to follow him," said Mr. Philander.

"Tut, tut, Mr. Philander," returned the professor. "A short time since you were advancing most logical argument in substantiation of your theory that camp lay directly south of us. I was skeptical, but you finally convinced me; so now I am positive that toward the south we must travel to reach our friends. Therefore I shall continue south."

"But, Professor Porter, this man may know better than either of us. He seems to be indigenous to this part of the world. Let us at least follow him for a short distance."

"Tut, tut, Mr. Philander," repeated the professor. "I am a difficult man to convince, but when once convinced my decision is unalterable. I shall continue in the proper direction, if I have to circumambulate the continent of Africa to reach my destination."

Further argument was interrupted by Tarzan, who, seeing that these strange men were not following him, had returned to their side.

Again he beckoned to them; but still they stood in argument.

Presently the ape-man lost patience with their stupid ignorance. He grasped the frightened Mr. Philander by the shoulder, and before that worthy gentleman knew whether he was being killed or merely maimed for life, Tarzan had tied one end of his rope securely about Mr. Philander's neck.

"Tut, tut, Mr. Philander," remonstrated Professor Porter; "it is most unbeseeming in you to submit to such indignities."

But scarcely were the words out of his mouth ere he, too, had been seized and securely bound by the neck with the same rope. Then Tarzan set off toward the north, leading the now thoroughly frightened professor and his secretary.

In deathly silence they proceeded for what seemed hours to the two tired and hopeless old men; but presently as they topped a little rise of ground they were overjoyed to see the cabin lying before them, not a hundred yards distant.

Here Tarzan released them, and, pointing toward the little building, vanished into the jungle beside them.

"Most remarkable, most remarkable!" gasped the professor. "But you see, Mr. Philander, that I was quite right, as usual; and but for your stubborn wilfulness we should have escaped a series of most humiliating, not to say dangerous accidents. Pray allow yourself to be guided by a more mature and practical mind hereafter when in need of wise counsel."

Mr. Samuel T. Philander was too much relieved at the happy outcome to their adventure to take umbrage at the professor's cruel fling. Instead he grasped his friend's arm and hastened him forward in the direction of the cabin.

It was a much-relieved party of castaways that found itself once more united. Dawn discovered them still recounting their various adventures, and speculating upon the identity of the strange guardian and protector they had found on this savage shore.

Esmeralda was positive that it was none other than an angel of the Lord, sent down especially to watch over them.

"Had you seen him devour the raw meat of the lion, Esmeralda," laughed Clayton, "you would have thought him a very material angel."

"Ah doan know nuffin' 'bout dat, Marse Clayton,"* rejoined Esmeralda; "but Ah 'specs de Lawd clean fergot to gib him any matches, He sent him down in sech a hurry to look after we-all. An' he suttinly cain't cook nuffin' 'thout matches—no, sah."

"There was nothing heavenly about his voice," said Jane Porter, with a little shudder at recollection of the awful roar which had followed the killing of the lioness.

"Nor did it precisely comport with my preconceived ideas of the dignity of divine messengers," remarked Professor Porter, "when the—ah—gentleman tied two highly respectable and erudite scholars neck to neck and dragged them through the jungle as though they had been cows."

CHAPTER XVII

BURIALS

As it was now quite light, the party, none of whom had eaten or slept since the previous morning, began to bestir themselves to prepare food.

The mutineers of the *Arrow* had landed a small supply of dried meats, canned soups and vegetables, crackers, flour, tea, and coffee for the five they had marooned, and these were hurriedly drawn upon to satisfy the craving of long-famished appetites.

The next task was to make the cabin habitable, and to this end it was decided to at once remove the gruesome relics of the tragedy which had taken place there on some bygone day.

Professor Porter and Mr. Philander were deeply interested in examining the skeletons. The two larger, they stated, had belonged to a male and female of one of the higher white races.

The smallest skeleton was given but passing attention, as its location, in the crib, left no doubt as to its having been the infant offspring of this unhappy couple.

As they were preparing the skeleton of the man for burial, Clayton discovered a massive ring which had evidently encircled the man's finger at the time of his death, for one of the slender bones of the hand still lay within the golden bauble.

Picking it up to examine it, Clayton gave a cry of astonishment, for the ring bore the crest of the house of Greystoke.

At the same time, Jane Porter discovered the books in the cupboard, and on opening to the fly-leaf of one of them saw the name, *John Clayton, London*. In a second book which she hurriedly examined was the single name, *Greystoke*.

"Why, Mr. Clayton," she cried, "what does this mean? Here are the names of some of your own people in these books."

"And here," he replied gravely, "is the great ring of the house of Greystoke which has been lost since my uncle, John Clayton, the former Lord Greystoke, disappeared, presumably lost at sea."

"But how do you account for these things being here, in this savage African jungle?" exclaimed the girl.

"There is but one way to account for it, Miss Porter," said Clayton. "The late Lord Greystoke was not drowned. He died here in this cabin and this poor thing upon the floor is all that is mortal of him."

"Then this must have been Lady Greystoke," said Jane Porter reverently, indicating the poor mass of bones upon the bed.

"The beautiful Lady Alice," replied Clayton, "of whose many virtues and remarkable personal charms I often have heard my mother and father speak. Poor, unhappy lady," he murmured sadly.

With deep reverence and solemnity the bodies of the late Lord and Lady Greystoke were buried beside their little African cabin, and between them was placed the tiny skeleton of the baby of Kala, the ape.

As Mr. Philander was placing the frail bones of the infant in a bit of sail cloth, he examined the skull minutely. Then he called Professor Porter to his side, and the two argued in low tones for several minutes.

"Most remarkable, most remarkable," said Professor Porter.

"Bless me," said Mr. Philander, "we must acquaint Mr. Clayton with our discovery at once."

"Tut, tut, Mr. Philander, tut, tut!" remonstrated Professor Archimedes Q. Porter. "'Let the dead past bury its dead.'"*

And so the white-haired old man repeated the burial service over this strange grave, while his four companions stood with bowed and uncovered heads about him.

From the trees Tarzan of the Apes watched the solemn ceremony; but most of all he watched the sweet face and graceful figure of Jane Porter.

In his savage, untutored breast new emotions were stirring. He could not fathom them. He wondered why he felt so great an interest in these people—why he had gone to such pains to save the three men. But he did not wonder why he had torn Sabor from the tender flesh of the strange girl.

Surely the men were stupid and ridiculous and cowardly. Even Manu, the monkey, was more intelligent than they. If these were creatures of his own kind he was doubtful if his past pride in blood was warranted.

But the girl, ah—that was a different matter. He did not reason here. He knew that she was created to be protected, and that he was created to protect her.

He wondered why they had dug a great hole in the ground merely to bury dry bones. Surely there was no sense in that; no one wanted to steal dry bones.

Had there been meat upon them he could have understood, for thus alone might one keep his meat from Dango, the hyena, and the other robbers of the jungle.

When the grave had been filled with earth the little party turned back toward the cabin, and Esmeralda, still weeping copiously for the two she had never heard of before today, and who had been dead twenty years, chanced to glance toward the harbor. Instantly her tears ceased.

"Look at dem low down white trash out dere!" she shrilled, pointing toward the *Arrow*. "They-all's a desecratin' us, right yere on dis yere perverted islan'."

And, sure enough, the *Arrow* was being worked toward the open sea, slowly, through the harbor's entrance.

"They promised to leave us firearms and ammunition," said Clayton. "The merciless beasts!"

"It is the work of that fellow they call Snipes, I am sure," said Jane Porter. "King was a scoundrel, but he had a little sense of humanity. If they had not killed him I know that he would have seen that we were properly provided for before they left us to our fate."

"I regret that they did not visit us before sailing," said Professor Porter. "I had purposed requesting them to leave the treasure with us, as I shall be a ruined man if that is lost."

Jane Porter looked at her father sadly.

"Never mind, dear," she said. "It wouldn't have done any good, because it is solely for the treasure that they killed their officers and landed us upon this awful shore."

"Tut, tut, child, tut, tut!" replied Professor Porter. "You are a good child, but inexperienced in practical matters," and Professor Porter turned and walked slowly away toward the jungle, his hands clasped beneath his long coat-tails and his eyes bent upon the ground.

His daughter watched him with a pathetic smile upon her lips, and then turning to Mr. Philander, she whispered:

"Please don't let him wander off again as he did yesterday. We depend upon you, you know, to keep a close watch upon him."

"He becomes more difficult to handle each day," replied Mr. Philander, with a sigh and a shake of his head. "I presume he is now off to report to the directors of the Zoo that one of their lions was at large last night. Oh, Miss Jane, you don't know what I have to contend with."

"Yes, I do, Mr. Philander; but while we all love him, you alone are best fitted to manage him; for, regardless of what he may say to you, he respects your great learning, and, therefore, has immense confidence in your judgment. The poor dear cannot differentiate between erudition and wisdom."

Mr. Philander, with a mildly puzzled expression on his face, turned to pursue Professor Porter, and in his mind he was revolving the question of whether he should feel complimented or aggrieved at Miss Porter's rather back-handed compliment.

Tarzan had seen the consternation depicted upon the faces of the little group as they witnessed the departure of the *Arrow*; so, as the ship was a wonderful novelty to him in addition, he determined to hasten out to the point of land at the north of the harbor's mouth and obtain a nearer view of the boat, as well as to learn, if possible, the direction of its flight.

Swinging through the trees with great speed, he reached the point but a moment after the ship had passed out of the harbor, so that he obtained an excellent view of the wonders of this strange, floating house.

There were some twenty men running hither and thither about the deck, pulling and hauling on ropes.

A light land breeze was blowing, and the ship had been worked through the harbor's mouth under scant sail, but now that they had cleared the point every available shred of canvas was being spread that she might stand out to sea as handily as possible.

Tarzan watched the graceful movements of the ship in rapt admiration, and longed to be aboard her. Presently his keen eyes caught the faintest suspicion of smoke on the far northern horizon, and he wondered over the cause of such a thing out on the great water.

At about the same time the look-out on the *Arrow* must have discerned it, for in a few minutes Tarzan saw the sails being shifted and shortened. The ship came about, and presently he knew that she was beating back toward land.

A man at the bows was constantly heaving into the sea a rope to the end of which a small object was fastened. Tarzan wondered what the purpose of this action might be.

At last the ship came up directly into the wind; the anchor was lowered; down came the sails. There was great scurrying about on deck.

A boat was lowered, and in it a great chest was placed. Then a dozen sailors bent to the oars and pulled rapidly toward the point where Tarzan crouched in the branches of a tree.

In the stern of the boat, as it drew nearer, Tarzan saw the rat-faced man.

It was but a few minutes later that the boat touched the beach. The men jumped out and lifted the great chest to the sand. They were on the north side of the point so that their presence was concealed from those at the cabin.

The men argued angrily for a moment. Then the rat-faced one, with several companions, ascended the low bluff on which stood the tree that concealed Tarzan. They looked about for several minutes.

"Here is a good place," said the rat-faced sailor, indicating a spot beneath Tarzan's tree.

"It is as good as any," replied one of his companions. "If they catch us with the treasure aboard it will all be confiscated anyway. We might as well bury it here on the chance that some of us will escape the gallows to come back and enjoy it later."

The rat-faced one now called to the men who had remained at the boat, and they came slowly up the bank carrying picks and shovels.

"Hurry, ——you!" cried Snipes.

"Stow it!" retorted one of the men, in a surly tone. "You're no admiral, you —— —— shrimp."

"I'm Cap'n here, though, I'll have you to understand, you swab," shrieked Snipes, with a volley of frightful oaths.

"Steady, boys," cautioned one of the men who had not spoken before. "It ain't goin' to get us nothing by fightin' amongst ourselves."

"Right enough," replied the sailor who had resented Snipes' autocratic tones; "but by the same token it ain't a-goin' to get nobody nothin' to put on airs in this bloomin' company neither."

"You fellows dig here," said Snipes, indicating a spot beneath the tree. "And while you're diggin', Peter kin be a-makin' of a map of the location, so's we kin find it again. You, Tom, and Bill, take a couple more down and fetch up the chest."

"Wot are you a-goin' to do?" asked he of the previous altercation. "Just boss?"

"Git busy there," growled Snipes. "You didn't think your Cap'n was a-goin' to dig with a shovel, did you?"

The men all looked up angrily. None of them liked Snipes, and his disagreeable show of authority since he had murdered King, the real head and ringleader of the mutineers, had only added fuel to the flames of their hatred.

"Do you mean to say that you don't intend to take a shovel, and lend a hand with this work? Your shoulder's not hurted so all-fired bad as that," said Tarrant, the sailor who had before spoken.

"Not by a —— sight," replied Snipes, fingering the butt of his revolver nervously.

"Then, by God," replied Tarrant, "if you won't take a shovel you'll take a pick ax."

With the words he raised his pick above his head, and, with a mighty blow, buried the point in Snipes' brain.

For a moment the men stood silently looking at the result of their fellow's grim humor. Then one of them spoke.

"Served the skunk jolly well right," he said.

One of the others commenced to ply his pick to the ground. The soil was soft and he threw aside the pick and grasped a shovel; then the others joined him. There was no further comment on the killing, but the men worked in a better frame of mind than they had since Snipes had assumed command.

When they had a trench of ample size to bury the chest, Tarrant suggested that they enlarge it and inter Snipes' body on top of the chest.

"It might 'elp fool any as 'appened to be diggin' 'ereabouts," he explained.

The others saw the cunning of the suggestion, and so the trench was lengthened to accommodate the corpse, and in the center a deeper hole was excavated for the box, which was first wrapped in sail cloth and then lowered to its place, which brought its top about a foot below the bottom of the grave. Earth was shovelled in and tramped down about the chest until the bottom of the grave showed level and uniform.

Two of the men rolled the rat-faced corpse unceremoniously into the grave, after first stripping it of its weapons and various other articles which the several members of the party coveted for their own.

They then filled the grave with earth and tramped upon it until it would hold no more.

The balance of the loose earth was thrown far and wide, and a mass of dead undergrowth spread in as natural a manner as possible over the new made grave to obliterate all signs of the ground having been disturbed.

Their work done the sailors returned to the small boat, and pulled off rapidly toward the *Arrow*.

The breeze had increased considerably, and as the smoke upon the horizon was now plainly discernible in considerable volume, the mutineers lost no time in getting under full sail and bearing away toward the southwest.

Tarzan, an interested spectator of all that had taken place, sat speculating on the strange actions of these peculiar creatures.

Men were indeed more foolish and more cruel than the beasts of the jungle! How fortunate was he who lived in the peace and security of the great forest!

Tarzan wondered what the chest they had buried contained. If they did not want it why did they not merely throw it into the water? That would have been much easier.

Ah, he thought, but they do want it. They have hidden it here because they intend returning for it later.

Tarzan dropped to the ground and commenced to examine the earth about the excavation. He was looking to see if these creatures had dropped anything which he might like to own. Soon he discovered a spade hidden by the underbrush which they had laid upon the grave.

He seized it and attempted to use it as he had seen the sailors do. It was awkward work and hurt his bare feet, but he persevered until he had partially uncovered the body. This he dragged from the grave and laid to one side.

Then he continued digging until he had unearthed the chest. This also he dragged to the side of the corpse. Then he filled in the smaller hole below the grave, replaced the body and the earth around and above it; covered it over with underbrush and returned to the chest.

Four sailors had sweated beneath the burden of its weight—Tarzan of the Apes picked it up as though it had been an empty packing case, and with the spade slung to his back by a piece of rope, carried it off into the densest part of the jungle.

He could not well negotiate the trees with this awkward burden, but he kept to the trails, and so made fairly good time.

For several hours he traveled a little north of east until he came to an impenetrable wall of matted and tangled vegetation. Then he took to the lower branches, and in another fifteen minutes he emerged into the amphitheater of the apes, where they met in council, or to celebrate the rites of the Dum-Dum.

Near the center of the clearing, and not far from the drum, or altar, he commenced to dig. This was harder work than turning up the freshly excavated earth at the grave, but Tarzan of the Apes was persevering and so he kept at his labor until he was rewarded by seeing a hole sufficiently deep to receive the chest and effectually hide it from view.

Why had he gone to all this labor without knowing the value of the contents of the chest?

Tarzan of the Apes had a man's figure and a man's brain, but he was an ape by training and environment. His brain told him that the chest contained something valuable, or the men would not have hidden it; his training had taught him to imitate whatever was new and unusual, and now the natural curiosity, which is as common to men as to apes, prompted him to open the chest and examine its contents.

But the heavy lock and massive iron bands baffled both his cunning and his immense strength, so that he was compelled to bury the chest without having his curiosity satisfied.

By the time Tarzan had hunted his way back to the vicinity of the cabin, feeding as he went, it was quite dark.

Within the little building a light was burning, for Clayton had found an unopened tin of oil which had stood intact for twenty years; a part of the supplies left with the Claytons by Black Michael.

The lamps also were still useable, and thus the interior of the cabin appeared as bright as day to the astonished Tarzan.

He had often wondered at the exact purpose of the lamps. His reading and the pictures had told him what they were, but he had no idea of how they could be made to produce the wondrous sunlight that some of his pictures had portrayed them as diffusing upon all surrounding objects.

As he approached the window nearest the door he saw that the cabin had been divided into two rooms by a rough partition of boughs and sailcloth.

In the front room were the three men; the two older deep in argument, while the younger, tilted back against the wall on an improvised stool, was deeply engrossed in reading one of Tarzan's books.

Tarzan was not particularly interested in the men, however, so he sought the other window. There was the girl. How beautiful her features! How delicate her snowy skin!

She was writing at Tarzan's own table beneath the window. Upon a pile of grasses at the far side of the room lay the negress, asleep.

For an hour Tarzan feasted his eyes upon her while she wrote. How he longed to speak to her, but he dared not attempt it, for he was convinced that, like the young men, she would not understand him, and he feared, too, that he might frighten her away.

At length she arose, leaving her manuscript upon the table. She went to the bed upon which had been spread several layers of soft grasses. These she rearranged.

Then she loosened the soft mass of golden hair which crowned her head. Like a shimmering waterfall turned to burnished metal by a dying sun it fell about her oval face; in waving lines, below her waist it tumbled.

Tarzan was spellbound. Then she extinguished the lamp and all within the cabin was wrapped in Cimmerian darkness.*

Still Tarzan watched without. Creeping close beneath the window he waited, listening, for half an hour. At last he was rewarded by the sounds of the regular breathing within which denotes sleep.

Cautiously he intruded his hand between the meshes of the lattice until his whole arm was within the cabin. Carefully he felt upon the desk. At last he grasped the manuscript upon which Jane Porter had been writing, and as cautiously withdrew his arm and hand, holding the precious treasure.

Tarzan folded the sheets into a small parcel which he tucked into the quiver with his arrows. Then he melted away into the jungle as softly and as noiselessly as a shadow.

CHAPTER XVIII

THE JUNGLE TOLL

EARLY the following morning Tarzan awoke, and the first thought of the new day, as the last of yesterday, was of the wonderful writing which lay hidden in his quiver.

Hurriedly he brought it forth, hoping against hope that he could read what the beautiful white girl had written there the preceding evening.

At the first glance he suffered the bitterest disappointment of his whole life; never before had he so yearned for anything as now he did for the ability to interpret a message from that golden-haired divinity who had come so suddenly and so unexpectedly into his life.

What if the message were not intended for him? It was an expression of her thoughts, and that was all sufficient for Tarzan of the Apes.

And now to be baffled by strange, uncouth characters the like of which he had never seen before! Why, they even tipped in the opposite direction from all that he had ever examined either in printed books or the difficult script of the few letters he had found.

Even the little bugs of the black book were familiar friends, though their arrangement meant nothing to him; but these bugs were new and unheard of.

For twenty minutes he poured over them, when suddenly they commenced to take familiar though distorted shapes. Ah, they were his old friends, but badly crippled.

Then he began to make out a word here and a word there. His heart leaped for joy. He could read it, and he would.

In another half hour he was progressing rapidly, and, but for an exceptional word now and again, he found it very plain sailing.

Here is what he read:

> WEST COAST OF AFRICA, ABOUT 10° DEGREES SOUTH
> LATITUDE.* (So Mr. Clayton says.)
>
> *February 3(?), 1909.*

DEAREST HAZEL:

It seems foolish to write you a letter that you may never see, but I simply must tell somebody of our awful experiences since we sailed from Europe on the ill-fated *Arrow*.

If we never return to civilization, as now seems only too likely, this will at least prove a brief record of the events which led up to our final fate, whatever it may be.

As you know, we were supposed to have set out upon a scientific expedition to the Congo. Papa was presumed to entertain some wondrous theory of an unthinkably ancient civilization, the remains of which lay buried somewhere in the Congo valley. But after we were well under sail the truth came out.

It seems that an old bookworm who has a book and curio shop in Baltimore discovered between the leaves of a very old Spanish manuscript a letter written in 1550 detailing the adventures of a crew of mutineers of a Spanish galleon bound from Spain to South America with a vast treasure of "doubloons" and "pieces of eight,"* I suppose, for they certainly sound weird and piraty.

The writer had been one of the crew, and the letter was to his son, who was, at the very time the letter was written, master of a Spanish merchantman.

Many years had elapsed since the events the letter narrated had transpired, and the old man had become a respected citizen of an obscure Spanish town, but the love of gold was still so strong upon him that he risked all to acquaint his son with the means of attaining fabulous wealth for them both.

The writer told how when but a week out from Spain the crew had mutinied and murdered every officer and man who opposed them; but they defeated their own ends by this very act, for there was none left competent to navigate a ship at sea.

They were blown hither and thither for two months, until sick and dying of scurvy, starvation, and thirst, they had been wrecked on a small islet.

The galleon was washed high upon the beach where she went to pieces; but not before the survivors, who numbered but ten souls, had rescued one of the great chests of treasure.

This they buried well up on the island, and for three years they lived there in constant hope of being rescued.

One by one they sickened and died, until only one man was left, the writer of the letter.

The men had built a boat from the wreckage of the galleon, but having no idea where the island was located they had not dared to put to sea.

When all were dead except himself, however, the awful loneliness so weighed upon the mind of the sole survivor that he could endure it no longer, and choosing to risk death upon the open sea rather than madness on the lonely isle, he set sail in his little boat after nearly a year of solitude.

Fortunately he sailed due north, and within a week was in the track of the Spanish merchantmen plying between the West Indies and Spain, and was picked up by one of these vessels homeward bound.

The story he told was merely one of shipwreck in which all but a few had perished, the balance, except himself, dying after they reached the island. He did not mention the mutiny or the chest of buried treasure.

The master of the merchantman assured him that from the position at which they had picked him up, and the prevailing winds for the past week he could have been on no other island than one of the Cape Verde* group, which lie off the West Coast of Africa in about 16° or 17° north latitude.

His letter described the island minutely, as well as the location of the treasure, and was accompanied by the crudest, funniest little old map you ever saw; with trees and rocks all marked by scrawly X's to show the exact spot where the treasure had been buried.

When papa explained the real nature of the expedition, my heart sank, for I know so well how visionary and impractical the poor dear has always been that I feared he had again been duped; especially when he told me he had paid a thousand dollars for the letter and map.

To add to my distress, I learned that he had borrowed ten thousand dollars more from Robert Canler, and had given his notes for the amount.

Mr. Canler had asked for no security, and you know, dearie, what that will mean for me if papa cannot meet them. Oh, how I detest that man!

We all tried to look on the bright side of things, but Mr. Philander, and Mr. Clayton—he joined us in London just for the adventure—both felt as skeptical as I.

Well, to make a long story short, we found the island and the treasure— a great iron bound oak chest, wrapped in many layers of oiled sail cloth, and as strong and firm as when it had been buried nearly two hundred years ago.

It was *simply filled* with gold coin, and was so heavy that four men bent beneath its weight.

The horrid thing seems to bring nothing but murder and misfortune to those who have to do with it, for three days after we sailed from the Cape Verde Islands our own crew mutinied and killed every one of their officers.

Oh, it was the most terrifying experience one could imagine—I cannot even write of it.

They were going to kill us too, but one of them, the leader, a man named King, would not let them, and so they sailed south along the coast to a lonely spot where they found a good harbor, and here they landed and have left us.

They sailed away with the treasure today, but Mr. Clayton says they will meet with a fate similar to the mutineers of the ancient galleon, because King, the only man aboard who knew aught of navigation, was murdered on the beach by one of the men the day we landed.

I wish you could know Mr. Clayton; he is the dearest fellow imaginable, and unless I am mistaken he has fallen very much in love with poor little me.

He is the only son of Lord Greystoke, and some day will inherit the title and estates. In addition, he is wealthy in his own right, but the fact that he is going to be an English Lord makes me very sad—you know what my sentiments have always been relative to American girls who married titled foreigners.* Oh, if he were only a plain American gentleman!

But it isn't his fault, poor fellow, and in everything except birth he would do credit to my darling old country, and that is the greatest compliment I know how to pay any man.

We have had the most weird experiences since we were landed here. Papa and Mr. Philander lost in the jungle, and chased by a real lion.

Mr. Clayton lost, and attacked twice by wild beasts. Esmeralda and I cornered in an old cabin by a perfectly awful man-eating lioness. Oh, it was simply "terrifical," as Esmeralda would say.

But the strangest part of it all is the wonderful creature who rescued us. I have not seen him, but Mr. Clayton and papa and Mr. Philander have, and they say that he is a perfectly god-like white man tanned to a dusky brown; with the strength of a wild elephant, the agility of a monkey, and the bravery of a lion.

He speaks no English and vanishes as quickly and as mysteriously after he has performed some valorous deed, as though he were a disembodied spirit.

Then we have another weird neighbor, who printed a beautiful sign in English and tacked it on the door of his cabin, which we have preempted, warning us to destroy none of his belongings, and signing himself "Tarzan of the Apes."

We have never seen him, though we think he is about, for one of the sailors, who was going to shoot Mr. Clayton in the back, received a spear in his shoulder from some unseen hand in the jungle.

The sailors left us but a meagre supply of food, so, as we have only a single revolver with but three cartridges left in it, we do not know how we can procure meat, though Mr. Philander says that we can exist indefinitely on the wild fruit and nuts which abound in the jungle.

I am very tired now, so I shall go to my funny bed of grasses which Mr. Clayton gathered for me, but will add to this from day to day as things happen.

Lovingly,
JANE PORTER.

TO HAZEL STRONG,* BALTIMORE, MD.

Tarzan sat in a brown study* for a long time after he finished reading the letter. It was filled with so many new and wonderful things that his brain was in a whirl as he attempted to digest them all.

So they did not know that he was Tarzan of the Apes. He would tell them.

In his tree he had constructed a rude shelter of leaves and boughs, beneath which, protected from the rain, he had placed the few treasures brought from the cabin. Among these were some pencils.

He took one, and beneath Jane Porter's signature he wrote:

I am Tarzan of the Apes.

He thought that would be sufficient. Later he would return the letter to the cabin.

In the matter of food, thought Tarzan, they had no need to worry—he would provide, and he did.

The next morning Jane Porter found her missing letter in the exact spot from which it had disappeared two nights before. She was mystified; but when she saw the printed words beneath her signature, she felt a cold, clammy chill run up her spine. She showed the letter, or rather the last sheet with the signature, to Clayton.

"And to think," she said, "that uncanny thing was probably watching me all the time that I was writing—oo! It makes me shudder just to think of it."

"But he must be friendly," reassured Clayton, "for he has returned your letter, nor did he offer to harm you, and unless I am mistaken he left a very substantial memento of his friendship outside the cabin door last night, for I just found the carcass of a wild boar there as I came out."

From then on scarcely a day passed that did not bring its offering of game or other food. Sometimes it was a young deer, again a quantity of strange, cooked food—cassava cakes pilfered from the village of Mbonga—or a boar, or leopard, and once a lion.

Tarzan derived the greatest pleasure of his life in hunting meat for these strangers. It seemed to him that no pleasure on earth could compare with laboring for the welfare and protection of the beautiful white girl.

Some day he would venture into the camp in daylight and talk with these people through the medium of the little bugs which were familiar to them and to Tarzan.

But he found it difficult to overcome the timidity of the wild thing of the forest, and so day followed day without seeing a fulfillment of his good intentions.

The party in the camp, emboldened by familiarity, wandered further and yet further into the jungle in search of nuts and fruit.

Scarcely a day passed that did not find Professor Porter straying in his preoccupied indifference toward the jaws of death. Mr. Samuel T. Philander, never what one might call robust, was worn to the shadow of a shadow through the ceaseless worry and mental distraction resultant from his Herculean efforts* to safeguard the professor.

A month passed. Tarzan had finally determined to visit the camp by daylight.

It was early afternoon. Clayton had wandered to the point at the harbor's mouth to look for passing vessels. Here he kept a great mass of wood, high piled, ready to be ignited as a signal should a steamer or a sail top the far horizon.

Professor Porter was wandering along the beach south of the camp with Mr. Philander at his elbow, urging him to turn his steps back before the two became again the sport of some savage beast.

The others gone, Jane Porter and Esmeralda had wandered into the jungle to gather fruit, and in their search were led further and further from the cabin.

Tarzan waited in silence before the door of the little house until they should return. His thoughts were of the beautiful white girl. They were always of her now. He wondered if she would fear him, and the thought all but caused him to relinquish his plan.

He was rapidly becoming impatient for her return, that he might feast his eyes upon her and be near her, perhaps touch her. The ape-man knew no god, but he was as near to worshipping his divinity as mortal man ever comes to worship.

While he waited he passed the time printing a message to her; whether he intended giving it to her he himself could not have told, but he took infinite pleasure in seeing his thoughts expressed in print—in which he was not so uncivilized after all. He wrote:

I am Tarzan of the Apes. I want you. I am yours. You are mine. We will live here together always in my house. I will bring you the best fruits, the tenderest deer, the finest meats that roam the jungle. I will hunt for you. I am the greatest of the jungle hunters. I will fight for you. I am the mightiest of the jungle fighters. You are Jane Porter, I saw it in your letter. When you see this you will know that it is for you and that Tarzan of the Apes loves you.

As he stood, straight as a young Indian, by the door, waiting after he had finished the message, there came to his keen ears a familiar sound. It was the passing of a great ape through the lower branches of the forest.

For an instant he listened intently, and then from the jungle came the agonized scream of a woman, and Tarzan of the Apes, dropping his first love letter upon the ground, shot like a panther into the forest.

Clayton, also, heard the scream, and Professor Porter and Mr. Philander, and in a few minutes they came panting to the cabin, calling out to each other a volley of excited questions as they approached. A glance within confirmed their worst fears.

Jane Porter and Esmeralda were not there.

Instantly, Clayton, followed by the two old men, plunged into the jungle, calling the girl's name aloud. For half an hour they stumbled on, until Clayton, by merest chance, came upon the prostrate form of Esmeralda.

He stooped beside her, feeling for her pulse and then listening for her heart beats. She lived. He shook her.

"Esmeralda!" he shrieked in her ear. "Esmeralda! For God's sake, where is Miss Porter? What has happened? Esmeralda!"

Slowly the black opened her eyes. She saw Clayton. She saw the jungle about her.

"Oh, Gaberelle!" she screamed, and fainted again.

By this time Professor Porter and Mr. Philander had come up.

"What shall we do, Mr. Clayton?" asked the old professor. "Where shall we look? God could not have been so cruel as to take my little girl away from me now."

"We must arouse Esmeralda first," replied Clayton. "She can tell us what has happened. Esmeralda!" he cried again, shaking the black woman roughly by the shoulder.

"O Gaberelle, Ah wants to die!" cried the poor woman, but with eyes fast closed. "Lemme die, deah Lawd, but doan lemme see dat awrful face again. Whafer yo' sen de devil 'roun' after po ole Esmeralda? She ain't done nuffin' to nobody, Lawd, hones' she ain't. She's puffickly indecent, Lawd; yas'm, deed she is."

"Come, come, Esmeralda," cried Clayton.

"The Lord isn't here; it's Mr. Clayton. Open your eyes."

Esmeralda did as she was bade.

"O Gaberelle! T'ank de Lawd," she said.

"Where's Miss Porter? What happened?" questioned Clayton.

"Ain' Miss Jane here?" cried Esmeralda, sitting up with wonderful celerity for one of her bulk. "Oh, Lawd, now Ah 'members! It done must have tooked her away," and the negress commenced to sob, and wail her lamentations.

"What took her away?" cried Professor Porter.

"A great big gi'nt all covered with hair."

"A gorilla, Esmeralda?" questioned Mr. Philander, and the three men scarcely breathed as he voiced the horrible thought.

"Ah done thought it was de devil, but Ah guess it mus' a-been one of dem gorilephants. Oh, my po baby, my po li'l honey," and again Esmeralda broke into uncontrollable sobbing.

Clayton immediately began to look about for tracks, but he could find nothing save a confusion of trampled grasses in the close vicinity, and his woodcraft was too meagre for the translation of what he did see.

All the balance of the day they sought through the jungle; but as night drew on they were forced to give up in despair and hopelessness, for they did not even know in what direction the thing had borne Jane Porter.

It was long after dark ere they reached the cabin, and a sad and grief-stricken party it was that sat silently within the little structure.

Professor Porter finally broke the silence. His tones were no longer those of the erudite pedant theorizing upon the abstract and the unknowable; but those of the man of action—determined, but tinged also by a note of indescribable hopelessness and grief which wrung an answering pang from Clayton's heart.

"I shall lie down now," said the old man, "and try to sleep. Early tomorrow, so soon as it is light, I shall take what food I can carry and continue the search until I have found Jane. I will not return without her."

His companions did not reply at once. Each was immersed in his own sorrowful thoughts, and each knew, as did the old professor, what the last words meant—Professor Porter would never return from the jungle.

At length Clayton arose and laid his hand gently upon Professor Porter's bent old shoulder.

"I shall go with you, of course," he said. "Do not tell me that I need even have said so."

"I knew that you would offer—that you would wish to go, Mr. Clayton; but you must not. Jane is beyond human assistance now. I simply go that I may face my Maker with her, and know, too, that what was once my dear little girl lies not alone and friendless in the awful jungle.

"The same vines and leaves will cover us, the same rains beat upon us; and when the spirit of her mother is abroad, it will find us together in death, as it has always found us in life.

"No; it is I alone who may go, for she was my daughter—all that was left on earth for me to love."

"I shall go with you," said Clayton simply.

The old man looked up, regarding the strong, handsome face of William Cecil Clayton intently. Perhaps he read there the love that lay in the heart beneath—the love for his daughter.

He had been too preoccupied with his own scholarly thoughts in the past to consider the little occurrences, the chance words, which would have indicated to a more practical man that these young people were being drawn more and more closely to one another. Now they came back to him, one by one.

"As you wish," he said.

"You may count on me, also," said Mr. Philander.

"No, my dear old friend," said Professor Porter. "We may not all go. It would be cruelly wicked to leave poor Esmeralda here alone, and three of us would be no more successful than one.

"There be enough dead things in the cruel forest as it is. Come—let us try to sleep a little."

CHAPTER XIX

THE CALL OF THE PRIMITIVE

FROM the time Tarzan left the tribe of great anthropoids in which he had been raised, it was torn by continual strife and discord. Terkoz proved a cruel and capricious king, so that, one by one, many of the older and weaker apes, upon whom he was particularly prone to vent his brutish nature, took their families and sought the quiet and safety of the far interior.

But at last those who remained were driven to desperation by the continued truculence of Terkoz, and it so happened that one of them recalled the parting admonition of Tarzan:

"If you have a chief who is cruel, do not do as the other apes do, and attempt, any one of you, to pit yourself against him alone. But, instead, let two or three or four of you attack him together. Then, if you will do this, no chief will dare to be other than he should be, for four of you can kill any chief who may ever be over you."*

And the ape who recalled this wise counsel repeated it to several of his fellows, so that when Terkoz returned to the tribe that day he found a warm reception awaiting him.

There were no formalities. As Terkoz reached the group, five huge, hairy beasts sprang upon him.

At heart he was an arrant coward, which is the way with bullies among apes as well as among men; so he did not remain to fight and die, but tore himself away from them as quickly as he could and fled into the sheltering boughs of the forest.

Two more attempts he made to rejoin the tribe, but on each occasion he was set upon and driven away. At last he gave it up, and turned, foaming with rage and hatred, into the jungle.

For several days he wandered aimlessly, nursing his spite and looking for some weak thing on which to vent his pent anger.

It was in this state of mind that the horrible, man-like beast, swinging from tree to tree, came suddenly upon two women in the jungle.

He was right above them when he discovered them. The first intimation Jane Porter had of his presence was when the great hairy body dropped to the earth beside her, and she saw the awful face and the snarling, hideous mouth thrust within a foot of her.

One piercing scream escaped her lips as the brute hand clutched her arm. Then she was dragged toward those awful fangs which yawned at her throat. But ere they touched that fair skin another mood claimed the anthropoid.

The tribe had kept his women. He must find others to replace them. This hairless white ape would be the first of his new household, and so he threw her roughly across his broad, hairy shoulders and leaped back into the trees, bearing Jane Porter away toward a fate a thousand times worse than death.

Esmeralda's scream of terror had mingled once with that of Jane Porter, and then, as was Esmeralda's manner under stress of emergency which required presence of mind, she swooned.

But Jane Porter did not once lose consciousness. It is true that that awful face, pressing close to hers, and the stench of the foul breath beating upon her nostrils, paralyzed her with terror; but her brain was clear, and she comprehended all that transpired.

With what seemed to her marvelous rapidity the brute bore her through the forest, but still she did not cry out or struggle. The sudden advent of the ape had confused her to such an extent that she thought now that he was bearing her toward the beach.

For this reason she conserved her energies and her voice until she could see that they had approached near enough to the camp to attract the succor she craved.

Poor child! Could she but have known it, she was being borne farther and farther into the impenetrable jungle.

The scream that had brought Clayton and the two older men stumbling through the undergrowth had led Tarzan of the Apes straight to where Esmeralda lay, but it was not Esmeralda in whom his interest centered, though pausing over her he saw that she was unhurt.

For a moment he scrutinized the ground below and the trees above, until the ape that was in him by virtue of training and environment, combined with the intelligence that was his by right of birth, told his wondrous woodcraft the whole story as plainly as though he had seen the thing happen with his own eyes.

And then he was gone again into the swaying trees, following the high-flung spoor which no other human eye could have detected, much less translated.

At boughs' ends, where the anthropoid swings from one tree to another, there is most to mark the trail, but least to point the direction of the quarry, for there the pressure is downward always, toward the small end of the branch, whether the ape be leaving or entering a tree; but nearer the center of the tree, where the signs of passage are fainter, the direction is plainly marked.

Here, on this branch, a caterpillar has been crushed by the fugitive's great foot, and Tarzan knows instinctively where that same foot would touch in the next stride. Here he looks to find a tiny particle of the demolished larva, oft-times not more than a speck of moisture.

Again, a minute bit of bark has been upturned by the scraping hand, and the direction of the break indicates the direction of the passage. Or some great limb, or the stem of the tree itself has been brushed by the hairy body, and a tiny shred of hair tells him by the direction from which it is wedged beneath the bark that he is on the right trail.

Nor does he need to check his speed to catch these seemingly faint records of the fleeing beast.

To Tarzan they stand out boldly against all the myriad other scars and bruises and signs upon the leafy way. But strongest of all is the scent, for Tarzan is pursuing up the wind, and his trained nostrils are as sensitive as a hound's.

There are those who believe that the lower orders are specially endowed by nature with better olfactory nerves than man, but it is merely a matter of development.

Man's survival does not hinge so greatly upon the perfection of his senses. His power to reason has relieved them of many of their duties, and so they have, to some extent, atrophied, as have the muscles which move the ears and scalp, merely from disuse.

The muscles are there, about your ears and beneath your scalp, and so are the nerves which transmit sensations to your brain, but they are under-developed in you because you do not need them.

Not so with Tarzan of the Apes. From early infancy his survival had depended upon acuteness of eyesight, hearing, smell, touch, and taste far more than upon the more slowly developed organ of reason.

The least developed of all, in Tarzan, was the sense of taste, for he could eat luscious fruits, or raw flesh, long buried, with almost equal appreciation; but in that he differed but slightly from more civilized epicures.

Almost silently the ape-man sped on in the track of Terkoz and his prey, but the sound of his approach reached the ears of the fleeing beast and spurred it on to greater speed.

Three miles were covered before Tarzan overtook them, and then Terkoz, seeing that further flight was futile, dropped to the ground in a small open glade, that he might turn and fight for his prize, or be free to escape unhampered if he saw that the pursuer was more than a match for him.

He still grasped Jane Porter in one great arm as Tarzan bounded like a leopard into the arena which nature had provided for this primeval-like battle.

When Terkoz saw that it was Tarzan who pursued him, he jumped to the conclusion that this was Tarzan's woman, since they were of the same kind—white and hairless—and so he rejoiced at this opportunity for double revenge upon his hated enemy.

To Jane Porter the strange apparition of this god-like man was as wine to sick nerves.

From the description which Clayton and her father and Mr. Philander had given her, she knew that it must be the same wonderful creature who had saved them, and she saw in him only a protector and a friend.

But as Terkoz pushed her roughly aside to meet Tarzan's charge, and she saw the great proportions of the ape and the mighty muscles and the fierce fangs, her heart quailed. How could any animal vanquish such a mighty antagonist?

Like two charging bulls they came together, and like two wolves sought each other's throat. Against the long canines of the ape was pitted the thin blade of the man's knife.

Jane Porter—her lithe, young form flattened against the trunk of a great tree, her hands tight pressed against her rising and falling bosom, and her eyes wide with mingled horror, fascination, fear, and admiration—watched the primordial ape battle with the primeval man for possession of a woman—for her.

As the great muscles of the man's back and shoulders knotted beneath the tension of his efforts, and the huge biceps and forearm held at bay those mighty tusks, the veil of centuries of civilization and culture was swept from the blurred vision of the Baltimore girl.

When the long knife drank deep a dozen times of Terkoz' heart's blood, and the great carcass rolled lifeless upon the ground, it was a primeval woman who sprang forward with outstretched arms toward the primeval man who had fought for her and won her.

And Tarzan?

He did what no red-blooded man needs lessons in doing. He took his woman in his arms and smothered her upturned, panting lips with kisses.

For a moment Jane Porter lay there with half-closed eyes. For a moment—the first in her young life—she knew the meaning of love.

But as suddenly as the veil had been withdrawn it dropped again, and an outraged conscience suffused her face with its scarlet mantle, and a mortified woman thrust Tarzan of the Apes from her and buried her face in her hands.

Tarzan had been surprised when he had found the girl he had learned to love after a vague and abstract manner a willing prisoner in his arms. Now he was surprised that she repulsed him.

He came close to her once more and took hold of her arm. She turned upon him like a tigress,* striking his great breast with her tiny hands.

Tarzan could not understand it.

A moment ago and it had been his intention to hasten Jane Porter back to her people, but that little moment was lost now in the dim and distant past of things which were but can never be again, and with it the good intention had gone to join the impossible.

Since then Tarzan of the Apes had felt a warm, lithe form close pressed to his. Hot, sweet breath against his cheek and mouth had fanned a new flame to life within his breast, and perfect lips had clung to his in burning kisses that had seared a deep brand into his soul—a brand which marked a new Tarzan.

Again he laid his hand upon her arm. Again she repulsed him. And then Tarzan of the Apes did just what his first ancestor would have done.

He took his woman in his arms and carried her into the jungle.

Early the following morning the four within the little cabin by the beach were awakened by the booming of a cannon. Clayton was the first to rush out, and there, beyond the harbor's mouth, he saw two vessels lying at anchor.

One was the *Arrow* and the other a small French cruiser. The sides of the latter were crowded with men gazing shoreward, and it was evident to Clayton, as to the others who had now joined him, that the gun which they had heard had been fired to attract their attention if they still remained at the cabin.

Both vessels lay at a considerable distance from shore, and it was doubtful if their glasses would locate the waving hats of the little party far in between the harbor's points.

Esmeralda had removed her red apron and was waving it frantically above her head; but Clayton, still fearing that even this might not be seen, hurried off toward the northern point where lay his signal pyre ready for the match.

It seemed an age to him, as to those who waited breathlessly behind, ere he reached the great pile of dry branches and underbrush.

As he broke from the dense wood and came in sight of the vessels again, he was filled with consternation to see that the *Arrow* was making sail and that the cruiser was already under way.

Quickly lighting the pyre in a dozen places, he hurried to the extreme point of the promontory, where he stripped off his shirt, and, tying it to a fallen branch, stood waving it back and forth above him.

But still the vessels continued to stand out; and he had given up all hope, when the great column of smoke, arising above the forest in one dense vertical shaft, attracted the attention of a lookout aboard the cruiser, and instantly a dozen glasses were leveled on the beach.

Presently Clayton saw the two ships come about again; and while the *Arrow* lay drifting quietly on the ocean, the cruiser steamed slowly back toward shore.

At some distance away she stopped, and a boat was lowered and dispatched toward the beach.

As it was drawn up a young officer stepped out.

"Monsieur Clayton, I presume?"* he asked.

"Thank God, you have come!" was Clayton's reply. "And it may be that it is not too late even now."

"What do you mean, Monsieur?" asked the officer.

Clayton told of the abduction of Jane Porter and the need of armed men to aid in the search for her.

"*Mon Dieu!*"* exclaimed the officer, sadly. "Yesterday and it would not have been too late. Today and it may be better that the poor lady were never found. It is horrible, Monsieur. It is too horrible."

Other boats had now put off from the cruiser, and Clayton, having pointed out the harbor's entrance to the officer, entered the boat with him and its nose was turned toward the little land-locked bay, into which the other craft followed.

Soon the entire party had landed where stood Professor Porter, Mr. Philander and the weeping Esmeralda.

Among the officers in the last boats to put off from the cruiser was the commander of the vessel; and when he had heard the story of Jane Porter's abduction, he generously called for volunteers to accompany Professor Porter and Clayton in their search.

Not an officer or a man was there of those brave and sympathetic Frenchmen who did not quickly beg leave to be one of the expedition.

The commander selected twenty men and two officers, Lieutenant d'Arnot and Lieutenant Charpentier. A boat was dispatched to the cruiser for provisions, ammunition, and carbines; the men were already armed with revolvers.

Then, to Clayton's inquiries as to how they had happened to anchor off shore and fire a signal gun, the commander, Captain Dufranne, explained that a month before they had sighted the *Arrow* bearing southwest under considerable canvas, and that when they had signaled her to come about she had but crowded on more sail.

They had kept her hull-up until sunset, firing several shots after her, but the next morning she was nowhere to be seen. They had then continued to cruise up and down the coast for several weeks, and had about forgotten the incident of the recent chase, when, early one morning a few days before, the lookout had descried a vessel laboring in the trough of a heavy sea and evidently entirely from under control.

As they steamed nearer to the derelict they were surprised to note that it was the same vessel that had run from them a few weeks earlier. Her fore-stay-sail and mizzen-spanker* were set as though an effort had been made to hold her head up into the wind, but the sheets had parted, and the sails were tearing to ribbons in the half gale of wind.

In the high sea that was running it was a difficult and dangerous task to attempt to put a prize crew aboard her; and as no signs of life had been seen above deck, it was decided to stand by until the wind and sea abated; but just then a figure was seen clinging to the rail and feebly waving a mute signal of despair toward them.

Immediately a boat's crew was ordered out and an attempt was successfully made to board the *Arrow*. The sight that met the Frenchmen's eyes as they clambered over the ship's side was appalling.

A dozen dead and dying men rolled hither and thither upon the pitching deck, the living intermingled with the dead. Two of the corpses appeared to have been partially devoured as though by wolves.

The prize crew soon had the vessel under proper sail once more and the living members of the ill-starred company carried below to their hammocks.

The dead were wrapped in tarpaulins and lashed on deck to be identified by their comrades before being consigned to the deep.

None of the living was conscious when the Frenchmen reached the *Arrow*'s deck. Even the poor devil who had waved the single despairing signal of distress had lapsed into unconsciousness before he had learned whether it had availed or not.

It did not take the French officer long to learn what had caused the terrible condition aboard; for when water and brandy were sought to restore the men, it was found that not only was there not any of either, but not a vestige of food of any description.

He immediately signalled to the cruiser to send water, medicine, and provisions, and another boat made the perilous trip to the *Arrow*.

When restoratives had been applied several of the men regained consciousness, and then the whole story was told. That part of it we know up to the sailing of the *Arrow* after the murder of Snipes, and the burial of his body above the treasure-chest.

It seems that the pursuit by the cruiser had so terrorized the mutineers that they had continued out across the Atlantic for several days after losing her; but on discovering the meagre supply of water and provisions aboard, they had turned back toward the east.

With no one on board who understood navigation, discussions soon arose as to their whereabouts; and as three days' sailing to the east did not raise land, they bore off to the north, fearing that the high north winds that had prevailed had driven them south of the southern extremity of Africa.

They kept on a north-northeasterly course for two days, when they were overtaken by a calm which lasted for nearly a week. Their water was gone, and in another day they would be without food.

Conditions changed rapidly from bad to worse. One man went mad and leaped overboard. Soon another opened his veins and drank his own blood.*

When he died they threw him overboard also, though there were those among them who wanted to keep the corpse on board. Hunger was changing them from human beasts to wild beasts.

Two days before they had been picked up by the cruiser they had become too weak to handle the vessel, and that same day three men died. On the following morning it was seen that one of the corpses had been partially devoured.

All that day the men lay glaring at each other like beasts of prey, and the following morning two of the corpses lay almost entirely stripped of flesh.

The men were but little stronger for their ghoulish repast, for the want of water was by far the greatest agony with which they had to contend. And then the cruiser had come.

When those who could had recovered, the entire story had been told to the French commander, but the men were too ignorant to be able to tell him at just what point on the coast the professor and his party had been marooned, so the cruiser had steamed slowly along within sight of land, firing occasional signal guns and scanning every inch of the beach with glasses.*

They had anchored by night so as not to neglect a particle of the shore line, and it had happened that the preceding night had brought them off the very beach where lay the little camp they sought.

The signal guns of the afternoon before had not been heard by those on shore, it was presumed, because they had doubtless been in the thick of the jungle searching for Jane Porter, where the noise of their own crashing through the underbrush would have drowned the report of a far distant gun.

By the time the two parties had narrated their several adventures, the cruiser's boat had returned with supplies and arms for the expedition.

Within a few minutes the little body of sailors and the two French officers, together with Professor Porter and Clayton, set off upon their hopeless and ill-fated quest into the untracked jungle.

CHAPTER XX

HEREDITY

WHEN Jane Porter realized that she was being borne away a captive by the strange forest creature who had rescued her from the clutches of the ape she struggled desperately to escape, but the strong arms, that held her as easily as though she had been but a day-old babe, only pressed a little more tightly.

So presently she gave up the futile effort and lay quietly, looking through half closed lids at the face of the man who strode easily through the tangled undergrowth with her.

The face above her was one of extraordinary beauty.

A perfect type of the strongly masculine, unmarred by dissipation, or brutal or degrading passions.* For, though Tarzan of the Apes was a killer of men and of beasts, he killed as the hunter kills, dispassionately, except on those rare occasions when he had killed for hate—though not the brooding, malevolent hate which marks the features of its own with hideous lines.

When Tarzan killed he more often smiled than scowled, and smiles are the foundation of beauty.

One thing the girl had noticed particularly when she had seen Tarzan rushing upon Terkoz—the vivid scarlet band upon his forehead, from above the left eye to the scalp; but now as she scanned his features she noticed that it was gone, and only a thin white line marked the spot where it had been.

As she lay more quietly in his arms Tarzan slightly relaxed his grip upon her.

Once he looked down into her eyes and smiled, and the girl had to close her own to shut out the vision of that handsome, winning face.

Presently Tarzan took to the trees, and Jane Porter, wondering that she felt no fear, began to realize that in many respects she had never felt more secure in her whole life than now as she lay in the arms of this strong, wild creature, being borne, God alone knew where or to what fate, deeper and deeper into the savage fastness of the untamed forest.

When, with closed eyes, she commenced to speculate upon the future, and terrifying fears were conjured by a vivid imagination, she had but to raise her lids and look upon that noble face so close to hers to dissipate the last remnant of apprehension.

No, he could never harm her; of that she was convinced when she translated the fine features and the frank, brave eyes above her into the chivalry which they proclaimed.

On and on they went through what seemed to Jane Porter a solid mass of verdure, yet ever there appeared to open before this forest god a passage, as by magic, which closed behind them as they passed.

Scarce a branch scraped against her, yet above and below, before and behind, the view presented naught but a solid mass of inextricably interwoven branches and creepers.

As Tarzan moved steadily onward his mind was occupied with many strange and new thoughts. Here was a problem the like of which he had never encountered, and he felt rather than reasoned that he must meet it as a man and not as an ape.

The free movement through the middle terrace, which was the route he had followed for the most part, had helped to cool the ardor of the first fierce passion of his new found love.

Now he discovered himself speculating upon the fate which would have fallen to the girl had he not rescued her from Terkoz.

He knew why the ape had not killed her, and he commenced to compare his intentions with those of Terkoz.

True, it was the order of the jungle for the male to take his mate by force; but could Tarzan be guided by the laws of the beasts? Was not Tarzan a Man? But how did men do? He was puzzled; for he did not know.

He wished that he might ask the girl, and then it came to him that she had already answered him in the futile struggle she had made to escape and to repulse him.

But now they had come to their destination, and Tarzan of the Apes with Jane Porter in his strong arms, swung lightly to the turf of the arena where the great apes held their councils and danced the wild orgy of the Dum-Dum.

Though they had come many miles, it was still but mid-afternoon, and the amphitheater was bathed in the half light which filtered through the maze of encircling foliage.

The green turf looked soft and cool and inviting. The myriad noises of the jungle seemed far distant and hushed to a mere echo of blurred sounds, rising and falling like the surf upon a remote shore.

A feeling of dreamy peacefulness stole over Jane Porter as she sank down upon the grass where Tarzan had placed her, and as she looked up at his great figure towering above her, there was added a strange sense of perfect security.

As she watched him from beneath half closed lids, Tarzan crossed the little circular clearing toward the trees upon the further side. She noted the graceful majesty of his carriage, the perfect symmetry of his magnificent figure and the poise of his well shaped head upon his broad shoulders.

What a perfect creature! There could be naught of cruelty or baseness beneath that god-like exterior. Never, she thought had such a man strode the earth since God created the first in his own image.*

With a bound Tarzan sprang into the trees and disappeared. Jane Porter wondered where he had gone. Had he left her there to her fate in the lonely jungle?

She glanced nervously about. Every vine and bush seemed but the lurking-place of some huge and horrible beast waiting to bury gleaming fangs in her soft flesh. Every sound she magnified into the stealthy creeping of a sinuous and malignant body.

How different now that he had left her!

For a few minutes, that seemed hours to the frightened girl, she sat with tense nerves waiting for the spring of the crouching thing that was to end her misery of apprehension.

She almost prayed for the cruel teeth that would give her unconsciousness and surcease from the agony of fear.

She heard a sudden, slight sound behind her. With a shriek she sprang to her feet and turned to face her end.

There stood Tarzan, his arms filled with ripe and luscious fruit.

Jane Porter reeled and would have fallen, had not Tarzan, dropping his burden, caught her in his arms. She did not lose consciousness, but she clung tightly to him, shuddering and trembling like a frightened deer.

Tarzan of the Apes stroked her soft hair, and tried to comfort and quiet her as Kala had him, when, as a little ape, he had been frightened by Sabor, the lioness, or Histah, the snake.

Once he pressed his lips lightly upon her forehead, and she did not move, but closed her eyes and sighed.

She could not analyze her feelings, nor did she wish to attempt it. She was satisfied to feel the safety of those strong arms, and to leave her future to fate; for the last few hours had taught her to trust this strange wild creature of the forest as she would have trusted but few of the men of her acquaintance.

As she thought of the strangeness of it, there commenced to dawn upon her the realization that she had, possibly, learned something else which she had never really known before—love. She wondered and then she smiled.

And still smiling, she pushed Tarzan gently away; and looking at him with a half-smiling, half-quizzical expression that made her face wholly entrancing, she pointed to the fruit upon the ground, and seated herself upon the edge of the earthen drum of the anthropoids, for hunger was asserting itself.

Tarzan quickly gathered up the fruit, and, bringing it, laid it at her feet; and then he, too, sat upon the drum beside her, and with his knife opened and prepared the various viands for her meal.

Together and in silence they ate, occasionally stealing sly glances at one another, until finally Jane Porter broke into a merry laugh in which Tarzan joined.

"I wish you spoke English," said the girl.

Tarzan shook his head, and an expression of wistful and pathetic longing sobered his laughing eyes.

Then Jane Porter tried speaking to him in French, and then in German; but she had to laugh at her own blundering attempt at the latter tongue.

"Any way," she said to him in English, "you understand my German as well as they did in Berlin."

Tarzan had long since reached a decision as to what his future procedure should be. He had had time to recollect all that he had read of the ways of men and women in the books at the cabin. He would act as he imagined the men in the books would have acted were they in his place.

Again he arose and went into the trees, but first he tried to explain by means of signs that he would return shortly, and he did so well that Jane Porter understood and was not afraid when he had gone.

Only a feeling of loneliness came over her and she watched the point where he had disappeared, with longing eyes, awaiting his return. As before, she was appraised of his presence by a soft sound behind her, and turned to see him coming across the turf with a great armful of branches.

Then he went back again into the jungle and in a few minutes reappeared with a quantity of soft grasses and ferns. Two more trips he made until he had quite a pile of material at hand.

Then he spread the ferns and grasses upon the ground in a soft flat bed, and above it he leaned many branches together so that they met a few feet over its center. Upon these he spread layers of huge leaves of the great elephant's ear, and with more branches and more leaves he closed one end of the little shelter he had built.

Then they sat down together again upon the edge of the drum and tried to talk by signs.

The magnificent diamond locket which hung about Tarzan's neck, had been a source of much wonderment to Jane Porter. She pointed to it now, and Tarzan removed it and handed the pretty bauble to her.

She saw that it was the work of a skilled artizan and that the diamonds were of great brilliancy and superbly set, but the cutting of them denoted that they were of a former day.

She noticed too that the locket opened, and, pressing the hidden clasp, she saw the two halves spring apart to reveal in either section an ivory miniature.*

One was of a beautiful woman and the other might have been a likeness of the man who sat beside her, except for a subtle difference of expression that was scarcely definable.

She looked up at Tarzan to find him leaning toward her gazing on the miniatures with an expression of astonishment. He reached out his hand for the locket and took it away from her, examining the likenesses within with unmistakable signs of surprise and new interest. His manner clearly denoted that he had never before seen them, nor imagined that the locket opened.

This fact caused Jane Porter to indulge in further speculation, and it taxed her imagination to picture how this beautiful ornament came into the possession of a wild and savage creature of the unexplored jungles of Africa.

Still more wonderful, how it contained the likeness of one who might be a brother, or, more likely, the father of this woodland demi-god who was even ignorant of the fact that the locket opened.

Tarzan was still gazing with fixity at the two faces. Presently he removed the quiver from his shoulder, and emptying the arrows upon the ground reached into the bottom of the bag-like receptacle and drew forth a flat object wrapped in many soft leaves and tied with bits of long grass.

Carefully he unwrapped it, removing layer after layer of leaves until at length he held a photograph in his hand.

Pointing to the miniature of the man within the locket he handed the photograph to Jane Porter, holding the open locket beside it.

The photograph only served to puzzle the girl still more, for it was evidently another likeness of the same man whose picture rested in the locket beside that of the beautiful young woman.

Tarzan was looking at her with an expression of puzzled bewilderment in his eyes as she glanced up at him. He seemed to be framing a question with his lips.

The girl pointed to the photograph and then to the miniature and then to him, as though to indicate that she thought the likenesses were of him, but he only shook his head, and then shrugging his great shoulders, he took the photograph from her and having carefully rewrapped it, placed it again in the bottom of his quiver.

For a few moments he sat in silence, his eyes bent upon the ground, while Jane Porter held the little locket in her hand, turning it over and over in an endeavor to find some further clew that might lead to the identity of its original owner.

At length a simple explanation occurred to her.

The locket had belonged to Lord Greystoke, and the likenesses were of himself and Lady Alice.

This wild creature had simply found it in the cabin by the beach. How stupid of her not to have thought of that solution before.

But to account for the strange likeness between Lord Greystoke and this forest god—that was quite beyond her, and it is not strange that she did not imagine that this naked savage was indeed an English nobleman.

At length Tarzan looked up to watch the girl as she examined the locket. He could not fathom the meaning of the faces within, but he could read the interest and fascination upon the face of the live young creature by his side.

She noticed that he was watching her and thinking that he wished his ornament again she held it out to him. He took it from her and taking the chain in his two hands he placed it about her neck, smiling at her expression of surprise at his unexpected gift.

Jane Porter shook her head vehemently and would have removed the golden links from about her throat, but Tarzan would not let her. Taking her hands in his, when she insisted upon it, he held them tightly to prevent her.

At last she desisted and with a little laugh raised the locket to her lips, and, rising, dropped him a little courtesy.

Tarzan did not know precisely what she meant, but he guessed correctly that it was her way of acknowledging the gift, and so he rose, too, and taking the locket in his hand, stooped gravely like some courtier of old, and pressed his lips upon it where hers had rested.

It was a stately and gallant little compliment performed with the grace and dignity of utter unconsciousness of self. It was the hallmark of his aristocratic birth, the natural outcropping of many generations of fine breeding, an hereditary instinct of graciousness which a lifetime of uncouth and savage training and environment could not eradicate.

It was growing dark now, and so they ate again of the fruit which was both food and drink for them, and then Tarzan rose and leading Jane Porter to the little bower he had erected, motioned her to go within.

For the first time in hours a feeling of fear swept over her, and Tarzan felt her draw away as though shrinking from him.

Contact with this girl for half a day had left a very different Tarzan from the one on whom the morning's sun had risen.

Now, in every fiber of his being, heredity spoke louder than training.

He had not in one swift transition become a polished gentleman from a savage ape-man, but at last the instincts of the former predominated, and over all was the desire to please the woman he loved, and to appear well in her eyes.

So Tarzan of the Apes did the only thing he knew to assure Jane Porter of her safety. He removed his hunting knife from its sheath and handed it to her hilt first, again motioning her into the bower.

The girl understood, and taking the long knife she entered and lay down upon the soft grasses while Tarzan of the Apes stretched himself upon the ground across the entrance.

And thus the rising sun found them in the morning.

When Jane Porter awoke, she did not at first recall the strange events of the preceding day, and so she wondered at her odd surroundings—the little leafy bower,* the soft grasses of her bed, the unfamiliar prospect from the opening at her feet.

Slowly the circumstances of her position crept one by one into her mind. And then a great wonderment arose in her heart—a mighty wave of thankfulness and gratitude that though she had been in such terrible danger, yet she was unharmed.

She moved to the entrance of the shelter to look for Tarzan. He was gone; but this time no fear assailed her for she knew that he would return.

In the grass at the entrance to her bower she saw the imprint of his body where he had lain all night to guard her. She knew that the fact that he had been there was all that had permitted her to sleep in such peaceful security.

With him near, who could entertain fear? She wondered if there was another man on earth with whom a girl could feel so safe in the heart of this savage African jungle. Why even the lions and panthers had no fears for her now.

She looked up to see his lithe form drop softly from a nearby tree. As he caught her eyes upon him his face lighted with that frank and radiant smile that had won her confidence the day before.

As he approached her Jane Porter's heart beat faster and her eyes brightened as they had never done before at the approach of any man.

He had again been gathering fruit and this he laid at the entrance of her bower. Once more they sat down together to eat.

Jane Porter commenced to wonder what his plans were. Would he take her back to the beach or would he keep her here? Suddenly she realized that the matter did not seem to give her much concern. Could it be that she did not care!

She began to comprehend, also, that she was entirely contented sitting here by the side of this smiling giant eating delicious fruit in a sylvan paradise far within the remote depths of an African jungle—that she was contented and very happy.

She could not understand it. Her reason told her that she should be torn by wild anxieties, weighted by dread fears, cast down by gloomy forebodings; but instead, her heart was singing and she was smiling into the answering face of the man beside her.

When they had finished their breakfast Tarzan went to her bower and recovered his knife. The girl had entirely forgotten it. She realized that it was because she had forgotten the fear that prompted her to accept it.

Motioning her to follow, Tarzan walked toward the trees at the edge of the arena, and taking her in one strong arm swung to the branches above.

The girl knew that he was taking her back to her people, and she could not understand the sudden feeling of loneliness and sorrow which crept over her.

For hours they swung slowly along.

Tarzan of the Apes did not hurry. He tried to draw out the sweet pleasure of that journey with those dear arms about his neck as long as possible, and so he went far south of the direct route to the beach.

Several times they halted for brief rests, which Tarzan did not need, and at noon they stopped for an hour at a little brook, where they quenched their thirst, and ate.

So it was nearly sunset when they came to the clearing, and Tarzan, dropping to the ground beside a great tree, parted the tall jungle grass and pointed out the little cabin to her.

She took him by the hand to lead him to it, that she might tell her father that this man had saved her from death and worse than death, that he had watched over her as carefully as a mother might have done.

But again the timidity of the wild thing in the face of human habitation swept over Tarzan of the Apes. He drew back, shaking his head.

The girl came close to him, looking up with pleading eyes. Somehow she could not bear the thought of his going back into the terrible jungle alone.

Still he shook his head, and finally he drew her to him very gently and stooped to kiss her, but first he looked into her eyes and waited to learn if she were pleased, or if she would repulse him.

Just an instant the girl hesitated, and then she realized the truth, and throwing her arms about his neck she drew his face to hers and kissed him—unashamed.

"I love you—I love you," she murmured.

From far in the distance came the faint sound of many guns. Tarzan and Jane Porter raised their heads.

From the cabin came Mr. Philander and Esmeralda.

From where Tarzan and the girl stood they could not see the two vessels lying at anchor in the harbor.

Tarzan pointed toward the sounds, touched his breast and pointed again. She understood. He was going, and something told her that it was because he thought her people were in danger.

Again he kissed her.

"Come back to me," she whispered. "I shall wait for you—always."

He was gone—and Jane Porter turned to walk across the clearing to the cabin.

Mr. Philander was the first to see her. It was dusk and Mr. Philander was very near sighted.

"Quickly, Esmeralda!" he cried. "Let us seek safety within; it is a lioness.* Bless me!"

Esmeralda did not bother to verify Mr. Philander's vision. His tone was enough. She was within the cabin and had slammed and bolted the door before he had finished pronouncing her name. The "Bless me" was startled out of Mr. Philander by the discovery that Esmeralda, in the exuberance of her haste, had fastened him upon the same side of the door as was the close-approaching lioness.

He beat furiously upon the heavy portal.

"Esmeralda! Esmeralda!" he shrieked. "Let me in. I am being devoured by a lion."*

Esmeralda thought that the noise upon the door was made by the lioness in her attempts to pursue her, so, after her custom, she fainted.

Mr. Philander cast a frightened glance behind him.

Horrors! The thing was quite close now. He tried to scramble up the side of the cabin, and succeeded in catching a fleeting hold upon the thatched roof.

For a moment he hung there, clawing with his feet like a cat on a clothesline, but presently a piece of the thatch came away, and Mr. Philander, preceding it, was precipitated upon his back.

At the instant he fell a remarkable item of natural history leaped to his mind. If one feigns death lions and lionesses are supposed to ignore one, according to Mr. Philander's faulty memory.

So Mr. Philander lay as he had fallen, frozen into the horrid semblance of death. As his arms and legs had been extended stiffly upward as he came to earth upon his back the attitude of death was anything but impressive.

Jane Porter had been watching his antics in mild eyed surprise. Now she laughed—a little choking, gurgle of a laugh; but it was enough. Mr. Philander rolled over upon his side and peered about. At length he discovered her.

"Jane!" he cried. "Jane Porter. Bless me!"

He scrambled to his feet and rushed toward her. He could not believe that it was she, and alive.

"Bless me! Where did you come from? Where in the world have you been? How—"

"Mercy, Mr. Philander," interrupted the girl, "I never can remember so many questions."

"Well, well," said Mr. Philander. "Bless me! I am so filled with surprise and exuberant delight at seeing you safe and well again that I scarcely know what I am saying, really. But come, tell me all that has happened to you."

CHAPTER XXI

THE VILLAGE OF TORTURE

As THE little expedition of sailors toiled through the dense jungle searching for signs of Jane Porter, the futility of their venture became more and more apparent, but the grief of the old man and the hopeless eyes of the young Englishman prevented the kind hearted D'Arnot from turning back.

He thought that there might be a bare possibility of finding her body, or the remains of it, for he was positive that she had been devoured by some beast of prey. He deployed his men into a skirmish line from the point where Esmeralda had been found, and in this extended formation they pushed their way, sweating and panting, through the tangled vines and creepers.

It was slow work. Noon found them but a few miles inland. They halted for a brief rest then, and after pushing on for a short distance further one of the men discovered a well marked trail.

It was an old elephant track, and D'Arnot after consulting with Professor Porter and Clayton decided to follow it.

The path wound through the jungle in a northeasterly direction, and along it the column moved in single file.

Lieutenant d'Arnot was in the lead and moving at a quick pace, for the trail was comparatively open. Immediately behind him came Professor Porter, but as he could not keep pace with the younger man D'Arnot was a hundred yards in advance when suddenly a half dozen black warriors arose about him.

D'Arnot gave a warning shout to his column as the blacks closed on him, but before he could draw his revolver he had been pinioned and dragged into the jungle.

His cry had alarmed the sailors and a dozen of them sprang forward past Professor Porter, running up the trail to their officer's aid.

They did not know the cause of his outcry, only that it was a warning of danger ahead.

They had rushed past the spot where D'Arnot had been seized when a spear hurled from the jungle transfixed one of the men, and then a volley of arrows fell among them.

Raising their rifles they fired into the underbrush in the direction from which the missiles had come.

By this time the balance of the party had come up, and volley after volley was fired toward the concealed foe. It was these shots that Tarzan and Jane Porter had heard.

Lieutenant Charpentier, who had been bringing up the rear of the column, now came running to the scene, and on hearing the details of the ambuscade ordered the men to follow him, and plunged into the tangled vegetation.

In an instant they were in a hand-to-hand fight with some fifty black warriors of Mbonga's village. Arrows and bullets flew thick and fast.

Queer African knives and French gun butts mingled for a moment in savage and bloody duels, but soon the natives fled into the jungle, leaving the Frenchmen to count their losses.

Four of the twenty were dead, a dozen others were wounded, and Lieutenant d'Arnot was missing. Night was falling rapidly, and their predicament was rendered doubly worse through the fact that they could not even find the elephant trail which they had been following.

There was but one thing to do, make camp where they were until daylight. Lieutenant Charpentier ordered a clearing made and a circular abatis of underbrush constructed about the camp.

This work was not completed until long after dark, the men building a huge fire in the center of the clearing to give them light to work by.

When all was safe as could be made from the attack of wild beasts and savage men, Lieutenant Charpentier placed sentries about the little camp and the tired and hungry men threw themselves upon the ground to sleep.

The groans of the wounded, mingled with the roaring and growling of the great beasts which the noise and firelight had attracted, kept sleep, except in its most fitful form, from the tired eyes. It was a sad and hungry party that lay through the long night praying for dawn.

The blacks who had seized D'Arnot, had not waited to participate in the fight which followed, but instead had dragged their prisoner a little way through the jungle and then struck the trail further on beyond the scene of the fighting in which their fellows were engaged.

They hurried him along, the sounds of battle growing fainter and fainter as they drew away from the contestants until there suddenly broke upon D'Arnot's vision a good sized clearing at one end of which stood a thatched and palisaded village.

It was now dusk, but the watchers at the gate saw the approaching trio and distinguished one as a prisoner ere they reached the portals.

A cry went up within the palisade. A great throng of women and children rushed out to meet the party.

And then began for the French officer the most terrifying experience which man can encounter upon earth—the reception of a white prisoner into a village of African cannibals.*

To add to the fiendishness of their cruel savagery was the poignant memory of still crueler barbarities practiced upon them and theirs by the white officers of that arch hypocrite, Leopold II of Belgium, because of whose atrocities they had fled the Congo Free State*— a pitiful remnant of what once had been a mighty tribe.

They fell upon D'Arnot tooth and nail, beating him with sticks and stones and tearing at him with claw-like hands. Every vestige of clothing was torn from him, and the merciless blows fell upon his bare and quivering flesh. But not once did the Frenchman cry out in pain. A silent prayer rose to his Maker that he be quickly delivered from his torture.

But the death he prayed for was not to be so easily had. Soon the warriors beat the women away from their prisoner. He was to be saved for nobler sport than this; and the first wave of their passion having subsided they contented themselves with crying out taunts and insults, and spitting upon him.

Presently they gained the center of the village. There D'Arnot was bound securely to the great post from which no live man had ever been released.

A number of the women scattered to their several huts to fetch pots and water, while others built a row of fires on which portions of the feast were to be boiled while the balance would be slowly dried in strips for future use, as they expected the other warriors to return with many prisoners.

The festivities were delayed awaiting the return of the warriors who had remained to engage in the skirmish with the white men, so that it was quite late when all were in the village, and the dance of death commenced to circle around the doomed officer.

Half fainting from pain and exhaustion, D'Arnot watched from beneath half closed lids what seemed but the vagary of delirium, or some horrid night-mare from which he must soon awake.

The bestial faces, daubed with color—the huge mouths and flabby hanging lips—the yellow teeth, sharp filed—the rolling, demon eyes—the shining naked bodies—the cruel spears. Surely no such creatures really existed upon earth—he must indeed be dreaming.

The savage, whirling bodies circled nearer. Now a spear sprang forth and touched his arm. The sharp pain and the feel of hot, trickling blood assured him of the awful reality of his hopeless position.

Another spear and then another touched him. He closed his eyes and held his teeth firm set—he would not cry out.

He was a soldier of France, and he would teach these beasts how an officer and a gentleman died.

Tarzan of the Apes needed no interpreter to translate the story of those distant shots. With Jane Porter's kisses still warm upon his lips he was swinging with incredible rapidity through the forest trees straight toward the village of Mbonga.

He was not interested in the location of the encounter, for he judged that that would soon be over. Those who were killed he could not aid, those who escaped would not need his assistance.

It was to those who had neither been killed or escaped that he hastened. And he knew that he would find them by the great post in the center of Mbonga's village.

Many times had Tarzan seen Mbonga's black raiding parties return from the northward with prisoners, and always were the same scenes enacted about that grim stake, beneath the flaring light of many fires.

He knew, too, that they seldom lost much time before consummating the fiendish purpose of their captures. He doubted that he would arrive in time to do more than avenge.

Tarzan had looked with complacency upon their former orgies, only occasionally interfering for the pleasure of baiting the blacks; but heretofore their victims had been men of their own color.

Tonight it was different—white men, men of Tarzan's own race—might be even now suffering the agonies of torture in that grim, jungle fortress.

On he sped. Night had fallen and he traveled high along the upper terrace where the gorgeous tropic moon lighted the dizzy pathway through the gently undulating branches of the tree tops.

Presently he caught the reflection of a distant blaze. It lay to the right of his path. It must be the light from the camp fire the two men had built before they were attacked—Tarzan knew nothing of the presence of the sailors.

So sure was Tarzan of his jungle knowledge that he did not turn from his course, but passed the glare at a distance of a half mile. It was the camp fire of the Frenchmen.

In a few minutes more Tarzan swung into the trees above Mbonga's village. Ah, he was not quite too late! Or, was he? He could not tell. The figure at the stake was very still, yet the black warriors were but pricking it.

Tarzan knew their customs. The death blow had not been struck. He could tell almost to a minute how far the dance had gone.

In another instant Mbonga's knife would sever one of the victim's ears—that would mark the beginning of the end, for very shortly after only a writhing mass of mutilated flesh would remain.

There would still be life in it, but death then would be the only charity it craved.

The stake stood forty feet from the nearest tree. Tarzan coiled his rope. Then there rose suddenly above the fiendish cries of the dancing demons the awful challenge of the ape-man.

The dancers halted as though turned to stone.

The rope sped with singing whir high above the heads of the blacks. It was quite invisible in the flaring lights of the camp fires.

D'Arnot opened his eyes. A huge black, standing directly before him, lunged backward as though felled by an invisible hand.

Struggling and shrieking, his body, rolling from side to side, moved quickly toward the shadows beneath the trees.

The blacks, their eyes protruding in horror, watched spell-bound.

Once beneath the trees, the body rose straight into the air, and as it disappeared into the foliage above, the terrified negroes, screaming with fright, broke into a mad race for the village gate.

D'Arnot was left alone.

He was a brave man, but he had felt the short hairs bristle upon the nape of his neck when that uncanny cry rose upon the air.

As the writhing body of the black soared, as though by unearthly power, into the dense foliage of the forest, D'Arnot felt an icy shiver run along his spine, as though death had risen from a dark grave and laid a cold and clammy finger on his flesh.

As D'Arnot watched the spot where the body had entered the tree he heard the sounds of movement there.

The branches swayed as though under the weight of a man's body—there was a crash and the black came sprawling to earth again—to lie very quietly where he had fallen.

Immediately after him came a white body, but this one alighted erect.

D'Arnot saw a clean limbed young giant emerge from the shadows into the firelight and come quickly toward him.

What could it mean? Who could it be? Some new creature of torture and destruction, doubtless.

D'Arnot waited. His eyes never left the face of the advancing man. Nor did those frank, clear eyes waver beneath his fixed gaze.

D'Arnot was reassured, but still without much hope, though he felt that that face could not mask a cruel heart.

Without a word Tarzan of the Apes cut the bonds which held the Frenchman. Weak from suffering and loss of blood, he would have fallen but for the strong arm that caught him.

He felt himself lifted from the ground. There was a sensation as of flying, and then he lost consciousness.

CHAPTER XXII

THE SEARCH PARTY

WHEN dawn broke upon the little camp of Frenchmen in the heart of the jungle it found a sad and disheartened group.

As soon as it was light enough to see their surroundings Lieutenant Charpentier sent men in groups of three in several directions to locate the trail, and in ten minutes it was found and the expedition was hurrying back toward the beach.

It was slow work, for they bore the bodies of six dead men, two more having succumbed during the night, and several of those who were wounded required support to move even very slowly.

Charpentier had decided to return to camp for reinforcements, and then make an attempt to track down the natives and rescue D'Arnot.

It was late in the afternoon when the exhausted men reached the clearing by the beach, but for two of them the return brought so great a happiness that all their suffering and heart breaking grief was forgotten on the instant.

As the little party emerged from the jungle the first person that Professor Porter and Cecil Clayton saw was Jane Porter, standing by the cabin door.

With a little cry of joy and relief she ran forward to greet them, throwing her arms about her father's neck and bursting into tears for the first time since they had been cast upon this hideous and adventurous shore.

Professor Porter strove manfully to suppress his own emotions, but the strain upon his nerves and weakened vitality were too much for him, and at length, burying his old face in the girl's shoulder, he sobbed quietly like a tired child.

Jane Porter led him toward the cabin, and the Frenchmen turned toward the beach from which several of their fellows were advancing to meet them.

Clayton, wishing to leave father and daughter alone, joined the sailors and remained talking with the officers until their boat pulled away toward the cruiser whither Lieutenant Charpentier was bound to report the unhappy outcome of his adventure.

Then Clayton turned back slowly toward the cabin. His heart was filled with happiness. The woman he loved was safe.

He wondered by what manner of miracle she had been spared. To see her alive seemed almost unbelievable.

As he approached the cabin he saw Jane Porter coming out. When she saw him she hurried forward to meet him.

"Jane!" he cried, "God has been good to us, indeed. Tell me how you escaped—what form Providence took to save you for—us."

He had never before called her by her given name. Forty-eight hours before it would have suffused Jane Porter with a soft glow of pleasure to have heard that name from Clayton's lips—now it frightened her.

"Mr. Clayton," she said quietly, extending her hand, "first let me thank you for your chivalrous loyalty to my dear father. He has told me how noble and self-sacrificing you have been. How can we ever repay you!"

Clayton noticed that she did not return his familiar salutation, but he felt no misgivings on that score. She had been through so much. This was no time to force his love upon her, he quickly realized.

"I am already repaid," he said. "Just to see you and Professor Porter both safe, well, and together again. I do not think that I could much longer have endured the pathos of his quiet and uncomplaining grief.

"It was the saddest experience of my life, Miss Porter; and then, added to it, there was my own grief—the greatest I have ever known. But his was so hopeless—it was pitiful. It taught me that no love, not even that of a man for his wife may be so deep and terrible and self-sacrificing as the love of a father for his daughter."

The girl bowed her head. There was a question she wanted to ask, but it seemed almost sacrilegious in the face of the love of these two men, and the terrible suffering they had endured while she sat laughing and happy beside a god-like creature of the forest, eating delicious fruits and looking with eyes of love into answering eyes.

But love is a strange master, and human nature is still stranger, so she asked her question, though she was not coward enough to attempt to justify herself to her own conscience. She felt self-hate, but she asked her question nevertheless.

"Where is the forest man who went to rescue you? Why did he not return?"

"I do not understand," said Clayton. "Whom do you mean?"

"He who has saved each of us—who saved me from the gorilla."

"Oh," cried Clayton, in surprise. "It was he who rescued you? You have not told me anything of your adventure, don't you know; tell me, do."

"But the wood man," she urged. "Have you not seen him? When we heard the shots in the jungle, very faint and far away, he left me. We had just reached the clearing, and he hurried off in the direction of the fighting. I know he went to aid you."

Her tone was almost pleading—her manner tense with suppressed emotion. Clayton could not but notice it, and he wondered, vaguely, why she was so deeply moved—so anxious to know the whereabouts of this strange creature. He did not suspect the truth, for how could he?

Yet a feeling of apprehension of some impending sorrow haunted him, and in his breast, unknown to himself, was implanted the first germ of jealousy and suspicion of the ape-man to whom he owed his life.

"We did not see him," he replied quietly. "He did not join us." And then after a moment of thoughtful pause: "Possibly he joined his own tribe—the men who attacked us." He did not know why he had said it, for he did not believe it; but love is a strange master.

The girl looked at him wide eyed for a moment.

"No!" she exclaimed vehemently, much too vehemently he thought. "It could not be. They were negroes—he is a white man—and a gentleman."

Clayton looked puzzled. The little green-eyed devil* taunted him.

"He is a strange, half-savage creature of the jungle, Miss Porter. We know nothing of him. He neither speaks nor understands any European tongue—and his ornaments and weapons are those of the West Coast savages."

Clayton was speaking rapidly.

"There are no other human beings than savages within hundreds of miles, Miss Porter. He must belong to the tribes which attacked us, or to some other equally savage—he may even be a cannibal."

Jane Porter blanched.

"I will not believe it," she half whispered. "It is not true. You shall see," she said, addressing Clayton, "that he will come back and that he will prove that you are wrong. You do not know him as I do. I tell you that he is a gentleman."

Clayton was a generous and chivalrous man, but something in the girl's breathless defense of the forest man stirred him to unreasoning jealousy, so that for the instant he forgot all that they owed to this wild demi-god, and he answered her with a half sneer upon his lip.

"Possibly you are right, Miss Porter," he said, "but I do not think that any of us need worry about our carrion-eating acquaintance. The chances are that he is some half-demented castaway who will forget us more quickly, but no more surely, than we shall forget him. He is only a beast of the jungle, Miss Porter."

The girl did not answer, but she felt her heart shrivel within her. Anger and hate against one we love steels our hearts, but contempt or pity leaves us silent and ashamed.

She knew that Clayton spoke merely what he thought, and for the first time she began to analyze the structure which supported her new found love, and to subject its object to a critical examination.

Slowly she turned and walked back to the cabin. She tried to imagine her wood-god by her side in the saloon of an ocean liner. She saw him eating with his hands, tearing his food like a beast of prey, and wiping his greasy fingers upon his thighs. She shuddered.

She saw him as she introduced him to her friends—uncouth, illiterate—a boor; and the girl winced.

She had reached her room now, and as she sat upon the edge of her bed of ferns and grasses, with one hand resting upon her rising and falling bosom, she felt the hard outlines of the man's locket beneath her waist.

She drew it out, holding it in the palm of her hand for a moment with tear-blurred eyes bent upon it. Then she raised it to her lips, and crushing it there buried her face in the soft ferns, sobbing.

"Beast?" she murmured. "Then God make me a beast; for, man or beast, I am yours."

She did not see Clayton again that day. Esmeralda brought her supper to her, and she sent word to her father that she was suffering from the reaction following her adventure.

The next morning Clayton left early with the relief expedition in search of Lieutenant d'Arnot. There were two hundred armed men this time, with ten officers and two surgeons, and provisions for a week.

They carried bedding and hammocks, the latter for transporting their sick and wounded.

It was a determined and angry company—a punitive expedition as well as one of relief. They reached the sight of the skirmish of the previous expedition shortly after noon, for they were now traveling a known trail and no time was lost in exploring.

From there on the elephant-track led straight to Mbonga's village. It was but two o'clock when the head of the column halted upon the edge of the clearing.

Lieutenant Charpentier, who was in command, immediately sent a portion of his force through the jungle to the opposite side of the village. Another detachment was dispatched to a point before the village gate, while he remained with the balance upon the south side of the clearing.

It was arranged that the party which was to take position to the north, and which would be the last to gain its station should commence the assault, and that their opening volley should be the signal for a concerted rush from all sides in an attempt to carry the village by storm at the first charge.

For half an hour the men with Lieutenant Charpentier crouched in the dense foliage of the jungle, waiting the signal. To them it seemed like hours. They could see natives in the fields, and others moving in and out of the village gate.

At length the signal came—a sharp rattle of musketry, and like one man, an answering volley tore from the jungle to the west and to the south.

The natives in the field dropped their implements and broke madly for the palisade. The French bullets mowed them down, and the French sailors bounded over their prostrate bodies straight for the village gate.

So sudden and unexpected the assault had been that the whites reached the gates before the frightened natives could bar them, and in another minute the village street was filled with armed men fighting hand to hand in an inextricable tangle.

For a few moments the blacks held their ground within the entrance to the street, but the revolvers, rifles and cutlasses of the Frenchmen crumpled the native spearmen and struck down the black archers with their bolts half-drawn.

Soon the battle turned to a wild rout, and then to grim massacre; for the French sailors had seen bits of D'Arnot's uniform upon several of the black warriors who opposed them.

They spared the children and those of the women whom they were not forced to kill in self-defense, but when at length they stopped, panting, blood covered and sweating, it was because there lived to oppose them no single warrior of all the savage village of Mbonga.

Carefully they ransacked every hut and corner of the village, but no sign of D'Arnot could they find. They questioned the prisoners by signs, and finally one of the sailors who had served in the French Congo* found that he could make them understand the bastard tongue that passes for language between the whites and the more degraded tribes of the coast, but even then they could learn nothing definite regarding the fate of D'Arnot.

Only excited gestures and expressions of fear could they obtain in response to their inquiries concerning their fellow; and at last they became convinced that these were but evidences of the guilt of these demons who had slaughtered and eaten their comrade two nights before.

At length all hope left them, and they prepared to camp for the night within the village. The prisoners were herded into three huts where they were heavily guarded. Sentries were posted at the barred gates, and finally the village was wrapped in the silence of slumber, except for the wailing of the native women for their dead.

The next morning they set out upon the return march. Their original intention had been to burn the village, but this idea was abandoned and the prisoners were left behind, weeping and moaning, but with roofs to cover them and a palisade for refuge from the beasts of the jungle.

Slowly the expedition retraced its steps of the preceding day. Ten loaded hammocks retarded its pace. In eight of them lay the more seriously wounded, while two swung beneath the weight of the dead.

Clayton and Lieutenant Charpentier brought up the rear of the column; the Englishman silent in respect for the other's grief, for D'Arnot and Charpentier had been inseparable friends since boyhood.

Clayton could not but realize that the Frenchman felt his grief the more keenly because D'Arnot's sacrifice had been so futile, since Jane Porter had been rescued before D'Arnot had fallen into the hands of the savages, and again because the service in which he had lost his life had been outside his duty and for strangers and aliens; but when he spoke of it to Lieutenant Charpentier, the latter shook his head.

"No, monsieur," he said, "D'Arnot would have chosen to die thus. I only grieve that I could not have died for him, or at least with him. I wish that you could have known him better, monsieur. He was indeed an officer and a gentleman—a title conferred on many, but deserved by so few.

"He did not die futilely, for his death in the cause of a strange American girl will make us, his comrades, face our ends the more bravely, however they may come to us."

Clayton did not reply, but within him rose a new respect for Frenchmen which remained undimmed ever after.

It was quite late when they reached the cabin by the beach. A single shot before they emerged from the jungle had announced to those in camp as well as on the ship that the expedition had been too late—for it had been prearranged that when they came within a mile or two of camp one shot was to be fired to denote failure, or three for success, while two would have indicated that they had found no sign of either D'Arnot or his black captors.

So it was a solemn party that awaited their coming, and few words were spoken as the dead and wounded men were tenderly placed in boats and rowed silently toward the cruiser.

Clayton, exhausted from his five days of laborious marching through the jungle and from the effects of his two battles with the blacks, turned toward the cabin to seek a mouthful of food and then the comparative ease of his bed of grasses, after two nights in the jungle.

By the cabin door stood Jane Porter.

"The poor lieutenant?" she asked. "Did you find no trace of him?"

"We were too late, Miss Porter," he replied sadly.

"Tell me. What had happened?" she asked.

"I cannot, Miss Porter, it is too horrible."

"You do not mean that they had tortured him?" she whispered.

"We do not know what they did to him *before* they killed him," he answered, his face drawn with fatigue and the sorrow he felt for poor D'Arnot—and he emphasized the word before.

"*Before* they killed him! What do you mean? They are not—? They are not—?"

She was thinking of what Clayton had said of the forest man's probable relationship to this tribe and she could not frame the awful word.

"Yes, Miss Porter, they were—cannibals," he said, almost bitterly, for to him too had suddenly come the thought of the forest man, and the strange, unaccountable jealousy he had felt two days before swept over him once more.

And then in sudden brutality that was as unlike Clayton as courteous consideration is unlike an ape, he blurted out:

"When your forest god left you he was doubtless hurrying to the feast."

He was sorry ere the words were spoken though he did not know how cruelly they had cut the girl. His regret was for his baseless disloyalty to one who had saved the lives of every member of his party, nor ever offered harm to one.

The girl's head went high.

"There could be but one suitable reply to your assertion, Mr. Clayton," she said icily, "and I regret that I am not a man, that I might make it."* She turned quickly and entered the cabin.

Clayton was an Englishman, so the girl had passed quite out of sight before he deduced what reply a man would have made.

"Upon my word," he said ruefully, "she called me a liar. And I fancy I jolly well deserved it," he added thoughtfully. "Clayton, my boy, I know you are tired out and unstrung, but that's no reason why you should make an ass of yourself. You'd better go to bed."

But before he did so he called gently to Jane Porter upon the opposite side of the sail cloth partition, for he wished to apologize, but he might as well have addressed the Sphinx. Then he wrote upon a piece of paper and shoved it beneath the partition.

Jane Porter saw the little note and ignored it, for she was very angry and hurt and mortified, but—she was a woman, and so eventually she picked it up and read it.

My Dear Miss Porter:

I had no reason to insinuate what I did. My only excuse is that my nerves must be unstrung—which is no excuse at all.

Please try and think that I did not say it. I am very sorry. I would not have hurt *you*, above all others in the world. Say that you forgive me.

Wm. Cecil Clayton.

"He did think it or he never would have said it," reasoned the girl, "but it cannot be true—oh, I know it is not true!"

One sentence in the letter frightened her: "I would not have hurt *you* above all others in the world."

A week ago that sentence would have filled her with delight, now it depressed her.

She wished she had never met Clayton. She was sorry that she had ever seen the forest god—no, she was glad. And there was that other note she had found in the grass before the cabin the day after her return from the jungle, the love note signed by Tarzan of the Apes.

Who could be this new suitor? If he were another of the wild denizens of this terrible forest what might he not do to claim her?

"Esmeralda! Wake up," she cried.

"You make me so irritable, sleeping there peacefully when you know perfectly well that the world is filled with sorrow."

"Gaberelle!" screamed Esmeralda, sitting up. "What am it now? A hipponocerous? Where am he, Miss Jane?"

"Nonsense, Esmeralda, there is nothing. Go back to sleep. You are bad enough asleep, but you are infinitely worse awake."

"Yasm honey, but what's de matter wif you-all precious? You acts sorter kinder disgranulated dis ebenin'."

"Oh, Esmeralda, I'm just plain ugly tonight," said the girl. "Don't pay any attention to me—that's a dear."

"Yasm, honey; now you-all go right to sleep. Yo' nerves am all on aidge. What wif all dese ripotamuses an' man eaten geniuses dat Marse Philander been a tellin' about—laws, it ain't no wonder we all get nervous prosecution."

Jane Porter crossed the little room, laughing, and kissing the faithful old black cheek, bid Esmeralda good night.

CHAPTER XXIII

BROTHER MEN

WHEN D'Arnot regained consciousness, he found himself lying upon a bed of soft ferns and grasses beneath a little "A" shaped shelter of boughs.

At his feet an opening looked out upon a green sward, and at a little distance beyond was the dense wall of jungle and forest.

He was very lame and sore and weak, and as full consciousness returned he felt the sharp torture of many cruel wounds, and the dull aching of every bone and muscle in his body as a result of the hideous beating he had received.

Even the turning of his head caused him such excruciating agony that he lay still with closed eyes for a long time.

He tried to piece out the details of his adventure prior to the time he lost consciousness to see if they would explain his present whereabouts—he wondered if he were among friends or foes.

At length he recollected the whole hideous scene at the stake, and finally recalled the strange white figure in whose arms he had sunk into oblivion.

D'Arnot wondered what fate lay in store for him now. He could neither see nor hear any signs of life about him.

The incessant hum of the jungle—the rustling of millions of leaves—the buzz of insects—the voices of the birds and monkeys seemed blended into a strangely soothing purr, as though he lay apart, far from the myriad life whose sounds came to him only as a blurred echo.

At length he fell in a quiet slumber, nor did he awake again until afternoon.

Once more he experienced the strange sense of utter bewilderment that had marked his earlier awakening, but soon he recalled the recent past, and looking through the opening at his feet he saw the figure of a man squatting on his haunches.

The broad, muscular back was turned toward him, but, tanned though it was, D'Arnot saw that it was the back of a white man, and he thanked his God.

The Frenchman called faintly. The man turned, and, rising, came toward the shelter. His face was very handsome—the handsomest, thought D'Arnot, that he had ever seen.

Stooping, he crawled into the shelter beside the wounded officer, and placed a cool hand upon his forehead.

D'Arnot spoke to him in French, but the man only shook his head—sadly, it seemed to the Frenchman.

Then D'Arnot tried English, but still the man shook his head. Italian, Spanish and German brought similar discouragement.

D'Arnot knew a few words of Norwegian, Russian, Greek, and also had a smattering of the language of one of the West Coast negro tribes—the man denied them all.

After examining D'Arnot's wounds the man left the shelter and disappeared. In half an hour he was back with fruit and a hollow gourd-like vegetable filled with water.

D'Arnot drank and ate a little. He was surprised that he had no fever. Again he tried to converse with his strange nurse, but the attempt was useless.

Suddenly the man hastened from the shelter only to return a few minutes later with several pieces of bark and—wonder of wonders— a lead pencil.

Squatting beside D'Arnot he wrote for a minute on the smooth inner surface of the bark; then he handed it to the Frenchman.

D'Arnot was astonished to see, in plain print-like characters, a message in English:

I am Tarzan of the Apes. Who are you? Can you read this language?

D'Arnot seized the pencil—then he stopped. This strange man wrote English—evidently he was an Englishman.

"Yes," said D'Arnot, "I read English. I speak it also. Now we may talk. First let me thank you for all that you have done for me."

The man only shook his head and pointed to the pencil and the bark.

"*Mon Dieu!*" cried D'Arnot. "If you are English why is it then that you cannot speak English?"

And then in a flash it came to him—the man was a mute, possibly a deaf mute.

So D'Arnot wrote a message on the bark, in English.

I am Paul d'Arnot, Lieutenant in the navy of France. I thank you for what you have done for me. You have saved my life, and all that

I have is yours. May I ask how it is that one who writes English does not speak it?

Tarzan's reply filled D'Arnot with still greater wonder:

I speak only the language of my tribe—the great apes who were Kerchak's; and a little of the languages of Tantor, the elephant, and Numa,* the lion, and of the other folks of the jungle I understand. With a human being I have never spoken, except once with Jane Porter, by signs. This is the first time I have spoken with another of my kind through written words.

D'Arnot was mystified. It seemed incredible that there lived upon earth a full grown man who had never spoken with a fellow man, and still more preposterous that such a one could read and write.

He looked again at Tarzan's message—"except once, with Jane Porter." That was the American girl who had been carried into the jungle by a gorilla.

A sudden light commenced to dawn on D'Arnot—this then was the "gorilla." He seized the pencil and wrote:

Where is Jane Porter?

And Tarzan replied, below:

Back with her people in the cabin of Tarzan of the Apes.

She is not dead then? Where was she? What happened to her?

She is not dead. She was taken by Terkoz to be his wife; but Tarzan of the Apes took her away from Terkoz and killed him before he could harm her.

None in all the jungle may face Tarzan of the Apes in battle, and live. I am Tarzan of the Apes—mighty fighter.

D'Arnot wrote:

I am glad she is safe. It pains me to write, I will rest a while.

And then Tarzan:

Yes, rest. When you are well I shall take you back to your people.

For many days D'Arnot lay upon his bed of soft ferns. The second day a fever had come and D'Arnot thought that it meant infection and he knew that he would die.

An idea came to him. He wondered why he had not thought of it before.

He called Tarzan and indicated by signs that he would write, and when Tarzan had fetched the bark and pencil, D'Arnot wrote:

Can you go to my people and lead them here? I will write a message that you may take to them, and they will follow you.

Tarzan shook his head and taking the bark, wrote:

I had thought of that—the first day; but I dared not. The great apes come often to this spot, and if they found you here, wounded and alone, they would kill you.

D'Arnot turned on his side and closed his eyes. He did not wish to die; but he felt that he was going, for the fever was mounting higher and higher. That night he lost consciousness.

For three days he was in delirium, and Tarzan sat beside him and bathed his head and hands and washed his wounds.

On the fourth day the fever broke as suddenly as it had come, but it left D'Arnot a shadow of his former self, and very weak. Tarzan had to lift him that he might drink from the gourd.

The fever had not been the result of infection, as D'Arnot had thought, but one of those that commonly attack whites in the jungles of Africa, and either kill or leave them as suddenly as D'Arnot's had left him.

Two days after, D'Arnot was tottering about the amphitheater, Tarzan's strong arm about him to keep him from falling.

They sat beneath the shade of a great tree, and Tarzan found some smooth bark that they might converse.

D'Arnot wrote the first message:

What can I do to repay you for all that you have done for me?

And Tarzan, in reply:

Teach me to speak the language of men.

And so D'Arnot commenced at once, pointing out familiar objects and repeating their names in French, for he thought that it would be easier to teach this man his own language, since he understood it himself best of all.

It meant nothing to Tarzan, of course, for he could not tell one language from another, so when he pointed to the word man which he had printed upon a piece of bark he learned from D'Arnot that it was pronounced *homme*, and in the same way he was taught to pronounce ape, *singe*, and tree, *arbre*.

He was a most eager student, and in two more days had mastered so much French that he could speak little sentences such as: "That is a tree," "this is grass," "I am hungry," and the like, but D'Arnot found that it was difficult to teach him the French construction upon a foundation of English.

The Frenchman wrote little lessons for him in English and had Tarzan repeat them in French, but as a literal translation was usually very poor French Tarzan was often confused.

D'Arnot realized now that he had made a mistake, but it seemed too late to go back and do it all over again and force Tarzan to unlearn all that he had learned, especially as they were rapidly approaching a point where they would be able to converse.

On the third day after the fever broke Tarzan wrote a message asking D'Arnot if he felt strong enough to be carried back to the cabin. Tarzan was as anxious to go as D'Arnot, for he longed to see Jane Porter again.

It had been hard for him to remain with the Frenchman all these days for that very reason, and that he had unselfishly done so spoke more glowingly for his nobility of character than even did his rescuing of the French officer from Mbonga's clutches.

D'Arnot, only too willing to attempt the journey, wrote:

But you cannot carry me all the distance through this tangled forest.

Tarzan laughed.

"*Mais oui*,"* he said, and D'Arnot laughed aloud to hear the phrase that he used so often glide from Tarzan's tongue.

So they set out, D'Arnot marveling as had Clayton and Jane Porter at the wondrous strength and agility of the ape-man.

Mid-afternoon brought them to the clearing, and as Tarzan dropped to earth from the branches of the last tree his heart leaped and bounded against his ribs in anticipation of seeing Jane Porter so soon again.

No one was in sight without the cabin, and D'Arnot was perplexed to note that neither the cruiser nor the *Arrow* was at anchor in the bay.

An atmosphere of loneliness pervaded the spot, which caught suddenly at both men as they strode toward the cabin.

Neither spoke, yet both knew before they opened the closed door what they would find beyond.

Tarzan lifted the latch and pushed the great door in upon its wooden hinges. It was as they had feared. The cabin was deserted.

The men turned and looked at one another. D'Arnot knew that his people thought him dead; but Tarzan thought only of the woman who had kissed him in love and now had fled from him while he was serving one of her people.

A great bitterness rose in his heart. He would go away, far into the jungle and join his tribe. Never would he see one of his own kind again; nor could he bear the thought of returning to the cabin. He would leave that forever behind him with the great hopes he had nursed there of finding his own race and becoming a man among men.

And the Frenchman? D'Arnot? What of him? He could get along as Tarzan had. Tarzan did not want to see him more. He wanted to get away from everything that might remind him of Jane Porter.

As Tarzan stood upon the threshold brooding, D'Arnot had entered the cabin. Many comforts he saw that had been left behind. He recognized numerous articles from the cruiser—a camp oven, some kitchen utensils, a rifle and many rounds of ammunition, canned foods, blankets, two chairs and a cot—and several books and periodicals, mostly American.

"They must intend returning," thought D'Arnot.

He walked over to the table that John Clayton had built so many years before to serve as a desk, and on it he saw two notes addressed to Tarzan of the Apes.

One was in a strong masculine hand and was unsealed. The other, in a woman's hand, was sealed.

"Here are two messages for you, Tarzan of the Apes," cried D'Arnot, turning toward the door; but his companion was not there.

D'Arnot walked to the door and looked out. Tarzan was nowhere in sight. He called aloud but there was no response.

"*Mon Dieu!*" exclaimed D'Arnot, "he has left me. I feel it. He has gone back into his jungle and left me here alone."

And then he remembered the look on Tarzan's face when they had discovered that the cabin was empty—such a look as the hunter sees in the eyes of the wounded deer he has wantonly brought down.

The man had been hard hit—D'Arnot realized it now—but why? He could not understand.

The Frenchman looked about him. The loneliness and the horror of the place commenced to get on his nerves—already weakened by the ordeal of suffering and sickness he had passed through.

To be left here alone beside this awful jungle—never to hear a human voice or see a human face—in constant dread of savage beasts and more terribly savage men—a prey to solitude and hopelessness. It was awful.

And far to the east Tarzan of the Apes was speeding through the middle terrace back to his tribe. Never had he traveled with such reckless speed. He felt that he was running away from himself—that by hurtling through the forest like a frightened squirrel he was escaping from his own thoughts. But no matter how fast he went he found them always with him.

He passed above the sinuous body of Sabor, the lioness, going in the opposite direction; toward the cabin, thought Tarzan.

What could D'Arnot do against Sabor—or if Bolgani, the gorilla, should come upon him—or Numa, the lion, or cruel Sheeta?

Tarzan paused in his flight.

"What are you, Tarzan?" he asked aloud. "An ape or a man?"

"If you are an ape you will do as the apes would do—leave one of your kind to die in the jungle if it suited your whim to go elsewhere.

"If you are a man, you will return to protect your kind. You will not run away from one of your own people, because one of them has run away from you."

D'Arnot closed the cabin door. He was very nervous. Even brave men, and D'Arnot was a brave man, are sometimes frightened by solitude.

He loaded one of the rifles and placed it within easy reach. Then he went to the desk and took up the unsealed letter addressed to Tarzan.

Possibly it contained word that his people had but left the beach temporarily. He felt that it would be no breach of ethics to read this letter, so he took the enclosure from the envelope and read:

To Tarzan of the Apes:

We thank you for the use of your cabin, and are sorry that you did not permit us the pleasure of seeing and thanking you in person.

We have harmed nothing, but have left many things for you which may add to your comfort and safety here in your lonely home.

If you know the strange white man who saved our lives so many times, and brought us food, and if you can converse with him, thank him, also, for his kindness.

We sail within the hour, never to return; but we wish you and that other jungle friend to know that we shall always thank you for what you did for strangers on your shore, and that we should have done infinitely more to reward you both had you given us the opportunity.

Very respectfully,

Wm. Cecil Clayton.

"'Never to return,'" muttered D'Arnot, and threw himself face downward upon the cot.

An hour later he started up, listening. Something was at the door trying to enter.

D'Arnot reached for the loaded rifle and placed it to his shoulder.

Dusk was falling, and the interior of the cabin was very dark; but the man could see the latch moving from its place.

He felt his hair rising upon his scalp.

Gently the door opened until a thin crack showed something standing just without.

D'Arnot sighted along the blue barrel at the crack of the door—and then he pulled the trigger.

CHAPTER XXIV

LOST TREASURE

WHEN the expedition returned, following their fruitless endeavor to succor D'Arnot, Captain Dufranne was anxious to steam away as quickly as possible, and all save Jane Porter had acquiesced.

"No," she said, determinedly, "I shall not go, nor should you, for there are two friends in that jungle who will come out of it some day expecting to find us awaiting them.

"Your officer, Captain Dufranne, is one of them, and the forest man who has saved the lives of every member of my father's party is the other.

"He left me at the edge of the jungle two days ago to hasten to the aid of my father and Mr. Clayton, as he thought, and he has stayed to rescue Lieutenant d'Arnot; of that you may be sure.

"Had he been too late to be of service to the lieutenant he would have been back before now—the fact that he is not back is sufficient proof to me that he is delayed because Lieutenant d'Arnot is wounded, or he has had to follow his captors further than the village which your sailors attacked."

"But poor D'Arnot's uniform and all his belongings were found in that village, Miss Porter," argued the captain, "and the natives showed great excitement when questioned as to the white man's fate."

"Yes, Captain, but they did not admit that he was dead, and as for his clothes and accouterments being in their possession—why more civilized peoples than these poor savage negroes strip their prisoners of every article of value whether they intend killing them or not.

"Even the soldiers of my own dear South* looted not only the living but the dead. It is strong circumstantial evidence, I will admit, but it is not positive proof."

"Possibly your forest man, himself, was captured or killed by the savages," suggested Captain Dufranne.

The girl laughed.

"You do not know him," she replied, a little thrill of pride setting her nerves a-tingle at the thought that she spoke of her own.

"I admit that he would be worth waiting for, this super-man* of yours," laughed the captain. "I most certainly should like to see him."

"Then wait for him, my dear captain," urged the girl, "for I intend doing so."

The Frenchman would have been a very much surprised man could he have interpreted the true meaning of the girl's words.

They had been walking from the beach toward the cabin as they talked, and now they joined a little group sitting on camp stools in the shade of a great tree beside the cabin.

Professor Porter was there, and Mr. Philander and Clayton, with Lieutenant Charpentier and two of his brother officers, while Esmeralda hovered in the background, ever and anon venturing opinions and comments with the freedom of an old and much indulged family servant.

The officers arose and saluted as their superior approached, and Clayton surrendered his camp-stool to Jane Porter.

"We were just discussing poor Paul's fate," said Captain Dufranne. "Miss Porter insists that we have no absolute proof of his death—nor have we. And on the other hand she maintains that the continued absence of your omnipotent jungle friend indicates that D'Arnot is still in need of his services, either because he is wounded, or still is a prisoner in a more distant native village."

"It has been suggested," ventured Lieutenant Charpentier, "that the wild man may have been a member of the tribe of blacks who attacked our party—that he was hastening to aid *them*—his own people."

Jane Porter shot a quick glance at Clayton.

"It seems vastly more reasonable," said Professor Porter.

"I do not agree with you," objected Mr. Philander. "He had ample opportunity to harm us himself, or to lead his people against us. Instead, during our long residence here, he has been uniformly consistent in his role of protector and provider."

"That is true," interjected Clayton, "yet we must not overlook the fact that except for himself the only human beings within hundreds of miles are savage cannibals. He was armed precisely as are they, which indicates that he has maintained relations of some nature with them, and the fact that he is but one against possibly thousands suggests that these relations could scarcely have been other than friendly."

"It seems improbable then that he is not connected with them," remarked the captain; "possibly a member of this tribe."

"Or," added another of the officers, "that otherwise he could even have lived a sufficient length of time among the savage denizens of the jungle, brute and human, to have become proficient in wood craft, or in the use of African weapons."

"You are judging him according to your own standards, gentlemen," said Jane Porter. "An ordinary white man such as any of you—pardon me, I did not mean just that—rather, a white man above the ordinary in physique and intelligence could never, I grant you, have lived a year alone and naked in this tropical jungle; but this man not only surpasses the average white man in strength and agility, but as far transcends our trained athletes and 'strong men' as they surpass a day old babe; and his courage and ferocity in battle are those of the wild beast."

"He has certainly won a loyal champion, Miss Porter," said Captain Dufranne, laughing. "I am sure that there be none of us here but would willingly face death a hundred times in its most terrifying forms to deserve the tributes of one even half so loyal—or so beautiful."

"You would not wonder that I defend him," said the girl, "could you have seen him as I saw him, battling in my behalf with that huge hairy brute.

"Could you have seen him charge the monster as a bull might charge a grizzly—absolutely without sign of fear or hesitation—you would have believed him more than human.

"Could you have seen those mighty muscles knotting under the brown skin—could you have seen them force back those awful fangs—you too would have thought him invincible.

"And could you have seen the chivalrous treatment which he accorded a strange girl of a strange race, you would feel the same absolute confidence in him that I feel."

"You have won your suit, my fair pleader," cried the captain. "This court finds the defendant not guilty, and the cruiser shall wait a few days longer that he may have an opportunity to come and thank the divine Portia."*

"Fo' de Lawd's sake honey," cried Esmeralda. "You all doan mean to tell *me* dat youse a-goin' to stay right yere in dis yere lan' of carnivable animals when you all done got de oppahtunity to escapade on dat crosier? Doan yo' tell me *dat*, honey."

"Why, Esmeralda! You should be ashamed of yourself," cried Jane Porter. "Is this any way to show your gratitude to the man who saved your life twice?"

"Well, Miss Jane, das all jes' as yo' say; but dat dere fores' lawd never did save us to stay yere. He done save us so we all could get *away* from yere. Ah expec' he be mighty peevish when he fin' we ain't got no mo' sense 'n to stay right yere after he done give us de chanct to get away.

"Ah hoped Ah'd never have to sleep in dis yere geological garden another night and listen to all dem lonesome noises dat come out of dat jumble after dark."

"I don't blame you a bit, Esmeralda," said Clayton, "and you certainly did hit it off right when you called them 'lonesome' noises. I never have been able to find the right word for them but that's it, don't you know, lonesome noises."

"You and Esmeralda had better go and live on the cruiser," said Jane Porter, in fine scorn. "What would you think if you *had* to live all of your life in that jungle as our forest man has done?"

"I'm afraid I'd be a blooming bounder as a wild man," laughed Clayton, ruefully. "Those noises at night make the hair on my head bristle. I suppose that I should be ashamed to admit it, but it's the truth."

"I don't know about that," said Lieutenant Charpentier. "I never thought much about fear and that sort of thing—never tried to determine whether I was a coward or a brave man; but the other night as we lay in the jungle there after poor D'Arnot was taken, and those jungle noises rose and fell around us I began to think that I was a coward indeed. It was not the roaring and growling of the big beasts that affected me so much as it was the stealthy noises—the ones that you heard suddenly close by and then listened vainly for a repetition of—the unaccountable sounds as of a great body moving almost noiselessly, and the knowledge that you didn't *know* how close it was, or whether it were creeping closer after you ceased to hear it? It was those noises—and the eyes.

"*Mon Dieu!* I shall see them in the dark forever—the eyes that you see, and those that you don't see, but feel; ah, they are the worst."

All were silent for a moment, and then Jane Porter spoke.

"And he is out there," she said, in an awe-hushed whisper. "Those eyes will be glaring at him tonight, and at your comrade Lieutenant d'Arnot. Can you leave them, gentlemen, without at least rendering them the passive succor which remaining here a few days longer might insure them?"

"Tut, tut, child," said Professor Porter. "Captain Dufranne is willing to remain, and for my part I am perfectly willing, perfectly willing—as I always have been to humor your childish whims."

"We can utilize the morrow in recovering the chest, Professor," suggested Mr. Philander.

"Quite so, quite so, Mr. Philander, I had almost forgotten the treasure," exclaimed Professor Porter. "Possibly we can borrow some men from Captain Dufranne to assist us, and one of the prisoners to point out the location of the chest."

"Most assuredly, my dear Professor, we are all yours to command," said the captain.

And so it was arranged that on the next day Lieutenant Charpentier was to take a detail of ten men, and one of the mutineers of the *Arrow* as a guide, and unearth the treasure; and that the cruiser would remain for a full week in the little harbor. At the end of that time it was to be assumed that D'Arnot was truly dead, and that the forest man would not return while they remained. Then the two vessels were to leave with all the party.

Professor Porter did not accompany the treasure-seekers on the following day, but when he saw them returning empty-handed toward noon, he hastened forward to meet them—his usual preoccupied indifference entirely vanished, and in its place a nervous and excited manner.

"Where is the treasure?" he cried to Clayton, while yet a hundred feet separated them.

Clayton shook his head.

"Gone," he said, as he neared the professor.

"Gone! It cannot be. Who could have taken it?" cried Professor Porter.

"God only knows, Professor," replied Clayton. "We might have thought the fellow who guided us was lying about the location, but his surprise and consternation on finding no chest beneath the body of the murdered Snipes were too real to be feigned.

"And then our spades showed us that *something* had been buried beneath the corpse, for a hole had been there and it had been filled with loose earth."

"But who could have taken it?" repeated Professor Porter.

"Suspicion might naturally fall on the men of the cruiser," said Lieutenant Charpentier, "but for the fact that sub-lieutenant Janviers here assures me that no men have had shore leave—that none has been on shore since we anchored here except under command of an officer.

"I do not know that you would suspect our men, but I am glad that there is now no chance for suspicion to fall on them," he concluded.

"It would never have occurred to me to suspect the men to whom we owe so much," replied Professor Porter, graciously. "I would as soon suspect my dear Clayton here, or Mr. Philander."

The Frenchmen smiled, both officers and sailors. It was plain to see that a burden had been lifted from their minds.

"The treasure has been gone some time," continued Clayton. "In fact the body fell apart as we lifted it, which indicates that whoever removed the treasure did so while the corpse was still fresh, for it was intact when we first uncovered it."

"There must have been several in the party," said Jane Porter, who had joined them. "You remember that it took four men to carry it."

"By jove!" cried Clayton. "That's right. It must have been done by a party of blacks. Probably one of them saw the men bury the chest and then returned immediately after with a party of his friends, and carried it off."

"Speculation is futile," said Professor Porter, sadly. "The chest is gone. We shall never see it more, nor the treasure that was in it."

Only Jane Porter knew what the loss meant to her father, and none there knew what it meant to her.

Six days later Captain Dufranne announced that they would sail early on the morrow.

Jane Porter would have begged for a further reprieve, had it not been that she too had begun to believe that her forest lover would return no more.

In spite of herself she began to entertain doubts and fears. The reasonableness of the arguments of these disinterested French officers commenced to convince her against her will.

That he was a cannibal she would not believe, but that he was an adopted member of some savage tribe at length seemed possible to her.

She would not admit that he could be dead. It was impossible to believe that that perfect body, so filled with triumphant life, could ever cease to harbor the vital spark—as soon believe that immortality were dust.

As Jane Porter permitted herself to harbor these thoughts, others equally unwelcome forced themselves upon her.

If he belonged to some savage tribe he had a savage wife—a dozen of them perhaps—and wild, half-caste children. The girl shuddered, and when they told her that the cruiser would sail on the morrow she was almost glad.

It was she, though, who suggested that arms, ammunition, supplies and comforts be left behind in the cabin, ostensibly for that intangible personality who had signed himself Tarzan of the Apes, and for D'Arnot should he still be living, but really, she hoped, for her forest god—even though his feet should prove of clay.*

And at the last minute she left a message for him, to be transmitted by Tarzan of the Apes.

Jane Porter was the last to leave the cabin, returning on some trivial pretext, after the others had started for the boat.

She knelt down beside the bed in which she had spent so many nights, and offered up a prayer for the safety of her primeval man, and crushing his locket to her lips she murmured:

"I love you, and because I love you I believe in you. But if I did not believe, still should I love. May God have pity on my soul that I should acknowledge it. Had you come back for me, and there had been no other way, I would have gone into the jungle with you—forever."

CHAPTER XXV

THE OUTPOST OF THE WORLD

WITH the report of his gun D'Arnot saw the door fly open and the figure of a man pitch headlong within onto the cabin floor.

The Frenchman in his panic raised his gun to fire again into the prostrate form, but suddenly in the half dusk of the open door he saw that the man was white and in another instant realized that he had shot his friend and protector, Tarzan of the Apes.

With a cry of anguish D'Arnot sprang to the ape-man's side, and kneeling, lifted the black head in his arms—calling Tarzan's name aloud.

There was no response, and then D'Arnot placed his ear above the man's heart. To his joy he heard its steady beating beneath.

Carefully he lifted Tarzan to the cot, and then, after closing and bolting the door, he lighted one of the lamps and examined the wound.

The bullet had struck a glancing blow upon the skull. There was an ugly flesh wound, but no signs of a fracture of the skull.

D'Arnot breathed a sigh of relief, and went about bathing the blood from Tarzan's face.

Soon the cool water revived him, and presently he opened his eyes to look in questioning surprise at D'Arnot.

The latter had bound the wound with pieces of cloth, and as he saw that Tarzan had regained consciousness he arose and going to the table wrote a message, which he handed to the ape-man, explaining the terrible mistake he had made and how thankful he was that the wound was not more serious.

Tarzan, after reading the message, sat on the edge of the couch and laughed.

"It is nothing," he said in French, and then, his vocabulary failing him, he wrote:

You should have seen what Bolgani did to me, and Kerchak, and Terkoz, before I killed them—then you would laugh at such a little scratch.

D'Arnot handed Tarzan the two messages that had been left for him.

Tarzan read the first one through with a look of sorrow on his face. The second one he turned over and over, searching for an opening—he had never seen a sealed envelope before. At length he handed it to D'Arnot.

The Frenchman had been watching him, and knew that Tarzan was puzzled over the envelope. How strange it seemed that to a fullgrown white man an envelope was a mystery. D'Arnot opened it and handed the letter back to Tarzan.

Sitting on a camp stool the ape-man spread the written sheet before him and read:

To Tarzan of the Apes:

Before I leave let me add my thanks to those of Mr. Clayton for the kindness you have shown in permitting us the use of your cabin.

That you never came to make friends with us has been a great regret to us. We should have liked so much to have seen and thanked our host.

There is another I should like to thank also, but he did not come back, though I cannot believe that he is dead.

I do not know his name. He is the great white giant who wore the diamond locket upon his breast.

If you know him and can speak his language carry my thanks to him, and tell him that I waited seven days for him to return.

Tell him, also, that in my home in America, in the city of Baltimore, there will always be a welcome for him if he cares to come.

I found a note you wrote me lying among the leaves beneath a tree near the cabin. I do not know how you learned to love me, who have never spoken to me, and I am very sorry if it is true, for I have already given my heart to another.

But know that I am always your friend,

JANE PORTER.

Tarzan sat with gaze fixed upon the floor for nearly an hour. It was evident to him from the notes that they did not know that he and Tarzan of the Apes were one and the same.

"I have given my heart to another," he repeated over and over again to himself.

Then she did not love him! How could she have pretended love, and raised him to such a pinnacle of hope only to cast him down to such utter depths of despair!

Maybe her kisses were only signs of friendship. How did he know, who knew nothing of the customs of human beings?

Suddenly he arose, and, bidding D'Arnot good night as he had learned to do, threw himself upon the couch of ferns that had been Jane Porter's.

D'Arnot extinguished the lamp, and lay down upon the cot.

For a week they did little but rest; D'Arnot coaching Tarzan in French. At the end of that time the two men could converse quite easily.

One night, as they were sitting within the cabin before retiring, Tarzan turned to D'Arnot.

"Where is America?" he said.

D'Arnot pointed toward the northwest.

"Many thousands of miles across the ocean," he replied. "Why?"

"I am going there."

D'Arnot shook his head.

"It is impossible, my friend," he said.

Tarzan rose, and, going to one of the cupboards, returned with a well thumbed geography.

Turning to a map of the world, he said:

"I have never quite understood all this; explain it to me, please."

When D'Arnot had done so, showing him that the blue represented all the water on the earth, and the bits of other colors the continents and islands, Tarzan asked him to point out the spot where they now were.

D'Arnot did so.

"Now point out America," said Tarzan.

And as D'Arnot placed his finger upon North America, Tarzan smiled and laid his palm upon the page, spanning the great ocean that lay between the two continents.

"You see it is not so very far," he said; "scarce the width of my hand."

D'Arnot laughed. How could he make the man understand?

Then he took a pencil and made a tiny point upon the shore of Africa.

"This little mark," he said, "is many times larger upon this map than your cabin is upon the earth. Do you see now how very far it is?"

Tarzan thought for a long time.

"Do any white men live in Africa?" he asked.

"Yes."

"Where are the nearest?"

D'Arnot pointed out a spot on the shore just north of them.

"So close?" asked Tarzan, in surprise.

"Yes," said D'Arnot; "but it is not close."

"Have they big boats to cross the ocean?"

"Yes."

"We shall go there tomorrow," announced Tarzan.

Again D'Arnot smiled and shook his head.

"It is too far. We should die long before we reached them."

"Do you wish to stay here then forever?" asked Tarzan.

"No," said D'Arnot.

"Then we shall start tomorrow. I do not like it here longer. I should rather die than remain here."

"Well," answered D'Arnot, with a shrug, "I do not know, my friend, but that I also would rather die than remain here. If you go, I shall go with you."

"It is settled then," said Tarzan. "I shall start for America tomorrow."

"How will you get to America without money?" asked D'Arnot.

"What is money?" inquired Tarzan.

It took a long time to make him understand even imperfectly.

"How do men get money?" he asked at last.

"They work for it."

"Very well. I will work for it, then."

"No, my friend," returned D'Arnot, "you need not worry about money, nor need you work for it. I have enough for two—enough for twenty. Much more than is good for one man, and you shall have all you need if ever we reach civilization."

So on the following day they started north along the shore. Each man carrying a rifle and ammunition, beside bedding and some food and cooking utensils.

The latter seemed to Tarzan a most useless encumbrance, so he threw his away.

"But you must learn to eat cooked food, my friend," remonstrated D'Arnot. "No civilized men eat raw flesh."

"There will be time enough when I reach civilization," said Tarzan. "I do not like the things and they only spoil the taste of good meat."

For a month they traveled north. Sometimes finding food in plenty and again going hungry for days.

They saw no signs of natives nor were they molested by wild beasts. Their journey was a miracle of ease.

Tarzan asked questions and learned rapidly. D'Arnot taught him many of the refinements of civilization—even to the use of knife and fork; but sometimes Tarzan would drop them in disgust and grasp his food in his strong brown hands, tearing it with his molars like a wild beast.

Then D'Arnot would expostulate with him, saying:

"You must not eat like a brute, Tarzan, while I am trying to make a gentleman of you. *Mon Dieu!* Gentlemen do not thus—it is terrible."

Tarzan would grin sheepishly and pick up his knife and fork again, but at heart he hated them.

On the journey he told D'Arnot about the great chest he had seen the sailors bury; of how he had dug it up and carried it to the gathering place of the apes and buried it there.

"It must be the treasure-chest of Professor Porter," said D'Arnot. "It is too bad, but of course you did not know."

Then Tarzan recalled the letter written by Jane Porter to her friend—the one he had stolen when they first came to his cabin, and now he knew what was in the chest and what it meant to Jane Porter.

"Tomorrow we shall go back after it," he announced to D'Arnot.

"Go back?" exclaimed D'Arnot. "But, my dear fellow, we have now been three weeks upon the march. It would require three more to return to the treasure, and then, with that enormous weight which required, you say, four sailors to carry, it would be months before we had again reached this spot."

"It must be done, my friend," insisted Tarzan. "You may go on toward civilization, and I will return for the treasure. I can go very much faster alone."

"I have a better plan, Tarzan," exclaimed D'Arnot. "We shall go on together to the nearest settlement, and there we will charter a boat and sail back down the coast for the treasure and so transport it easily.

"That will be safer and quicker and also not require us to be separated. What do you think of that plan?"

"Very well," said Tarzan. "The treasure will be there whenever we go for it; and while I could fetch it now, and catch up with you in a moon or two, I shall feel safer for you to know that you are not alone on the trail.

"When I see how helpless you are, D'Arnot, I often wonder how the human race has escaped annihilation all these ages which you tell me about. Why, Sabor, single handed, could exterminate a thousand of you."

D'Arnot laughed.

"You will think more highly of your genus when you have seen its armies and navies, its great cities, and its mighty engineering works. Then you will realize that it is mind, and not muscle, that makes the human animal greater than the mighty beasts of your jungle.

"Alone and unarmed, a single man is no match for any of the larger beasts; but if ten men were together, they would combine their wits and their muscles against their savage enemies, while the beasts, being unable to reason, would never think of combining against the men.

"Otherwise, Tarzan of the Apes, how long would you have lasted in the savage wilderness?"

"You are right, D'Arnot," replied Tarzan, "for if Kerchak had come to Tublat's aid that night at the Dum-Dum, there would have been an end of me. But Kerchak could never think far enough ahead to take advantage of any such opportunity.

"Even Kala, my mother, could never plan ahead. She simply ate what she needed when she needed it, and if the supply was very scarce, even though she found plenty for several meals, she would never gather any ahead.

"I remember that she used to think it very silly of me to burden myself with extra food upon the march, though she was quite glad to eat it with me, if the way chanced to be barren of sustenance."

"Then you knew your mother, Tarzan?" asked D'Arnot, in surprise.

"Yes. She was a great, fine ape, larger than I, and weighing twice as much."

"And your father?" asked D'Arnot.

"I did not know him. Kala told me he was a white ape, and hairless like myself. I know now that he must have been a white man."

D'Arnot looked long and earnestly at his companion.

"Tarzan," he said at length, "it is impossible that the ape, Kala, was your mother. If such a thing can be, which I doubt, you would have inherited some of the characteristics of the ape, but you have not—you are pure man, and, I should say, the offspring of highly bred and intelligent parents.

"Have you not the slightest clue to your past?"

"Not the slightest," replied Tarzan.

"No writings in the cabin that might have told something of the lives of its original inmates?"

"I have read everything that was in the cabin with the exception of one book which I know now to be written in a language other than English. Possibly you can read it."

Tarzan fished the little black diary from the bottom of his quiver, and handed it to his companion.

D'Arnot glanced at the title page.

"It is the diary of John Clayton, Lord Greystoke, an English nobleman, and it is written in French," he said.

Then he proceeded to read the diary that had been written over twenty years before, and which recorded the details of the story which we already know—the story of adventure, hardships and sorrow of John Clayton and his wife Alice, from the day they left England until an hour before he was struck down by Kerchak.

D'Arnot read aloud. At times his voice broke, and he was forced to stop reading for the pitiful, hopelessness that spoke between the lines.

Occasionally he glanced at Tarzan; but the ape-man sat upon his haunches, like a carven image, his eyes fixed upon the ground.

Only when the little babe was mentioned did the tone of the diary alter from the habitual note of despair which had crept into it by degrees after the first two months upon the shore.

Then the passages were tinged with a subdued happiness that was even sadder than the rest.

One entry showed an almost hopeful spirit.

Today our little boy is six months old. He is sitting in Alice's lap beside the table where I am writing—a happy, healthy, perfect child.

Somehow, even against all reason, I seem to see him a grown man, taking his father's place in the world—the second John Clayton—and bringing added honors to the house of Greystoke.

There—as though to give my prophecy the weight of his endorsement—he has grabbed my pen in his chubby fist and with his inkbegrimed little fingers has placed the seal of his tiny finger prints upon the page.

And there, on the margin of the page, were the partially blurred imprints of four wee fingers and the outer half of the thumb.

When D'Arnot had finished the diary the two men sat in silence for some minutes.

"Well! Tarzan of the Apes, what think you?" asked D'Arnot. "Does not this little book clear up the mystery of your parentage?

"Why, man, you are Lord Greystoke."

Tarzan shook his head.

"The book speaks of but one child," he replied. "Its little skeleton lay in the crib, where it died crying for nourishment, from the first time I entered the cabin until Professor Porter's party buried it, with its father and mother, beside the cabin.

"No, that was the babe the book speaks of—and the mystery of my origin is deeper than before, for I have thought much of late of the possibility of that cabin having been my birthplace.

"I am afraid that Kala spoke the truth," he concluded sadly.

D'Arnot shook his head. He was unconvinced, and in his mind had sprung the determination to prove the correctness of his theory, for he had discovered the key which alone could unlock the mystery, or consign it forever to the realms of the unfathomable.

A week later the two men came suddenly upon a clearing in the forest.

In the distance were several buildings surrounded by a strong palisade. Between them and the enclosure stretched a cultivated field in which a number of negroes were working.

The two halted at the edge of the jungle.

Tarzan fitted his bow with a poisoned arrow, but D'Arnot placed a hand upon his arm.

"What would you do, Tarzan?" he asked.

"They will try to kill us if they see us," replied Tarzan. "I prefer to be the killer."

"Maybe they are friends," suggested D'Arnot.

"They are black," was Tarzan's only reply.

And again he drew back his shaft.

"You must not, Tarzan!" cried D'Arnot. "White men do not kill wantonly. *Mon Dieu!* but you have much to learn.

"I pity the ruffler who crosses you, my wild man, when I take you to Paris. I will have my hands full keeping your neck from beneath the guillotine."

Tarzan lowered his bow and smiled.

"I do not know why I should kill the blacks back there in my jungle, yet not kill them here. Suppose Numa, the lion, should spring out upon us, I should say, then, I presume: Good morning, Monsieur Numa, how is Madame Numa; eh?"

"Wait until the blacks spring upon you," replied D'Arnot, "then you may kill them. Do not assume that men are your enemies until they prove it."

"Come," said Tarzan, "let us go and present ourselves to be killed," and he started straight across the field, his head high held and the tropical sun beating upon his smooth, brown skin.

Behind him came D'Arnot, clothed in some garments which had been discarded at the cabin by Clayton when the officers of the French cruiser had fitted him out in more presentable fashion.

Presently one of the blacks looked up, and beholding Tarzan, turned, shrieking, toward the palisade.

In an instant the air was filled with cries of terror from the fleeing gardeners, but before any had reached the palisade a white man emerged from the enclosure, rifle in hand, to discover the cause of the commotion.

What he saw brought his rifle to his shoulder, and Tarzan of the Apes would have felt cold lead once again had not D'Arnot cried loudly to the man with the leveled gun:

"Do not fire! We are friends!"

"Halt, then!" was the reply.

"Stop, Tarzan!" cried D'Arnot. "He thinks we are enemies."

Tarzan dropped into a walk, and together he and D'Arnot advanced toward the white man by the gate.

The latter eyed them in puzzled bewilderment.

"What manner of men are you?" he asked, in French.

"White men," replied D'Arnot. "We have been lost in the jungle for a long time."

The man had lowered his rifle and now advanced with outstretched hand.

"I am Father Constantine of the French Mission* here," he said, "and I am glad to welcome you."

"This is Monsieur Tarzan, Father Constantine," replied D'Arnot, indicating the ape-man; and as the priest extended his hand to Tarzan, D'Arnot added: "and I am Paul d'Arnot, of the French Navy."

Father Constantine took the hand which Tarzan extended in imitation of the priest's act, while the latter took in the superb physique and handsome face in one quick, keen glance.

And thus came Tarzan of the Apes to the first outpost of civilization.

For a week they remained there, and the ape-man, keenly observant, learned much of the ways of men; while black women sewed upon white duck garments for himself and D'Arnot that they might continue their journey properly clothed.

CHAPTER XXVI

THE HEIGHT OF CIVILIZATION*

ANOTHER month brought them to a little group of buildings at the mouth of a wide river, and there Tarzan saw many boats, and was filled with the old timidity of the wild thing by the sight of many men.

Gradually he became accustomed to the strange noises and the odd ways of civilization, so that presently none might know that two short months before, this handsome Frenchman in immaculate white ducks, who laughed and chatted with the gayest of them, had been swinging naked through primeval forests to pounce upon some unwary victim, which, raw, was to fill his savage belly.

The knife and fork, so contemptuously flung aside a month before, Tarzan now manipulated as exquisitely as did the polished D'Arnot.

So apt a pupil had he been that the young Frenchman had labored assiduously to make of Tarzan of the Apes a polished gentleman in so far as nicety of manners and speech were concerned.

"God made you a gentleman at heart, my friend," D'Arnot had said; "but we want His works to show upon the exterior also."

As soon as they had reached the little port, D'Arnot had cabled his government of his safety, and requested a three-months leave, which had been granted.

He had also cabled his bankers for funds, and the enforced wait of a month, under which both chafed, was due to their inability to charter a vessel for the return to Tarzan's jungle after the treasure.

During their stay at the coast town "Monsieur Tarzan" became the wonder of both whites and blacks because of several occurrences which to Tarzan seemed the merest of nothings.

Once a huge black, crazed by drink, had run amuck and terrorized the town, until his evil star had led him to where the black haired French giant lolled upon the veranda of the hotel.

Mounting the broad steps, with brandishing knife, the negro made straight for a party of four men sitting at a table sipping the inevitable absinthe.*

Shouting in alarm, the four took to their heels, and then the black spied Tarzan.

With a roar he charged the ape-man, while half a hundred heads peered from sheltering windows and doorways to witness the butchering of the poor Frenchman by the giant black.

Tarzan met the rush with the fighting smile that the joy of battle always brought to his lips.

As the negro closed upon him, steel muscles gripped the black wrist of the uplifted knife-hand, and a single swift wrench left the hand dangling below a broken bone.

With the pain and surprise, the madness left the black man, and as Tarzan dropped back into his chair the fellow turned, crying with agony, and dashed wildly toward the native village.

On another occasion as Tarzan and D'Arnot sat at dinner with a number of other whites, the talk fell upon lions and lion hunting.

Opinion was divided as to the bravery of the king of beasts—some maintaining that he was an arrant coward, but all agreeing that it was with a feeling of greater security that they gripped their express rifles* when the monarch of the jungle roared about a camp at night.

D'Arnot and Tarzan had agreed that his past be kept secret, and so none other than the French officer knew of the ape-man's familiarity with the beasts of the jungle.

"Monsieur Tarzan has not expressed himself," said one of the party. "A man of his prowess who has spent some time in Africa, as I understand Monsieur Tarzan has, must have had experiences with lions—yes?"

"Some," replied Tarzan, dryly. "Enough to know that each of you are right in your judgment of the characteristics of the lions—you have met. But one might as well judge all blacks by the fellow who ran amuck last week, or decide that all whites are cowards because one has met a cowardly white.

"There is as much individuality among the lower orders, gentlemen, as there is among ourselves.

"Today we may go out and stumble upon a lion which is over-timid—he runs away from us. Tomorrow we may meet his uncle or his twin-brother, and our friends wonder why we do not return from the jungle.

"For myself, I always assume that a lion is ferocious, and so I am never caught off my guard."

"There would be little pleasure in hunting," retorted the first speaker, "if one is afraid of the thing he hunts."

D'Arnot smiled. Tarzan afraid!

"I do not exactly understand what you mean by fear," said Tarzan. "Like lions, fear is a different thing in different men, but to me the only pleasure in the hunt is the knowledge that the hunted thing has power to harm me as much as I have to harm him.

"If I went out with a couple of rifles and a gun bearer, and twenty or thirty beaters, to hunt a lion, I should not feel that the lion had much chance, and so the pleasure of the hunt would be lessened in proportion to the increased safety which I felt."

"Then I am to take it that Monsieur Tarzan would prefer to go naked into the jungle, armed only with a jack knife, to kill the king of beasts," laughed the other, good naturedly, but with the merest touch of sarcasm in his tone.

"And a piece of rope," added Tarzan.

Just then the deep roar of a lion sounded from the distant jungle, as though to challenge whoever dared enter the lists with him.

"There is your opportunity, Monsieur Tarzan," bantered the Frenchman.

"I am not hungry," said Tarzan simply.

The men laughed, all but D'Arnot. He alone knew that a savage beast had spoken its simple reason through the lips of the ape-man.

"But you are afraid, just as any of us would be, to go out there naked, armed only with a knife and a piece of rope," said the banterer. "Is it not so?"

"No," replied Tarzan. "Only a fool performs any act without reason."

"Five thousand francs is a reason," said the other. "I wager you that amount you can not bring back a lion from the jungle under the conditions we have named—naked and armed only with a knife and a piece of rope."

Tarzan glanced toward D'Arnot and nodded his head.

"Make it ten thousand," said D'Arnot.

"Done," replied the other.

Tarzan arose.

"I shall have to leave my clothes at the edge of the settlement, so that if I do not return before daylight I shall have something to wear through the streets."

"You are not going now," exclaimed the wagerer—"at night?"

"Why not?" asked Tarzan. "Numa walks abroad at night—it will be easier to find him."

"No," said the other, "I do not want your blood upon my hands. It will be foolhardy enough if you go forth by day."

"I shall go now," replied Tarzan, and went to his room for his knife and rope.

The men accompanied him to the edge of the jungle, where he left his clothes in a small storehouse.

But when he would have entered the blackness of the undergrowth they tried to dissuade him; and the wagerer was most insistent of all that he abandon his foolhardy venture.

"I will accede that you have won," he said, "and the ten thousand francs are yours if you will but give up this foolish attempt, which can only end in your death."

Tarzan laughed, and in another moment the jungle had swallowed him.

The men stood silent for some moments and then slowly turned and walked back to the hotel veranda.

Tarzan had no sooner entered the jungle than he took to the trees, and it was with a feeling of exultant freedom that he swung once more through the forest branches.

This was life! ah, how he loved it! Civilization held nothing like this in its narrow and circumscribed sphere, hemmed in by restrictions and conventionalities. Even clothes were a hinderance and a nuisance.

At last he was free. He had not realized what a prisoner he had been.

How easy it would be to circle back to the coast, and then make toward the south and his own jungle and cabin.

Now he caught the scent of Numa, for he was traveling up wind. Presently his quick ears detected the familiar sound of padded feet and the brushing of a huge, furclad body through the undergrowth.

Tarzan came quietly above the unsuspecting beast and silently stalked him until he came into a little patch of moonlight.

Then the quick noose settled and tightened about the tawny throat, and, as he had done it a hundred times in the past, Tarzan made fast the end to a strong branch and, while the beast fought and clawed for freedom, dropped to the ground behind him, and leaping upon the great back, plunged his long thin blade a dozen times into the fierce heart.

Then with his foot upon the carcass of Numa, he raised his voice in the awesome victory cry of his savage tribe.

For a moment Tarzan stood irresolute, swayed by conflicting emotions of loyalty to D'Arnot and a mighty lust for the freedom of his own jungle. At last the vision of a beautiful face, and the memory of warm lips crushed to his dissolved the fascinating picture he had been drawing of his old life.

The ape-man threw the warm carcass of Numa across his shoulders and took to the trees once more.

The men upon the veranda had sat for an hour, almost in silence.

They had tried ineffectually to converse on various subjects, and always the thing uppermost in the mind of each had caused the conversation to lapse.

"*Mon Dieu*," said the wagerer at length, "I can endure it no longer. I am going into the jungle with my express and bring back that mad man."

"I will go with you," said one.

"And I"—"And I"—"And I," chorused the others.

As though the suggestion had broken the spell of some horrid nightmare they hastened to their various quarters, and presently were headed toward the jungle—each man heavily armed.

"God! What was that?" suddenly cried one of the party, an Englishman, as Tarzan's savage cry came faintly to their ears.

"I heard the same thing once before," said a Belgian, "when I was in the gorilla country. My carriers said it was the cry of a great bull ape who has made a kill."

D'Arnot remembered Clayton's description of the awful roar with which Tarzan had announced his kills, and he half smiled in spite of the horror which filled him to think that the uncanny sound could have issued from a human throat—from the lips of his friend.

As the party stood finally near the edge of the jungle, debating as to the best distribution of their forces, they were startled by a low laugh near them, and turning, beheld advancing toward them a giant figure bearing a dead lion upon its broad shoulders.

Even D'Arnot was thunderstruck, for it seemed impossible that the man could have so quickly dispatched a lion with the pitiful weapons he had taken, or that alone he could have borne the huge carcass through the tangled jungle.

The men crowded about Tarzan with many questions, but his only answer was a laughing depreciation of his feat.

To Tarzan it was as though one should eulogize a butcher for his heroism in killing a cow, for Tarzan had killed so often for food and for self-preservation that the act seemed anything but remarkable to him. But he was indeed a hero in the eyes of these men—men accustomed to hunting big game.

Incidentally, he had won ten thousand francs, for D'Arnot insisted that he keep it all.

This was a very important item to Tarzan, who was just commencing to realize the power which lay behind the little pieces of metal and paper which always changed hands when human beings rode, or ate, or slept, or clothed themselves, or drank, or worked, or played, or sheltered themselves from the rain or cold or sun.

It had become evident to Tarzan that without money one must die. D'Arnot had told him not to worry, since he had more than enough for both, but the ape-man was learning many things and one of them was that people looked down upon one who accepted money from another without giving something of equal value in exchange.

Shortly after the episode of the lion hunt, D'Arnot succeeded in chartering an ancient tub for the coastwise trip to Tarzan's land-locked harbor.

It was a happy morning for them both when the little vessel weighed anchor and made for the open sea.

The trip to the beach was uneventful, and the morning after they dropped anchor before the cabin, Tarzan, garbed once more in his jungle regalia, and carrying a spade, set out alone for the amphitheater of the apes where lay the treasure.

Late the next day he returned, bearing the great chest upon his shoulder, and at sunrise the little vessel was worked through the harbor's mouth and took up her northward journey.

Three weeks later Tarzan and D'Arnot were passengers on board a French steamer bound for Lyons, and after a few days in that city D'Arnot took Tarzan to Paris.

The ape-man was anxious to proceed to America, but D'Arnot insisted that he must accompany him to Paris first, nor would he divulge the nature of the urgent necessity upon which he based his demand.

One of the first things which D'Arnot accomplished after their arrival was to arrange to visit a high official of the police department, an old friend; and to take Tarzan with him.

Adroitly D'Arnot led the conversation from point to point until the policeman had explained to the interested Tarzan many of the methods in vogue for apprehending and identifying criminals.

Not the least interesting to Tarzan was the part played by finger prints in this fascinating science.

"But of what value are these imprints," asked Tarzan, "when, after a few years the lines upon the fingers are entirely changed by the wearing out of the old tissue and the growth of new?"

"The lines never change," replied the official. "From infancy to senility the finger prints of an individual change only in size, except as injuries alter the loops and whorls. But if imprints have been taken of the thumb and four fingers of both hands one must needs lose all entirely to escape identification."*

"It is marvellous," exclaimed D'Arnot. "I wonder what the lines upon my own fingers may resemble."

"We can soon see," replied the police officer, and ringing a bell he summoned an assistant to whom he issued a few directions.

The man left the room, but presently returned with a little hard wood box which he placed on his superior's desk.

"Now," said the officer, "you shall have your finger prints in a second."

He drew from the little case a square of plate glass, a little tube of thick ink, a rubber roller, and a few snowy white cards.

Squeezing a drop of ink onto the glass, he spread it back and forth with the rubber roller until the entire surface of the glass was covered to his satisfaction with a very thin and uniform layer of ink.

"Place the four fingers of your right hand upon the glass, thus," he said to D'Arnot. "Now the thumb. That is right. Now place them in just the same position upon this card, here, no—a little to the right. We must leave room for the thumb and the fingers of the left hand. There, that's it. Now the same with the left."

"Come, Tarzan," cried D'Arnot, "let's see what your whorls look like."

Tarzan complied readily, asking many questions of the officer during the operation.

"Do finger prints show racial characteristics?" he asked. "Could you determine, for example, solely from finger prints whether the subject was Negro or Caucasian?"

"I think not," replied the officer, "although some claim that those of the negro are less complex."*

"Could the finger prints of an ape be detected from those of a man?"

"Probably, because the ape's would be far simpler than those of the higher organism."*

"But a cross between an ape and a man might show the characteristics of either progenitor?" continued Tarzan.

"Yes, I should think likely," responded the official; "but the science has not progressed sufficiently to render it exact enough in such matters. I should hate to trust its findings further than to differentiate between individuals.

"There it is absolute. No two people born into the world probably have ever had identical lines upon all their digits. It is very doubtful if any single finger print will ever be exactly duplicated by any finger other than the one which originally made it."

"Does the comparison require much time or labor?" asked D'Arnot.

"Ordinarily but a few moments, if the impressions are distinct."

D'Arnot drew a little black book from his pocket and commenced turning the pages.

Tarzan looked at the book in surprise. How did D'Arnot come to have his book?

Presently D'Arnot stopped at a page on which were five tiny little smudges.

He handed the open book to the policeman.

"Are these imprints similar to mine or Monsieur Tarzan's, or can you say that they are identical with either?"

The officer drew a powerful glass from his desk and examined all three specimens carefully, making notations meanwhile upon a pad of paper.

Tarzan realized now what was the meaning of their visit to the police officer.

The answer to his life's riddle lay in these tiny marks.

With tense nerves he sat leaning forward in his chair, but suddenly he relaxed and dropped back, smiling.

D'Arnot looked at him in surprise.

"You forget that for twenty years the dead body of the child who made those finger prints lay in the cabin of his father, and that all my life I have seen it lying there," said Tarzan bitterly.

The policeman looked up in astonishment.

"Go ahead, captain, with your examination," said D'Arnot, "we will tell you the story later—provided Monsieur Tarzan is agreeable."

Tarzan nodded his head.

"But you are mad, my dear D'Arnot," he insisted. "Those little fingers are buried on the west coast of Africa."

"I do not know as to that, Tarzan," replied D'Arnot. "It is possible, but if you are not the son of John Clayton then how in heaven's name did you come into that God forsaken jungle where no white man other than John Clayton had ever set foot?"

"You forget—Kala," said Tarzan.

"I do not even consider her," replied D'Arnot.

The friends had walked to the broad window overlooking the boulevard as they talked. For some time they stood there gazing out upon the busy throng beneath, each wrapped in his own thoughts.

"It takes some time to compare finger prints," thought D'Arnot, turning to look at the police officer.

To his astonishment he saw the official leaning back in his chair hastily scanning the contents of the little black diary.

D'Arnot coughed. The policeman looked up, and, catching his eye, raised his finger to admonish silence.

D'Arnot turned back to the window, and presently the police officer spoke.

"Gentlemen," he said.

Both turned toward him.

"There is evidently a great deal at stake which must hinge to a greater or lesser extent upon the absolute correctness of this comparison. I therefore ask that you leave the entire matter in my hands until Monsieur Desquerc, our expert, returns. It will be but a matter of a few days."

"I had hoped to know at once," said D'Arnot. "Monsieur Tarzan sails for America tomorrow."

"I will promise that you can cable him a report within two weeks," replied the officer; "but what it will be I dare not say. There are resemblances, yet—well, we had better leave it for Monsieur Desquerc to solve."

CHAPTER XXVII

THE GIANT AGAIN

A TAXICAB drew up before an old-fashioned residence upon the outskirts of Baltimore.

A man of about forty, well built and with strong, regular features, stepped out, and paying the chauffeur dismissed him.

A moment later the passenger was entering the library of the old home.

"Ah, Mr. Canler!" exclaimed an old man, rising to greet him.

"Good evening, my dear Professor," cried the man, extending a cordial hand.

"Who admitted you?" asked the professor.

"Esmeralda."

"Then she will acquaint Jane with the fact that you are here," said the old man.

"No, Professor," replied Canler, "for I came primarily to see you."

"Ah, I am honored," said Professor Porter.

"Professor," continued Robert Canler, with great deliberation, as though carefully weighing his words, "I have come this evening to speak with you about Jane.

"You know my aspirations, and you have been generous enough to approve my suit."

Professor Archimedes Q. Porter fidgeted in his armchair. The subject always made him uncomfortable. He could not understand why. Canler was a splendid match.

"But Jane," continued Canler, "I cannot understand her. She puts me off first on one ground and then another. I have always the feeling that she breathes a sigh of relief every time I bid her good by."

"Tut—tut," said Professor Porter. "Tut—tut, Mr. Canler. Jane is a most obedient daughter. She will do precisely as I tell her."

"Then I can still count on your support?" asked Canler, a tone of relief marking his voice.

"Certainly, sir; certainly, sir," exclaimed Professor Porter. "How could you doubt it?"

"There is young Clayton, you know," suggested Canler. "He has been hanging about for months.

"I don't know that Jane cares for him; but beside his title they say he has inherited a very considerable estate from his father, and it might not be strange, if he finally won her, unless—" and Canler paused.

"Tut—tut, Mr. Canler; unless—what?"

"Unless, you see fit to request that Jane and I be married at once," said Canler, slowly and distinctly.

"I have already suggested to Jane that it would be desirable," said Professor Porter sadly, "for we can no longer afford to keep up this house, and live as her associations demand."

"What was her reply?" asked Canler.

"She said she was not ready to marry anyone yet," replied Professor Porter, "and that we could go and live upon the farm in northern Wisconsin which her mother left her.

"It is a little more than self-supporting. The tenants have always made a living from it, and been able to send Jane a trifle beside, each year.

"She is planning on our going up there the first of the week. Philander and Mr. Clayton have already gone to get things in readiness for us."

"Clayton has gone there?" exclaimed Canler, visibly chagrined. "Why was not I told? I would gladly have gone and seen that every comfort was provided."

"Jane feels that we are already too much in your debt, Mr. Canler," said Professor Porter.

Canler was about to reply, when the sound of footsteps came from the hall without, and Jane Porter entered the room.

"Oh, I beg your pardon!" she exclaimed, pausing on the threshold. "I thought you were alone, papa."

"It is only I, Jane," said Canler, who had risen, "won't you come in and join the family group? We were just speaking of you."

"Thank you," said Jane Porter, entering and taking the chair Canler placed for her. "I only wanted to tell papa that Tobey is coming down from the college tomorrow to pack his books. I want you to be sure, papa, to indicate all that you can do without until fall. Please don't carry this entire library to Wisconsin, as you would have carried it to Africa, if I had not put my foot down."

"Was Tobey here?" asked Professor Porter.

"Yes, I just left him. He and Esmeralda are exchanging religious experiences on the back porch now."

"Tut—tut, I must see him at once!" cried the professor. "Excuse me just a moment, children," and the old man hastened from the room.

As soon as he was out of ear-shot Canler turned to Jane Porter.

"See here, Jane," he said bluntly. "How long is this thing going on like this?

"You haven't refused to marry me, but you haven't promised either.

"I want to get the license tomorrow, so that we can be married quietly before you leave for Wisconsin. I don't care for any fuss or feathers, and I'm sure you don't either."

The girl turned cold, but she held her head bravely.

"Your father wishes it, you know," added Canler.

"Yes, I know."

She spoke scarcely above a whisper.

"Do you realize that you are buying me, Mr. Canler?" she said finally, and in a cold, level voice. "Buying me for a few paltry dollars? Of course you do, Robert Canler, and the hope of just such a contingency was in your mind when you loaned papa the money for that hair-brained escapade, which but for a most mysterious circumstance would have been surprisingly successful.

"But you, Mr. Canler, would have been the most surprised. You had no idea that the venture would succeed. You are too good a business man for that. And you are too good a business man to loan money for buried-treasure seeking, or to loan money without security—unless you had some special object in view.

"You knew that without security you had a greater hold on the honor of the Porters than with it. You knew the one best way to force me to marry you, without seeming to force me.

"You have never mentioned the loan. In any other man I should have thought that the prompting of a magnanimous and noble character. But you are deep, Mr. Robert Canler. I know you better than you think I know you.

"I shall certainly marry you if there is no other way, but let us understand each other once and for all."

While she spoke Robert Canler had alternately flushed and paled, and when she ceased speaking he arose, and with a cynical smile upon his strong face, said:

"You surprise me, Jane. I thought you had more self control—more pride.

"Of course you are right. I am buying you, and I knew that you knew it, but I thought you would prefer to pretend that it was otherwise. I should have thought your self-respect and your Porter pride would have shrunk from admitting, even to yourself, that you were a bought woman.

"But have it your own way, dear girl," he added lightly. "I am going to have you, and that is all that interests me."

Without a word the girl turned and left the room.

Jane Porter was not married before she left with her father and Esmeralda for her little Wisconsin farm, and as she coldly bid Robert Canler good by as her train pulled out, he called to her that he would join them in a week or two.

At their destination they were met by Clayton and Mr. Philander in a huge touring car belonging to the former, and quickly whirled away through the dense northern woods toward the little farm which the girl had not visited before since childhood.

The farm house, which stood on a little elevation some hundred yards from the tenant house, had undergone a complete transformation, during the three weeks that Clayton and Mr. Philander had been there.

The former had imported a small army of carpenters and plasterers, plumbers and painters from a distant city, and what had been but a dilapidated shell when they reached it was now a cosy little two story house filled with every modern convenience procurable in so short a time.

"Why, Mr. Clayton, what have you done?" cried Jane Porter, her heart sinking within her as she realized the probable size of the expenditure that had been made.

"S-sh," cautioned Clayton. "Don't let your father guess. If you don't tell him he will never notice, and I simply couldn't think of him living in the terrible squalor and sordidness which Mr. Philander and I found. It was so little when I would do so much, Jane. For his sake, please, never mention it."

"But you know that we can't repay you," cried the girl. "Why do you want to put me under such terrible obligations?"

"Don't, Jane," said Clayton sadly. "If it had been just you, believe me, I wouldn't have done it, for I knew from the start that it would only hurt me in your eyes, but I couldn't think of that dear old man living in the hole we found here.

"Won't you please believe that I did it just for him and give me that little crumb of pleasure at least?"

"I do believe you, Mr. Clayton," said the girl, "because I know you are big enough and generous enough to have done it just for him—and, oh Cecil, I wish I might repay you as you deserve—as you would wish."

"Why can't you, Jane?"

"Because I love another."

"Canler?"

"No."

"But you are going to marry him. He told me as much before I left Baltimore."

The girl winced.

"I do not love him," she said, almost proudly.

"It is because of the money, Jane?"

She nodded.

"Then am I so much less desirable than Canler? I have money enough, and far more, for every need," he said bitterly.

"I do not love you, Cecil," she said, "but I respect you. If I must disgrace myself by such a bargain with any man, I prefer that it be one I already despise. I should loathe the man to whom I sold myself without love, whomsoever he might be.

"You will be happier," she concluded, "alone—with my respect and friendship, than with me and my contempt."

He did not press the matter further, but if ever a man had murder in his heart it was William Cecil Clayton, Lord Greystoke, when, a week later, Robert Canler drew up before the farm house in his purring six cylinder.*

A week passed; a tense, uneventful, but uncomfortable week for all the inmates of the little Wisconsin farm house.

Canler was insistent that Jane marry him at once.

At length she gave in from sheer loathing of the continued and hateful importuning.

It was agreed that on the morrow Canler was to drive to town and bring back the license and a minister.

Clayton had wanted to leave as soon as the plan was announced, but the girl's tired, hopeless look kept him. He could not desert her.

Something might happen yet, he tried to console himself by thinking. And in his heart, he knew that it would require but a tiny spark to turn his hatred for Canler into the blood lust of the killer.

Early the next morning Canler set out for town.

In the east smoke could be seen lying low over the forest, for a fire had been raging for a week not far from them, but the wind still lay in the west and no danger threatened them.

About noon Jane Porter started off for a walk. She would not let Clayton accompany her. She wanted to be alone, she said, and he respected her wishes.

In the house Professor Porter and Mr. Philander were immersed in an absorbing discussion of some weighty scientific problem. Esmeralda dozed in the kitchen, and Clayton, heavy-eyed after a sleepless night, threw himself down upon the couch in the living room and soon dropped into a fitful slumber.

To the east the black smoke clouds rose higher into the heavens, suddenly they eddied, and then commenced to drift rapidly toward the west.

On and on they came. The inmates of the tenant house were gone, for it was market day, and none there was to see the rapid approach of the fiery demon.

Soon the flames had spanned the road to the south and cut off Canler's return. A little fluctuation of the wind now carried the path of the forest fire to the north, then blew back and the flames nearly stood still as though held in leash by some master hand.

Suddenly, out of the north-east, a great black car came careening down the road.

With a jolt it stopped before the cottage, and a black haired giant leaped out to run up onto the porch. Without a pause he rushed into the house. On the couch lay Clayton. The man started in surprise, but with a bound was at the side of the sleeping man.

Shaking him roughly by the shoulder, he cried:

"My God, Clayton, are you all mad here? Don't you know you are nearly surrounded by fire? Where is Miss Porter?"

Clayton sprang to his feet. He did not recognize the man, but he understood the words and was upon the veranda in a bound.

"Scott!"* he cried, and then, dashing back into the house, "Jane! Jane! where are you?"

In an instant Esmeralda, Professor Porter and Mr. Philander had joined the two men.

"Where is Miss Jane?" cried Clayton, seizing Esmeralda by the shoulders and shaking her roughly.

"Oh, Gaberelle, Marse Clayton, she done gone for a walk."

"Hasn't she come back yet?" and, without waiting for a reply, Clayton dashed out into the yard, followed by the others.

"Which way did she go?" cried the black haired giant of Esmeralda.

"Down dat road," cried the frightened black, pointing toward the south where a mighty wall of roaring flames shut out the view.

"Put these people in the other car," shouted the stranger to Clayton. "I saw one as I drove up—and get them out of here by the north road.

"Leave my car here. If I find Miss Porter we shall need it. If I don't, no one will need it. Do as I say," as Clayton hesitated, and then they saw the lithe figure bound away across the clearing toward the northwest where the forest still stood, untouched by flame.

In each rose the unaccountable feeling that a great responsibility had been raised from their shoulders; a kind of implicit confidence in the power of the stranger to save Jane Porter if she could be saved.

"Who was that?" asked Professor Porter.

"I do not know," replied Clayton. "He called me by name and he knew Jane, for he asked for her. And he called Esmeralda by name."

"There was something most startlingly familiar about him," exclaimed Mr. Philander, "and yet, bless me, I know I never saw him before."

"Tut—tut!" cried Professor Porter. "Most remarkable! Who could it have been, and why do I feel that Jane is safe, now that he has set out in search of her?"

"I can't tell you, Professor," said Clayton soberly, "but I know I have the same uncanny feeling."

"But come," he cried, "we must get out of here ourselves, or we shall be shut off," and the party hastened toward Clayton's machine.

When Jane Porter turned to retrace her steps homeward, she was alarmed to note how near the smoke of the forest fire seemed, and as she hastened onward, her alarm became almost a panic when she perceived that the rushing flames were rapidly forcing their way between herself and the cottage.

At length she was compelled to turn into the dense thicket and attempt to force her way to the west in an effort to circle around the flames and regain her home.

In a short time the futility of her attempt became apparent and then her one hope lay in retracing her steps to the road and flying for her life to the south toward the town.

The twenty minutes that it took her to regain the road was all that had been needed to cut off her retreat as effectually as her advance had been cut off before.

A short run down the road brought her to a horrified stand, for there before her was another wall of flame. An arm of the parent conflagration had shot out a half mile south of its mate to embrace this tiny strip of road in its implacable clutches.

Jane Porter knew that it was useless again to attempt to force her way through the undergrowth.

She had tried it once, and failed. Now she realized that it would be but a matter of minutes ere the whole space between the enemy on the north and the enemy on the south would be a seething mass of billowing flames.

Calmly the girl kneeled down in the dust of the roadway and prayed to her Maker to give her strength to meet her fate bravely, and to deliver her father and her friends from death.

She did not think to pray for deliverance for herself; for she knew there was no hope—not even God could save her now.

Suddenly she heard her name being called aloud through the forest:

"Jane! Jane Porter!" It rang strong and clear, but in a strange voice.

"Here!" she called in reply. "Here! In the roadway!"

Then through the branches of the trees she saw a figure swinging with the speed of a squirrel.

A veering of the wind blew a cloud of smoke about them and she could no longer see the man who was speeding toward her, but suddenly she felt a great arm about her. Then she was lifted up, and she felt the rushing of the wind and the occasional brush of a branch as she was borne along.

She opened her eyes.

Far below her lay the undergrowth and the hard earth.

About her was the waving foliage of the forest.

From tree to tree swung the giant figure which bore her, and it seemed to Jane Porter that she was living over in a dream the experience that had been hers in that far African jungle.

Oh, if it were but the same man who had borne her so swiftly through the tangled verdure on that other day; but that were impossible. Yet who else in all the world was there with the strength and agility to do what this man was now doing?

She stole a sudden glance at the face close to hers, and then she gave a little frightened gasp—it was he!

"My man!" she murmured. "No, it is the delirium which precedes death."

She must have spoken aloud, for the eyes that bent occasionally to hers lighted with a smile.

"Yes, your man, Jane Porter; your savage, primeval man come out of the jungle to claim his mate—the woman who ran away from him," he added almost fiercely.

"I did not run away," she whispered. "I would only consent to leave when they had waited a week for you to return."

They had come to a point beyond the fire now, and he had turned back to the clearing.

Side by side they were walking toward the cottage. The wind had changed once more and the fire was burning back upon itself—another hour like that and it would be burned out.

"Why did you not return?" she asked.

"I was nursing D'Arnot. He was badly wounded."

"Ah, I knew it!" she exclaimed.

"They said you had gone to join the blacks—that they were your people."

He laughed.

"But you did not believe them, Jane?"

"No;——what shall I call you?" she asked. "What is your name?"

"I was Tarzan of the Apes when you first knew me," he said.

"Tarzan of the Apes!" she cried—"and that was your note I answered when I left?"

"Yes, whose did you think it was?"

"I did not know; only that it could not be yours, for Tarzan of the Apes had written in English, and you could not understand a word of any language."

Again he laughed.

"It is a long story, but it was I who wrote what I could not speak—and now D'Arnot has made matters worse by teaching me to speak French instead of English."

"Come," he added, "jump into my car, we must overtake your father, they are only a little way ahead."

As they drove along, he said:

"Then when you said in your note to Tarzan of the Apes that you loved another—you might have meant me?"

"I might have," she answered, simply.

"But in Baltimore—Oh, how I have searched for you—they told me you would possibly be married by now. That a man named Canler had come up here to wed you. Is that true?"

"Yes."

"Do you love him?"

"No."

"Do you love me?"

She buried her face in her hands.

"I am promised to another. I cannot answer you, Tarzan of the Apes," she cried.

"You have answered. Now, tell me why you would marry one you do not love."

"My father owes him money."

Suddenly there came back to Tarzan the memory of the letter he had read—and the name Robert Canler and the hinted trouble which he had been unable to understand then.

He smiled.

"If your father had not lost the treasure you would not feel forced to keep your promise to this man Canler?"

"I could ask him to release me."

"And if he refused?"

"I have given my promise."

He was silent for a moment. The car was plunging along the uneven road at a reckless pace, for the fire showed threateningly at their right, and another change of the wind might sweep it on with raging fury across this one avenue of escape.

Finally they passed the danger point, and Tarzan reduced their speed.

"Suppose I should ask him?" ventured Tarzan.

"He would scarcely accede to the demand of a stranger," said the girl. "Especially one who wanted me himself."

"Terkoz did," said Tarzan, grimly.

Jane Porter shuddered and looked fearfully up at the giant figure beside her, for she knew that he meant the great anthropoid he had killed in her defense.

"This is not an African jungle," she said. "You are no longer a savage beast. You are a gentleman, and gentlemen do not kill in cold blood."

"I am still a wild beast at heart," he said, in a low voice, as though to himself.

Again they were silent for a time.

"Jane Porter," said the man, at length, "if you were free, would you marry me?"

She did not reply at once, but he waited patiently.

The girl was trying to collect her thoughts.

What did she know of this strange creature at her side? What did he know of himself? Who was he? Who, his parents?

Why, his very name echoed his mysterious origin and his savage life.

He had no name. Could she be happy with this jungle waif? Could she find anything in common with a husband whose life had been spent in the tree tops of an African wilderness, frolicking and fighting with fierce anthropoids; tearing his food from the quivering flank of fresh-killed prey, sinking his strong teeth into raw flesh, and tearing away his portion while his mates growled and fought about him for their share?

Could he ever rise to her social sphere? Could she bear to think of sinking to his? Would either be happy in such a horrible misalliance?

"You do not answer," he said. "Do you shrink from wounding me?"

"I do not know what answer to make," said Jane Porter sadly. "I do not know my own mind."

"You do not love me, then?" he asked, in a level tone.

"Do not ask me. You will be happier without me. You were never meant for the formal restrictions and conventionalities of society—civilization would become irksome to you, and in a little while you would long for the freedom of your old life—a life to which I am as totally unfitted as you to mine."

"I think I understand you," he replied quietly. "I shall not urge you, for I would rather see you happy than to be happy myself.

"I see now that you could not be happy with—an ape."

There was just the faintest tinge of bitterness in his voice.

"Don't," she remonstrated. "Don't say that. You do not understand."

But before she could go on a sudden turn in the road brought them into the midst of a little hamlet.

Before them stood Clayton's car surrounded by the party he had brought from the cottage.

CHAPTER XXVIII

CONCLUSION*

AT THE sight of Jane Porter, cries of relief and delight broke from every lip, and, as Tarzan's car stopped beside the other, Professor Porter caught his daughter in his arms.

For a moment no one noticed Tarzan, sitting silently in his seat.

Clayton was the first to remember, and, turning, held out his hand.

"How can we ever thank you?" he exclaimed. "You have saved us all.

"You called me by name at the cottage, but I do not seem to recall yours, though there is something very familiar about you.

"It is as though I had known you well under very different conditions a long time ago."

Tarzan smiled as he took the proffered hand.

"You are quite right, Monsieur Clayton," he said, in French. "You will pardon me if I do not speak to you in English. I am just learning it, and while I understand it fairly well I speak it very poorly."

"But who are you?" insisted Clayton, speaking in French this time himself.

"Tarzan of the Apes."

Clayton started back in surprise.

"By Jove!" he exclaimed. "It is true."

And Professor Porter and Mr. Philander pressed forward to add their thanks to Clayton's, and to voice their surprise and pleasure at seeing their jungle friend so far from his savage home.

The party now entered the modest little hostelry, where Clayton soon made arrangements for their entertainment.

They were sitting in the little, stuffy parlor when the distant chugging of an approaching automobile caught their attention.

Mr. Philander, who was sitting near the window, looked out as the machine drew in sight, finally stopping beside the other cars.

"Bless me!" said Mr. Philander, a shade of annoyance in his tone. "It is Mr. Canler. I had hoped, er—I had thought or—er—how very happy we should be that he was not caught in the fire," he ended lamely.

"Tut—tut! Mr. Philander," said Professor Porter. "Tut—tut! I have often admonished my pupils to count ten before speaking. Were I you, Mr. Philander, I should count at least a thousand, and then maintain a discreet silence."

"Bless me, yes!" acquiesced Mr. Philander. "But who is the clerical appearing gentleman with him?"

Jane Porter blanched.

Clayton moved uneasily in his chair.

Professor Porter removed his spectacles nervously, and breathed upon them, but replaced them on his nose without wiping.

The ubiquitous Esmeralda grunted.

Only Tarzan did not comprehend.

Presently Robert Canler burst into the room.

"Thank God!" he cried. "I feared the worst, until I saw your car, Clayton. I was cut off on the south road and had to go away back to town, and then strike east to this road. I thought we'd never reach the cottage."

No one seemed to enthuse much. Tarzan eyed Robert Canler as Sabor eyes her prey.

Jane Porter glanced at him and coughed nervously.

"Mr. Canler," she said, "this is Monsieur Tarzan, an old friend."

Canler turned and extended his hand. Tarzan rose and bowed as only D'Arnot could have taught a gentleman to do it, but he did not seem to see Canler's hand.

Nor did Canler appear to notice the oversight.

"This is the Reverend Mr. Tousley, Jane," said Canler, turning to the clerical party behind him. "Mr. Tousley, Miss Porter."

Mr. Tousley bowed and beamed.

Canler introduced him to the others.

"We can have the ceremony at once, Jane," said Canler. "Then you and I can catch the midnight train in town."

Tarzan understood the plan instantly. He glanced out of half closed eyes at Jane Porter, but he did not move.

The girl hesitated. The room was tense with the silence of taut nerves.

All eyes turned toward Jane Porter, awaiting her reply.

"Can't we wait a few days?" she asked. "I am all unstrung. I have been through so much today."

Canler felt the hostility that emanated from each member of the party. It made him angry.

"We have waited as long as I intend to wait," he said roughly. "You have promised to marry me. I shall be played with no longer. I have the license and here is the preacher. Come Mr. Tousley; come Jane. There are witnesses a-plenty—more than enough," he added with a disagreeable inflection, and taking Jane Porter by the arm, he started to lead her toward the waiting minister.

But scarcely had he taken a single step ere a heavy hand closed upon his arm with a grip of steel.

Another hand shot to his throat and in a moment he was being shaken high above the floor, as a cat might shake a mouse.

Jane Porter turned in horrified surprise toward Tarzan.

And, as she looked into his face, she saw the crimson band upon his forehead that she had seen that other day in far distant Africa, when Tarzan of the Apes had closed in mortal combat with the great anthropoid—Terkoz.

She knew that murder lay in that savage heart, and with a little cry of horror she sprang forward to plead with the ape-man. But her fears were more for Tarzan than for Canler. She realized the stern retribution which justice metes to the murderer.

Before she could reach them, however, Clayton had jumped to Tarzan's side and attempted to drag Canler from his grasp.

With a single sweep of one mighty arm the Englishman was hurled across the room, and then Jane Porter laid a firm white hand upon Tarzan's wrist, and looked up into his eyes.

"For my sake," she said.

The grasp upon Canler's throat relaxed.

Tarzan looked down into the beautiful face before him.

"Do you wish this to live?" he asked in surprise.

"I do not wish him to die at your hands, my friend," she replied. "I do not wish you to become a murderer."

Tarzan removed his hand from Canler's throat.

"Do you release her from her promise?" he asked. "It is the price of your life."

Canler, gasping for breath, nodded.

"Will you go away and never molest her further?"

Again the man nodded his head, his face distorted by fear of the death that had been so close.

Tarzan released him, and Canler staggered toward the door. In another moment he was gone, and the terror stricken preacher with him.

Tarzan turned toward Jane Porter.

"May I speak with you for a moment, alone," he asked.

The girl nodded and started toward the door leading to the narrow veranda of the little hotel. She passed out to await Tarzan and so did not hear the conversation which followed.

"Wait," cried Professor Porter, as Tarzan was about to follow.

The professor had been stricken dumb with surprise by the rapid developments of the past few minutes.

"Before we go further, sir, I should like an explanation of the events which have just transpired.

"By what right, sir, did you interfere between my daughter and Mr. Canler?

"I had promised him her hand, sir, and regardless of our personal likes or dislikes, sir, that promise must be kept."

"I interfered, Professor Porter," replied Tarzan, "because your daughter does not love Mr. Canler—she does not wish to marry him. That is enough for me to know."

"You do not know what you have done," said Professor Porter. "Now he will doubtless refuse to marry her."

"He most certainly will," said Tarzan, emphatically.

"And further," added Tarzan, "you need not fear that your pride will suffer, Professor Porter, for you will be able to pay the Canler person what you owe him the moment you reach home."

"Tut—tut, sir!" exclaimed Professor Porter. "What do you mean, sir?"

"Your treasure has been found," said Tarzan.

"What—what is that you are saying?" cried the professor. "You are mad, man. It cannot be."

"It is, though. It was I who stole it, not knowing either its value or to whom it belonged. I saw the sailors bury it, and, ape-like, I had to dig it up and bury it again elsewhere.

"When D'Arnot told me what it was and what it meant to you I returned to the jungle and recovered it. It had caused so much crime and suffering and sorrow that D'Arnot thought it best not to attempt to bring the treasure itself on here, as had been my intention, so I have brought a letter of credit instead.

"Here it is, Professor Porter," and Tarzan drew an envelope from his pocket and handed it to the astonished Professor, "two hundred and forty-one thousand dollars.

"The treasure was most carefully appraised by experts, but lest there should be any question in your mind, D'Arnot himself bought it and is holding it for you, should you prefer the treasure to the credit."

"To the already great burden of the obligations we owe you, sir," said Professor Porter, with trembling voice, "is now added this greatest of all services. You have given me the means to save my honor."

Clayton, who had left the room a moment after Canler, now returned.

"Pardon me," he said. "I think we had better try to reach town before dark and take the first train out of this forest. A native just rode by from the north, who reports that the fire is moving slowly in this direction."

This announcement broke up further conversation, and the entire party went out to the waiting machines.

Clayton, with Jane Porter, the professor and Esmeralda occupied Clayton's car, while Tarzan took Mr. Philander in with him.

"Bless me!" exclaimed Mr. Philander, as the car moved off after Clayton's machine. "Who would ever have thought it possible! The last time I saw you you were a veritable wild man, skipping about among the branches of a tropical African forest, and now you are driving me along a Wisconsin road in a French automobile. Bless me! But it is most remarkable."

"Yes," assented Tarzan, and then, after a pause; "Mr. Philander, do you recall any of the details of the finding and burying of three skeletons found in my cabin beside that African jungle?"

"Very distinctly, sir, very distinctly," replied Mr. Philander.

"Was there anything peculiar about any of those skeletons?"

Mr. Philander eyed Tarzan narrowly.

"Why do you ask?"

"It means a great deal to me to know," replied Tarzan. "Your answer may clear up a mystery. It can do no worse, at any rate, than to leave it still a mystery.

"I have been entertaining a theory concerning those skeletons for the past two months, and I want you to answer my question to the best of your knowledge—were the three skeletons you buried all human skeletons?"

"No," said Mr. Philander, "the smallest one, the one found in the crib, was the skeleton of an anthropoid ape."

"Thank you," said Tarzan.

In the car ahead, Jane Porter was thinking fast and furiously. She had felt the purpose for which Tarzan had asked a few words with her, and she knew that she must be prepared to give him an answer in the very near future.

He was not the sort of person one could put off, and somehow that very thought made her wonder if she did not really fear him.

And could she love where she feared?

She realized the spell that had been upon her in the depths of that far-off jungle, but there was no spell of enchantment now in prosaic Wisconsin.

Nor did the immaculate young Frenchman appeal to the primal woman in her, as had the stalwart forest god.

Did she love him? She did not know—now.

She glanced at Clayton out of the corner of her eye. Was not here a man trained in the same school of environment in which she had been trained—a man with social position and culture such as she had been taught to consider as the prime essentials to congenial association?

Did not her best judgment point to this young English nobleman, whose love she knew to be of the sort a civilized woman should crave, as the logical mate for such as herself?

Could she love Clayton? She could see no reason why she could not. Jane Porter was not coldly calculating by nature, but training, environment and heredity had all combined to teach her to reason even in matters of the heart.

That she had been carried off her feet by the strength of the young giant when his great arms were about her in the distant African forest, and again today, in the Wisconsin woods, seemed to her only attributable to a temporary mental reversion to type on her part—to the psychological appeal of the primeval man to the primeval woman in her nature.

If he should never touch her again, she reasoned, she would never feel attracted toward him. She had not loved him, then. It had been nothing more than a passing hallucination, superinduced by excitement and by personal contact.

Excitement would not always mark their future relations, should she marry him, and the power of personal contact eventually would be dulled by familiarity.

Again she glanced at Clayton. He was very handsome and every inch a gentleman. She should be very proud of such a husband.

And then he spoke—a minute sooner or a minute later might have made all the difference in the world to three lives—but chance stepped in and pointed out to Clayton the psychological moment.

"You are free now, Jane," he said. "Won't you say yes—I will devote my life to making you very happy."

"Yes," she whispered.

That evening in the little waiting room at the station Tarzan caught Jane Porter alone for a moment.

"You are free now, Jane," he said, "and I have come across the ages out of the dim and distant past from the lair of the primeval man to claim you—for your sake I have become a civilized man—for your sake I have crossed oceans and continents—for your sake I will be whatever you will me to be. I can make you happy, Jane, in the life you know and love best. Will you marry me?"

For the first time she realized the depths of the man's love—all that he had accomplished in so short a time solely for love of her. Turning her head she buried her face in her arms.

What had she done? Because she had been afraid she might succumb to the pleas of this giant, she had burned her bridges behind her—in her groundless apprehension that she might make a terrible mistake, she had made a worse one.

And then she told him all—told him the truth word by word, without attempting to shield herself or condone her error.

"What can we do?" he asked. "You have admitted that you love me. You know that I love you; but I do not know the ethics of society by which you are governed. I shall leave the decision to you, for you know best what will be for your eventual welfare."

"I cannot tell him, Tarzan," she said. "He too, loves me, and he is a good man. I could never face you nor any other honest person if I repudiated my promise to Mr. Clayton.

"I shall have to keep it—and you must help me bear the burden, though we may not see each other again after tonight."

The others were entering the room now and Tarzan turned toward the little window.

But he saw nothing without—within he saw a patch of greensward surrounded by a matted mass of gorgeous tropical plants and flowers, and, above, the waving foliage of mighty trees, and, over all, the blue of an equatorial sky.

In the center of the greensward a young woman sat upon a little mound of earth, and beside her sat a young giant. They ate pleasant fruit and looked into each other's eyes and smiled. They were very happy, and they were all alone.

His thoughts were broken in upon by the station agent who entered asking if there was a gentleman by the name of Tarzan in the party.

"I am Monsieur Tarzan," said the ape-man.

"Here is a message for you, forwarded from Baltimore; it is a cablegram from Paris."

Tarzan took the envelope and tore it open. The message was from D'Arnot.

It read:

Finger prints prove you Greystoke. Congratulations.

D'Arnot.

As Tarzan finished reading Clayton entered, and came toward him with extended hand.

Here was the man who had Tarzan's title, and Tarzan's estates, and was going to marry the woman whom Tarzan loved—the woman who loved Tarzan. A single word from Tarzan would make a great difference in this man's life.

It would take away his title and his lands and his castles, and—it would take them away from Jane Porter also.

"I say, old man," cried Clayton, "I haven't had a chance to thank you for all you've done for us. It seems as though you had your hands full saving our lives in Africa and here.

"I'm awfully glad you came on here. We must get better acquainted. I often thought about you, you know, and the remarkable circumstances of your environment.

"If it's any of my business, how the devil did you ever get into that bally jungle?"

"I was born there," said Tarzan, quietly. "My mother was an Ape, and of course she couldn't tell me much about it. I never knew who my father was."[1]

THE END

---

[1] The further adventures of Tarzan, and what came of his noble act of self-renunciation, will be told in the next book of Tarzan. [*Burroughs's note.*]

APPENDIX I
READERS' LETTERS

[The editorial reviews and letters in this appendix originally appeared in the 'Table-Talk', or letters to the editor, section of *The All-Story Magazine*, which published *Tarzan of the Apes* in their October 1912 issue. The selections come from the issues of Dec. 1912, 955–60; Jan. 1913, 238–40; Feb. 1913, 478, 480; and June 1913, 478–9.]

THE GLOAT DEPARTMENT

CAMP E. S. OTIS, PANAMA,
Sept. 14, 1912.

EDITOR OF ALL-STORY MAGAZINE:

Your October number of ALL-STORY is fine. Let me send you the voice of hundreds of soldiers here for Norman Bean, or, in his correct name, Edgar Rice Burroughs,* and his great story of "Tarzan of the Apes."

Everybody's talking about it, and every one thinks it's great. Some say that Bean should write another about "Tarzan" because he lost the girl, while others wonder if he can get used to living in civilization. What about it, Mr. Editor?

Yours for the other story,
THE SOLDIERS OF THE 10TH INF. U.S. ARMY.
Las Cascadas, Panama.

———

WILMINGTON, Del., Sept. 11, 1912.

DEAR SIR:

I thought I would write and tell you what I thought of E. R. Burroughs's masterpiece in the October ALL-STORY, "Tarzan of the Apes."

I think it is the best magazine story ever written.

It was simply *swell*.

I read a good many magazines, and it is the best story I ever read.

A PLEASED READER.

———

BLOOMINGTON, Ill., Sept. 12, 1912.

DEAR SIR:

I have just finished reading "Tarzan of the Apes," and to say that it is the best story I ever read would be putting it mildly. It is full of life and action, besides being unique in its plot.

I did not lay down the magazine until I had finished "Tarzan," and since then I have been trying to figure out what *Tarzan* did after he was refused by *Jane Porter*.

It seems against human nature that he should declare that his mother was an ape just after it had been proven that he was a man.

What did he do? Did he go back to the jungle or remain in civilization? The story is so engrossing that I am burning to find out what became of him.

Cannot you persuade the author to write a kind of sequel? I know many of the other readers feel as I do. That story was the "best ever."

Respectfully,

A. J. J.

————

SPOKANE, Wash., Sept. 10, 1912.

DEAR SIR,

I have read THE ALL-STORY MAGAZINE for the past year, and I think "Tarzan of the Apes" is a swell story, except the ending, which was rotten.

Yours truly,

O. B.

————

NEWPORT NEWS, Va., Sept. 13, 1912.

DEAR SIR:

Have been a reader of THE ALL-STORY MAGAZINE for some time, and am well pleased with it.

The story, "Tarzan of the Apes," in your last issue, was an exceptionally interesting one. I admired *Tarzan's* strength and prowess, pitied his ignorance while in the jungle, and sympathized with him in his sorrow, when, after many months, he had found his soul-mate and was rejected.

I was sorry when I reached the end of the romance, which ended so unhappily for the hero, and, if it is at all plausible, I for one wish that a sequel could be written which would tell us more of "Tarzan of the Apes."

Yours as a devoted reader,

D. A. H.

————

DETROIT, Mich., Sept. 18, 1912.

GENTLEMEN:

"Tarzan of the Apes," which appeared in the October number of THE ALL-STORY, is, I think, one of the most intensely absorbing stories I've ever read, but Mr. Burroughs's climax seems to me to fall flat.

Acts of sacrifice such as *Tarzan* commits when he refuses to recognize his parentage are in keeping with the middle of a story, but at the end, in these days of love-stories, some friend (*D'Arnot*) turns up and "sets things right," and the hero and heroine "live happily ever after." *Clayton* is a good character, but I can't see where he's done anything to merit the sacrifice *Tarzan* makes.

Can't you persuade Mr. B. to write a sequel to this story, wherein *T.* will be treated as his character deserves?

It don't make much difference what becomes of *Clayton*. *Miss Porter* can simply break the engagement, or, for all I care, Mr. B. can kill *Clayton* in a train-wreck. I hope Mr. B. will see fit to write such a sequel, because I've "talked over" this story with a number of persons, and they all agreed that it would be improved upon by this addition.

Hoping soon to read this sequel in THE ALL-STORY, of which I have always been an enthusiastic reader, I am,

Sincerely yours,

J. O. B.

_____

SPRINGFIELD, Mass., Sept. 17, 1912.

DEAR SIR:

In "Tarzan of the Apes" the author stumbled into what has often proved an effective trap for the unwary. One of his principal quadruped characters is *Sabor, the tiger*, who is thoughtlessly placed on the continent of Africa, where he does not belong.

The tiger is not and never has been included in the fauna of the African continent. Neither history, science, nor the personal experience of the explorer or hunter records the tiger as being indigenous to Africa.

The newspaper cartoonists blundered into the same pitfall at the time of Colonel Roosevelt's hunting trip,* and the surprising thing is that no one seemed to care enough about the matter to correct them.

G. J. M.

_____

WOODLAWN, Pa., Sept. 17, 1912.

DEAR SIR:

I want to fall in line with the rest of your boosters and express my opinion of your magazine. I have been a reader for about five years, and have yet to find anything to beat it.

Just finished "Tarzan of the Apes," and think it is the best ever. I like the ending where the reader may feel a little disappointment on the outcome. "Under the Moon of Mars," by the same author, is another winner with a good finish.

No doubt, most of your readers like to see the hero marry the heroine, but let us have more of the kind that you can't guess the outcome.

Yours Truly,

C. R. L.

There are many other letters about "Tarzan." Most all of them are complimentary, though lots of folks don't seem to like the finish and are sitting round and barking for a sequel.

It would seem that no editorial comment were necessary. But we are tempted to say—oh, why should we?

Mr. Burroughs wrote us a letter the other day, and he ended by saying: "About a score of readers have threatened my life unless I promise to write a sequel to 'Tarzan'—shall I?"

We wonder.

LURE OF GOLD

We have a good deal of correspondence with Mr. Burroughs *in re* a follow-up story for *Tarzan*. Many more letters have come in, so many that we cannot print anywhere near all of them. Even Mr. Burroughs in his modesty said that, while he was tickled to death with the nice things we printed in the Table-Talk last month, he was afraid people would get bored with any more "Tarzan" letters or chatter. He didn't exactly say that, but something like it.

A QUESTION OF SEQUELS

It seems to us, though, that we might print one or two more that were especially pleasant and especially wanted a sequel.

We believe that we can persuade Mr. Burroughs to frame up a few more stunts for *Tarzan*.

When we learn the good news for sure, we will fire off guns, ring bells, and put every one generally wise to what is going to happen.

————

1409 Rhode Island Street,
LAWRENCE, Kansas, Sept. 25, 1912.

EDITOR ALL-STORY MAGAZINE,
   Care Frank A. Munsey Co.,
      New York.

DEAR SIR:

I have read your October "Table-Talk." It is good. I can appreciate better now why the Munsey publications are such a success.

I bought an October ALL-STORY at Wichita, *en route* to Lawrence. I began to read "Tarzan of the Apes." My university friends with me upon the train promptly pronounced me a "grouch." For the story fascinated me such that football and the old frat were simply overshadowed.

I reached Lawrence only half-way through "Tarzan of the Apes." There I received a wire to return to Kiowa, Kansas, on a business matter of my father's.

I forgot to slip the October ALL-STORY into my grip. At the depot I missed it and tried to purchase another. They were sold out.

I rushed up town only to find the news-depots with none unsold. The train news-boy and the Fred Harvey stands* for three successive stops were unable to supply me. After two hundred miles of chafing I found a solitary copy at Wichita. I finished the story.

At Wellington I discovered two more copies of your magazine for October. I bought them both. I slashed the less desirable half of the remaining pages from the binders.

At Harper I mailed three rolled "Tarzan of the Apes" to as many friends. I was afraid they might have missed a very good thing.

After all of this 'tis useless for me to say that I think the story more than ordinarily good.

When I had finished the article I felt the keenest sorrow for Mr. Burroughs's "Tarzan of the Apes." No—he had become *my* Tarzan. For several seconds I sat deeply touched.

Further, if you will bear a moment more, after "Tarzan of the Apes," my appetite for further reading failed me.

"The Spaniard"* looked uninteresting beyond expression. I felt sorry, indeed, for the author of an article which was destined to follow "Tarzan of the Apes" (for I've written a bit myself).

But imagine my surprise when, as I hastily ran over Mr. Comstock's little narrative, I found my already overflowing imagination absorb every thought, and when I had finished, crave for more.

Sincerely,

G. W. von S.

————

Oly, Sept. 17, 1912.

Editor of The All-Story,

There are so many stories in The All-Story I like I cannot single out any particular few for preference! But "Tarzan of the Apes" was, as my brother would say, "a dinger." But when the end of a story would make a lady swear, that's some provoking.

Mr. Bean must have grown tired or had a grouch, hence the ending of the Ape-man. Many stories end like Tarzan. The author floats along upon a sea of ideas, when, "all ter [*sic*] once," the think-feast is over—and, end—that's all! They don't always go [*sic*] to suit the reader, but—

Jane wasn't far from an "Ape-a-renas" herself. But Tarzan had left Ape-dom behind, and she admits she loves him! Was it because he was still a monkey that Tarzan let go all holds and let the other fellow have the whole basket of peaches?

I hope Tarzan goes back to the island and stays there. The rest of the story was so good, except the end. I'm only mad at Tarzan, Mr. Bean, so come again soon; shall be watching for you, sir!

Also John D. Swain and Ella B. Argo*—I may as well include the rest. I like them all.

A constant reader,

Mrs. A. C. P. F.

————

Spokane, Washington, Sept. 10, 1912.

Dear Sir:

I have just finished the complete book in the October issue, entitled "Tarzan of the Apes," and never saw anything in print that could get on the same block with it up to the last page—but gee!—the finish is rotten.

Yours for a better finish,

F. G. R.

WITH THE HELP OF THE MAIL CLERK

Letters still come in about "Tarzan." Also about the proposed sequel. We have done our best with Mr. Burroughs, and now we can only lie down and wait. He is a good-humored man, however, and we should not be surprised if at some odd moment he would flash something on us.

———

TORONTO, Canada.

THE EDITOR OF THE ALL-STORY MAGAZINE.

175 Fifth Avenue, New York City.

DEAR SIR:

Hope you are back from your annual loaf, feeling fit—no swelled head or cold feet.

Table-Talk accumulates interest. We enjoy it.

I want you to tell Burroughs, through Table-Talk, that "Tarzan of the Apes" is a glorious yarn. All good. It gets you. But, oh, the punishment put upon Tarzan! He didn't get his mate.

My wife and daughter nearly cried because Jane Porter was at last only a mutt, and I feel rotten about it myself. Poor old Tarzan! If he won't tell, why doesn't D'Arnot?

Do not leave Tarzan suffering. He is worth more. Tell Burroughs to get him his mate. We hope there will be a sequel.

Very sincerely yours,

J. A. C.

———

THE TIGERS IN "TARZAN"

BOSTON, Massachusetts.

EDITOR OF THE ALL-STORY MAGAZINE.

MY DEAR SIR:

It seems to me that it is about time that some one came to the rescue of our friend Mr. Burroughs and his much belabored African tiger, "Sabor."

Perhaps the following will be of interest, which I quote from the introduction to Mr. Jekyll's very interesting book, "Jamaican Song and Story."*

"All over South Africa leopards are called 'tigers' by Dutch, English, and Germans. 'Tiger' is used in the same sense in German Kamerun, and probably elsewhere in West Africa."

Mr. Burroughs undoubtedly knows all this, but probably like some others of us, he is too busy wearing out the point of his fountain-pen to start a primary-school class "for critics only."

Personally I should not hesitate to introduce a "tiger" into the sacred purlieus of Gramercy Park itself if the situation seemed to require one, though I understand that the *felis tigris* of the metropolis is usually supposed to be of the blind variety.

As a suggestion, why doesn't Mr. Burroughs gather together all his "tiger" critics in that little hut on the edge of the African jungle, get old "Sabor" headed in the right direction, and—let go of his tail?

THE AUTHOR OF "THE DOMINANT CHORD."*

CAPE TOWN, South Africa.

EDITOR OF THE ALL-STORY.

DEAR SIR:

The "know-alls" who criticize the author of "Tarzan of the Apes" for introducing a tiger into his story of South Africa don't know everything.

From the Cape to Zambezi you can scarcely pick up a newspaper but the chances are that a record is there of a "tiger" hunt, or of a "tiger" having destroyed sheep, *et cetera*.

Colonials all call it a "tiger" over here; specifically it may be known as a leopard or a panther, but to South Africans—Dutch or English speaking—it is a tiger.

H. J. B.

APPENDIX II

HENRY M. STANLEY, *IN DARKEST AFRICA*

[The mythical and often problematic portrayals of Africa and Africans in *Tarzan of the Apes* are greatly indebted to Henry Morton Stanley's accounts of his explorations and colonial work on the continent. In addition to Stanley, many other sources for Burroughs's mythical Africa have been suggested, some of which are excerpted in the introduction. See the Select Bibliography for full information on the text.]

From Vol. 1, Chapter III, 'By Sea to the Congo River'

I have settled several little commissions at Zanzibar satisfactorily. One was to get the Sultan* to sign the concessions which Mackinnon* tried to obtain a long time ago. As the Germans have magnificent territory east of Zanzibar, it was but fair that England should have some portion for the protection she has accorded to Zanzibar since 1841. The Germans appeared to have recognized this, as you may see by the late Anglo-German Agreement.* France had already obtained an immense area in West Africa. All the world had agreed to constitute the domain of King Leopold, on which he had spent a million sterling, as the Independent State of the Congo.* Portugal, which is a chronic grumbler, and does little, and that little in a high-handed, illiberal manner, has also been graciously considered by the European Powers; but England, which had sent out her explorers . . . had obtained nothing, and probably no people had taken such interest in the Dark Continent, or had undergone such sacrifices in behalf of the aborigines, as the English. Her cruisers for the last twenty years had policed the ocean along the coast to suppress slave-catching; her missions were twenty-two in number, settled between East and West Africa. The concession that we wished to obtain embraced a portion of the East African coast, of which Mombasa and Melindi* were the principal towns. For eight years, to my knowledge, the matter had been placed before His Highness, but the Sultan's signature was difficult to obtain.

Arriving at Zanzibar, I saw the Sultan was aging, and that he had not long to live.[1] Englishmen could not invest money in the reserved "sphere of influence" until some such concessions were signed.

"Please God," said the Sultan, "we shall agree; there will be no further doubt about the matter." But his political anxieties are wearing him fast, and unless this matter is soon completed it will be too late.

[1] Seyyid Barghash dies six months later. [*Stanley's note*]

From Vol. 1, Chapter VIII, 'From Panga Falls to Ugarrowwa's'

When the column was across I had a murder case to inquire into. For on the 12th,* at Engweddé, one of our Zanzibaris had been killed with a rifle bullet outside of camp, and it was supposed that some vengeful ruffian in the column had shot him. Meantime, I had suggested to two head men to take forty scouts and re-cross the creek, to explore if there were any opportunities for foraging on the next day to the south-west of the creek. My little court had just sat down for the inquiry, and a witness was relating his evidence, when the rifles were heard firing with unusual energy. Lieutenant Stairs* mustered some fifty men, and proceeded on the double-quick to the river. Under the impression that ninety breech-loaders were quite sufficient we resumed the investigation, but as volley after volley rang out, with continued cracking of scouts' rifles, the Doctor, Nelson,* and myself hastened to the scene with a few more men. The first person I saw was Lieutenant Stairs, with his shirt torn open, and blood streaming from an arrow-wound in the left breast, about the region of the heart, and I heard a pattering on the leaves around me, and caught a glimpse of arrows flying past. After consigning our poor friend to Parke's care I sought for information. There were numbers of men crouching about, and firing in the most senseless fashion at some suspicious bushes across the creek. There were certainly obstinate savages hidden behind them, but I failed to get a glimpse of one. The creek I soon found lay between us. I was told that as the boat was crossing the creek a body of natives had suddenly issued on the other side and shot their arrows into them; that surprised by the discharge they had crouched in the bottom of the boat to escape the arrows, and had paddled the boat back to the landing-place with their hands. They had then picked up their rifles and blazed away at them. Simultaneously Lieutenant Stairs had rushed in among them and fired at the enemy, who were of a bolder kind than any they had yet met. In a short time he had received an arrow in the breast, which he had torn off while retreating, and five other men had been punctured. Almost as soon as I had finished receiving these particulars, I saw for the first time a dark shadow creep along the ground between two bushes, and fired into the centre of it, and a curiously weird wail responded to it. Two minutes later the arrows had ceased their patter among the leaves. Having posted a strong guard of the best shots along the bank to observe any movement on the opposite bank of the creek, the rest of the people were withdrawn.

[. . .] On the 14th, at dawn, pushed over the creek two companies to hunt up the enemy that had done us such damage; a company was also sent, under Captain Nelson, to the forest inland. In a few minutes we heard a volley, and a second, and then incessant rifle fire, showing that the enemy were of a resolute character. There were some crack shots in No. 1 Company, but it was scarcely possible to do much damage in a thick bush against a crafty enemy, who knew that they possessed most dangerous weapons, and who were ignorant of the deadly force of the pellets that searched the bushes. About 300 rounds had been fired, and silence followed. Four only of these had been fatal, and our party received four wounds from arrows smeared over freshly with a copal–colored substance. One dead body was brought to me for examination. The head had a crop of long hair banded by a kind of coronet of iron; the neck had a string of iron drops, with a few monkey teeth among them. The teeth were filed into points. The distinguishing mark of the body appears to form double rows of tiny cicatrices across the chest and abdomen. The body was uncircumcised. Another dead body brought to the landing-place had a necklace of human teeth, and a coronet of shining plated iron, and the forehead and several wristlets of the same metal, polished; on the left arm was the thick pad of silk cotton covered with goat skin, to protect the arm from the bow string.

After the natives had been chased away on all sides from the vicinity, the people commenced to forage, and succeeded in bringing to Avisibba during the day sufficient plantains to give eighty per man—four days' rations.

Lieutenant Stairs' wound was one-fifth of an inch in diameter, an inch and a quarter below the heart, and the pointed head of the arrow had penetrated an inch and a half deep. The other men were wounded in the wrists, arms, and one in the fleshy part of the back. At this period we did not know what this strange copal-coloured substance was with which the points had been smeared, nor did we know what were its peculiar effects when dry or wet; all that the Doctor could do at this time was to inject water in the wounds and cleanse them. The "old hands" of the Zanzibaris affirmed it was poison extracted from the India rubber (Landolphia) by boiling; that the scum after sufficient boiling formed the poison. A native declared that it was made of a species of arum, which, after being bruised, was boiled; that the water was then poured out into another pot, and boiled again until it had left a strong solution, which was mixed with fat, and this was the substance on the arrows. The odour was acrid, with a suspicion of asafœtida. The men proved its deadly properties by remarking that elephants and all big game were killed by it. All these stories caused us to be very anxious, but our ignorance was excessive, I admit. We could only look on with wonder at the small punctures on the arms, and express our opinion that such small wounds could not be deadly, and hope, for the sake of our friend Stairs and our nine wounded men, that all this was mere exaggeration.

The arrows were very slender, made of a dark wood, twenty-four inches long, points hardened by slow baking in the warm atmosphere above the hut fires; at the butt end was a slit, in which a leaf was introduced to guide the flight; the sharp points were as sharp as needles, and half an inch from the point began a curving line of notches for about two inches. The arrow heads were then placed in the prepared and viscid substance, with which they were smeared; large leaves were then rolled round a sheaf before they were placed in the quiver. Another substance was pitch black in colour, and appeared more like Stockholm tar when fresh, but had a very disagreeable smell. In a quiver there would be nearly a hundred arrows. When we observed the care taken of these arrows, rolled up in green leaves as they were, our anxiety for our people was not lessened.

APPENDIX III

PETER THE WILD BOY

[Tarzan is often cited in discussions of so-called 'feral' children. Several such stories existed before Burroughs wrote his novel, and that of Peter the Wild Boy was one of the most famous. The following selection comes from Henry Wilson's *Wonderful Characters: Comprising Memoirs and Anecdotes of the Most Remarkable Persons of Every Age and Nation*, vol. ii (London: J. Robins and Co. Albion Press, 1821), 152-60.]

On the continent of Europe, the regions of which are interspersed with vast forests and uncultivated tracts, various individuals of the human species have at different times been discovered in a state no better than that of the brute creation. With nearly all of them this has been the case to such a degree, that it has been found impossible to obtain from them any information respecting the circumstances which reduced them to such a deplorable situation, or of the manner in which they contrived to preserve their lives amidst the numerous perils by which they were surrounded. Most of these unfortunate beings were so completely brutalized as to be utter strangers to the faculty of speech and totally incapable of acquiring it—a fact which demonstrates how much man is indebted to the society of his fellow-creatures for many of the eminent advantages possessed by him over the other classes of animated nature.

One of the most singular of these human brutes, as they may justly be denominated, was Peter the Wild Boy, whose origin and history, previous to this discovery, must, from the reasons already mentioned, remain for ever a secret. He was found in the year 1725, in a wood near Hamelin, about twenty-five miles from Hanover, walking on his hands and feet, climbing trees like a squirrel, and feeding on grass and moss; and in the month of November was conveyed to Hanover by the superintendent of the House of Correction at Zell. At this time he was supposed to be about thirteen years old, and could not speak. This singular creature was presented to King George I,* then at Hanover, while at dinner. The king caused him to taste of all the dishes at the table; and in order to bring him by degrees to relish human diet, he directed that he should have such provision as he seemed best to like, and such instructions as might best fit him for human society.

Soon after this, the boy made his escape into the same wood, where he concealed himself among the branches of a tree, which was sawed down to recover him. He was brought over to England at the beginning of 1726, and exhibited to the king and many of the nobility. In this country he was distinguished by the appellation of Peter the Wild Boy which he ever afterwards retained.

He appeared to have scarcely any ideas, was uneasy at being obliged to wear clothes, and could not be induced to lie on a bed, but sat and slept in a corner of the room, whence it was conjectured that he used to sleep on a tree for security against wild beasts. He was committed to the care of Dr. Arbuthnot,* at whose house he either was, or was to have been baptized; but notwithstanding all the doctor's pains, he never could bring the wild youth to the use of speech, or the pronunciation of words. As every effort of this kind was found to be in vain, he was placed with a farmer at a small distance from town, and a pension was allowed him by the king, which he enjoyed till his death.

The ill success of these efforts seems to have laid curiosity asleep, till Lord Monboddo* again called the public attention to this phenomenon. That nobleman had been collecting all the particulars he could meet with concerning Peter, in order to establish a favourite but truly whimsical hypothesis. The plan of his work on the "Origin and Progress of Language," necessarily involved the history of civilization and general knowledge. His lordship carried his researches to a period far beyond the records of history, when men might be supposed to possess no means of the vocal communication of their thoughts but natural and inarticulate sounds. Abstracting, in imagination, from the rational superiority of man, whatever seems to depend on his use of artificial language, as a sign of thought, he represents the earlier generations of the human race, as having been little, if at all, exalted in intelligence above the ape and the oran outang, whose form bears a resemblance to the human. The spirit of paradox even inclined him to believe that those rude men, who wanted articulate language must have had tails, of which they might gradually have divested themselves, either by attentions to the breed, like those of a Cully or a Bakewell, or by continual docking, till the tail was utterly extirpated.

In a very witty and ludicrous piece, by Dean Swift,* entitled, "It cannot rain but it pours,"—he gives an account of this wonderful wild man, as he calls him, replete with satire and ridicule, but containing many particulars concerning him that were undoubtedly true. Lord Monboddo, therefore concluded that the other facts mentioned by that witty writer, though no where else to be found, are likewise authentic, whatever may be thought of the use and application he makes of them: such as, that in the circle at court he endeavoured to kiss the young Lady Walpole;* that he put on his hat before the king, and laid hold of the Lord Chamberlain's staff; that he expressed his sensations by certain sounds which he had framed to himself, and particularly that he neighed something like a horse, in which way he commonly expressed his joy; that he understood the language of birds and beasts, by which they express their appetites and feelings; that his senses were more acute than those of the tame man; and, lastly, that he could sing sometimes. These facts, his lordship contends, the dean must have known, for he was at London at the time, and of Swift's integrity in not stating any facts that were untrue, even in a work of humor, his lordship has no doubt. The dean farther said, that it was evident, by several tokens, that this wild boy had a father and mother like one of us. "This," says Lord Monboddo, "I believe also to be true; because I was told by a person yet living, that when he was caught he had a collar about his neck with something written upon it."

In Peter the Wild Boy, Lord Monboddo conceived that he had discovered a corroboration of his eccentric opinion. His lordship, accordingly, went to see him, and the result of his inquiries is thus stated in his "Ancient Metaphysics:"—

"[. . .] He feeds at present as the farmer and his wife do, but, as I was told by an old woman, who remembered to have seen him when he first came to Hertfordshire, which she computed to be about fifty-five years before; he then fed much on leaves, particularly of cabbage, which she saw him eat raw. He was then, as she thought, about fifteen years of age, walked upright, but could climb trees like a squirrel. At present he not only eats flesh, but has acquired a taste for beer, and even for spirits, of which he inclines to drink more than he can get [. . .]"

His lordship afterwards requested Mr. Burgess of Oxford, to make farther inquiries for him on the spot, concerning Peter, and that gentleman transmitted him an account, which was in substance as follows:—

Peter, in his youth, was very remarkable for his strength, which always appeared so much superior, that the stoutest young men were afraid to contend with him. His vigour continued unimpaired till the year 1781, when he was suddenly taken ill, fell down before the fire, and for a time lost the use of his right side. I met with an old gentleman, a surgeon of Hempstead, who remembers to have seen Peter in London, between the years 1724, and 1726. [. . .]

Till the spring of 1782, which was soon after his illness, he always appeared remarkably animated by the influence of the spring, singing all day; and if it was clear, half the night. He is much pleased at the sight of the moon and stars; he will sometimes stand out in the warmth of the sun, with his face turned up towards it in a strained attitude, and he likes to be out in a starry night, if not cold. These particulars naturally lead to the inquiry, whether he has, or seems to have any idea of the great author of all these wonders. I thought this a question of so much curiosity, that when I left Broadway, I rode back several miles to ask whether he had ever betrayed any sense of a Supreme Being. I was told, that when he first came into that part of the country, different methods were taken to teach him to read, and to instruct him in the principles of religion, but in vain. He learned nothing, nor did he ever show any feeling of the consciousness of a God. [. . .]

He ran away several times since he was at Broadway, but never since he has been with his present master. In 1745, or 1746, he was taken up as a spy from Scotland; as he was unable to speak, the people supposed him obstinate, and threatened him with punishment for his contumacy; but a lady who had seen him in London, acquainted them with the character of their prisoner, and directed them whither to send him. In these excursions he used to live on raw herbage, berries, and young tender roots of trees. [. . .]

To these accounts we have nothing farther to add, than that Peter did not long survive the visits of Lord Monboddo and his friend. He died at the farm in the month of February, 1785, at the supposed age of 73 years.

APPENDIX IV

RALPH WALDO EMERSON, 'SELF-RELIANCE'

['Self-Reliance' originally appeared in Ralph Waldo Emerson's *Essays*. Emerson (1803–82) was a leading American author and philosopher of the nineteenth century, and the major figure of the so-called Transcendentalists. That Burroughs knew Emerson's work is evidenced by his *The Cave Girl*, which was originally serialized in *All-Story* from July to September 1913. The protagonist of the tale is Waldo Emerson Smith-Jones, a 'not overly courageous' man who, by being thrust away from civilization, has 'forced upon him the development of attributes of self-reliance, courage, initiative, and resourcefulness' (*All-Story* (July 1913), 622; (Aug. 1913), 891). Similar Emersonian themes of self-reliance run throughout the previously published *Tarzan of the Apes*, as do the related topics of 'manliness' and race mentioned in this passage.]

The nonchalance of boys who are sure of a dinner, and would disdain as much as a lord to do or say aught to conciliate one, is the healthy attitude of human nature. How is a boy the master of society; independent, irresponsible, looking out from his corner on such people and facts as pass by, he tries and sentences them on their merits, in the swift, summary way of boys, as good, bad, interesting, silly, eloquent, troublesome. He cumbers himself never about consequences, about interests; he gives an independent, genuine verdict. You must court him: he does not court you. But the man is, as it were, clapped into jail by his consciousness. As soon as he has once acted or spoken with eclat, he is a committed person, watched by the sympathy or the hatred of hundreds whose affections must now enter into his account. There is no Lethe* for this. Ah, that he could pass again into his neutral, godlike independence! Who can thus lose all pledge, and having observed, observe again from the same unaffected, unbiased, unbribable, unaffrighted innocence, must always be formidable, must always engage the poet's and the man's regards. Of such an immortal youth the force would be felt. He would utter opinions on all passing affairs, which being seen to be not private but necessary, would sink like darts into the ear of men, and put them in fear.

These are the voices which we hear in solitude, but they grow faint and inaudible as we enter into the world. Society everywhere is in conspiracy against the manhood of every one of its members. Society is a joint-stock company in which the members agree for the better securing of his bread to each shareholder, to surrender the liberty and culture of the eater. The virtue in most request is conformity. Self-reliance is its aversion. It loves not realities and creators, but names and customs.

Whoso would be a man, must be a nonconformist. He who would gather immortal palms must not be hindered by the name of goodness, but must explore if it be goodness. Nothing is at last sacred but the integrity of our own mind. Absolve you to yourself, and you shall have the suffrage of the world. I remember an answer which when quite young I was prompted to make to a valued adviser who was wont to importune me with the dear old doctrines of the church. On my saying, What have I to do with the sacredness of traditions, if I live wholly from within? my friend suggested—"But these impulses may be from below, not from above." I replied, 'They do not seem to me to be such; but if I am the devil's child, I will live then from the devil.' No law can be sacred to me but that of my nature. Good and bad are but names very readily transferable to that or this; the only right is what is after my constitution, the only wrong what is against it. A man is to carry himself in the presence of all opposition as if every thing were titular and ephemeral but he. I am ashamed to think how easily we capitulate to badges and names, to large societies and dead institutions. [. . .]

But now we are a mob. Man does not stand in awe of man, nor is the soul admonished to stay at home, to put itself in communication with the internal ocean, but it goes abroad to beg a cup of water of the urns of men. We must go alone. Isolation must precede true society. I like the silent church before the service begins, better than any preaching. How far off, how cool, how chaste the persons look, begirt each one with a precinct or sanctuary. So let us always sit. Why should we assume the faults of our friend, or wife, or father, or child, because they sit around our hearth, or are said to have the same blood? All men have my blood and I have all men's. Not for that will I adopt their petulance or folly, even to the extent of being ashamed of it. But your isolation must not be mechanical, but spiritual, that is, must be elevation. At times the whole world seems to be in conspiracy to importune you with emphatic trifles. Friend, client, child, sickness, fear, want, charity, all knock at once at thy closet door and say, 'Come out unto us.'—Do not spill thy soul; do not all descend; keep thy state; stay at home in thine own heaven; come not for a moment into their facts, into their hub-bub of conflicting appearances, but let in the light of thy law on their confusion. The power men possess to annoy me, I give them by a weak curiosity. No man can come near me but through my act. "What we love that we have, but by desire we bereave ourselves of the love."

If we cannot at once rise to the sanctities of obedience and faith, let us at least resist our temptations, let us enter into the state of war, and wake Thor and Woden,* courage and constancy in our Saxon breasts. This is to be done in our smooth times by speaking the truth. Check this lying hospitality and lying affection. Live no longer to the expectation of these deceived and deceiving people with whom we converse. Say to them, O father, O mother, O wife, O brother, O friend, I have lived with you after appearances hitherto. Henceforward I am the truth's. Be it known unto you that henceforward I obey no law less than the eternal law. I will have no covenants but proximities. I shall endeavor to nourish my parents, to support my family, to be the chaste husband of one wife,—but these relations I must fill after a new and unprecedented way. I appeal from your customs. I must be myself.

EXPLANATORY NOTES

Full details of references in these notes can be found in the Select Bibliography, above. I have also consulted the one other annotated edition of *Tarzan of the Apes*, ed. John Seelye (New York: Penguin, 1990).

5 *British Colonial Office*: this office was created in 1854, although a permanent undersecretary for colonial affairs had been in existence since 1825.

British . . . rubber: British colonies on the west coast of the continent included Sierra Leone, Gambia, the British Gold Coast (now Ghana), and Nigeria. The other 'European power' is Belgium, which, under Leopold II, frequently engaged in the kind of exploitation described here, and which is mentioned later in the novel. It should be noted, though, that similar accusations were also levelled against the administrators of the French Congo. See Introduction, p. xvi–xvii.

Congo . . . Aruwimi: the Congo is the second longest river in Africa, and runs from the south-east of what is now Democratic Republic of the Congo northwards, and then south-west to the Atlantic. The Aruwimi is a Congo tributary in the north-east of the country.

6 *Queen*: Queen Victoria (1819–1901; ruled 1837–1901).

1888: the date means that Clayton's trip took place during Henry Morton Stanley's expedition up the Congo, recounted in his *In Darkest Africa* (1890).

Lady Alice: also the name of a boat Stanley used to travel on the Congo.

Freetown: the capitol of Sierra Leone, founded by freed African American slaves who had left with the British after the American Revolution.

Fuwalda: given the anarchic nature of the ship, Burroughs could be playing on the name of William Buwalda, a US soldier who was court-martialled in 1908 for attending an anarchist rally, and who subsequently served a sentence of hard labour in Alcatraz.

7 *St. Helena*: a volcanic island in the Pacific under British rule, and famously the island to which Napoleon Bonaparte (1769–1821) was exiled.

8 *England's . . . navy*: the Royal Navy of the Victorian period was the most significant global military force.

10 *'Ell's . . . pay'*: Burroughs consistently renders working-class characters' speech in dialect form, here attempting to mimic a working-class English accent.

a pill: a bullet.

11 *'Ancient Mariner'*: a reference to the poem 'The Rime of the Ancient Mariner' (1798), by Samuel Taylor Coleridge (1772–1834).

11 *Mutiny . . . years ago*: the most famous mutiny, that on *HMS Bounty*, took place in 1789, almost exactly a hundred years before the time of the action here.

14 *cleft . . . chin*: this type of blow is common in such epic poems as *The Song of Roland*.

17 *wild and lonely shore*: this phrase opens and closes Ode II of the 'Odes to Nea' in *Epistles, Odes, and Other Poems* (1806), by popular Irish writer Thomas Moore; the poem focuses on a couple taking 'lonely walks' together on the shore.

18 *gloomy wood*: a reference to the opening lines of the *Inferno*, the first book of Dante's famous poem *The Divine Comedy*. A well-known translation by Henry Francis Cary (1772–1844), which was still being published in Burroughs's time, reads: 'In the midway of this our mortal life, | I found me in a gloomy wood, astray | Gone from the path direct: and e'en to tell, | It were no easy task, how savage wild | That forest, how robust and rough its growth, | Which to remember only, my dismay | Renews, in bitterness not far from death' (i. 1–7).

20 *elephant's ear*: several species of plants share this common name, including colocasia (taro), xanthosoma, and caladium, many of which are widely grown in West Africa.

21 *Turks . . . blankets*: this is a standard orientalist image, though 'carpets' would be more common than 'blankets'; carpets were a significant form of artistic expression across the Ottoman Empire.

24 *anthropoid ape*: 'human-like' or humanoid ape, a common scientific term, from the nineteenth century onwards, for apes, often used in early scientific literature specifically for gorillas, chimpanzees, orang-utans, and gibbons. Burroughs's apes are imaginary creatures, seeming to form a 'missing link' in the human evolutionary line, which he continues in the representation of the male residents of Opar in the sequel, *The Return of Tarzan*.

30 *forehead . . . kind*: much of the physical detail here and later mimics that of general descriptions of apes, but also echoes many of the racist assertions of contemporary evolutionary science. See, for example, Robert Hartmann's comparisons, in his textbook *Anthropoid Apes* (New York: D. Appleton and Co., 1886) of 'anthropoid apes' and 'the lower races' of humanity, which echo this racism even as he tries to complicate it.

32 *hunger . . . ape*: the nursing echoes that of Romulus and Remus, legendary founders of Rome, who were suckled by a wolf. See Introduction, above.

36 *inalienable rights*: here, and elsewhere, Burroughs echoes the Declaration of Independence: 'We hold these truths to be self-evident, that all men are created equal, that they are endowed by their Creator with certain unalienable Rights, that among these are Life, Liberty and the pursuit of Happiness.' This document, adopted in 1776, declared the independence of the thirteen United States from Britain.

38 *huge lioness*: in *All-Story*, Sabor was a tiger, and a male, as opposed to the female lion ('huge' is also missing from *All-Story* in this description). Several letters to the editor of *All-Story* (reprinted in Appendix I) discuss the issue of the presence of tigers in the original publication.

40 *the van*: an abbreviation of 'vanguard', meaning the front of a group (usually of people).

41 *another race*: the terms 'race' and 'species' were much more interchangeable in early science, and were still popularly mixed in Burroughs's day, a slipperiness that fed into the racist implications of some anthropological and zoological research.

47 *Stygian blackness*: black as Styx, the mythological river of Hades.

48 *but now . . . former self*: the magazine version does not contain this lengthy section of text which paints Kala in a more 'motherly' light, ending the chapter at 'with him'.

50 *pathos . . . learning*: for a discussion of the allegorical nature of this scene, see the Introduction, p. xii.

52 *And . . . read*: Tarzan's ability to learn a language in this manner is clearly a device of fantasy, though it does resemble—in a hyperbolic manner—Noam Chomsky's theory that children are born with an inherent ability to acquire language. See, for example, Chomsky's *Aspects of the Theory of Syntax* (1969).

53 *palm of victory*: the leaf of the palm tree is often used as a symbol of victory.

in a hollow . . . hills: this section, added after the *All-Story* publication, and other additions in this chapter serve to further the ceremonial, quasi-religious aspect of the Dum-Dum, making it seem more 'human-like'.

Many travelers . . . sounds: explorer Paul Du Chaillu writes that, when a gorilla beats his chest the noise 'resound[s] like an immense bass-drum' (Du Chaillu, *Explorations and Adventures in Equatorial Africa* (New York: Harper, 1861; repr. New York: Negro Univ. Press, 1969), p. 987).

54 *which stands . . . meeting place*: another passage added for the book publication that does not appear in *All-Story*, which plays into the novel's comments on evolution (see Introduction, p. xii).

57 *lese-majesté*: literally, an injury to the Majesty, meaning an insult to a ruler or sovereign (French).

58 *Tarzan of the Apes*: this is the first occurrence of this term in which 'Apes' is capitalized, turning it into a title. In *All-Story*, the phrase only occurs in the body of the text with a lower-case 'apes', making it more descriptive and less of an honorific.

59 *pisang and scitamine*: pisang is a banana or plantain plant; scitamine (more commonly scitamineae) is a family of plants that includes banana, ginger, and turmeric.

60 *Numa*: Numa Pompilius was the legendary second king of Rome, who succeeded Romulus. See Plutarch, *Plutarch's Lives*, 127–59.

65 *savage . . . interior*: many European depictions of the interior of Africa, such as Du Chaillu's *Explorations and Adventures* and Mary H. Kingsley's *Travels in West Africa*, frequently commented on the 'savageness' of the aboriginal population, including many descriptions of purported cannibal tribes.

gorged . . . a-plenty: i.e., both groups of black warriors are cannibals.

66 *pursuit of happiness*: this is another of Burroughs's references to the American Declaration of Independence (see note to p. 36).

Mbonga: the name could be based on one in Du Chaillu's *Explorations and Adventures*: near the beginning of that text, the author meets 'Mbango, a chief or head-man among the Corisco people' (p. 52). Du Chaillu also discusses the 'Mbenga tribe' (p. 49).

arrows . . . prick: see Henry Morton Stanley's discussion of poison arrows, which this passage echoes, in Appendix II, above.

72 *drawing . . . tree*: this murder, as well as later similar killings, bears a certain resemblance to the extra-legal lynchings of African Americans in the US. It also echoes a passage from Du Chaillu: 'Finally was rehearsed the story which is current among all the tribes who at all know the gorilla: that this animal lies in wait in the lower branches of trees, watching for people who go to and fro; and, when one passes sufficiently near, grasps the luckless fellow with his powerful feet, and draws him up into the tree, where he quietly chokes him' (p. 87).

76 *human skulls*: Burroughs's description of a cannibal village echoes the more sensationalist accounts of African exploration. Du Chaillu, for example, describes sleeping in a cannibal village: 'I slept, and was not interrupted, though, on going out next morning, I saw a pile of ribs, leg and arm bones, and skulls (human) piled up at the back of my house' (p. 106). Such images of cannibals became staples of depictions of native Africans.

81 *Sheeta, the leopard*: originally, in *All-Story*, 'Sabor, the tiger'; Burroughs does not carry this change through to the reference, a few paragraphs after this point, to the 'savage and cruel' Sabor, which no longer follows logically from the preceding statement about 'Sheeta'.

90 *Mungo*: Mungo Park was a Scottish surgeon and famous early explorer of Africa. He recounts his travels in *Travels in the Interior Districts of Africa: Performed in the Years 1795, 1796, and 1797* (London: Murray, 1816).

96 *men . . . escape*: this phrase replaces 'fleeing quarry' in the *All-Story* version, which is a change that at once humanizes the Africans while also making it even clearer that Tarzan's actions are murderous.

101 *ducks*: pants made from strong fabric that is often used for sails and men's (esp. sailors') work clothing.

Solomon . . . colors: Solomon, biblical king of Israel, is often represented as wearing colourful clothing (see Matthew 6: 28–9, where Jesus disparages Solomon's clothing in comparison to the lilies of the field). Esmeralda is depicted as a stereotypical 'mammy' figure.

102 *TARZAN*: the fact that Tarzan can spell his name is a distinct problem in the plot, given that Burroughs earlier goes to lengths to explain that Tarzan has no idea of the relation between written letters and their phonetic equivalents (writing that Tarzan 'could only write the word ["man"] in English; he could not pronounce it' (p. 86)). One also must wonder why Tarzan never tried to write to the people of Mbonga's village (see Jeff Berglund, *Cannibal Fictions: American Explorations of Colonialism, Race, Gender, and Sexuality* (Madison: Univ. of Wisconsin Press, 2006), 84).

Archimedes Q. Porter: Archimedes was a scientist in ancient Greece, who is also associated with the stereotype of the absent-minded professor due to an anecdote that has him running naked through the streets shouting 'Eureka!' ('I have found it!') after discovering, while taking a bath, the relation between the displacement of water and the volume of objects.

104 *Samuel T. Philander*: philander, as either the common verb or rarer noun, relates to male flirtatiousness or casual sexuality. Given that such a description of Mr Philander seems out of keeping with his character, Burroughs is drawing a broad comedy here.

105 *continued . . . indecision*: this phrase is an addition made after the *All-Story* publication: many of the additional descriptions of Clayton seem to make him a weaker figure than he was in the *All-Story* version, perhaps because his tragic fate in the sequel was already decided.

106 *Zanzibar . . . dark continent*: Zanzibar was a sultanate and British protectorate in East Africa, now part of Tanzania. The reference to the 'dark continent', combined with that to Zanzibar, alludes to Stanley's *In Darkest Africa*. See the Introduction, pp. xvi–xvii, as well as Appendix II, above.

Cape Town: during the period in which the novel is set, Cape Town would have been the capital of the British Cape Colony. Given the rough timeline of the novel, though, this reference would appear just before the British formed the Union of South Africa, again with Cape Town as the capital.

114 *Gaberelle*: 'Gabriel', the archangel. Burroughs writes Esmeralda's speech in an exaggerated dialect, in keeping not only with certain trends in US literature, but also, given the intentional comic effect, with vaudeville performances, more marked because Burroughs does not write any of the white American or upper-class British speech in dialect.

114 *builded*: Burroughs here uses the more poetic, often biblical, past participle of 'build', giving more majesty to Clayton's effort.

119 *and she . . . second time*: this long section, in which Jane attempts to kill Esmeralda, intending to commit suicide afterwards, was the most significant deletion in the popular Ballantine editions of the novel.

122 *Ferdinand and Isabella . . . Spain*: Ferdinand II (1452–1516), King of Aragon (1479–1516), and Isabella I (1451–1504), Queen of Castile and León (1474–1504), conquered Granada in 1492, defeating Muhammad XII, the last Muslim ruler of what is now Spain.

Moslemism: Islam.

123 *genus Felis*: the professor's Latin identification of the lion's genus is incorrect. Lions are correctly identified as genus *Panthera* in the family Felidae. The genus *Felis* actually refers to several small cats, including the domestic cat.

Felis carnivora: Mr Philander is wrong not only in his Latin identification of the lion with the genus *Felis*, but also in the fact that Carnivora more properly applies to a much larger order of placental (as opposed to marsupial) mammals. Mr Philander is obviously trying to translate 'carnivore', but since all cats are carnivores, this distinction doesn't help his description.

126 *graven image*: Exodus 20: 4, 'Thou shalt not make unto thee any graven image'; one of the Ten Commandments.

128 *up and doing*: a popular phrase from *Poor Richard's Almanack*, by Benjamin Franklin (1706–90): 'The Day is short, the Work great, the Workmen lazy, the Wages high, the Master urgeth; up, then, and be doing' (Franklin, *Autobiography and Other Writings*, ed. Ormond Seavey (Oxford: OUP, 1998, 284). Professor Porter's version is closer to the later use of the phrase by Henry Wadsworth Longfellow (1807–82) in the poem 'A Psalm of Life': 'Let us, then, be up and doing, | With a heart for any fate; | Still achieving, still pursuing, | Learn to labor and to wait' (Longfellow, *Poems and Other Writings*, ed. J. D. McClatchy (New York: Library of America, 2000), 4). See note to p. 132.

129 *Marse Clayton*: 'Marse' or 'Mars' is a common rendering of a southern US pronunciation of 'Master'.

132 *'Let . . . dead'*: another quotation from Longfellow's 'A Psalm of Life': 'Trust no Future, howe'er pleasant! | Let the dead Past bury its dead! | Act,—act in the living Present! | Heart within, and God o'erhead!' (Longfellow, *Poems and Other Writings*, 4). See note to p. 128.

139 *Cimmerian darkness*: in Homer's *Odyssey*, the Cimmerian people live in a land surrounded by fog or clouds, and so never see daylight.

141 *10° . . . LATITUDE*: Jane mistakenly spells out 'degrees' after already using the symbol for it; this puts Tarzan's cabin in what is now Angola.

142 *Spain . . . 'pieces of eight'*: from the sixteenth century onwards, Spain, and later Portugal, colonized areas of South America. A 'doubloon' is a Spanish gold coin; 'pieces of eight' refers to the Spanish silver dollar, or *peso*, worth 8 *reals* and marked with the figure 8. These terms became popularly associated with pirates through such works as *Treasure Island* by Robert Louis Stevenson (1850–94).

143 *Cape Verde*: a group of islands that was a Portuguese colony, and is now an independent nation. Cape Verde was a centre of the transatlantic slave trade.

144 *married titled foreigners*: a common practice for young women of rich families in the post-Civil War US. See Maureen E. Montgomery, *Gilded Prostitution* (London: Routledge, 1989).

145 *Hazel Strong*: Hazel plays a much larger role in the immediate sequel to the novel, *The Return of Tarzan*.

brown study: absorbed in his own thoughts.

146 *Herculean efforts*: the Roman name for the Greek hero Heracles, son of the god Zeus. In Greek mythology, Heracles, after killing his children, must perform twelve superhuman tasks as a penance. Here, Burroughs portrays what passes as 'Herculean' in the civilized world, juxtaposing this image to the 'forest god' Tarzan. Heracles/Hercules is depicted in ways that resonate with Tarzan as well, particularly the fact that the former dresses in a lion's skin.

150 *who may . . . you*: Tarzan here develops the basic tenets of Lockean democracy—that a government rules under an implied social contract with the people, and if a government rules in such a way as to violate its subjects' inalienable rights, then the subjects have the right to revolt. This tenet was one of the foundations of the American Revolution. See Locke, *Second Treatise of Government*, ed. C. B. Macpherson (Indianapolis: Hackett Publishing, 1980), 111).

154 *like a tigress*: Jane is the only 'tiger' in Africa, and the only remaining 'tiger' reference to be carried over from the *All-Story* version to the book-version of the novel.

155 *"Monsieur . . . presume"*: the officer's greeting mimics that of Henry Morton Stanley (1841–1904) to David Livingstone (1813–73)—'Dr. Livingstone, I presume?'—after finding Livingstone, who was reportedly 'lost' in Africa.

156 *"Mon Dieu!"*: My God! (French).

157 *fore-stay-sail and mizzen-spanker*: a fore-stay sail is a sail hoisted on the rope (or stay) that supports the mast that is nearest the bow of a ship; 'mizzen-spanker' is a bit redundant, as both terms are often used interchangeably to refer to the principal sail on the mizzen-mast of a ship (the mast that is aft the mainmast).

158 *Soon . . . own blood*: another allusion to Coleridge's 'Rime of the Ancient Mariner' (see note to p. 11), in which the Mariner is also forced by thirst to drink his own blood.

glasses: telescopes or other magnifying lens device.

160 *dissipation . . . passions*: throughout the nineteenth century, it was believed that one could produce profound, negative effects on one's health by indulging in base or frivolous pursuits, so much that the word 'dissipation' acquired the meaning of a wasting of life by overindulging in pleasure: Henry David Thoreau, in *Walden*, mentions a similar kind of dissipation.

162 *Never . . . own image*: a reference to Genesis 1: 27, 'So God created man in his own image, in the image of God created he him; male and female created he them.'

164 *ivory miniature*: small watercolour portrait, on ivory.

167 *leafy bower*: an allusion to Adam and Eve's 'blissful Bower' in Milton's *Paradise Lost* (iv. 690).

169 *lioness*: originally, a tiger; an interesting misidentification in the *All-Story* version, given Jane's description earlier as a 'tigress'.

lion: the *All-Story* version also has 'lion' here, indicating Mr Philander's confusion, since he had just seen a 'tiger'.

173 *African cannibals*: the following description of the cannibalism ritual is wholly fictional, though it did reproduce and help popularize this pernicious stereotype.

Leopold II . . . State: Leopold II (1835–1909) is best known for founding (under the auspices of an organization called the 'International Association of the Congo') the Congo Free State in 1885; for the tasks leading up to this moment, he employed Henry Morton Stanley as an explorer and diplomat (see Appendix II). Under Leopold's rule, several atrocities were committed in the Congo region.

179 *green-eyed devil*: jealousy.

182 *French Congo*: a French colony that bordered on the Congo Free State.

184 *suitable . . . it*: Jane is implying that, if she were permitted, she would challenge Clayton to a duel.

188 *Kerchak's . . . Numa*: it is again unclear how Tarzan can know how to transliterate these names, which he only knows aurally, into a language the phonetics of which he cannot understand.

190 *"Mais oui"*: 'But of course' (French; literally, 'But yes').

194 *my . . . South*: Jane is referring to the soldiers of the Confederacy in the US Civil War. She is from Baltimore, Maryland, which was a slave-holding state, but one that bordered free states. Burroughs's father, George, fought for the Union.

195 *super-man*: an echo of the concept of the *Übermensch*, developed by Friedrich Nietzsche in *Thus Spoke Zarathustra* (1885).

196 *Portia*: in Shakespeare's *Merchant of Venice* (*c*.1598), Portia dresses as a man in order to act as a lawyer for Antonio.

200 *feet . . . clay*: In the Book of Daniel, Daniel has a dream of a statue with 'feet part of iron and part of clay' (Daniel 2: 33); the phrase 'feet of clay' has come to stand for vulnerability in an otherwise strong or idealized person.

210 *Father Constantine . . . Mission*: religious missions to convert Africans to Christianity went hand-in-hand with imperial projects. It is worth noting in this context that Father Constantine shares his name with Constantine I, the first emperor of the Holy Roman Empire, at another moment in history when imperial activities and Christianity mixed together.

211 *Height of Civilization*: in *All-Story*, this chapter is titled 'The Light of Civilization'.

sipping . . . absinthe: absinthe is an alcoholic drink made from various plants, including wormwood, and was especially popular in France at the end of the nineteenth century.

212 *express rifles*: rifles constructed to discharge a bullet with a high initial velocity and a low trajectory (*OED*).

217 *identification*: fingerprints began to be studied as a means of identification in the nineteenth century, and started to be regularly used by police services by the early twentieth century.

218 *although . . . less complex*: such a claim, based on racist pseudo-scientific assumptions, is, of course, untrue. This clause was deleted in the later Ballantine edition of the novel.

ape's . . . organism: another unsupported theory. In fact, koala fingerprints are said to be nearly identical to those of humans.

225 *purring six cylinder*: a car with a six-cylinder engine, indicating a large, expensive car. Six-cylinder-engine cars would have been a relatively new product.

227 *"Scott"*: an abbreviated form of the mild exclamation 'Great Scott!'

233 CONCLUSION: in *All-Story*, this chapter is titled 'Lord Ape-Man'.

Appendix I

242 *Norman . . . Burroughs*: Burroughs's first work, *Under the Moon of Mars*, was published under the pseudonym 'Norman Bean': Burroughs had wanted the name to read 'Normal Bean', but a typographic error was introduced. Afterwards, he published under his full name.

244 *Colonel . . . trip*: Theodore Roosevelt, the twenty-sixth president of the United States, went on safari in Africa in 1909, just after the end of his presidency.

246 *Fred Harvey stands*: Fred Harvey created the first US restaurant chain, which was tied to the rail-lines, and also offered news-stand services.

246 *"The Spaniard"*: 'The Spaniard', by Frank Comstock, follows *Tarzan of the Apes* in the October 1912 *All-Story* (pp. 373–5).

247 *John . . . Argo*: both authors of stories that appeared in the same issue as *Tarzan*. John D. Swain, 'The Goat of Dolores Valdez' (pp. 417–23); Ella B. Argo, 'On the Zodiac Turnpike' (pp. 472–6).

248 *"Jamaican . . . Story"*: Walter Jekyll (ed.), *Jamaican Song and Story: Annancy Stories, Digging Sings, Ring Tunes, and Dancing Tunes*, introd. Alice Werner (London: Folk-Lore Society/David Nutt, 1907), p. xxiv.

249 *DOMINANT CHORD*: Edward Kimball's *The Dominant Chord* was serialized in *All-Story* from October 1911 to January 1912.

Appendix II

250 *Sultan*: Barghash ibn Said (1837–88), Sultan of Zanzibar (ruled 1870–88).

Mackinnon: Sir William Mackinnon (1823–93), shipping magnate and imperialist.

Anglo–German Agreement: signed in 1890, this agreement defined the 'spheres of influence' in Africa for both Great Britain and Germany.

Independent State of the Congo: see note to p. 173.

Mombasa and Melindi: Mombasa is a large city in Kenya, on the Indian Ocean coast; Malindi, also in Kenya on the same coast, lies approximately 75 miles (120 kilometres) to the north-east.

251 *For on the 12th*: information provided in the margins of the text identifies the events described in this section as happening on 13–14 August 1887, at Avisibba.

Lieutenant Stairs: William Grant Stairs (1863–92), Canadian-born British military officer.

Doctor, Nelson: the doctor is Thomas Heazle Parke (1857–93), a British army medical officer; R. H. Nelson (dates unknown), was a British military officer.

Appendix III

254 *King George I*: George I (1660–1727), King of Great Britain and Ireland and Elector of Hanover.

255 *Dr. Arbuthnot*: John Arbuthnot [Arbuthnott] (bap. 1667, d. 1735): physician and satirist, friend of Jonathan Swift.

Lord Monboddo: James Burnett, Lord Monboddo (bap. 1714, d. 1799), judge and philosopher.

Dean Swift: Jonathan Swift (1667–1745), famous satirist and dean of St Patrick's Cathedral, Dublin. Swift is credited with writing the satirical essay 'It cannot rain but it pours: or, London strow'd with rarities' about Peter the Wild Boy (in which he also mentions Romulus and Remus).

Lady Walpole: probably Mary Magdalen (née Lombard), Lady Walpole (1694?–1783).

Appendix IV

258 *Lethe*: in Greek myth, a river in Hades the waters of which, if drunk, would make the drinker forget his or her past.

260 *Thor and Woden*: in Anglo-Saxon and Norse myth, Thor was the god of thunder, while Woden (or Odin) was seen as the chief god.

	Late Victorian Gothic Tales
JANE AUSTEN	Emma
	Mansfield Park
	Persuasion
	Pride and Prejudice
	Selected Letters
	Sense and Sensibility
MRS BEETON	Book of Household Management
MARY ELIZABETH BRADDON	Lady Audley's Secret
ANNE BRONTË	The Tenant of Wildfell Hall
CHARLOTTE BRONTË	Jane Eyre
	Shirley
	Villette
EMILY BRONTË	Wuthering Heights
ROBERT BROWNING	The Major Works
JOHN CLARE	The Major Works
SAMUEL TAYLOR COLERIDGE	The Major Works
WILKIE COLLINS	The Moonstone
	No Name
	The Woman in White
CHARLES DARWIN	The Origin of Species
THOMAS DE QUINCEY	The Confessions of an English Opium-Eater
	On Murder
CHARLES DICKENS	The Adventures of Oliver Twist
	Barnaby Rudge
	Bleak House
	David Copperfield
	Great Expectations
	Nicholas Nickleby
	The Old Curiosity Shop
	Our Mutual Friend
	The Pickwick Papers

CHARLES DICKENS	A Tale of Two Cities
GEORGE DU MAURIER	Trilby
MARIA EDGEWORTH	Castle Rackrent
GEORGE ELIOT	Daniel Deronda
	The Lifted Veil and Brother Jacob
	Middlemarch
	The Mill on the Floss
	Silas Marner
SUSAN FERRIER	Marriage
ELIZABETH GASKELL	Cranford
	The Life of Charlotte Brontë
	Mary Barton
	North and South
	Wives and Daughters
GEORGE GISSING	New Grub Street
	The Odd Women
EDMUND GOSSE	Father and Son
THOMAS HARDY	Far from the Madding Crowd
	Jude the Obscure
	The Mayor of Casterbridge
	The Return of the Native
	Tess of the d'Urbervilles
	The Woodlanders
WILLIAM HAZLITT	Selected Writings
JAMES HOGG	The Private Memoirs and Confessions of a Justified Sinner
JOHN KEATS	The Major Works
	Selected Letters
CHARLES MATURIN	Melmoth the Wanderer
JOHN RUSKIN	Selected Writings
WALTER SCOTT	The Antiquary
	Ivanhoe

American Literature

Authors in Context

British and Irish Literature

Children's Literature

Classics and Ancient Literature

Colonial Literature

Eastern Literature

European Literature

History

Medieval Literature

Oxford English Drama

Poetry

Philosophy

Politics

Religion

The Oxford Shakespeare

A complete list of Oxford World's Classics, including Authors in Context, Oxford English Drama, and the Oxford Shakespeare, is available in the UK from the Marketing Services Department, Oxford University Press, Great Clarendon Street, Oxford OX2 6DP, or visit the website at www.oup.com/uk/worldsclassics.

In the USA, visit www.oup.com/us/owc for a complete title list.

Oxford World's Classics are available from all good bookshops. In case of difficulty, customers in the UK should contact Oxford University Press Bookshop, 116 High Street, Oxford OX1 4BR.

*The
Oxford
World's
Classics
Website*

www.oup.com/uk/worldsclassics

- Information about new titles
- Explore the full range of Oxford World's Classics
- Links to other literary sites and the main OUP webpage
- Imaginative competitions, with bookish prizes
- Articles by editors
- Extracts from Introductions
- Special information for teachers and lecturers

www.oup.com/uk/worldsclassics